About the Author

Malcolm Gerloch was born in 1939 in Hull, East Yorkshire. He was educated at Hymers College there, and subsequently at Imperial College in London where he spent six years working for his bachelor and first doctorate degrees. After two years in post-doctoral research in magnetochemistry and ligand-field theory at the University of Manchester, he was appointed lecturer before moving, the following year, to University College, London. After three years, he was appointed to a post as Assistant Director of Research in chemistry in the University of Cambridge. He was awarded the degree of Doctor of Science there in 1980 and promoted to Reader in Inorganic Chemistry in 1984. He retired in 1999 and is an Emeritus Fellow of Trinity Hall. He and his wife, Gwyneth, now live in Canberra, Australia where they enjoy many of the usual pleasures of what might have been expected to be a quiet life in retirement. At 78, Malcolm began writing non-scientific books to add to his four technical books and over 120 research papers. He currently boasts some dozen children's books, together with a collection of short stories and a couple of autobiographical accounts of life before and after retirement; he has recently completed his second novel. Malcolm has two daughters, three grandsons and innumerable stray cats.

By the Same Author

Short stories
> Old Harald and Other Stories

Memoirs
> Second-Best Luck
> Such a Silly Mistake

Novels
> The Hut
> Arnold Forbutt Esquire (in press)

Children's stories

> *Series:*
> Bird
> Bahs
> Flea
> Spike
> Blue
> Hols
> The Humans in our Family
> Other Creatures
> Jubilee!

> *Assorted*
> Rosie 'N' Co.
> Zada
> Chook (with Gwyneth Gerloch)
> A Strange Tale or Three

THE HUT

Malcolm Gerloch

THE HUT

Pegasus

PEGASUS PAPERBACK

© Copyright **2023**
Malcolm Gerloch

The right of Malcolm Gerloch to be identified as author of
this work has been asserted by him in accordance with the
Copyright, Designs and Patents Act 1988

All Rights Reserved

No reproduction, copy or transmission of this publication
may be made without written permission.
No paragraph of this publication may be reproduced,
copied or transmitted save with the written permission of the publisher, or in accordance
with the provisions
of the Copyright Act 1956 (as amended).

Any person who does any unauthorised act in relation to
this publication may be liable to criminal
prosecution and civil claims for damage.

A CIP catalogue record for this title is
available from the British Library

ISBN-978 1 80468 000 1

Pegasus is an imprint of
Pegasus Elliot MacKenzie Publishers Ltd.
www.pegasuspublishers.com

First Published in **2023**

Pegasus
Sheraton House Castle Park
Cambridge CB3 0AX England

Printed & Bound in Great Britain

Acknowledgements

Several good friends have carefully read this book in manuscript and provided a great deal of encouragement and thoughtful, insightful commentary for which I am immensely grateful: Maria Altman, Sue King, Edith Richie and Michael Young. Once again, my wife, Gwyneth, has provided me with a sounding board, running commentary and repeated proofreading throughout the whole process: for this and her love I am eternally indebted.

Part I

1

Harvey Trentham had finally received an invitation to stay at *The Hut*. He was, however, more than a little intrigued that his uncle should suggest a visit at this particular time.

Gerald had occasionally mentioned the place over the years and Harvey had tried to find out more about it for himself, but without much success. None of his computer searches had yielded anything relevant, and he could only surmise that the name was merely a private sobriquet. From what little his uncle had told him, that was probably right, for Gerald had described a place where he and those of like-mind might occasionally spend a week or more in quiet ease. Apparently, "like-mind" was short for tasteful, costly, by invitation only, and above all, private.

Gerald was a man of substantial, inherited means, who had long ago taken his nephew under his generous wing, especially following the tragic death of Harvey's parents in a quite shocking road accident. Harvey's mother had been Gerald's older sister. Harvey, however, had no siblings and even though he had grown to be a busy and confident boy of nineteen at the time of the accident, and just as he was to begin his university course, he took the loss of his parents very hard. Gerald had been, and indeed continued to be, a rock for him. Time had healed, as it should, however imperfectly.

Instinctively, Harvey had always been tactful enough not to press Gerald to introduce him to *The Hut,* but he had listened with curiosity to the odd, rare, teasing snippet of information which his uncle sometimes dropped. So it was, that when Gerald proposed taking him to this special haunt, and intriguingly at this particular time, Harvey felt able, at last, to ask direct questions about the place. Even then, Gerald had provided a mere soupçon of information, and his nephew felt it appropriate not to press too hard. What Harvey did recognise, however, was that his uncle savoured both quietude and good conversation, fine music, good victuals and comfort. Certainly, he abhorred noise and vulgarity.

Harvey, despite being a member of a younger generation, concurred on all fronts. Mind you, being described as a member of a younger generation, which had happened on several occasions in Gerald's presence, was pushing things a bit far, for there was barely a dozen years between them.

Harvey, whose career some might have over-excitedly described as that of a superior variety of business sleuth, had been contacted just one week ago by Michael Montayne, the owner of this place, to provide professional assistance with an upcoming difficulty. Harvey assumed that Gerald's invitation to accompany him at this time was linked to Montayne's project. Indeed it was, although Gerald knew no more than that Michael had suggested that he bring his nephew along when next he visited *The Hut*. Michael always kept secrets secret, perhaps even when such care was unnecessary. Moreover, Michael's subtlety was such that Gerald had been quite unaware that he had been manoeuvred into making this visit, at this time. Not that Gerald minded one bit. It was always a pleasure to renew his acquaintance with *The Hut* and with Michael.

Nevertheless, Gerald had smiled at Harvey's intrigued expression and assured him that all would become clear when they had settled in. In different circumstances and from anyone else, Harvey would have smelled a very large rat and not agreed to go. After all, *The Hut* could be the centre of a vice ring, a dubious right-wing political group, a religious monstrosity or something even worse. Gerald would never countenance meeting with any such group; of that Harvey was more than sure. Trust was what it was all about, and Harvey had plenty of that. In any case, Harvey was looking forward to meeting Michael Montayne in the flesh.

Gerald had told Harvey to pack for an elegant holiday, to include smart, formal and casual wear, and tennis togs too, if he were so inclined.

It seemed that they were off to some place towards the west, Harvey casually observed, as Gerald drove them through the countryside, for he had been given no clue about the precise location of their destination, not that it couldn't have been worked out with just a modicum of attention. The sun was out, and everything looked fresh. By now they had left anything resembling a main road some while back and were, more slowly, navigating a narrow B-road.

'We are nearly there,' said Gerald, after a long spell of silence. 'I would normally drive right up to the hall but there's another way which provides a wonderful welcoming view. As it's a warm day, I propose to take you for a walk while I explain a few things.'

They were driving downhill along a well-wooded stretch of road as Gerald spoke. Then Harvey saw what seemed to be a simple clearing on the left. As they approached, a large, opaque, sliding gate set into a high stone wall came into view. Gerald looked carefully in his rear-view mirror before slowly pulling into it. However, he didn't steer the car so as to drive through the gate, but rather positioned the car parallel to it. He checked his rear-view mirror once again before reversing a short way within the clearing and into an area which was shielded from view by several bushes on both driver and passenger sides. Because of a curve in the short drive into which Gerald had reversed, public view from the front was also denied.

Simple, but clever, Harvey mused. On second thoughts, discreet was a better description.

'We'll leave the car here. I have arranged for someone from *The Hut* to drive it the rest of the way and take our luggage to our suite.'

On cue, a neatly dressed man appeared from behind another bush.

'Great timing, Gordon,' Gerald observed.

'Welcome back, sir. We've put you in suite number eight this time. Everything is ready for you and otherwise just as before.'

'Good! Gordon, this is my nephew, Harvey,' Gerald replied.

'Welcome to *The Hut*, sir. I hope you will enjoy your visit,' Gordon said with simple formality, nodding courteously but briefly to Harvey. 'Could I set your passes, please, gentlemen?'

Gerald brought out his smartphone, indicating that Harvey should do the same, and placed it close to one proffered by Gordon. Their phones each made a ping once they got within a few inches of Gordon's device. Harvey remembered now that Gerald had insisted that he download some special app before they set off. He had fiddled with it before they left, but as it apparently did nothing, he had assumed that it had downloaded incorrectly and resolved to ask his uncle about the matter later on. Now he realised that all was well.

'Remember to refresh your passes each morning at the desk, gentlemen,' Gordon said.

He climbed into Gerald's car and carefully drove off. He had obviously checked for traffic as he did so, but it was clear to Harvey that there wasn't too much of that on this road.

Gerald led Harvey into a gap in the innermost hedge through which Gordon had appeared. It led to a small, postern gate which Gerald opened with his mobile phone.

So that's what the airdrop was for, thought Harvey.

Once inside the property, they found themselves in a spacious area with an open shelter on the left in which a large tractor was housed. There was a similar, but smaller shelter immediately opposite where a couple of small electric vehicles, rather like golf carts, were parked.

'We could take one of those,' Gerald said, 'but I think you'll enjoy the walk much more.'

They followed a small private road to the right of the yard and began to descend a barely double-width and quite steep path curving sharply to the left. All around were well-established trees of a variety of species: tall pines mixed in with less substantial, but more plentiful birch, the occasional fern and even a few rhododendrons and holly bushes in amongst them. The planting was close but not dense enough to create any sense of dankness. On the contrary, everything smelt fresh.

The road twisted and turned as they descended. It took another fifty yards or so for Harvey to see that the public road, which they had just left, ran alongside a very steep fault or cliff in the land and that the chicane they were now descending had been constructed upon a less steep part of the land but one, nevertheless, heading towards the same near-level footing of the main cliff.

'Gosh, this is all very private, Gerald,' he said. 'You could have no idea of the existence of this place from the road.'

'Indeed, but just wait for the next bit,' Gerald replied.

It was obvious that he enjoyed the prospect of showing it off.

The slope of the path began to ease, and Harvey thought he could see an end to it up ahead, for they were in sight of a much wider section, circular and sealed, with an exit to the right. As they reached that circle, Gerald took hold of his nephew's shoulders and twisted him slightly so that he was looking directly at that exit.

'Now look at that!'

Extended before them, on ground sloping down just a little, lay a dead straight, paved road, just wide enough for two vehicles to pass safely, almost disappearing – or so it seemed to Harvey, at first glance – into the distance. It did end, however, probably about half a mile away. Parallel to this road, set back by some twenty yards on either side, were two lines of handsome lime trees, forming a magnificent avenue leading up to an imposing country house of some kind. What kind, Harvey could not quite see at this distance.

'So, this is *The Hut*!' he said to his uncle.

'Well, that is the hall and these its grounds, but *The Hut* is more a concept than an estate,' he replied. 'While we're here, you will have every opportunity to explore the acres of which this avenue is just an introduction and, indeed, I'll point out some other features of the terrain as we walk. But now, dear boy, is the time for me to explain a little more about *The Hut*, I think. As will become clearer when we get closer, the house is moderately large, as well as being handsome and old. It was bequeathed to Michael Montayne by his father many years ago, along with a sizable, but nonetheless inadequate, sum of money. Inadequate, because it barely covered the death duties associated with the whole, otherwise magnificent, bequest. There was certainly nothing left over to pay the wages of the many servants required in such a place, let alone for repairs which are an ongoing nightmare in an estate like this. It had, of course, been Michael's home all his life, and that of many of his forebears, so he hated the idea of selling the property or even of coming to some kind of agreement with the National Trust, which might have allowed him to live in it, but only on their terms. Michael, as you will come to know, is a man of considerable gentility. He is well-educated and gregarious and, largely by virtue of his privileged upbringing, of course, has powerful and wealthy friends in many walks of life. Yes, of course, you can see the silver spoon in his mouth. I know. Much like me, but on a larger scale. But it wasn't his fault that he was born into such society any more than it is the fault of any child born into a poor family.

'Anyway, social science aside, Michael had a problem, and in due course he found an answer. He sold a majority share in the whole estate to a cruise company. In effect, *The Hut* is formally akin to a cruise ship! If that seems too vulgar for you, Harvey, remember two things: not all cruises are cheap and vulgar; and Michael retains a share in this enterprise. The deal he made with that company is that he and his family continue to live in the place, that he designs the facilities, and that while he does not manage the enterprise, he does direct the manager. Furthermore, Michael selects the clientele. Essentially, the place is Michael's to play with, but he only owns ten percent or so of it! Or something like that, for, to tell the truth, I'm not altogether *au fait* with the details. And, Harvey, you will really like this man. I guarantee it!'

'I see. That's a fascinating story, but I still have one question,' Harvey replied. 'Why all the secrecy? Why is everything so hush-hush?'

'Ah! That's because of Michael's clientele, Harvey. Many would judge Michael as something of a snob, for he insists on guests who are to his liking or are friends of such people and so properly vouched for; guests who are well-educated and can mix well in a collegiate assembly for a week or more; people who enjoy conversation, good food and wine, music and occasional sophisticated cabaret; and sadly, but quite essentially, guests who can afford the high charges imposed by this organisation. Those fees have to cover the restoration and modernisation cost of the house, the upkeep of both house and grounds, which you can already see are magnificent, and the many servants required to sustain as splendid an environment as Michael insists on providing, including both food and entertainment. And, finally, privacy. After all that, there has to be some non-trivial return for the cruise company, of course.'

'I guess that the secrecy is all about that word "privacy",' suggested Harvey.

'Indeed. Some of Michael's guests are well known to the public –film stars, politicians, men and women of industry. Many are titled, some ennobled, and some even members of one royal family or another, for *The Hut* is discreetly known throughout the world. These people, in particular, do not want paparazzi chasing them all over the place. They simply want a little peace and quiet. Often they are merely looking for a simple holiday where they can blend in with ordinary people – or perhaps I should say, "more ordinary" – as a change from their usual, glamorous or, perhaps, formal lives. And amongst this group of highly privileged people are some who are not brash or vulgar, who enjoy many of the things Michael enjoys. They receive invitations to attend *The Hut*. Those of unlike mind do not. Michael promises to do his very best to preserve the privacy of all his guests and, in due course, you may come to see a little of how he goes about it. You have already come across one aspect of his care: namely that you would have been unable to find out anything about this place on Google or anywhere else you might have used in a search. There is nothing on paper for you to read about your holiday. It is all done by word of mouth – just as I'm doing now.'

'But you introduced me to that fellow, Gordon, by my real name.'

'Well spotted! However, I take it that, like me, you have nothing to conceal; that you have no paparazzi or other spies seeking you out; that you are not sloping off with some woman, or man for that matter, you shouldn't be with. So I made a point of following conventional pleasantries. You wouldn't have noticed, by the way – but you will – that all servants around the place address guests as sir or madam. They almost never use their names, even if they know them, nor do they make any use of their titles, if they have them. All guests are free to introduce themselves to both other guests and to servants, if they so wish, by their first names – no surnames. Those names may be true or false. That is nobody else's concern. All guests understand this rule and are expected to abide by it throughout their stay at *The Hut*. Oh, look! There's a spy.'

Gerald pointed to movement in some bushes about fifty yards to their left. Harvey looked but saw nothing... until a couple of deer appeared, grazing in long grass.

'Plenty to see around this place!' smiled his host.

The interruption brought Harvey's attention back to his surroundings. Now he saw something he hadn't seen at first. The avenue of limes was doubled up, as it were, by parallel rows of beech set some ten to fifteen metres further back from the road and planted in the gaps between the limes in zigzag formation, so providing an even denser curtain of foliage to define this magnificent driveway to the house. Harvey saw exactly why Gerald had suggested walking rather than driving. This way, details were clear, things which would likely be missed from a vehicle. Indeed, on the left,

Harvey noticed an irregularity in the line of beech trees. One was missing, left out so as to provide an unsealed track which curved back and to the side, off into the dense, but copse-like thicket beyond.

'Where does that go?' he asked his uncle.

'To large sheds where the groundsmen and others store most of their equipment. You can explore them for yourself later,' Gerald replied.

They resumed their walk towards the house and Harvey continued his revue of the layout of the estate, at least so far as he could see it. To his right, behind the double row of avenue trees, the land was covered in meadow-length grass as far as the extended woodland at the foot of, and indeed up the face of, the cliff marking one boundary of the estate. As he looked closer, he saw mown paths within that meadow. It was all reminiscent of the fairway and rough of a golf course, he thought. On his left, on the other hand, it appeared that all the land behind the row of beech trees was given over to woodland. In places that woodland seemed rather dense; in others, sparse with obvious indications of paths, worn by use if not design. Altogether it was clear that there were many opportunities for good long walks without undue repetition. Harvey enjoyed walking.

'How did you first come to hear about this place, Gerald?' asked Harvey.

'I knew Michael as a young man at university and before his parents died. As a teenager he had once told me that he had anticipated the problems he would face because of looming death duties, and he had begun to dream of how he might overcome the problem. Of course, he knew *intimately* of no suitably rich people or companies who might help at that time, so his ideas were just more of a dream than a plan. At one time, he considered trying to form a consortium of people like me, each of whom could chip in a substantial sum, but it soon became clear to him that such a path would be difficult and, more importantly for Michael, would involve continual supervision and, worse, was likely to be unstable. A commitment from a single source was his preferred option. I'm not sure how or when he came to know Geoffrey Etherington who heads that cruise company I told you about, but he counts that as one of the happiest meetings of his life. Anyway, a deal was struck, and in due course the thing was done. Michael spent three years planning and supervising the remodelling of the house, and of the gardens to some extent, while he slowly began to recruit his staff.

Of course, he inherited some staff with the estate, and many of those remain. Indeed, the only ones who don't are those who have died or retired. Staff loyalty is very strong here. I believe they are well paid as well.'

'You mentioned earlier Michael's affection for a collegiate style of entertaining, I think,' said Harvey. 'What's all that about?

'Oh! Merely his preference for dining with his guests around one large table rather than in an hotel style with separate tables. He wants his guests to get to know each other and build loyalty, I suppose. It's all very pleasant, really. Ah! And then there is the simplification of the menu.' He grinned.

'How do you mean?'

'There isn't one! You will have had an enquiry, by now, asking whether there are any ingredients your body won't tolerate. And, of course, you can lie and so include things you simply don't like, but it's best to trust the chefs here, you will find. Anyway, appropriate action is taken to accommodate guests' problems, but otherwise, the same meals are served to all guests.'

'Sounds like my college days!'

'Yes, except for the quality of the dishes provided. They are quite splendid and highly varied. Michael has some really top-class chefs in the place. You like food as much as I do. Trust me: you will enjoy it all.'

'Is there a seating plan? Does Michael sit in with us at the top of the table?'

'No, nothing like that. You sit where you like, and the great man does the same. Occasionally, he dines in his private quarters. After all, this is his home.' Gerald broke off from his descriptions as they approached a statue in the middle of the Grand Avenue.

By this time, they had covered about two thirds of its length, and they had arrived at a little crossroad with a statue of a twin-headed bird perched upon a pedestal in the middle of it. At first, Harvey thought it silly to break the long vista down which they had gained an ever-growing reveal of the house. But actually it hadn't, because the more distant stretch of road they had already traversed had been slightly inclined downwards, so that they had looked over the top of the statue until they were within a short distance of it. The road beyond the statue, ending at the house, was dead level. In any case, the statue, though not at all insignificant, was not too large to have obscured their view. Instead, it had merely diffused their view somewhat, so that as they walked round it and looked once more toward their goal, the true magnificence of the house was suddenly revealed in full clarity. The statue, it seemed, was a tease – a hiatus in their approach to intimacy. Like a kid eating his ice-cream cone at the seaside, Harvey first studied the statue for its own sake, as well as to stretch out his enjoyment of the main course. Gerald knew he would do that and stepped back to let him.

The two-headed bird – Harvey could not tell what kind of bird, but it was certainly mythical – was carved from sandstone, he thought; no longer sharp, owing to the weathering of the years… *How long?* he wondered. A couple of centuries, maybe. Maybe much less. The creature stood about seven or eight feet high and was set upon a latticed, bronze plinth aged with a dull-green patina. Overall, the construction was perhaps twelve feet high and was set upon a wide plinth whose purpose was clearly to prevent vehicles – presumably horse-drawn carriages in earlier times – from hitting and damaging the bird with two heads. *Why two heads?* Harvey wondered. They did not align symmetrically with the avenue. One faced the house, while the other looked left; away from the cliff, whose height, by the way, was now only half of what it had been where they had begun their walk, reflecting the downward slope of the road they had left earlier.

The crossroad itself was clearly of minor importance. It was unsealed and, as far as Harvey could see, went into nothingness within a few hundred yards or so. More importantly, however, was that the terrain on both sides of the road was now grassed more carefully and, it appeared, was regularly mown. By far the greatest change was that those avenue trees were dispensed with beyond the crossroad. Instead, the relatively well-manicured grass on either side came right up to the road verge. There was a splendid, old oak tree about fifty yards further on to the right, and nearer to the house a clump of three or four yews. Each feature made its own strong statement without detracting from the view of the house, and Harvey guessed that the same would be true of the view from the building. It seemed that they had reached a more formal part of the estate, albeit with reduced symmetry, now that they were within clear sight of the house.

Ah yes! The house. Harvey turned away from the statue at last and focussed his attention on the building. He had been wondering about this building ever since he and Gerald stopped to admire the deer because, grand though it was, it was out of place in the Wiltshire (Was it Wiltshire? Maybe

Gloucestershire or Hereford?) countryside. Architecturally, it was very close to being a French chateau of the mid-eighteenth century.

'Gerald…' Harvey began.

'Michael's forebears were French – I would guess about four or five generations ago. Certainly, the builder and first owner of this place was French, although his wife was English. I believe he came to some sort of arrangement with her, that if she insisted on living in England rather than France, he would insist on a French lifestyle. There are extensions at the back of the place, which you cannot yet see, which were added sometime in the nineteenth century and, disgusting though it may seem to the architectural purist, they have an English eighteenth century feel about them. So the place is a bit of a freak from several points of view.'

'What I can see from here is quite wonderful, though, and the decision to establish the approach we have just walked along could not be more fitting,' Harvey enthused. 'Hang on, I've just thought of something. To make proper use of this impressive drive, one would have to ride – in a carriage, no doubt – from the place where we first saw the whole vista. But no carriage could navigate that steep, winding little road from where we left your car.'

'Quite right, Harvey. You will remember that I abruptly turned you to face the chateau as soon as we reached that circular feature at the bottom of the winding descent. Had I given you a couple of seconds more, you would have noticed that another road entered that circle from the opposite side. However, because it enters via a sort of chicane, one doesn't get a long view of it. That road continues for a fair way before reaching a pair of rather splendid wrought iron gates, which are really the main entrance to this place. You will appreciate the significance of that entry point in a day or two when I have explained the neighbouring countryside, including the village which borders this estate, and which we might go and explore together tomorrow, unless Michael has planned something.'

Harvey turned back to admire the façade of the chateau once more. 'Does Michael refer to this place as a chateau?' he asked.

'Very occasionally, but mostly he calls it *The Hut*. His little joke.'

The front elevation was perfectly symmetrical, left to right. There were four stories – maybe five if there was a cellar. *Surely likely*, thought Harvey.

The ground and first floor windows were very tall. Above each pair was a much smaller window. There were three such vertical columns of fenestration on either side of a central group of three, the latter set into a wall which protruded about a foot further out than the walls on either side. Thus, nine columns of windows defined the front face of the building. All windows were set in stone and similarly mullioned. The lower three openings in the mid-section of the grand façade, however, were given over to three very tall double doors with semi-circular lights above.

'Good grief, Gerald,' Harvey exclaimed. 'This is an exquisite building. Those doors, for example, must be twelve foot high if they're an inch! I presume they open into a grand entrance hall?'

Gerald was fully prepared for Harvey's enthusiasm, for he knew of his interest in all matters architectural from the time when his nephew had taken a course in that subject as an "extra" during his sixth-form days.

'Actually, no. The hall inside at that point is certainly as high as you would suppose from those magnificent doors, but it covers only a modest area. I suspect that the arrangement dates from when the building became used as the special hotel it now is. There's a reception desk in there, but little else. Immediately behind that small entrance hall lies perhaps the most important feature of the place –the dining hall – as you will see this evening.'

'But that must mean that the hall is rather dark, surely, not having light from the front?' Harvey asked.

'Again, no, because it takes some light from some small internal windows opening high into the entrance vestibule, and also because the hall extends a long way back so that there are sizeable windows at the rear. In any case, by the time we all sit down for dinner, artificial illumination is the main light source.'

Harvey's attention returned to the front of the building. Four fluted pilasters with simple capitals, so forming a dummy portico, marked the separation and boundaries of these three doors.

'Those pilasters are so well done,' he said.

'And what, pray, are pilasters?' asked Gerald. 'Are you showing off your 'A' levels again?'

'Oh, come, come, my dear uncle, if bits and pieces have been given names, we should use them.'

Harvey's rebuke was noted and duly ignored by Gerald.

'Well?' he asked.

'Okay, pilasters are those half-columns framing the doors. They look like round columns which are half set into the building but, actually, are merely constructed from semicircular stones cemented onto the front of the wall behind. As you see, in this case each stone is carved into a succession of small scallops so that long grooves are formed, running the length of each half-column; hence fluted.'

There were vertical, semicircular stone lintels providing eyebrows above each doorway and each tall window above them. All other lintels were straight and horizontal. Each lintel protruded markedly, so providing the windows with some relief from dripping water in the rain, as well as serving to clearly define the geometry of the structure. The facades, left, right and middle were all painted in a cream colour, while the quoins of the central section and of the extremities of the whole house were of sandstone.

'Those quoins really set the whole of the central section off to perfection – and, indeed, mark the boundaries of the whole building beautifully.'

'Coins?' teased Gerald. 'What? Five bob or a quid?'

'Oh, dear, oh dear! I bet you mentally spelled that with four letters,' Harvey moaned.

'No, five! It's plural.'

'All right, all right. Quoins are those very large stones set into the corners of the walls – indeed, making the corners – in that zig-zag pattern. If you require yet more education, please arrange for your cheque to clear PDQ.'

'Oh! The arrogance of youth!' Gerald mocked.

His interruptions, however, failed to prevent Harvey returning to his examination of this grand building. Five steps surrounded the four pilasters announcing the main entrance. The steps gave way onto a five-yard-wide terrace which was pebbled in off-white stone, the whole of which was itself a further five steps above a generous, ground-level pebbled square across the front of the building and towards which the Grand Avenue was directed. Above all this, was the crowning glory of the roof.

What a roof! It probably defined the French aesthetic more than anything. A very steep, and therefore tall, hipped and fine-shingled structure with a pronounced lower lip and overhang, the latter characterised by a markedly gentler slope, was peppered with handsome, tall, brick chimneys picked out, once more, with pronounced stone quoins, together with collars and caps. Overall, Harvey mused, the main part of the roof resembled Napoleon Bonaparte's hat. Maybe not. There were four chimneys in the front, and more were visible along each side. Most likely there were yet more at the rear of the building, as well. One third of the way up the roof, and aligned with the fenestration on the façade, were six small dormer-style windows, presumably providing light for servants' quarters – in former times, if not now. There were only six of these, three on each side of the central part of the façade line. Aligned above the central portico and its pediment, and thus three windows wide, was a square-based, curved roof whose slope, at the bottom, approached the vertical and, at the top, was about forty-five degrees. Altogether it resembled an upturned bowl, but with a square cross-section. It was capped off with a short square turret in the same near-black hue as all the roof shingles, and it appeared to be somewhat higher than the chimney caps.

'So French, so beautiful. Michael must be so proud of this place!' Harvey murmured eventually. 'I guess the same was true of his forebears.'

Gerald concurred, 'He is, and they were.'

All in all, the main part of the building was probably half as deep as it was wide; clearly a substantial country home. However, as Gerald had mentioned to Harvey earlier, there were large additions on either side of the main structure, set back so as to overlap and join the main building about one third of the way from the rear. These two wings, of a less insistent style, rose to three stories but were, overall, about two-thirds of the height of the main part of the house. Their ground floors extended a distance equal to that of six windows worth of the main structure; in other words equal to two thirds of its width. Although the height of the ground floor windows in the wings were the same as those in the main structure, the spacing which characterised the latter was not maintained. Instead, nearly all of the ground floor front was glazed, albeit with appropriate narrow columns at regular intervals for obvious structural reasons. Furthermore, at ground floor level only, the glazing was set back some way under a narrow peristyle, simultaneously providing a colonnade and window shade. The left and right wings were identical. Their second and third floors were characterised by markedly more modest room and window-heights than those in the main building. The ground area in front of each wing was laid to lawn, except for narrow, pebbled paths immediately in front of the buildings. Overall, these two wings, presumably added in the nineteenth century, roughly doubled the size of the house. Some hut!

The two men began walking again, and Harvey started to scan the grounds. Over in the right-hand corner, he caught sight of a couple of tennis courts and, in front of the right wing itself, was a croquet lawn which was currently in use by a couple of ladies who were so deeply immersed in the play that they failed to notice the approach of Gerald and his nephew.

'They seem to be taking that game rather seriously,' Gerald remarked, although, at the sound of his voice, one of the players turned in recognition.

'Gerald!' she cried out. 'I heard you were coming. How delightful to see you again!'

Gerald steered Harvey towards the ladies. He and the older of the two players lightly embraced.

'And lovely to see you here again, Hillary! Have you been here long? We have just arrived. I have been giving my nephew, Harvey here, the *Introduction of the Long March*!'

'Always the best way, I think,' Hillary replied. 'Hello Harvey, a pleasure to meet you. I hope you'll enjoy your stay here. May I introduce my young cousin, Isobel?'

'Izzy, please. Hello, Gerald; hello, Harvey. Nice to meet. Do you play croquet, by any chance?'

'Yes, we both do,' replied Harvey.

'Oh, good!' replied Isobel gleefully. 'We can set up a pairs match.'

'I think we might first settle into our suite,' Gerald replied, smiling, 'but it is nice to find other croquet players. I had no idea you indulged, Hillary.'

'You'll soon discover why, Gerald,' she said with a laugh.

Harvey thought she had a lovely laugh – almost a chuckle, really.

2

For the third time that week, Michael headed for the river moorings to watch the narrow boats and occasional posh motorboats coming and going and often staying. He was especially fascinated by the compact, long, narrow, floating homes and by how skilfully their owners navigated the canal and nearby locks which joined the river a couple of miles further upstream.

As for all small boys, hobbies come and go. Watching boats had taken his fancy for over two months now. On this occasion, he had decided to go and see the goings-on in the evening. It was midsummer, the day had been warm and sunny and the citizens of Tomberwater were in for a long, gentle dusk.

Michael had no brothers or sisters, something his uncles and aunts openly expressed sorrow about, but Michael felt no anguish over the matter.

He had left his grand house after teatime, through the kitchen garden and out of a side gate which opened directly onto the main road. The road skirted his family estate and nearly into the centre of the village before turning right abruptly to go around the rest of Tomberwater and pass parallel to the river along an embankment which ran adjacent to the main river wharf. Michael could have taken that route, but it was quicker to duck into the village itself and to turn this way and that through some of the older, narrow streets. Everyone in the village knew that route; only strangers would go "roundabout". In any case, halfway along his route was the village pub, the *Tomber Pot,* as every villager knew, and the old street cobbles were pretty well worn in that area.

Michael had nearly reached the *Pot* that evening, when two older-looking boys, who were clearly rough types, accosted him. He didn't recall having seen them before but that might not have been too surprising. It was hardly Michael's fault that he happened to be passing by just at the time when these two toughs were in the mood for a scrap.

'Where yer goin' fancy boy?' provoked one of them; the one with ginger hair and black fingernails.

'Decided to mix with us locals, then?' his fatter mate jeered. 'We *are* honoured, I'm sure'.

'I'm just minding my own business. Why don't you mind yours?' retaliated Michael, bravely but recklessly, and far too provocatively for a quiet life, as he realised the instant he'd opened his mouth.

Michael was not yet nine years old, and the wisdom required to know when to keep your mouth shut had not yet come upon him; but that didn't mean that he couldn't work things out, even if it was too late. And by that time, of course, it was too late. The younger, slightly fatter youth gave Michael a push towards his mate who pushed him back. Michael shouted at them to stop, but to no avail. Indeed, his speaking merely provoked them to renew their assault until the whole thing turned into an all-in fight. Michael was game enough to fight back, but he had no chance against two larger and meaner boys. They began to give him a proper thumping.

Michael was lucky, though, for Mr. Gaston, the publican of the *Pot,* had just seen what had happened through the front window of the pub and rushed out of the front door. In three strides he reached the brawling mob and, with a nifty, twisting motion, pulled Michael's antagonists off by their ears which, at that moment, looked as if they might separate from their unkempt skulls.

'Right, you two. I know who you are and I'll be telling your dad when he comes in later, don't you fear. I saw what you did, and I heard. Just let people be. And while you're at it, get a wash.' He turned to Michael, and with a flick on his head, said, 'I should get off home now, if I were you. But don't worry. I don't think the Roland boys will be troubling you again.'

'Thanks, Mr. Gaston,' Michael mumbled with some embarrassment, as he sheepishly and shakily went off.

At first he thought he might continue to the wharf as planned, but he felt very shaken and reckoned that going home was a better idea. It was only when he met his father some while later that he realised that signs of his fight were clear for all to see. His right eye was closing, a tell-tale bruise was developing and a tear near his jacket pocket, which he hadn't noticed before, was pointed out to him by his dad.

'How did it begin?' his dad asked gently. 'I know how it ended, because Mr. Gaston telephoned me ten minutes ago.'

Michael described his earlier contretemps, adding that he thought that he had been silly to respond to the boys in the way he had.

'Yes, that's probably right. You do well to understand that. However, that was no excuse for their behaviour. I gather from Mr. Gaston that you gave a good account of yourself under the circumstances. Why were you there at that time in the evening, by the way?'

Arthur Montayne was a kindly man and allowed his son every freedom of movement, for he trusted his son completely. He put his arm gently around Michael's shoulders as the boy explained about his fascination with the narrow boats.

'Why don't you show me them tomorrow, Michael?' he suggested.

The deal was struck.

The next day, in the early afternoon, they strolled down to the village wharf, and Michael began to point out to his father the special paintwork and decorations on each of a line of five narrowboats moored there. He was obviously less interested in a couple of much smaller clinker-built motorboats moored at the end of the line. The narrowboats had been moored in the same spot for several weeks now, as Michael knew full well, and seemed deserted. But then they always did, Michael explained, although he had seen people climb aboard from time to time. In any case, four of them had small plant pots with geraniums and similar flowers in them aligned in rows on their roofs. They were more like homes on water than boats, in Michael's opinion.

Then he noticed someone in the narrowboat somewhat further away, moored at a separate and less-used spot. As they approached, he recognised that person as none other than Mr. Gaston from the *Tomber Pot*. He was dressed in some overalls, had a cigarette hanging from his mouth and was busy smoothing a piece of wood with a long jackplane.

'Hello, George,' Arthur greeted him. 'I didn't know you did woodwork as well as running a pub.' Turning then to his son, he explained, 'Mr. Gaston owns this boat as well as the pub, Michael.'

Michael had had no idea that his dad and Mr. Gaston knew each other, apart, of course, from that phone call the previous evening. But then there was a lot that Michael was yet to know about his dad.

'Come aboard!' Mr. Gaston offered a helping hand to Michael as they climbed into the cockpit. 'I hear that you are interested in canal boats, young sir. Open those doors,' he said, 'and go in and explore. Take your time.'

Like a boy with a lolly, Michael needed no further encouragement. He trod very carefully down three steep steps, through the double doors and inside the boat, typically treating everything he found with the utmost respect. Michael was like that. Mr Gaston knew it. As he rummaged about inside, he was aware that his father and Mr. Gaston were talking, but he couldn't make out any words. His first impression of the boat was of how much wider it seemed, compared with what he had seen outside. His second was of how neat, clean and cosy the cabin was, for the outside of the boat was obviously in need of some repair and paint. He had spotted that long ago just by comparing this boat with those further along the wharf. The saloon he had entered had a central aisle with seats on either side, beyond which was clearly a galley. He knew the right word for a small boat kitchen. There were cupboards on the left and a small work area on the right with cooking rings and a neat, small oven at the far end, and yet more cupboards underneath. Above the cooking rings hung several pans and skillets. It was surprisingly light inside the boat, Michael noted.

Immediately beyond the kitchen area was a table attached and set at right angles to the starboard side, with two double bench seats on either side of it; soft seats, upholstered in a dark-blue material. He found it a bit tight to pass from the central aisle in the sitting-cum-kitchen area to the dining space in which the aisle had now moved to the port side, but he could see that every inch of space had been put to the best use. Michael climbed over the corner of the seat nearest him as he manoeuvred himself into the port side aisle and the past the table.

The next section, adjacent to the aisle, was boarded in. He opened a door in the middle of it and looked inside to find a neat, very compact toilet, basin and shower/bath. Everything you might need was there, albeit in a tight space. Michael thought it was a very clever design.

He carried on past the bathroom. Next came a bedroom with a full double bed facing forward, and beyond were centrally positioned double doors, much like the ones he had entered the boat by, on the far side of a small sitting area at the end of the bed. There were cupboards on either side of those doors. One was fitted out as a wardrobe, he discovered, and the other had shelves and drawers for general storage. He opened the double doors to find himself outside once again and, by way of three steps, up onto a small open foredeck. He turned round and saw Mr. Gaston and his father still chatting back in the cockpit. They seemed a long way away. Outside, the boat felt very long and narrow.

Michael went back inside and through the boat to join his father and Mr. Gaston. The publican turned to Michael and asked him what he thought of his home on the water.

'I think it's super, Mr. Gaston. I hadn't realised how much space there would be in there or how smart everything would seem.'

'Well, I'm beginning to fix up the outside now, Michael. Your father tells me you are interested in the decorations on narrowboats. Would you like to give me a hand?'

Michael was overjoyed. The few friends he had were from rich families, whose aspirations sometimes irritated him; indeed, he had told his father of his views on more than one occasion. To his growing pleasure of late, he had begun to realise that his dad was not only happy to accept Michael's opinions on that subject but seemed to agree with them.

So, without even consulting his dad and, of course, not realising that the two adults had been discussing the whole question while Michael was exploring the boat, he enthusiastically replied, 'Oh! Mr. Gaston, I would so like that. When can I come?'

'Well, today's Tuesday. Come over on Thursday morning – say about ten o'clock. Come in some old clothes, or bring overalls, and we'll make a start. I don't work on the boat every day, because I have to work in the *Pot*, but on some days my wife takes charge there, and anyway, she's teaching the ropes to my son, Ken, who will take over the place one day, like as not.'

As Michael walked home with his father, he said, 'I hope you don't mind my helping Mr. Gaston on his boat, Dad?'

'Not at all, Michael. It's your holidays right now, so you do what you want as long as you're sensible, and I know you are. Of course, when term starts again, school comes first. But, for the moment, I think it's good that you have found a different sort of interest, and I trust Mr. Gaston to look after you.'

'I hadn't realised that you knew him before yesterday, Father. Have you known him long?'

'I'll let you into a little secret, Michael. George Gaston and I have not only known each other for years but have been very good friends. We don't advertise that widely, so it's sort of secret. Okay?'

'Of course. You can trust me,' Michael assured his father, who smiled and gave a slight nod. 'Is Mother in on it?' he continued.

'To some extent, Michael. I'll tell you more about it all one day.'

*

Thursday turned out to be another warm day – indeed, that summer had been one of the sunniest, he could remember – when Michael, dressed in his old, "gardening" clothes, turned up at Mr. Gaston's canal boat at ten o'clock on the dot. Nobody seemed to be about, though. Michael knocked on the side of the boat and called out Mr. Gaston's name, but there was no response. Assuming that Mr. Gaston would be along soon, Michael amused himself by looking carefully at the outside of the boat to see what needed doing to it. That wasn't difficult to see, for, in marked contrast with the pristine interior, the outside was dirty and discoloured, and in some places there was some damage to the wooden skin. Mind you, while that was true of the upper part of the boat, the lower part – the basic hull – seemed to have been recently overhauled. There was no obvious damage and it had been painted black, with two rubbing bands at the top and bottom of the gunwale plank picked out in white between. And her name was painted in white between those bands on either side – or so Michael presumed – of the prow: *Maisy Pot*. So it seemed to Michael that the renovation was nearly complete; just the top level outside remained to be done, and that shouldn't take long, he reckoned.

George Gaston turned up around a quarter past.

'Morning, young Michael! Have you had a look around her? There's just the upper section outside to do. I had her in dry dock last year and mended and repainted her bottom. She had an argument with a lock gate a couple of years ago, and there's a bit of damage to the superstructure on the starboard side. That's the first thing that needs attention now. I had begun shaving a piece of wood for that when you and your dad turned up on Tuesday, but I can't fit it standing on the boat, so we'll have to turn her round. Can you lift that mooring line from the capstan on the dock near the bow, throw it into the fore well and then jump into the cockpit?'

Michael enjoyed learning the proper names for the different parts of the boat. Mr. Gaston lifted the aft mooring line from its mooring and tossed it into the boat before climbing aboard and into the cockpit. After some moments, Michael heard the engine turn over. It made far less noise than he had expected, though. There was more of a throb than any obvious mechanical noises.

There was no traffic on the river. Michael only then realised that Mr. Gaston must have seen all that before he began this operation. He also saw, some small distance ahead, that the river widened considerably, and as *Maisy Pot* slowly slid forwards, he guessed that Mr. Gaston was aiming for that wide bit of the river so as to turn this very long boat around. Mr. Gaston shouted at Michael to take hold of a long push pole which rested against one of the rails running along the top of the superstructure.

'If necessary, just help me in the turn if I look as if I'm going to hit the bank'.

Michael felt quite panicky for he only vaguely understood what Mr. Gaston was asking him to do; and anyway, would he be strong enough?

But he took the pole, rested it against the portside gunwale and was pleased to hear Mr. Gaston call out, 'Yes, that's right. You chose the correct side to stand by at.'

Mr. Gaston was manoeuvring the boat very carefully, reversing the engine at some moments so that he had managed to get the long canalboat turned at right angles to the bank.

'See if you can touch the bottom with your pole, Michael,' he called out.

To his surprise, Michael found that he could. He had thought the river would be much deeper than that.

'Keep a firm hold of the pole and see if you can push on it a bit.'

Michael pushed on the pole which went into the muddy bottom, but only a short distance.

'Try and hold it right there, Michael. If you lose control, try and pull the pole out. If you can't, let go! Don't fall in!'

Mr. Gaston played with his engine and rudder with some complex delicacy, and Michael felt he was losing control of the pole for a moment, but the pressure went away and the *Maisy Pot* began to swing round nicely.

'Pull the pole out now, Michael,' called Mr. Gaston.

It needed an almighty heave, but Michael did it and put the pole back on the roof.

'Well done, shipmate!' called his master.

It was only then that Michael realised that the river itself was flowing – slowly, admittedly – and that Mr. Gaston had taken advantage of that to help the turn. Michael was learning fast. By now the boat was turned fully around and was making for the mooring from which it had left some while earlier. All that had to be done now was to jump out with the mooring line when told to and to slip the loop over the capstan once more. That was easy enough because Mr. Gaston had brought the boat into the wharf with exacting slowness and care. Michael ran to the stern to complete the job without being told. He felt very proud of himself.

Mr. Gaston had a huge grin on his face. 'That was very smooth. Tell your dad when you get home.'

Michael looked at the starboard side of the superstructure for the first time and saw a long tear (he couldn't think of a better word for it) in between two of the windows.

'I see what you mean about an argument, Mr. Gaston,' he said. 'Lucky the window frame wasn't smashed as well, I guess.'

'Yes, quite right. I'm hoping I won't have to take that out when I repair the woodwork. We'll see.'

When everything had settled down, Michael asked Mr. Gaston how he might be able to help in that repair or maybe something else.

'Your dad tells me that you are rather good at painting and decorating.'

That was a bit of an exaggeration, Michael thought, for it could only have been based on his painting his bedroom last year. He smiled but said nothing.

'I'd like you to help with the painting of the superstructure, Michael, and if you feel like it, maybe we can decorate *Maisy Pot* together.'

Although he already knew what the other canal boats looked like, Michael instinctively looked at the nearest one further along the wharf. Its superstructure was painted on a glossy, dark-green background and yellow lines had been used to pick out rectangular panels around each window. The panel nearest the bow didn't include a window but was decorated with a painting of some oversize loaves of bread.

In answer to Michael's quizzical look, Mr. Gaston told him, 'That boat is owned by Steve Hutton who also owns the baker's shop down the road from *The Pot*. We're great pals. Actually, it was Steve who first got me interested in narrowboats. Anyway, we could take a cue from what he's done. Maybe you would like to think of some ideas, Michael. Here, have a sandwich.'

That was really all they got done that day. It might not seem much, but when Michael looked at his watch as he was walking through the side door of the Big House, as Mr. Gaston had called it, it was just past three o'clock. Mr. Gaston had told Michael that he wouldn't be working on the boat for a few days and suggested that Michael return on the following Wednesday if he still wanted to help.

During the next few days, Michael made three separate drawings of ideas he thought up for decorating *Maisy Pot*. One was of a couple of pints of beer tilted away from one another; another was of a large bunch of brightly coloured flowers; and the third was an abstract picture in the style of Georges Braque, a cubist whom Michael had only just discovered. He wasn't too sure whether Mr. Gaston would take to the abstract stuff, but if he didn't, there were the other two suggestions.

Wednesday came around and saw Michael with a bundle of papers under his arm marching up to Mr. Gaston's boat. Mr. Gaston was already working on the repair. He had a small bench with a clamp on the wharf and he was busy planing a mahogany plank there. He had cut around the tear in the superstructure and set in some small ribs of less expensive timber in between the inner and outer skins of the structure. The inner skin formed the panelling from inside the boat while the outer one faced the outside world.

'Why are you making the repair out of mahogany, Mr. Gaston?' asked Michael. 'Surely that's a rather expensive wood, isn't it?'

'Thank you for trying to save my money, Michael. The reason, though, is that the rest of the outer skin is mahogany, and I'd hate to botch the job for a ha'porth of tar. In any case, I'm still considering whether I might prefer to strip off all the old paint and varnish the top instead. What do you think?'

'I like the idea of varnished wood,' he said, 'but wouldn't that be an awful lot of work, stripping off the old paint? It would have to be done perfectly, wouldn't it?'

'Quite right, young feller. Like you, I prefer a varnished finish, but I'm not too sure I fancy the paint-stripping job. What have got there?' he asked, when he saw Michael's bundle.

Michael showed his paintings. Mr. Gaston was amazed at how much work Michael had done. He was obviously very pleased.

'I've made three suggestions,' Michael explained, quite unnecessarily, of course, as George Gaston riffled through the papers. 'What do you think?'

George continued to show his surprise, and then growing pleasure, with Michael's work, once more shuffling the papers back and forth. Now it was Michael's turn to be surprised, for Mr. Gaston picked out the abstract picture.

'I think I like this one,' he said, holding up Michael's homage to Braque. 'There won't be many other boats with a cubist picture on the side!'

Michael really hadn't thought that Mr. Gaston would pick that one, and in any case, he hadn't expected Mr. Gaston to know about abstract painting. Michael felt that he had learned an important lesson that day. Just because a man was a publican didn't mean he lacked an education. Anyway, he was delighted with Mr. Gaston's choice and asked when they might begin to copy it onto the side of the boat.

'There's a lot to do first, Michael,' replied George. 'Look, while I do this bit of repair work, why don't you have a go at scraping off the old paint? Just do it for a small area so that we can get an idea how difficult it will be. I think you should begin with a dry scraper. You never know, we might be in luck and find that that is all that is required. If not, we might consider using a paint stripper. But one thing at a time, eh?'

By summer's end, it was all finished. They had decided to paint the outside. It had been too hard to clean off the old paint for varnishing. It turned out to be a fortunate choice, anyway, because Mr. Gaston chose a dark blue finish with gold striping – which was very smart – and that made a wonderful backdrop to Michael's cubism. He had painted two pictures, one on either side of the fore section of the superstructure. George Gaston had let him get on with them by himself, which was a grand act of trust, which both Michael and his father appreciated greatly.

It was while he was painting the second picture that Mr. Gaston told Michael to call him George. He also invited Michael to join him and his family for a couple of days upriver when it was finished. There was just enough time left of his holiday before returning to his posh school.

As he joined the Gaston family, Michael was introduced for the first time to Mrs. Gaston, a happy, cheerful woman, and their son, Ken. Ken had just turned seventeen and seemed to Michael to be a rather clever lad. Indeed he was, and he was increasingly running the *Pot* these days.

'Who's in charge of the *Pot*, George?' asked Michael, for he had become used to the idea of Ken and his mother running the place when George and he were working on the boat.

'We're taking a few days' holiday for a change, Michael, so we've got a sub in. It's somebody we've had in before. He's reliable and honest, so we don't worry.'

'Mind you, he costs a lot,' added Ken.

Michael and George did all the work at first, Ken and his mother being all too happy to sit back and enjoy the treat. That suited Michael, as well, for he had been longing to be first mate to George on the narrowboat. In any case, by the time they had travelled a fair way and moored along a deserted stretch of the river, it fell to Mary, as Michael came to know her, to cook up a meal in that galley he had seen so long ago. She had come on board with a steak and kidney stew ready to heat up, so most of her work had been done earlier. The smell from the galley soon made *Maisy Pot* seem like a real home. George didn't even ask, as he poured a beer for Michael along with all members of the Gaston family. Later, George and Mary went into the fore section where the double bed had been prepared, while Michael and Ken took the two side benches in the saloon, which on removal of the back cushions, turned into a couple of very comfortable single beds.

The river outside was like a mill pond. Everything was silent as they extinguished the boat lights which were placed at intervals along the inner walls and roof. It was so easy to fall asleep.

After taking it in turns to use the bathroom the next morning, which was, Michael saw, a difficulty with this style of living but one he thought he could get used to, Ken drummed up a good breakfast for everyone. The sun began to warm them. They cast off once more, this time with Ken and his dad doing the "driving", as Mary put it. Michael and Mary went out onto the foredeck where they felt like the lord and lady of the manor. They both laughed for it was not forgotten that Michael's dad was exactly that. They had a good chat all morning, and Michael began to feel that he really was part of this lovely family.

As ten o'clock came round, they came upon a T-junction in the river and George manoeuvred *Maisy Pot* into it. He explained to Michael that this was the beginning of the local canal system. Michael knew that narrow boats had been especially designed for these narrow waterways. He also knew that there would be several locks to navigate as they traversed higher ground, and he looked forward to the experience of going through one.

He got his chance about an hour later. Just in front of the lock itself, the canal widened; indeed, it widened sufficiently for a narrow boat to turn around. Michael had been wondering about that, for how else would they have been able to return to base? So that was one problem solved. However, they were not going to turn round. Instead, they moored loosely against the bank some way back from the lock. Michael wondered why they had done that, until he saw another canal boat actually in the lock.

'Come and watch, Michael,' said George, and he jumped off *Maisy Pot* onto the bank.

They climbed up a short embankment and then Michael saw and understood how the lock worked. A section of waterway called the chamber, he was told, about one and a half times longer than *Maisy Pot,* was blocked at each end by pairs of huge timber gates. Actually, the gate at the far end, in front of the higher part of the canal – it was higher by some three feet, Michael guessed – had just been closed by a man he assumed was the master or assistant of the narrow boat which was tied up inside the closed section of the lock. He also saw that the gate closed from the outside so that when water was let out from the locked section, the pressure of the higher water kept the gate closed. When he had finished closing the upper gate, the man walked round to a place near the lower gate and took a large, metal handle, with a square socket at its end, from a holder, inserted it onto a square, iron spindle and began to turn the spindle round. A noise of rushing water began from under the near-side lock gate. The man continued to turn the spindle, and Michael then saw that it was coupled to a vertical rack and pinion which, in turn, raised a horizontal barrier – called a sluice gate, George told him – below the near-side gate. The more the man turned that spindle, the greater the outflow of water from under the lower gates and the lower the level of the water in the chamber so that, before Michael's delighted eyes, the narrow boat inside the lock began to descend towards the water level outside and downstream. It all took some time, but that was okay because there was a lot to learn, and it all took time. Eventually, water flow from the chamber dwindled to a trickle, and the man stopped opening the sluice gate and turned his attention to the main lower gates themselves. It was only when the water levels inside the chamber and outside in the canal became equal that the gates could be opened, not by any regulation, but simply because of water pressure. If the water in the chamber was higher than outside, the water pushed so hard against the gate that nobody could move it. Once the levels became equal, it was easy to push on a long bar attached to the top of each gate and make them swing.

George walked over to open the gate on the other bank to help the man from the other narrow boat. Michael understood that such comradely spirit was the essence of canal navigation. He also saw that the gates were made oversize, so that they came together when still protruding somewhat into the higher-level water. That meant that there was no chance of water pressure being able to push the gates the wrong way. Michael now also understood why the chamber was a fair bit longer than a narrow boat: there had to be sufficient spare room to let the lower gates fold back into the chamber. It was all very clever, Michael thought. He wasn't the first to think that.

The other narrow boat chugged out of the lock through the open gates, so leaving an invitation for the *Maisy Pot* to chug upstream and replace it in the lock chamber. The whole process was reversed, and as the water level in the chamber rose when the upper sluice was opened, *Maisy* rose with it. The upper gates were opened, and they began their journey out of the lock and into the next stretch of canal. It had taken nearly an hour to clear both canal boats from that lock. Nothing happened quickly on the canals, Michael began to realise.

They stopped for a salad lunch soon after that, navigated a second lock about two hours later and moored for the night around six. Mary heated up another stew which she had prepared in the pub beforehand; this time, rabbit, which Michael adored.

It was only just after breakfast when it dawned on Michael that he had a problem. He had to be back at school in two days' time, and there was no way that the *Maisy Pot* could return by then. He really should have thought of this before! He began to feel panicky and explained his problem to George. George just smiled and told him not to worry; all would be well. Michael couldn't see how, but he remained silent – at least, for the rest of the morning.

Around midday, they moored up alongside a pub which, George explained, was well loved by canal boaters. As they all walked through the front door, Michael saw his dad, smiling and waving them over to his table.

'Thought you could skive off school for a few days, eh?' he grinned.

He had planned all this beforehand with George, of course. They all enjoyed their lunch and chatted for a while before Michael was sent off to collect his belongings from the boat and to drive off with his dad in his Alvis. It took no more than an hour to get home that way.

That was the end of Michael's summer holiday that year. Although Michael's interests moved onto other things in the later years, he remained close friends with the Gaston family for the rest of his life, not least because of a profoundly disturbing event on his next trip on the canal with George and Ken.

*

Michael was keen to renew his experience with narrowboats when he returned home at the end of term. The weather was chilly by now and few people ventured onto the canal without some urgent business reason or other, but Michael felt the draw as soon as he got home. So, it was organised. A short trip, this time with Ken and George together. The plan was just to go far enough to pass through two locks and then to return to base. They were all dressed in warm clothes, for this really was a silly adventure. Michael even got the chance to take the helm for a while, George looking on carefully, of course.

They had been going for forty minutes or so when Ken appeared with mugs of tea. Only as he began to sip from his mug did Michael realise just how cold it was out on the water. He had been concentrating so hard that he hadn't felt the cold. He began to apologise to George and Ken for dragging them out in such weather. They didn't mind in the least. If anything, they argued, there was something more authentic, more real, about a trip in this weather.

'Even better if it rains!' George added. 'Your head gets soaked, your hands get numb and it's hard to navigate, but it's one hell of an experience.'

Michael felt a little better after that. And he was enjoying himself. There were no other boats waiting at the first lock and the lower doors were open, following the departure of a canal boat obviously going in the opposite direction to theirs, so it took them no more than twenty minutes to get through and be on their way again.

Ken took a turn at the wheel, as he called it, while Michael climbed along the top of *Maisy Pot* to sit with his legs dangling over the fore-well. He knew, somehow, that this might be his last trip in *Maisy Pot* for some while. He was absolutely not bored with narrowboats, but he felt restive. He had grown up significantly during the last term. He was aware of it vaguely and knew the change had been more than what he had experienced at the same time last year. If asked what exactly the change in him was, he would have been unable to say. *Just a feeling*, he might have explained. He was happy sitting up near *Maisy*'s prow, just staring into space, his mind a blank.

They made good time, arriving at the second lock in a little short of two hours. However, there was another canalboat ahead of them moored in front and to the side of the lock, waiting for a third boat to finish coming through. In view of the long wait ahead of them, while they tied up behind the waiting boat, Ken made another brew, this time with a plate of biscuits. After ten minutes, the lock levels had equalized, the gates were opened and the leading boat emerged. The canalboat immediately ahead of them manoeuvred into mid-stream and slowly slipped into the vacant lock. The low-level gates were closed, and the sluice gate was opened a little.

As the *Maisy Pot* moved up along the bank in readiness for its turn, Michael could hear again the familiar sound of water rushing into the lock from up-stream. Two people had disembarked from the boat in the lock, a lame man and a boy, presumably his son, who seemed to be round about Michael's age. The man was turning the spigot on the sluice gate while the boy was, well, essentially mucking about on the narrow ledge atop the gates. Suddenly, and before Michael's startled eyes, the boy slipped, yelled and fell into the lock. His father, if that was his relationship to the lad, stopped turning the sluice handle immediately and shouted. Michael steaked across the grassy mound between *Maisy*'s mooring and the lock gates, pulling off his topcoat as he ran and flinging it onto the ground. The water in the lock was of course very low, for the sluice gate had only been open a short while. Just before he reached the lock, the boy's dad had jumped, fully clothed, into the water. By the time Michael had reached the lock side, the man had gathered his boy into his arms but, for some reason, was thrashing about.

'What's the matter?' Michael shouted down at him.

'I've got my foot caught under the sluice gate,' he yelled back, 'and my son can't swim.'

Michael very nearly jumped into the lock himself but then thought that he might get caught up himself so, rather than jumping, he climbed down an iron ladder attached to the side of the lock, jumped down from above the last couple of rungs, swum the few yards towards the pair and took the boy in his arms.

'Let go!' he told the trapped man. 'I have him.'

The boy's father gently released his son into Michael's grasp, not without some misgivings in view of Michael's youth and stature and shouted over the noise of the water rushing into the lock from under the sluice gate, 'Be very careful. It's slippery under foot.'

The water was too deep for Michael to walk with the boy; after all, it had to be deep enough to float the narrowboat, so Michael made use of his life-saving knowledge from school. However, it was one thing to practice your skills in a warm, clean, more or less calm swimming pool, and quite another to do the job clothed in a cold, wet, woolly jumper and pants in the frothing, cold, dirty water of a canal lock.

'I know what I'm doing,' he told the boy. 'Trust me, now. Lie back while I hold you. You can breathe, or hold your breath a little if you must, while I tow you to that ladder. It isn't far. Trust me. Relax.'

The boy did as he was told. *Thank God for that*, thought Michael. He had practised this manoeuvre many times in the pool at school, so he was confident he knew what to do. In any case, it wasn't far to tow the boy.

They got there and Michael told the lad to turn, take a firm grip on the ladder and find a foothold. After that, it was all plain sailing. By the time the boy had climbed the few steps to the bank above, Ken had arrived and helped him off the ladder and onto *terra firma*.

Michael turned back immediately to help the boy's father. 'What can I do to help?' he yelled at him. 'Would it be helpful to open the sluice gate more?'

'I'm not sure that will help,' the man replied. "I think I've caught my foot in some netting or something.'

'I'll see if I can get a look,' Michael replied and made a brief dive into the cold water to see if he could see anything.

But it was too dark and murky down there, and the water was rushing past at some lick.

He came up for air. 'I can't see down there. I'll drop down and see if I can feel anything.'

Well, drop down wasn't a good description, because buoyancy and the rushing water made it very difficult to reach down. He tried again, also without success. The trapped man was beginning to look anxious. Michael tried a third time.

When he came back up for air, he yelled, 'I can feel it. Like you said, some netting, I think. I'll get some cutters.'

'Please don't leave me. I'm not sure I can keep my head above water for much longer by myself.'

It was obvious that he was becoming panicky by now. Michael stayed with him and yelled up to Ken above. It was quite difficult to make himself heard, but he got his message across. Ken disappeared. Michael held the trapped man as best he could, but he too was becoming nervous about keeping his balance. This brought a whole new meaning, it seemed, to "walking on water".

There came a shout from Ken and a heavy pair of cutters (too heavy, really, but maybe there had been no choice) hanging from a rope. *That's a good move*, Michael thought. *It would be a disaster to drop those in the water.* Michael grabbed the cutters, told the trapped man to do his best to stay upright and ducked down into the freezing froth in search of the netting. Fortunately he found it immediately and began to tear at it with the cutters. He was aware that he had banged the man's ankle at one point, but he carried on regardless. He nudged the man on his shin. He got the message and pulled his leg up – he was free. He swam into a resting position for a moment to make sure that his rescuer was safe. Michael came up for air, Ken pulled the cutters up and away, and the rescuer and rescued made their way to the iron ladder and safety.

They were both shaking as they climbed up and onto the lock side: Michael because of the cold, and the freed man because of his ordeal.

'How's my son?' he called out.

He was assured that he was well and enjoying a cup of hot, sweet tea as they spoke. They all went to the *Maisy Pot,* then, for a cup of warmth, too. George had found some absorbent towels and blankets and he wrapped them up snuggly, as he had done for the boy a little earlier. In due course, they all calmed down and began to warm up.

Then came the business of exchanging names. The lame man was called Brendon Plater and his son was called Nigel. Nigel was roughly one year younger than Michael. He seemed to Michael to be a bright lad. After some more talk, although it has to be said that the Platers weren't really in the mood for much talk right then, *Maisy*'s guests got up to leave. Not, of course, before yet another round of profuse thanks, to Michael in particular.

George suggested that they not bother to go through the lock now but, in view of the time, turn round and go back home.

As they got under way, George said quietly to Michael, 'You did really well there, Michael.'

'It was a brilliant idea to tie the cutters to a rope,' Michael replied.

3

Michael matured a lot during the next three years. He was a good student and achieved fair – if not always brilliant – grades in his exams. Of course, his father had sent him to a good public school where he boarded all term. That had been difficult in the first year and there had been tears, but nothing could drag him away now. He still enjoyed being home in the holidays, though, and now he had a new interest: jazz. He had bought a small record player with his generous pocket money and, during term time, had sloped off into the local town to seek out new records from the music shop there. He was reasonably open-minded in his choices, liking Mulligan's bebop as well as trad.

His father was glad that the walls of the rooms in their big house were thick. When Mike was playing his music in his room, it couldn't be heard downstairs. So it was, that early in those summer holidays, Michael came to hear of a local jazz session to be held at the beer garden of the *Tomber Pot* at eight o'clock in the evening on Saturday next. Good that it was outside, otherwise he'd have to pretend that he was over sixteen. Mind you, that would have been difficult, as everybody knew everybody else in Tomberwater; certainly, the village bobby knew Michael. Michael reckoned he would look the other way.

He strolled down to the pub around a quarter to eight and was a little surprised to see that the beer garden was almost full already. Michael hadn't expected many other people in their sleepy village to be jazz lovers. Once again, he realised that he had formed a judgement based on nothing. It was a habit he must learn to ditch.

The jazz band for the night called themselves *The Tomber Jazzmen*. Hardly original, Michael thought, but it would do; and anyway, it was their music which mattered rather than their name.

In one corner of the yard, next to the pub piano, they'd set up a simple drumkit: base drum, snare and symbols. Shortly after eight, without introduction from George, Mary or Ken Gaston, four youths, about seventeen or eighteen years old, Michael thought, walked into the limelight or, to be more exact, into the area around the piano and drums which was illuminated by four hanging light bulbs covered in differently coloured shades. In addition to the percussion section, they sported a trumpet and a trombone. The latter shone in all its contemporary glory while the trumpet had an uneven, dirty-looking patina all over.

The Tomber Jazzmen were billed to play traditional jazz. From the start, it was clear that the trumpet was the lead. With a couple of foot stomps and a nod of his instrument, the band began, beautifully together, with the oldie of the oldies *When the Saints Go Marchin' In.* However corny their choice of opener was – and that number is frequently banal in the hands of insensitive musicians – they kept it all together very well indeed, in particular because of the mastery and forward thrust of the trumpet, and they had their audience clapping along with them in no time at all. Michael really hadn't expected anything so good to come out of this little village of theirs. There followed *Basin Street Blues, Beale Street Blues, Baby Won't You Please Come Home* and several of that ilk. They finished their first set with *Tiger Rag* and brought the house down.

As the musicians passed by Michael on their way to the bar, with applause continuing all around them, Michael stood up, grabbed the trumpeter by his free hand and shook it vigorously, shouting above the din, 'That was superb! I never knew there was such a good band around here. Thank you very much.'

The trumpeter looked at him in some confusion for a split second as the band members passed by.

Michael waited for the bar crowd to thin out before he walked up and asked Ken for a lemonade. Ken brought him half a pint of bitter and nobody seemed to notice.

All so civilised, thought Michael, as he made his way back to the beer garden where, in due course, the band reassembled and began their second set of the evening. They were almost as good as before – perhaps a little scrappy here and there – but Michael remained delighted with his evening's entertainment, as did everybody else, as far as he could see.

He left immediately afterwards, and when he arrived back home, he was pleased to see his father around and told him of how much he had enjoyed the concert. Michael overdid it a bit, really, for his praise for the band was perhaps just a little more than they deserved. He asked his father whether he had previously heard of *The Tomber Jazzmen*. He hadn't, but that was no great surprise, for his musical leanings were elsewhere, and he suggested that Michael ask Ken Gaston or his dad, maybe.

A few days later, Michael did just that. George Gaston hesitated for a split second before telling Michael that the two lead players, trumpet and trombone, were the Roland boys.

Mike looked blank for a moment before replying. 'You mean those two kids who thumped me three years ago?'

'That's right, Michael. Jazz is just their hobby, of course. They both have proper jobs during the day.'

'Well, I'll be damned. I certainly didn't recognise them. I don't now, even after you've told me. For one thing, they look quite smart and they no longer have dirty fingernails; at least the trumpeter didn't. Anyway, George, I think they were great. They all played very well, I thought, and I really enjoyed the evening. I told them so.'

'Oh! I'm so pleased you did that. They have changed a lot in the last three years and holding down jobs has turned them into men. They're actually quite a responsible pair of lads these days. Barry – he's the younger one and plays the trombone – is a mechanic in Gerry Madden's garage down the road; services most of the cars in Tomber.'

'What does the other one do?'

George looked slightly embarrassed as he replied, 'Gordon's a gardener.'

'Any idea when they play their next gig, George?' Michael asked.

'I'll find out and let you know, Mike.'

Michael was dimly aware that that was probably the first time that George had called him Mike. He felt somehow proud about it.

Over the next six weeks or so, Michael followed *The Tomber Jazzmen* around local villages, enjoying their strident, confident playing. He opened a couple of conversations with them about their pieces. Michael couldn't play a note himself but had amassed quite an impressive knowledge of how the numbers were played by various famous bands on record. He was pleased that the Rolands weren't upset by comparisons he made, for they were as enthusiastic about their heroes as was Michael. He told them one day that although he liked trad jazz a lot, his favourite form was bebop.

'Miles Davies, Thelonious Monk…' he began, but was interrupted by Gordon,

'Charlie Parker, Gerry Mulligan, Chet Baker. I couldn't agree more, Mike,' he said. 'The only reason we don't play bebop ourselves is that it's too hard! We have lots of records, though. Would you like to come round and listen to them sometime?'

Michael was ecstatic to find kindred spirits in such a small place as Tomberwater and district and accepted Gordon's invitation on the spot. So began regular meetings between the boys, even though Michael was their junior by four and five years and, more to the point, even though they had fought each other three years earlier. All that was forgotten amidst their shared love of jazz, and their friendship grew and filled that summer holiday with joy for both Michael and the Rolands.

Michael's schooling and examinations began to take up more of his time over the next few years, so his role as groupie to *The Tomber Jazzmen* came to a natural end. Nevertheless, Michael kept in close touch with Gordon and Barry during his holidays, and that the friendship matured and firmed.

It was not until two years later that Michael asked Gordon what he did in his work. He had completely forgotten that George Gaston had told him that he was a gardener back when he learned that Barry was a garage mechanic.

Gordon smiled at Michael and said, 'You're not very observant, Mike. I work for your mother at the Big House. You've passed me by several times in the last couple of years.'

'Oh, God! I'm sorry, Gordon. I wasn't ignoring you; I just didn't know,' Michael replied in great confusion.

'I know, I know. You walk around in some sort of dream half the time, Mike. I understand. Really.'

'How long have you been one of our gardeners, Gordon?'

'It must be about three years now, Mike.'

'Are you happy with the job, Gordon? I do hope you are,' Mike replied.

'More than happy, mate, and the pay is better than I'd get anywhere else. So, unless you sack me, I'm staying!'

Michael put his arm round Gordon's neck for a moment. 'Good,' he said.

Great friendships can have very inauspicious beginnings.

*

Michael Montayne was a good student. He worked hard and was well above average in his grades. He was also popular among his fellows at school, most of whom came from extremely privileged backgrounds. Yet his school had built a reputation of caring for both development and education. By some people's lights, it might have been called somewhat left-wing. Teachers there, however, took the issue to their charges head on.

'It's not a question of left or right,' they insisted. 'It's a question of decency.'

It seemed that all Michael's teachers sang from the same hymn sheet, for the insistence on decency was repeated many times by most, maybe all, of his teachers over the years. Indeed, the word appeared in the school motto, even if it was in Latin.

Michael once mentioned this to his father.

'Why do you think we chose that school for you, Michael?' was his reply.

It seems his dad sang along, too.

In due course, Michael sat for his 'A' levels and passed in three subjects: French with an A grade, and English and Italian with a B. Though a little disappointed, Michael recognised the justice of the result, and there was no moaning. His father and mother both expressed their pleasure at the outcome, and Michael felt that their praise was genuine. He had already obtained conditional offers for places at four universities, probably as much for the maturity he displayed at the interview as anything, and without hesitation but equally without any real understanding why, he chose Bristol. After Oxbridge, it was in the top half-dozen universities in England. He had thought about places in Scotland and Ireland, but somehow they didn't appeal to him. So, like thousands of other schoolboys and girls, he chose his route almost with his eyes shut. Of course, in Michael's case, there was a big difference.

He came from a privileged background. The prospect of entering university was seen in his family, and most certainly in his milieu, as something of a "rounding off" –an opportunity to enlarge one's circle even more. The fact that Michael had shown some talent for languages early on – indeed, his spoken French was more or less fluent – was regarded by some of his parent's friends as just a piece of fun, while Michael understood that learning about French culture and literature was much more to his taste.

He enrolled at Bristol in their Modern Languages course. To be fair, many of his parents' friends and acquaintances were sensitive people and understood Michael's aspirations. But occasionally, along came someone who was not.

One of those happened along round about the time that Michael was hot into jazz. There had been yet another of his parents' dinner parties which Michael had attended. He had been doing that more often as he grew older. It had been his choice, usually, whether to attend or not, and when he was younger, boredom had decided his decision to give many of these occasions a miss.

Anyway, about two years before his 'A' levels, conversation at one of these dinners had turned to how Michael occupied himself these days. Already sensing a patronising aspect of the question, Michael was somewhat guarded as he told his questioner about his love of jazz and of his friendship with a local jazz band. He was asked if the band was famous – on the stage, for example. No, Michael explained, they were just a group of local boys with like-mind. Arthur Montayne added that a couple of years earlier, Michael had spent his long vacation helping the local publican renovate his narrow boat.

'Oh!' laughed Michael's questioner. 'Slumming it in the hols, eh?'

Michael had been well brought up and he should have known better, but he lost it. 'These were, and still are, good friends of mine. Their lack of privilege does not diminish them one jot!' he exclaimed; he almost shouted it.

His antagonist shut up immediately, turned to another guest at the table and tried to bring the subject round to whatever was in that day's headlines. That did it for Michael. He got up from the table, nodded to his parents and walked briskly out of the room. In the morning, he apologised to his father for his unseemly behaviour.

'No need, Mike. He will not be a guest here again.'

Once again, Michael had reason to appreciate his parents' innate decency. The occasion stood out in his memory, for nothing quite like that ever happened again. Generally, Michael was coming to enjoy these dinner parties more and more. He was growing up and beginning to understand what was being said, and even more, what was not being said. He was also coming to realise that the conversation around his parents' table was anything but trivial. Certainly, it might be fun – it often was – but the humour was clever and, as far as Michael was concerned, informative. He had been aware for many years that several of his parents' guests were titled, and on two occasions, he was sure, had some foreign royal connection, though exactly what that was he had no idea.

Everyone at the table addressed each other by their Christian names – or maybe that should have been forenames, Michael thought on occasion – so that their handles were never on show. Exactly how or why his parents had come to know such people, Michael had no idea. He asked his father once but only received a brief "Oh, we've been friends for years."

By osmosis, really, Michael came to know many bright, articulate and sometimes eminent people, and as the years went by, they began to remember him. He continued to enjoy the company of the village people, the Rolands and the Gastons in particular. He saw no difficulty in being friends with people from very different walks of life.

So it continued throughout his three years in Bristol. He enjoyed his subject and performed better there than at school, quite probably because of the advantages he had unconsciously assimilated around his parents' dinner table. His spoken Italian had become pretty much as fluent as his French, and he had become more than useful at German and Spanish – both, of course, being new languages to Michael. He had taken strongly to French and Italian literature and was increasingly interested in French and European history in general, so much so, that he began to wish that he had chosen to read History instead of languages. His tutors pointed out that he couldn't do everything and that he would have the rest of his life to catch up on history, at least to a satisfying extent. Unless, that was, he intended to take another degree afterwards. Michael was tempted to do that, in a way, but he knew that he would leave academe after finishing his degree and get cracking in the real world. What as, however, he had little idea.

He didn't miss out on a social life, either. He had played a bit of tennis with his father in his teen years and continued with that at university. He never achieved great heights, but then, he wasn't interested in trying to. It was just a bit of exercise and a social thing as far as he was concerned. And he was right, because it was tennis that brought Michael and Rachael together. There was no flash of light; no tempestuous love affair.

They met in the bar of the tennis club and agreed to partner for a doubles match with a couple of Michael's other friends. It just worked well for them, and a friendship grew. It continued to grow, month on month. Neither was short on looks, and neither was short on friends and acquaintances. They just fitted and, increasingly, they grew to realise that this would last. Rachael also came from a "good" home, though nothing like as rich as Michael's, and she had happy and loving parents, so they had a lot in common.

Michael invited Rachael to Tomberwater for a weekend to meet his folks and, of course, to see what they thought of her. God help them if they had found fault, of course, but the thing had to be done. He needn't have worried. His parents clearly approved his choice, indeed did so from the first moment, and Rachael equally obviously fell for them. And so it continued to grow. He proposed a couple of months before his finals and shortly after having met her parents who had come to Bristol for a weekend's break. He liked them, and it was reciprocated. So, one up for tennis.

Michael also attended a dining club at the university. Of course, he was merely continuing the lifestyle he had enjoyed at home. Most others in the club were doing the same. Pretty much all members were from financially privileged backgrounds, of course, but, as Michael had observed years before, that was no more his fault than it was the fault of someone from a poor background starting off broke. Neither was it any guarantee of human decency.

Unfortunately, some members of the club were awful snobs. As often as not they were the less financially secure, but such was a rule of thumb more than a hard and fast affair.

Anyway, Michael found two or three of his fellow members to his liking, and a friendship blossomed. One in particular was the son of what Michael presumed would be described as a shipping magnate. Geoffrey

Etherington's family appeared pretty well-off to Michael, though he had no real interest in whether they had more or less than his own family. Not only would he never have asked such a question of Geoffrey, he actually had absolutely no interest in the answer, an indifference which was almost certainly not shared by Geoffrey.

Friendships forged at university, however, were often very deep and frequently lasted a lifetime. Geoffrey was the second of Michael's friends to spend a weekend at the family pile and, like Rachael before him, he clicked with his hosts almost immediately. He joined Michael at home on several more occasions, once while Rachael was there, and he disappeared with Arthur Montayne on one occasion for a couple of hours' exploration of the estate. Geoffrey, by the way, had chosen to read Economics and had every intention of joining his father in the shipping business.

Michael got a first! He was ecstatic and in no doubt that he deserved it. Rachael got a first in History, and Michael was equally in no doubt of the justice done. Geoffrey thundered home with the top first in his faculty. On the evening of the day the results appeared on their respective notice boards, the three firm friends went out and got very expensively pissed. Arthur and Helen Montayne came up for degree day, as did Martin and Ellie Thorndell, Rachael's mum and dad and Bob and Doris Etherington, Geoffrey's parents, whom Michel met for the first time. It was a delightful occasion; everybody was very proud of their children or themselves – or both.

The Etheringtons insisted on hosting the group to dinner at The Grand Hotel. The occasion was a delight. The food and wine were quite exceptional, the party appeared to be treated like royalty and the service was faultless. Michael discovered later that the Etheringtons owned the place.

The next time these nine people spent time together was at Rachael and Michael's wedding. That took place a little less than three months after degree day. They had chosen to have only one hundred guests between them – their nearest and dearest, they insisted. The wedding was to be held, by agreement with Martin and Ellie Thorndell, at Saint Jean Church in Tomberwater, and the reception at Tomberwater Hall, Michael's family home. Geoffrey Etherington was the best man, and Susan Holleck, an old friend of Rachael's from childhood, was the bridesmaid. As well as Rachael and Michael's closest university friends and their families, the Gastons and Rolands of Tomberwater were included in the guest list.

At the end of the long, lovely day, Michael and Rachael sloped off down to Tomberwater wharf, climbed aboard *Maisy Pot*, and under Michael's deft handling – and what a surprise to Rachael that was – chugged quietly up-river for the first week of their married life together.

*

Michael's parents offered the newlyweds the first floor of the west wing of the Big House. It was a generous allotment, comprising their own suite of bedroom, dressing room and sitting room, together with a guest suite with three bedrooms and large lounge. Rachael and Michael were delighted with the Montayne's generosity.

Usually, all four family members met for the first meal of the day in the breakfast room, though rarely simultaneously. Hot breakfast was provided in tureens on the side, with all cold items placed on a separate table alongside. Each member of the household drifted in as he or she liked. It was all very casual. Lunches were mostly taken in one end of the kitchen and occasionally in the breakfast room. Dinner was an altogether more formal affair. It wasn't their habit to dress formally for family dinners, but black tie, or very occasionally white tie, was the order of the day when there were houseguests. Whatever the level of formality with regard to dress, self-service was never tolerated. Domenic, as butler, and Margaret, as housekeeper and chief of table, served either on their own, or with others brought in as the occasion demanded. Of course, Michael had been used to such proceedings all his life – or all of it at home – but Rachael had not. Her family were far from poverty-stricken, but their five-bedroom house in suburban northeast London did not boast servants, let alone suites.

Surprisingly, though not to Michael, Rachael found no difficulty in assuming the mantle of bride to the wealthy. She was adored by all but especially by Helen, who took to the role of mother-in-law like a duck to water. Often Helen would take Rachael firmly by the arm and march her out into the garden where she explained what changes she was trying to bring about, and she insisted that Rachael offer up suggestions. If Gordon Roland was around at the time, he would be dragged into these discussions and his opinions avidly sought. They grew into a strong threesome in the Tomberwater household, for on matters of the gardens, the other males around the place were given short shrift.

Rachael began to develop an interest in the history of the house and of the family. It was undoubtedly the historian in her. She found a couple of small, inconsequential volumes on the subject in the library. They were, without doubt, turgid accounts, but given the natural intensity of her interest, proved quite informative. One evening, she spoke about her reading to Michael.

'Oh yes!' he replied, somewhat dismissively. 'Those old things. Read them years ago. They do go on a bit. Still, did you find them interesting?'

She certainly did, especially when she came to realise that the whole village of Tomberwater owed its existence to the founding family. After some prodding, she got Michael to talk about his forebears. It wasn't that he was reluctant or secretive, just that it was "old hat" to him, and he hadn't thought about it all for years. Michael's father's father's father – he wasn't quite sure how many generations back it was – was a phenomenally wealthy Frenchman, Philippe Montaigne, who fell madly in love with an English rose, Catherine Harman. He proposed and she accepted but with one condition. She insisted that they make their home in England. There seemed to be no records of why she was adamantly against a life in France, but as things turned out – the much later Revolution and all that – she had made a good choice.

Catherine knew of this bit of countryside and took her new husband to see it. He fell in love with it, for its geology as much as anything. He found this roughly level piece of land of sixty acres or so, which he thought large enough for a country house estate without being too much of a burden, bordered on one side by a natural cliff, and on the other by a pleasantly flowing river. There was no village there at that time, so Philippe resolved to build one from scratch, recognising that he would need its inhabitants to service his proposed country seat. It was Philippe who named his little village, Tomberwater: *Tomber*, which was French for "to fall", referring to the sudden fall of the land on one side, and *water* came from the river, of course. It was very artificial, but then, so are most place names. The only difference is that this naming was relatively recent – mid-seventeenth century – and that the village had been created in one go rather than having evolved, as it were, over decades or even centuries. Philippe made one condition to his bride, effectively as a *quid pro quo* for her insistence on domicile in England. He would build their residence in the French style, using French builders who he would bring over for the job. The village buildings were built in the English vernacular of those times by English builders from neighbouring shires. The land upon which the village was built remained as freehold to the estate for a very long time, but after a few generations of Montaignes had managed to squander money too freely, the village land was sold off piecemeal, and all village properties now were freehold to the present occupants. All, that is, except for the pub – whose name had changed over the years but always with the blessing of the "Squire". The pub was still part of the grand estate, although its rent was maintained at an unusually low figure. From time to time, publicans of what was now called the *Tomber Pot* had tried to negotiate a buy-out, but each attempt had been strongly rebuffed. Rachael was unable to find any clue about why the pub should have been singled out in this way, and when she asked Michael about it, he realised for the first time that he had no idea either; he had never thought about the matter. When he raised the matter with his father, all he got was a noncommittal, "Oh, it's boring; I'll tell you about it someday".

As for the "chateau" itself, two substantial wings had been added after about a hundred years, one on either side and to the rear of the original building, but by then, access to French builders was more difficult or simply not sought. Although their style fitted reasonably well with that of the main building, the differing heritage of the extensions was clear for all to see. Nevertheless, Michael's forbear minus two, as it were, did a tasteful job, and the extensions proved to be no pain to the eye.

While all this learning was going on, Rachael was increasingly being involved in the gardens of Tomberwater Hall. Her mother-in-law had always been engrossed in that side of the estate and clearly sought to establish a successor while the going was good. Rachael had absolutely no problem with that, for she had loved gardens and garden planning for years. She had had no actual experience of anything so grand – suburbia hadn't offered anything like it, of course – but her love of her own family garden as a small child had blossomed into reading about the ideas and visiting the great gardens of Gertrude Jekyll and Vita Sackville-West, and others before them. So now she had her chance! Well, maybe not yet, for she had a lot to learn about what was around the place already, and in any case, notwithstanding Helen's great love for the gardens, their maintenance was in the hands of the small team of gardeners led by Mr. Patrick Louthy who cared deeply for the estate, his job and his opinions.

Early on in her life at the hall, Rachael had explored the place, as was only natural, and discovered that more than half of the rooms were shut off, and in those where she was able to gain access, she found dust, cobwebs, and furnishings swathed in huge dustsheets. She had asked Michael about it and learned that such had been the case for most, if not all, of his life.

'It's for the same reason we only have half a dozen gardeners and two cooks, for example,' he had replied. 'We aren't exactly broke, but how shall I say – a trifle distrait. This is obviously a huge estate to maintain in the style I imagine it to have been when it was first built; before Montaigne became Montayne. I have heard Father worry and snuffle about money all my life, but because I never actually felt short of anything, I have assumed that things aren't too serious. Mind you, Father is beginning to take me into his confidence a bit these days. Even so, I don't think anything too serious is afoot.'

As it happened, it was only about three months after that conversation with his wife that Michael really was taken into Arthur's confidence in a more serious way than ever before. Arthur took the line that now that Michael was married and settled down, he thought it time to appraise his son of some basic facts of life as far as the Tomberwater Estate was concerned. Not only had there been insufficient income from various investments to support anything like the original estate – and such had been the case all through Arthur's life and stewardship – but matters were rapidly coming to a head. Obviously, as Arthur assured his son yet again, everything would come to Michael on his death – after provision for his widow, of course. However, that was more of a threat than a promise these days, for big changes to the laws concerning inheritance of large estates had been introduced a decade earlier in 1949. Former regulations had had relatively little effect on anything really, but the estate duties of Sir Stafford Cripps meant business.

'The point, Michael, is that when you take this over, it is almost certain that duties and taxes will necessitate your selling the place; assuming, that is, that you could find anyone rich enough to buy it. It will be the end of our beloved home and way of life. I am very well aware that one may live in comfort with far less; that most people in the world do not face the dilemma we have. But that's not the point, of course. We have to grapple with things as they are, and have been, *for us*. So, I am truly sorry, my boy, that I cannot hand you anything like the life I have enjoyed – or, indeed, which you have enjoyed so far.'

Michael had never before seen his father so despondent.

'You have been aware of all this for a long time then? And never shared your worries with Mother or me?'

Arthur turned to Michael and simply said, 'I regarded it as my problem to solve. Unfortunately, I do not know how to do so.'

The discussion finished at that point, and Michael had several weeks in which to come to terms with these shattering tidings. He had known of the existence of estate duties for some time but had assumed that there were sufficient funds in other assets to meet the problem when it arose. When next he raised the matter with his father, he thought he might try a different angle.

'Dad, you mentioned some investments that have helped you maintain the place; in the manner to which we are well accustomed, at least. Even that must take a lot of money, I imagine?'

'Yes, it does, and we only just scrape through,' Arthur said glumly.

'Is there no way of increasing those investments? What are they, anyway?'

'They're shares in a small number of companies which produce dividends in a steady but small way. They have been carefully and cautiously purchased, and they represent something as near stable in that field as you can get. If I were to sell some and buy more flashy stock, shall we say, it could well bring in more money but at a significantly greater risk. Overall, there's little room for manoeuvre. Anyway, Michael, think about it and let's see if you can come up with any ideas. In the top drawer of the filing cabinet in my study, you will find details of all our investments, should you wish to look over them.'

And thus it was left for several weeks until Michael excitedly asked his father for another discussion on the subject.

'Father, just to recapitulate; while we can jog along financially at the moment, upon your death, taxes will claim more than half of the value of your total estate, the value of which would be determined by the tax authorities. Right?'

'I see you have been reading up on the subject, Michael. And yes, I agree with your summary.'

'I have looked at your portfolio of shares, Dad, and I have just one question. A major component of the portfolio is your holdings in *Marchant Voyages*. When did you buy those shares?'

'I didn't. I inherited them from your grandfather. Why do you ask?'

'Do you know anything about the company?'

Arthur paused for a split second before replying. Michael didn't notice anything.

'Not really, except that they don't yield any dividend. Our advisor has managed all the other shares, which are quoted on the public exchange. I have left all that to him. Is there something wrong?'

'Not at all. It's just that we know the owner of *Marchant Voyages*. It's none other than Geoffrey's dad, Robert Etherington! And are you aware of how much of their stock we own?'

'Goodness! No, I don't know the extent of our holdings.'

'It amounts to nearly fifteen percent of that company's total value. It's also the largest holding in our portfolio. Those shares are currently worth about sixteen million pounds.'

'Yes, but don't forget, Michael, that the costs of maintaining the estate and our lifestyle are substantial. There is still nowhere enough in the kitty to cover the taxes when I die.'

'I agree with that, Father. I just wanted to know if there was any reason for so large a holding in *Marchant Voyages* before I put a proposal to you.'

Arthur was silent for a moment before replying. 'Well, as far as I am concerned, there is no special reason for it. Perhaps your grandfather had one, but if so, I have no idea what it was. Anyway, how does our knowing the owner of *Marchant Voyages* help our problem?'

'I am wondering whether we can do a deal with *Marchant Voyages*, such that we sell Tomberwater estate to them as a specialist hotel, run by us and with permanent accommodation for us. You know, presumably, that they already own a number of prestigious hotels around Britain and the

Baltic, as well as a cruise ship, as they call it. Tomberwater could be a special part of their portfolio. Of course, a lot of money would be needed to bring the house up to the sort of standard required; money which we could never raise ourselves. I think I have some more detailed ideas which they might find attractive. What do you think of the idea in outline, though?'

'I would never have thought of that,' Arthur replied, with a somewhat curious half-smile on his face.

So began a tortured fortnight for the Montaynes. Arthur had to come to terms with the idea of losing the estate even during his lifetime. Then, at Michael's insistence, his mother and wife both had to be brought into the decision process, even though Arthur was the legal owner of everything. Actually, that turned out to be something of a relief to Arthur, a shared responsibility to lighten his burden, even if it meant that four people would now have to be convinced of every little detail before making a move. As Michael observed, they were beginning to see this business as a business. He stopped short of saying that sentiment should be overruled, for an essential part of his plan was to provide for a family lifestyle such that their accustomed privileges were maintained. Of course, money raised from the sale would still be subject to inheritance tax, but that might be reduced by selling the estate at a much-reduced price, together with guarantees of the results they sought. If the family could agree on all that, they would then put the plan to *Marchant Voyages*.

Helen saw the advantages right away and had no difficulty with the surrender of the deeds. She had watched Arthur becoming ever more worried for several years. For her, it seemed that Michael had brought matters to a head. Rachael, on the other hand, had no memories of a family background going back for ever, nor had she been brought up with servants and acres of land. No, she did not marry Michael for his family's wealth, but now that it was all laid out before her, she was appalled. However, she was a very useful foil in the discussions which filled those weeks, for being an intelligent woman, she was able to put her view strongly and logically, admitting immediately the nature of her outsider's bias. Equally, being intelligent, she was able to concede points when they were made well.

Eventually, a plan close to Michael's original ideas was agreed to by the whole family, not with reluctance in the end, but with a sense of adventure.

Michael made the first move towards *Marchant Voyages* via his best man. Geoffrey, who had joined his father's shipping and hotel empire straight after taking his degree, was more than sympathetic to the proposal, far more so than Michael had expected. Geoffrey promised to put the matter to his father and report back in due course. The die was cast. All that remained now was for Michael and his family to twiddle their thumbs and wait.

Not for too long, as it turned out. In merely three days, Geoffrey telephoned Michael to suggest a meeting of all parties, but without lawyers in the first instance.

The meeting was to be convened at ten o'clock in the morning at Tomber Hall. Geoffrey greeted Michael very warmly. There were smiles all round so far as Rachael, Helen and Doris Etherington were concerned, as one may have hoped, but that was nothing compared with the warmth on show between Arthur Montayne and Bob Etherington. Michael looked questioningly at his father who simply raised his finger and murmured that all would become clear very soon.

Coffee had been provided, and when all were seated, Arthur opened the meeting very simply but with a revelation which startled everyone else in the Montayne family.

'Bob and I have been talking long and hard during the last couple of days...'

Michael was astounded at this.

'And we have agreed that I would begin proceedings by acquainting my family with a little history. You might enjoy this, Rachael. Between us, Bob and I can probably provide a reasonably complete history of our families going back over one hundred and twenty years, at least, and we are willing to spend the necessary time going through it all if you wish, but not now. In the hope of keeping this meeting down to the hours remaining in this day – we shall provide lunch in due course – I shall merely sketch the important features that will help us to get down to the business plan proposed by Michael a couple of days ago.

'It will become apparent that Bob and I have known these histories for a long time, indeed for pretty much all of our lives. That's because our families have been tied together in business for something like one hundred years; if not more. Michael, please don't explode! I told you I'd explain everything. Have a little patience. It is entirely natural that Michael should ask, "Why the hell didn't I mention this when he first proposed this plan?" Well, the answer is that the… collaboration, shall I call it… between our families has a totally dishonourable past. I shall not beat about the bush, everybody. We were criminals! Not figuratively, you understand, but literally!

'I'm unsure how much history you each know – apart from Rachael, of course – but the lesser-known history of Britain and France, to name but two countries, during the sixty or so years beginning around the mid-nineteenth century, is soaked – do you like that, Bob? – with illicit booze. It mostly began with the French shipping brandy out of their country to Britain, and it soon found its way to North America as well. Duties were avoided at every turn, of course – French and English – so that smuggling became rife. It wasn't just in Cornwall that such things happened, famous though that is. It happened everywhere. Later on, the traffic became two-way to some extent in that Londoners, in particular – although the craze spread (or should I say, flowed?) elsewhere – developed a taste for gin. Mothers' ruin. You might know of the famous cry in the eighteen nineties, "Drunk for a penny: dead drunk for tuppence." Anyway, there are many books written on this subject, and if you want any more, you can sing it yourself; I think that phrase came from that era, too, but I'm not an historian, so don't take my word for it. You can take my word, however, when I tell you that Bob's and my forebears were deeply into it all. The two new wings of Tomber Hall, as we quaintly refer to them, were built by my great, great – I'm sorry, there are too many greats to recall right now – grandfather, who still had pots of money from our founding forebear, Phillipe Montaigne, by the way, in – and some might argue, in anticipation of – the mid-nineteenth century. Anyway, one of those wings never came to be used for accommodation. Instead, it became what I can only describe as a distillery. Who would believe that such goings-on took place in the middle of rural England in a grand country seat?

'Of course, it's one thing to store illicit booze and then, later, to make another illicit liquor; it's quite another to organise their shipment and distribution. That's where the Etheringtons came into the picture. It seems that great, great, etcetera Montaigne and great, great, etcetera Etherington became acquainted, then friends, and later, business associates, as the Mafia might say. Don't misunderstand my little joke; I don't suggest for a second that our families actually indulged in physical wrongdoings of any kind. I am sure that their criminality was restricted to booze-running and tax evasion. I am equally sure that such goings-on ceased before our grandfathers' time – or very nearly so, maybe.' Arthur grinned a little sheepishly and went on immediately with, 'The point I want to emphasise very strongly indeed right here and now, however, is that no such illegalities have been indulged in by me or by Bob; except, of course, by keeping our family histories quiet. "The sins of the father shall not be carried over to the son", or something like that. Not only have both Bob and I lived otherwise blameless lives, we have raised our children to be upstanding citizens, too. Michael, I had hoped never to have had the need to tell you all this – I know that Bob has taken a contrary view with Geoffrey, which has always been his choice, of course – but our new circumstances demand that we share all our knowledge with all of our immediate family members. And that is why you are all at this meeting today, of course.'

Seeing Michael was about to burst forth, Arthur continued, 'Michael, I'll finish very soon, but I must first say something about our respective financial circumstances today. In our smuggling heyday, the Montaignes and the Etheringtons had a roughly equal share – so far as I am able to ascertain, and I understand that Bob agrees – in the illicit trade. In addition, we had Tomber Hall and Estate; and separately, the Etheringtons had their home in Yorkshire. Since going straight – I think that's the correct expression these days – *our* family have been singularly bad financial managers, let alone money-makers, while the Etheringtons have been stupendously successful in that area. The fact that our shares in *Marchant Voyages* amount to only about fifteen percent is a reflection of the stupendous growth the Etheringtons have made in their shipping and hotel business, and I sincerely congratulate Bob on his splendid success. When Michael came to me with his plan to save something of our glorious, privileged past, I was amazed and delighted. I didn't tell you of our history at that time, Michael, because I wanted to discuss the proposal independently with Bob and to assure him that you had come up with your proposals without any reference to our joint family history. I believe that Bob is convinced of this.'

Bob interrupted to say, firmly, that he was, not least because of Geoffrey's assessment of Michael. Geoffrey was fast becoming an astute asset to *Marchant Voyages* at this time.

Arthur continued, 'I'm about done for now. I wanted you to know how our families have been entwined for generations – albeit for dishonourable reasons – so that Michael's proposal can be discussed in total honesty within our two families.'

Helen stood at this point and said, with the sweetest of expressions on her face, 'I think it's time for a drink. I know that lunch is some time away yet, but… I hope you agree?'

She rang for service. A good move, really, for it allowed everyone to collect his and her thoughts, to come to some kind of terms with Arthur's momentous revelations. It was also useful for Rachael, who was clearly shocked by her father-in-law's revelations.

Helen, on the other hand, was rather enjoying herself. No, she hadn't heard this story before. Arthur hadn't given her a "heads up", as we say today, but her bubbly sense of fun overcame any thoughts of accepting guilt for someone else's crimes. Rachael, though a highly intelligent young lady, had been brought up within, shall we say, a less expansive milieu. Shades of grey were somewhat less accessible for her.

Time, however, is a great healer. And so was a good lunch. (Helen had wondered why Arthur had issued some rather generous instructions to the kitchen the day before.)

Doris Etherington, of course, had been told all about the murky family past – was quite inured to it by now – and so took all Arthur had said in her stride. So it was, that when their meeting reconvened in any sort of formal way, everybody was suitably primed, on board and equally criminal at one (or was that two?) remove. No one was looking for financial ruin. Everyone hoped for an amicable and mutually beneficial solution to the Montaynes' problem.

So, dear reader, you need not wade through the endless details of the agreement that was forged that day. We shall leave all that to the lawyers who enjoy such things. A short outline will do. Essentially, the two families merged their assets into the creation of a new enterprise called *Marchant Enterprises*. Michael, Geoffrey, Bob and Arthur formed the Board of Directors and Bob also took on the role of Managing Director, or CEO, as we'd say today, but long before that term became well-known, Bob retired and Geoffrey took over. Tomber Hall became a glorified hotel – but with rather special characteristics, some of which we have heard, but there are more – with a manager to oversee everyday matters. The whole building underwent a face-lift, involving new rooms and suites being carved out of the former accommodation, and new decoration throughout. Substantial private quarters were reserved for the Montayne family members who, nevertheless, involved themselves in many of the public aspects of the hotel. *Marchant Enterprises* was launched so that Tomber Hall, *per se*, ceased to exist. The Montaynes nurtured and developed contacts of the sort they felt happy to entertain in "their" home; contacts who were, however, paying guests. They paid for splendid accommodation, first-rate food from the revamped kitchens and its specially introduced staff, good conversation from their hosts when they weren't away developing further contacts around the world, and above all, a very high degree of privacy. That privacy was not to be confused with nefarious concealment, however, for the families agreed from the outset that their predecessors' criminality was not to be emulated in any way.

As the years passed, other aspects of the *Marchant Enterprises* corporation developed. Cruise ships became an important part of the business, and the standards offered by those ships varied quite widely between companies, and in the case of *Marchant Enterprises,* within different arms of the greatly enlarged enterprise.

Geoffrey, by now in full control, had shown extraordinary flair. Right from the beginning when he had shown such support for Michael Montayne's plan, Geoffrey had taken a very long view, understanding that it would take quite a long time before Tomber Hall would move into profit. But it did, and his patience was rewarded. That had much to do with Michael's ingenuity, not only in forming strong friendships around the world with suitable paying guests, but by exploiting some of the hardware, as it were, of the Montaigne family history. As we shall see, that linked to the Gaston family as well.

4

Loose ends. There are always loose ends. For example, did you wonder why the *Tomber Pot* was never put up for sale? Arthur remembered about it just in time before the lawyers got to work on the *Great Agreement*. The point, however, is that when the Montaignes and the Etheringtons were in cahoots in the booze-shifting business, how do you suppose all that liquor found its way into storage at Tomber Hall? For that matter, why had the Montaignes got into bootlegging in the first place? The answer lies in geography. You see, being located very near to the river – originally, of course, merely because of the beauty of the place – offered splendid access to a natural (and, later with the canal system, man-made) highway. One is tempted to talk of highway robbery at this point, but that would be far too opportunistic. The point was that barrels of hooch could be brought to the estate by barge, and by narrowboat when advantage of the rapidly developing canal system was taken. However, it takes time to unload a specially modified narrowboat, and one wouldn't want to be seen doing that by inquisitive bystanders. Admittedly, such bystanders were very likely to be villagers of Tomberwater who might be expected to keep mum, in view, at the very least, of many of their homes still being the property of the Tomber Estate. But you cannot be too careful. So, some rather special physical arrangements were built to assist the business operations.

They built a tunnel; all the way from the wharf to the hall. In fact, this tunnel was constructed while those "new" wings were added to the original building, thus affording some further degree of secrecy for the whole operation. "Why are they digging up the main approach to the hall?" might have been a question of the day. "It's all part of the great building operations", might have been the reply – which was true, of course. The Grand Avenue, as the dramatic approach to the hall had been called right from the earliest days of the Tomber Estate, was originally lined with limes along its full length – that is, right up to within fifty feet of the front façade.

It was decided to build the tunnel under the roadway rather than diagonally across the open grounds, for any movement of the topsoil or any discoloration of the over-lying grass, either of which would assuredly develop over time, might draw attention to the tunnel below. However, the roots of the avenue of lime trees on either side of the approach road had already reached the subsoil of the roadway, and as the trees developed further, might be expected to damage the brickwork of the tunnel. So those trees had to go; only as far as the crossroad, some two hundred yards from the house. At that point, the tunnel joined another running across the property. A left turn coming away from the hall led, in only fifty yards or so, to a disguised emergency exit within a gardeners' storage depot. A right turn led all the way out of the estate property and onto the wharf. At the T-junction so created, a statue was placed above, mounted upon a perforated plinth. The idea of the perforations was to provide additional fresh air for the tunnel below. However, heavy brandy barrels were to be carried along the long tunnel on wheeled trolleys, and these would have some difficulty turning round a sharp right-angle bend under that statue. So an additional gentler curve in the tunnel was added there to sweeten the right angle and so to facilitate the booze traffic. Once more, there were to be no tell-tale discolorations to overlying grass, so a circular path around the statue was built wide enough, not only for carriages above ground to navigate, but also to overlay the curved turn of the tunnel beneath with suitable hard standing. This had the added advantage that, when using the tunnel at night, no lights could be seen through the ventilation perforations in the statue's plinth, for the curve in the tunnel was constructed, not only to feed into the main approach to the house, but also to curve in front of the statue to link with the short part of the tunnel which led to the emergency exit inside the gardeners' depot. A short ventilation tunnel from the statue to the curve around it was only a narrow affair, large enough merely for servicing those perforations, should that ever be necessary.

Overall, they had been very clever. Originally, the last part of the main tunnel ended under the house, just behind the main entrance hall, where it met up with two exits. One was a short flight of steps up into a vestibule behind the main hall, and the other curved around into a large cellar where the barrels were to be stored. Beyond that was a separate cellar area, laid out as a wine cellar for the normal activities of the household. Access between the two cellars was by a secret metal sliding door, made to look like brickwork.

The other end of the tunnel ended at that wharf on the river, but there was yet more subterfuge built into the system there. Obviously one cannot navigate and moor a narrowboat, unload it, cast off and be on your way in the twinkling of an eye; of the eye of a spy. So a small "loop" was dredged into the hall side of the river, so that when the coast was seen to be clear, a narrowboat could be diverted out of the river into this private inlet. Further, the inlet was hidden by a stone wall and camouflaged with bushes and other greenery, and its entrance and exit was further hidden by curtains of stout netting interwoven with vines of various kinds. The netting had the added advantage of letting light into a loading wharf inside the enclosure. Thus, apart from the arrival and departure of a narrowboat, which would be overseen by guards on the lookout for prying eyes, an unloading boat would be completely hidden from external view. Oh yes! They had, indeed, been very clever.

There was one further wrinkle in all this. The tunnel heading away from the "crossroad" toward the wharf passed almost directly under the *Tomber Pot*. It was decided to recruit staff to operate this system from amongst the citizenry of Tomberwater itself. They were to be very well paid for their labour; or to be more exact, for their labour *and* their loyalty. It was therefore decided to build a very short side-tunnel under the *Pot* with access to the pub cellar. The labourers on the project would thus access the tunnel through the village pub. Once again, that access was through a hidden door at the back of the pub cellar.

This whole complex system was quite likely unnecessary. After all, it was all deep in the English countryside near a respectable country seat. Nobody would ever suspect and come looking. But it paid to be careful, and they were.

So now we come to the first of those "loose ends". All that business concerning the *Tomber Pot* could only be arranged with the participation of the pub landlord. At that time, few of the village houses had been put up for sale, but it was clear that from the moment this subterranean intrigue was contemplated and certainly before it was constructed, the *Tomber Pot* would never be put on sale. It was equally clear that the landlord of *The Pot*, and his successors, would have to be in on the plot, be well cared for financially, and generally be regarded as persons of particular importance to the Tomber estate.

As all this was explained to Michael, he remembered how special the relationship between George Gaston and his father had seemed to him when he was a young lad mucking about with George's refurbished narrowboat, and how his father had seemed to know everything about the Gastons and their doings almost the moment anything actually happened. And now Ken Gaston was in line to take over the *Pot*. Therefore, George and Ken Gaston had to be in on the *Great Agreement*. Their futures would have to be safe. On that they must be completely reassured.

When Michael and Arthur met up with George and Ken – in the *Maisy Pot*, for privacy and old times' sake – it wasn't long before Ken asked an obvious question.

'Can we now buy *The Pot*, then? After all, all that stuff about smuggling is at least two generations old.'

It was therefore necessary to bring the Gastons more fully into their confidence. Michael explained that privacy was going to be the watchword of the proposed hotel, or retreat as he preferred to call it – that some guests might want to slip in or out of the hall unseen.

'Not for any illegal reasons,' he hastened to assure them, 'but maybe simply to avoid the press, for example.'

Michael had only vaguely formulated his plans on this question and didn't want, or feel able, to explain further, but he was adamant that the standing of *The Pot* should remain intact. Similarly, he insisted, the publican and his family, now and into the future, would enjoy the same privileges they enjoyed today. That would be written into the *Great Agreement*. He also assured his friends, for they *were* his friends and he intended that they remain so, that when he came to firm up the details of any exploitation of those tunnels and so on, they would be consulted at every stage.

As if by accident, Arthur reached into a bag he had brought along to their meeting and solemnly cracked open a bottle of some decidedly not insignificant French champagne. He did this with such a practised art, with such respect for the wine, that the cork was removed almost silently, and no bubbles deigned to leave the bottle before George brought out four flutes from a cupboard behind him. There followed a few sombre moments and a toast to seal the promise.

*

It took nearly three years for the alterations/modernisation of Tomber Hall. Every room, new and old, was decorated to the highest standard, but it had been decided not to retain the old style everywhere. While the dining room, for example, was kept in period, albeit with some imaginative and sensitive colourings – and very grand it looked too – three of the lounges and drawing rooms were set up in modern styling. The same was true of the breakfast room set out with sideboards for self-service. A music room had been carved out of one of the largest rooms from the old building and provided with a superb Bechstein grand piano with a figured walnut case. There was space for some thirty seats in the room should audiences ever get that large, but the seating, though very comfortable, was casual. A smaller room was set out with several small tables, some two-seaters for chess or backgammon, and four-seaters for bridge and other card games. Another large room at basement level was set out with a bar, several small and larger tables, and a small stage for occasional cabaret performances. Accommodation was provided as separate rooms or as suites. All were elegant, some more modern than others and all were very expensive. Prices were all-inclusive and meals were superb, but there was no *a la carte* menu for dinner. Enquiries about patrons' allergies and particular dislikes were made in advance of their stay, but dinner dishes were selected by the management –Michael and Rachael, in due course – and taken at a single large table in collegiate style. Good conversation was to be a cornerstone of the hospitality of this exclusive retreat.

Throughout the hall, flowers were displayed almost everywhere. Helen and Rachael had insisted on this feature and they were in charge of it all. The day-to-day management of such displays was in the hands of the General Manager and his staff, of course. Rachael and Helen saw to it that standards were maintained. Part of the achievement of that floral effusion was the growing of large and varied supply in the estate gardens, and that brought the ladies into regular and understanding cooperation with the gardeners. Helen had had such a rapport with the head gardener and his lieutenant for years, and on joining the family, Rachael had joyfully taken to sharing that task. Of course, by the time that the hall was up on its feet as an hotel, there had been a considerable enlargement of the gardening staff so that the estate grounds overall could be returned to something like their former glory, such that the founder, Philippe Montaigne, would have approved. An arborist had been appointed as part of the team.

Unfortunately, only a year after the retreat was up and running, the head gardener reached sixty-five and could not be prevailed upon to stay in post a month longer. He had been a gardener at the hall for more than fifty years and argued that enough was enough. Nobody argued, and he was given a fine send-off and a handsome retirement present. There was nobody else on the gardening staff with the experience and gravitas to promote to head gardener, so one had to be found from outside. That took some time, for discretion was an essential ingredient of the job. There was a tied gardener's cottage with the job, which was large enough for a small family, so the successful applicant found himself automatically in a loyalty-providing situation.

Shortly after his appointment, he entered discussions with management for adjustments in the staff he inherited, including pay rises for particular service and skills. Michael involved himself in some of these discussions, and with no objection from the new man, Gordon Roland was promoted to deputy head gardener. He hadn't been at all upset when he had been bypassed for the top job. He knew he wasn't ready for it and probably never would be, for the head man had a diploma or something which had required a lot of book work, but Gordon was as proud as punch to be made his deputy. It had helped, of course, to have been a close friend of Michael, the big boss of the place.

The Rolands still played the occasional jazz gig around the area, and Michael equally occasionally appeared at these with Rachael who shared his taste to a considerable degree.

One of several services which *The Retreat* – which Michael had decided was to be called *The Hut* in future, for he liked the gentle humour of the name – was the provision of several vehicles of differing grandeur for the occasional use of guests. The idea here was to provide a level of privacy for those who particularly needed it. From the outset, Michael had conceived of two "getaway" schemes, thinking of famous visitors especially, who might want to dodge the press on occasion. The main such will be described later, for it is quite complex and we can well do without any further tortuous elaborations right here and now.

The second, and rather modest, affair was to offer "away days", in which guests might be driven into the countryside – in an hotel car, perhaps, rather than their own, for the sake of a little privacy – to stay a while in one of three rather superior hotels around (all of which had been owned and managed by *Marchant Voyages* but were now incorporated within the new entity we know as *The Hut*, so guaranteeing continued discretion). One, for example, was a renowned golfing hotel, for those inclined to a life of frustration when trying to put little balls into little holes, rewarded only by a drink at the nineteenth. Guests who might take advantage of this service, Michael had envisaged, could be people of some eminence, used to but occasionally irritated by an especially sumptuous lifestyle, who simply wanted to experience a short break in the milieu of the "common man". As Michael explained, when he first put all this to the founding committee, all things are relative.

Anyway, his ideas were accepted, and in due course, adopted, but of course required appropriate hardware; namely, a small fleet of vehicles. There had always been extensive garaging, or stabling in the old days, at the back of the hall, so it was a simple job to replace these with facilities which were more appropriate to the modern age. Over and above that, of course, this fleet of vehicles – and there are more to be described later – would need appropriate mechanical upkeep and servicing. So it was that Barry Roland, who was now in charge of the village garage, was co-opted on a part-time basis to the staff of *The Hut*. Needless to say, both gardening and workshop activities were to take second place to jazz on several evenings in the year. Michael accepted that principle without demur.

5

Hillary and Isobel, having finished their game of croquet, had meandered into the bar. They were sitting at a small table and had ordered their drinks when Hillary nonchalantly asked Isobel what she thought of him.

'He's just right for you, if you really want to know,' she replied.

'What? Who are you talking about, Izzy?' Hillary was clearly startled. 'Harvey? I'm old enough to be his mother – well, much older sister, anyway,' she bridled.

'Goodness, cousin, have you never heard of cougars? Everyone is entitled to a toy-boy these days, aren't they?'

'Stop it. You're laughing at me, Izzy. I have no such inclinations towards Harvey at all. Now, behave yourself. I was referring to *you*. What do *you* think of Harvey?'

'He's all right, I suppose. A bit lanky. I prefer a bit of meat on a man, myself.'

'Oh, do stop it, Izzy. I think he's a rather good-looking boy, myself.'

'I would have thought you'd have far more interest in Gerald, Hillary. He obviously shines for you.'

'We're not talking about me, Izzy. We're talking about you. Now stop it, do.'

'I couldn't agree more, Hillary. We'll stop all this right now. I wonder what Uncle Michael has chosen for tonight's dinner. I'm beginning to get interested.'

'I'm not sure Michael would like to hear you addressing him like that. I know what you mean, though. I find it rather nice to be coddled.'

The ladies continued to enjoy their drinks and their chat, turning to smile at other guests who were slowly beginning to congregate in the bar, obviously sharing the need for a wee snifter before their meal.

'Who is that elegant, older fellow over there, Hillary? I think he's new, isn't he? We've been here for three days now, but this is the first time I've noticed him.'

'Well, who knows, Izzy? Remember, the rules of *The Hut* are that only first names are advertised – and they may well be false, anyway – but I have seen him here previously. I believe he's a count or something noble like that. Spanish, I think, but that's all I know about him.'

It was at that moment that the gentleman in question was joined by an equally elegant lady with jet-black hair – Isobel guessed them to be in their fifties – who made no bones about inspecting everyone else in the room. There was nothing haughty in her manner. She was simply curious and completely open about it. She caught Isobel's eye and smiled, somewhat wickedly, Isobel thought. She returned the smile with a grin. The moment passed as each continued her own examination of her fellow guests.

At another table sat two middle-aged men with two much younger women. Unlike the Spanish count and his wife, as Isobel mentally labelled the previous pair, these four did not appear to be paired up in matrimony. Nor, however, did it seem to Isobel, that they were actually tied in any other personal way. She could, of course, be completely wrong – and, if pushed, would have readily admitted her prejudice – but she regularly insisted, to Hillary, at least, that she had a nose for these things. But if these four were not romantically linked, what was the connection? One of the women caught her looking, seemed quite unconcerned with her scrutiny, and responded with a brief, watery smile.

Isobel was about to let her gaze move onto yet other guests, when Gerald and Harvey walked up to their table.

'Mind if we join you, ladies?' Gerald asked, and sat down before receiving a reply.

Hillary patted his hand. 'Of course you may. How are your rooms? Come to that, where have you been put this time?'

Gerald made a naughty purse of his lips. 'I'm showing off this time. We have taken a suite on the second floor, East: *The Quiet*, it's humorously called.'

'Michael is like that, isn't he?' replied Hillary.

'I'm not sure that he takes the credit this time. I have a feeling that room and suite names are down to Rachael.'

Harvey looked quizzical.

'Rachael is Michael's wife. I imagine she will join us for dinner. She often does and has done so for the past twenty-odd years,' Hillary explained. 'She is a delight. You are sure to like her, Harvey. Gerald does, don't you, my dear?'

Isobel caught Harvey's eye at that endearment and grinned. Hillary was too busy to notice.

'Isobel, as an old hand now, you should give Harvey a guided tour of the place after dinner.'

Isobel smiled sweetly, slightly excessively so perhaps, and assured one and all that she would be delighted to do so.

The butler appeared in his tails.

'Ladies and gentlemen, dinner is served,' he announced in a firm, unwavering voice which was, however, neither forced nor loud.

Without undue haste, everybody in the bar got up from their tables and quite informally paraded into the dining room. Some gentlemen graciously offered their arms to their ladies, others merely held back a little to usher their companions forward. The Spanish count and countess led the way with a modicum of formality. Harvey noted that none of the guests were formally dressed; neatly, yes; formally, no.

As guests passed into the dining hall – you had to label so splendid an environment with a suitably grand word – they were greeted by Michael and Rachael, not in any formal way as for a snake passing a starting gate, but with a genteel shout from across the large dining table. He expressed his hope that everyone had passed a pleasant day and, as usual, directed all to be seated wherever they liked.

'We have five new guests today and one returnee, unless that should be returner. At this stage, I bid them welcome and hope to chat to each as the evening progresses.'

There followed a modicum of local arranging, much by Gerald and Hillary, such that Gerald and Hillary, as returners, sat nearly opposite to Michael, while Isobel was manoeuvred into place on Gerald's left, and with Harvey on *her* left, the two ended diagonally opposite Rachael. The Spanish count and countess sat between Michael and his wife.

Everyone almost immediately fell into small talk in so relaxed a manner that Harvey could feel the bonhomie immediately. He had imagined a far more restrained and formal air to the dinner. This was such a pleasant surprise.

The table had been laid out beautifully with splendid, though not ostentatious, solid silver cutlery and several modest but elegant, solid silver candle sticks rather than ornate candelabra, and with tasteful glassware. At the head of each place lay a small menu card. Harvey picked his up to see what was coming, for he realised that he was, by now, quite peckish.

Michael, a man of about forty-three or so, Harvey guessed, leaned forward a little towards him. 'It's Harvey, isn't it? I seem to recall that you're with our old friend, Gerald. Nice to meet you. Hope you will enjoy your stay.'

He turned his head slightly and greeted Gerald.

How casual and innocent, Harvey thought.

'So good to see you here again, Gerald. We must have a game of chess later. I want my revenge.'

Harvey returned to his menu. He had been warned a little about the lack of choice at *The Hut*, but less about how little that would matter. There were four courses this evening with a "half-choice" offered for the first course. *Langoustine Papillotes with Foie Gras* was coming for the first course, but below this was printed: *Sp: Sautéed Foie Gras with Apples.*

Isobel leaned over to Harvey. 'The "special" is for people who have previously indicated an intolerance of shellfish,' she explained.

'Poor things. Life can be hard, it seems,' Harvey replied with a wide grin. 'Is this typical for dinner at *The Hut*, or are we newcomers being pandered to?'

'No special pandering here, Harvey. I've been here several days so far, and every evening meal has been a delight; very varied, but always beautifully thought out and prepared.'

At this point, the butler appeared on Harvey's right and asked, 'It's Mr. Harvey, isn't it, sir?' he enquired. After Harvey concurred, he went on, 'I won't disturb you again, sir, but I just wanted to welcome you to *The Hut*. Please ask me if there's anything special you require or whether there are any amendments to your special requirements list.'

He discreetly disappeared just as another waiter came along serving everyone with something in a very small handle-less beaker. This *amuse bouche* could be described as a warm, moderately thick, light-green soup.

Harvey joined the others right away in tasting this small, unannounced offering.

'Leek, I think,' Harvey said to Isobel.

'Yes, I agree, but there's a flavour over that. What is it? I know it well, but it's subtle.'

Harvey was so pleased to find a fellow gourmet. 'There's a touch of curry, I believe,' he suggested.

'Of course! You're quite right. Do you cook yourself, Harvey?' she asked. 'I mean cook, comma, yourself; not cook yourself!' she giggled.

Harvey grinned before replying. 'Actually, I do. Enough, at least, to have learned how difficult it is to produce something of refinement. For the most part, I try to cook simple things, but well.'

At that point, Isobel was distracted by Rachael leaning across the table to introduce her to the Spanish count. It turned out that he was using the name Carlos and, Rachael learned, his wife was Valentina.

So maybe I guessed their nationality, at least, thought Isobel.

Harvey turned his attention back to his menu. The second course was labelled, very simply, as *Duck with Coriander*.

Before he could look further, Harvey was interrupted by Hillary: 'Harvey, tomorrow, would you be a dear and show Isobel the long walk and the woods near the gardeners' hut which I understand Gerald pointed out to you earlier today? I haven't taken her in that direction and I gather that you have only glimpsed it yourself, so it should be a pleasant outing. The weather's forecast to be fine.'

'It would be a pleasure,' Harvey replied, and with a smile, relayed the plan to Isobel.

'How nice of my cousin to think of it,' she replied, with an especially sweet smile. She turned back to Carlos, the Spaniard.

A wine waiter appeared, offering a barely chilled *Savenniere*. Soon thereafter, a waitress appeared with the first course, already plated up in a subtle fashion. On one side of an oval plate, which had been put down carefully so that its major axis lay sideways, left to right, was a langoustine shell on the left, next to a small pile of baked tail meat in the middle of the plate. Next and in line with these was a neat parcel of julienned carrot and leek sprinkled with tarragon, and finally, on the right, a slice of baked *foie gras*. Altogether, there was not very much food on the plate, but what there was was so rich, not only to the eye but also to the stomach. Harvey thought about the dish as he ate. It was so simple, but when cooked to perfection as was this, it was an elegant piece of magic. And the choice of the *Clos de la Coulée-de-Serrant* seemed so right. He didn't know the wine but mentally applauded the sommelier's choice.

Isobel turned back to Harvey and said, 'The appearance of a dish takes you half-way there, I think.'

'I couldn't agree more. If this standard continues for the whole of our stay, I'll be a very happy bunny,' he grinned.

It will, it will,' she replied.

From across the table, Rachael looked at Isobel with an enquiring eye.

'We were agreeing that this lovely dish – Harvey's first at *The Hut* – is a piece of perfection,' Isobel explained.

Rachael beamed. 'Oh! I'm so pleased. I remember asking for that about two months ago. You know, Michael and I have monthly meetings with our chef and sommelier to plan menus. After about two months wait, each dish comes along as something of a surprise to us! We have served this dish before, I believe, but not for some time.

'Changing the subject, Isobel, Hillary tells me that you do something clever in the city. Is that right?'

'Hillary is my favourite cousin, but she is inclined to exaggerate somewhat. But I do work in the city. I work with the British branch of a well-known American bank. I'm a researcher. I get paid to read up on any and all literature pertaining to any particular company, world-wide, that my superiors deem worthy of interest –sometimes with a takeover in mind, sometimes with a view to investment, sometimes with the intention of dumping holdings. I don't actually make those decisions, but I do furnish my boss with the necessary ammunition. I've only been in the job for about three years now. It will take more years and more experience before I even get a go at the sharp end. It is equally possible that I might leave to join another bank in order to get promotion. That's the way things work with our business. I'm very happy with things at the moment, though.'

'Maybe you've met or heard of Geoffrey Etherington? He's the boss of *Marchant Enterprises* who, as you probably know, own *The Hut* amongst many other things. He was Michael's best man at our wedding many years ago.'

'I've heard of *Marchant Enterprises* from Hillary,' Isobel replied.

The exchange faded away as plates were cleared. Harvey had been making small talk with Valentina, confirming that she and her husband were Spanish. She, in turn, was asking about the relationship between Harvey and Isobel.

'Oh no!' Harvey said hastily. 'We only met a couple of hours ago.'

'Please forgive me,' Valentina replied with some bluster. 'You seemed to know each other better than that, I thought. I pride myself upon having a nose – I think that's a correct expression, isn't it? – of having a nose for these things. My nose is clearly in need of a blow!'

Hillary caught most of this exchange and gave Gerald a (hopefully) concealed poke with her elbow. She noticed, however, that the countess seemed to have seen this gesture. Valentina said nothing but smiled fleetingly at Hillary. Hillary briefly pursed her lips, but her eyes smiled back.

The duck arrived in the form of several slices of rare breast together with a fan of caramelised apple wedges, all sitting in a coriander-flavoured sauce. Bowls of a neat green salad with individual cruets in the form of pairs of cut-glass oil and red wine vinegar bottles were distributed about the table. It was so simple and so effective, and as far as Harvey was concerned, just right. The wine waiters appeared immediately after service with splendid bottles of a *Corton*.

Harvey leaned over to Isobel. 'You know, I do like the way only modest quantities of food are served. This way, you savour every mouthful.'

'It's a lovely way to slim, I suppose,' she replied with a grin, 'and I suppose we could always smuggle chocolate bars into our dorms afterwards.'

'Who are you smuggling into your dorm, Isobel?' giggled Hillary from the far side of Gerald.

'Are you listening to our conversation, Hill?' asked Isobel with mock anger. 'Is nothing private here?'

'Behave yourselves, you two,' Gerald interrupted. 'I must agree with you, though, Harvey. Dinner so far has been splendid, tasty and tasteful.'

'So you were listening too, Uncle?' Harvey replied. 'Maybe I should rise to make a general announcement and to raise a glass to the management?'

'Can't help it, old boy, your enthusiasm is so noticeable and infectious.'

Valentina had caught the exchanges, too. 'I do like people who like their food and all good things in life,' she laughed openly.

The count heard her laugh and joined in. 'Is my wife bothering you? She is a nosey type, I know, and cannot help meddling in other people's affairs.'

Was it his accent, or had he pronounced the word as "affaires" deliberately? Harvey wondered and glanced at Isobel. She had a pursed and twisted little grin on her face, and her eyes were lit up with amusement. It seemed that the Spanish couple understood each other perfectly.

Plates were cleared with a speed and precision that did credit to the meal. Harvey had not noticed any signs made by the butler, but when it happened, it happened all at once and from every part of the table simultaneously. It was the same a few minutes later when a small, subtle – *was it lime?* Harvey wondered – sorbet appeared in front of each guest. Harvey glanced again at his menu. *What next?* he wondered. His menu offered no real clue. *Le Royal* it said. He would have to wait and see. He caught Isobel's eyes. She was wondering, too.

'I guess we must just be patient little teddy-bears and see what mummy has concocted,' she said.

There arrived something obviously delicate which looked as if it were coated in slivers of wood. In the middle of each plate was a circular timbale, about two inches across and the same depth, of a deep-cream-cum-pale-orange mousse whose top was grained with a – probably chocolate – swirl. Placed all around the central mousse were thin broken wafers of what looked like white chocolate, similarly grained in the same swirly pattern as the top of the mousse itself. Sitting on top of the mousse – and that is what it turned out to be – was a miniature mandarin, which actually turned out to be a gooseberry coated in confectioners' sugar. Within seconds of service, a small glass of orange curaçao was presented to each guest.

Harvey glanced at Isobel.

'You're dribbling,' she laughed.

Conversation was in full throttle around the whole table. There had been a momentary quieting as the dessert had been served, but the volume re-established itself moments later. After the dessert plates were removed from the table, but this time without the almost military precision in presentation of previous courses, large bowls of various fruits were placed here and there along the central line of the communal table, together with cheese boards and bowls of biscuits. In between these offerings were placed several bottles and decanters. The decanters proved to contain port – *Warres*, Harvey was told – a *Barsac* and a fine, very dry *Bordeaux*. There were also a couple of bottles of a splendid old brandy. A cluster of appropriate glasses were placed next to each guest.

'For our new guests: please help yourselves to whatever takes your fancy. Rachael and I will probably clear up any remnants afterwards.'

'He's made that joke almost every night for the last twenty years or so,' moaned Rachael with a laugh.

Michael continued: 'We'd appreciate it if smokers would take whatever they want into the adjacent smoking room. If you have any breath left, please speak up so that the rest of us can hear you.'

'And that,' Rachael added.

A few guests drifted off into the smoking room taking a couple of decanters with them, but most stayed in the dining room.

Gerald observed to Harvey, speaking across Hillary, that while everyone was clearly well watered, nobody seemed remotely near to losing control. 'Yet another thing I like about staying here. If anyone wishes to move around the table now that there are some free seats, please do so. It is quite normal to do this.'

Michael chirped in from across the table, 'It's a polite way to get away from me.'

'Yes, Michael. We've heard that joke before, as well,' replied Gerald. 'Once again, my dear old friend, you have made a delightful evening. I thank you.'

Harvey leaned over towards Isobel once more and said quietly, 'I'd like to get acquainted with those two older men and their young ladies. I'm curious about them. Join me to find out something?'

'Yes. I've been curious, too. I hadn't realised that you had noticed them.'

'Insulting me already, then?' Harvey retaliated. They got up from their seats and, glasses in hand, found a couple of empty seats roughly opposite the foursome in question.

'Mind if we join you for a while?' Harvey asked. 'I'm Harvey, and my friend is called Isobel.'

They sat down without waiting for a reply, and Harvey explained that he had only just arrived at *The Hut* and wanted to make contact with everyone "for friendship's sake." There was no immediate response from one of the men, but the other nodded briefly and with considerable hesitation said that they were at *The Hut* for private business discussions with their assistants, that they had only just arrived in the place and were only just settling in.

Isobel took a turn to make these most reticent fellow guests ease up a little.

'What did you think of that dessert?' she said. 'I thought it was absolutely delicious. That chocolate mousse was to die for, didn't you think?'

'Yes. It was nice,' one of the young females replied, with what can only be described as a watery smile, at best.

'Like you, I have just arrived today,' Harvey joined in. 'Isobel has been here for over a week, and she tells me that meal standards are uniformly high. I almost wish I could eat non-stop!'

He smiled broadly at the quartet of stony-faced bores before him. Inside, he had reached a point of exasperation.

'Yes, but one must not over-feed,' replied the man who had previously spoken.

Harvey tried once more. He looked directly at the other man and asked if he agreed with that injunction.

'Of course!' came the reply.

Success! thought Harvey. *Though was it worth all the effort?*

'Well, goodnight,' he replied. 'We shall take a short walk now.'

He took hold of Isobel's hand and gently pulled her away and out of the room before he realised what he was doing.

'Oh, I'm sorry, Isobel, but I couldn't maintain so high a level of human intercourse any longer. I do hope that I haven't deprived you of any excitement.'

Isobel laughed, saying, 'I think I mentioned it before, Harvey. Please call me Izzy. And as for pulling me away – I shall learn to live with it.'

'Did you catch an accent from the second guy? German, perhaps?'

'Hmm, maybe. And his construction was slightly odd, I thought,' she replied.

'Nosey buggers, aren't we?' Harvey grinned. 'But I just sensed something… something different about that group. I wanted to know what. Did you feel anything, Izzy?'

'Yes, I did. I first spotted it when Hillary and I were in the bar earlier this afternoon. I heard nothing. It was just something about their furtive manner, I suppose. Aren't we awful? After all, people have every right to look any way they please. It's none of our business!'

'Especially in this place where privacy is sacrosanct, eh? Still, it's only human to be nosey. I mean no harm. But I am curious though!' He grinned at Isobel who nodded in sympathy.

'Talking about being nosey, Harvey, may I ask what your line of work is? You heard that I am in banking,' she added, as an inducement.

'Well, I'm not a million miles from what you do, in a way. You could best describe me as a facilitator. I do any necessary detective work for businesspeople – and corporations and such – who wish to be well prepared before making deals. For people who need to know what makes their marks tick.'

'You make it sound as if you're a spy!' Isobel replied.

'In a way, I am. But completely legal, let me add, totally within the law. I would say, that while you research the paperwork of your bank's marks, I research their personalities.'

'Maybe I object to your use of the epithet, mark,' Isobel murmured.

'Oh! I'm sorry. I am so used to explaining myself to hard characters,' Harvey replied. 'Would you prefer "targets"?'

'Only marginally,' Isobel said. 'Anyway, it's only a word. I'm sure that someone with your deep love of food cannot be mean! After all, there isn't enough time in life to satisfy your gourmandising and to be mean as well.' She poked her tongue out just a fraction.

'I protest! I resent that "gourmandising",' Harvey protested. 'I may not be a complete gourmet, but that is a bit mean.'

'I think you'll survive,' she replied, grinning widely. 'Fancy a coffee or something?'

And so the evening ended almost as it had begun.

6

'I think it's all going rather well, don't you?'

Hillary was giggling to Gerald over their morning coffee.

'It might be,' he replied, 'but I'm not at all sure that Isobel, at least, doesn't know what you're trying to do. You did lay it on a bit thick last evening.'

'Yes, I probably did, but that might not be a bad thing. When you wave a flag in front of people's faces, they tend to take notice. At least Harvey is taking her out and about today. We can do no more.'

'But you'll try, I dare say,' Gerald said, with a twitch on his mouth. 'Meanwhile, how do you fancy a game or two of tennis today? I'll let you win!'

'Bloody cheek. I'll thrash you… and you know it.'

It was a good day for a game. Hardly a cloud in the sky, little breeze, and it was already beginning to warm up.

'Good. I'll see you at the courts in ten,' he replied and left to change his clothes.

Meanwhile, Isobel and Harvey, having finished their breakfast a little earlier, had already set forth on a determined, slow stroll in the grounds to the left of the Grand Avenue. That was well-mown grass, albeit not manicured like the lawns close to the house. The cliff which had taken so much of Harvey's attention on the day of his arrival was now to their left, and the seemingly random mixing of rhododendrons – some of which were coming into flower – hazel and alder along the lower slopes leading to the cliff formation were repeated ahead of them, as they came level with the two-headed bird capping the stone plinth at the "crossroads" along the Grand Avenue.

'Do you prefer to walk along the avenue, or are you happy to explore this wooded area?' Harvey asked.

'This is fine,' she replied. 'This way we might run into surprises. I always enjoy surprises.'

So they continued. There were plenty of leaves underfoot, a little damp yet from the overnight dew, but they hadn't to fight their way through. Taller trees now sprinkled the bushes: oaks, some pines and sycamore. There seemed nothing planned or formal about it all. Just a wooded area to form a mass background to the more formal stuff close to the house. The planting, however, was sufficiently open that the atmosphere remained fresh rather than at all dank.

Out of the mess, as it were, they suddenly came across a large shed built of tarred timber and with a corrugated iron roof which, from the evident lack of rust, was obviously well cared for. It had one small window, well draped with cobwebs, and a substantial timber double-door which was not padlocked, as they soon discovered.

'Gardeners' shed, I suppose,' Harvey suggested.

But when they opened the door and walked in, they found it to be some sort of hide. They hadn't previously noticed an opening high at the rear, covered with top-hinged wooden shutters, and bench seating provided in front.

'Ah! For twitchers.'

'I wonder what kind of birds they find interesting around here,' mused Isobel.

Harvey nosed around the shed for a while, tapping on a wooded plinth on which the twitchers' bench was placed.

'Looking for treasure, Harvey?' Isobel asked, but he was noncommittal.

'Habit. I'm curious about everything.'

'It's remarkable,' Isobel said, changing the subject, 'how well into the woods it feels, even though we have only left the margin a couple of minutes ago. And it's so quiet. I suppose that makes it ideal for bird watching.'

'It's certainly very private. And also rather large for a hide, don't you think?' Harvey noted.

'Maybe it's used to store middling-sized gardening equipment, as well,' Isobel suggested. 'There must be a lot of gear to maintain an estate this size.'

'I suppose so,' Harvey grunted. 'Anyway, if you've seen enough, let's move on.'

They carefully shut the doors of the shed behind them and continued their stroll in roughly the same direction, namely directly away from the house and parallel to the cliff – not that that was visible from within the wood. Very soon they had left the hide – as they had agreed to call it – behind and well out of view so that, once more, they were completely surrounded by trees and bushes. They were suddenly startled by some movement ahead and to their right.

'What's that?' Isobel said with a start.

The sound of her voice, however, made everything clear as a small, equally startled deer ran across their field of view and dashed away.

'Oh, how sweet!' she exclaimed. 'A deer. It looked ever so young, don't you think?'

'Yes, dear.' Harvey chortled at his little dad-joke.

Isobel rolled her eyes. 'Oh! The benefits of a higher education. Oxford, I presume.'

'Actually, yes, but that doesn't preclude one from mixing with *hoi polloi* on occasion.'

'Even with a studied omission of the definite article,' she replied.

Harvey grinned with his mouth firmly closed, but his eyes shone.

'And,' Isobel continued, 'thank you, sir, for the endearment. Hillary would be proud of you. Gerald too, I suspect.'

'What *do* you mean by that?' Harvey asked, but with a touch too much of ingénue about him.

'You spotted it too, then?' Isobel replied. 'Last night, Hillary – with Gerald's approval, I thought – was pushing the two of us as close together as they could.'

'Yes, it was rather obvious, wasn't it? Mind you, if you don't mind my saying so, I haven't found keeping you company in any way onerous, my dear.'

'Why, sir, I do thank you. Mind you, we could have a bit of fun of our own, couldn't we?'

'What do you have in mind?'

They had come to a halt.

'Have you noticed that Gerald and Hillary seem to be particularly close? It could simply be because of their shared plans to push us together, but I sensed something a little stronger than that. What do you think?'

'Now you come to mention it… mind you, it could be the evening's alcohol, of course.'

'Maybe, but I feel like a bit of retaliatory fun. Why don't we do some manoeuvring of our own? And you never know, we might be just the catalyst they require!'

Harvey raised his hand as Isobel completed the high five.

'We must give the matter some thought,' he said, and began to walk on.

'Sorry, changing the subject again: I know there's a large gardeners' complex on the other side of the Grand Avenue, and I wouldn't mind having a look at it. But I suggest we stay on this side of the avenue until we reach the end of the estate, which isn't far now, go and explore the main entrance and take in the gardening complex on the way back. I would think that might take us an hour and a half or more. Okay with you?'

'Fine. I'm on holiday. Got all the time in the world,' she replied.

They continued their stroll, and after a while, encountered yet more pine trees. Indeed, with those and the now rising ground, the going was beginning to be rather more of an effort than a casual morning stroll was expected to provide. They decided to turn right towards the Grand Avenue, and by the time they arrived at those two lines of limes, they found themselves almost at the end of the avenue itself. Harvey took Isobel's hand, led her to the middle of the road and turned her to face the hall in the distance. She, like him the day before, found the view breath-taking.

'Oh! Thank you for agreeing to show me this. I don't really know why I didn't explore this part of the estate for myself. I guess I was too preoccupied with croquet and Hillary.'

They turned away from the long view and walked the last eighty yards or so of the avenue until they reached the circle where Harvey had first seen the long view. He pointed out the steeply sloping road down which he and Gerald had first come.

'At the top of that short road, you come to a gate and cleverly disguised car parking – slot, shall I say? – where one can be well-shielded from inquisitive eyes on the main road outside. Unless you are eager to see every little nook and cranny, Izzy, I suggest that we go this way, which I understand leads to the main entrance to the estate.'

'Sure, I'll take your lead,' she replied, and they began a gentle, level walk along the approach road which was every bit as wide as the Grand Avenue itself.

They encountered no traffic whatsoever. There was fairly dense shrubbery on either side of the road, almost all of which was of rhododendrons and alder. Clearly the planting idea was that as the rhododendron flowers faded, the white alder "cabbages" would take over, but even where there was a deciduous alder, it had been double planted behind with some evergreen bush of similar height but with which Harvey was unfamiliar, so that a dense screen existed on either side of the approach road.

'The privacy continues,' Harvey observed.

'Yes, but aren't the rhodies beautiful!' Isobel observed. 'I like rhododendrons, even when they're not in flower. I love those sculptured leaves.'

Apart from the short chicane-like beginning to the approach road as they left the Grand Avenue and the top circle – obviously a device to slow any traffic but more to increase the surprise on entering the Grand Avenue itself – the road was dead straight. They couldn't see any gates ahead, though. It looked as if the chicane idea was repeated so as to shield the road from outside.

'More privacy,' mumbled Harvey, as they got close to the expected feature.

It was as they had anticipated, the road making a gentle S before reaching its end, barred by a most beautiful pair of high, wrought-iron gates. Set into the pickets, between the finials at the top of each gate, was a small emblem in painted iron. These were simple representations of small bunches of grapes.

'I wonder if there was a small vineyard here originally,' Isobel said. 'We must ask about that when we return to the hall.'

The gates opened out into a short area before joining the main road. The road was more or less level, unlike that by which Harvey and Gerald had approached *The Hut* on the previous afternoon. However, there was one feature in common between the two entrances, it seemed, for there was a small parking area to one side of the main gate, which was itself gated off, so that once parked there, a vehicle would be hidden from inquisitive eyes on the main road.

'There really is a mania for privacy, isn't there?' Harvey said, more to himself than to Isobel. 'Can we get out, do you think?'

There was a small postern gate to the left of the main gates, just before the special vehicle "hide". It was, however, locked.

'Use your app,' Isobel said.

'Ah, yes! I'd forgotten that.'

Harvey removed his mobile phone from his pocket, tapped *The Hut* app he had downloaded on checking in and placed his phone close to a small hut symbol on the gatepost. The postern gate swung open and they walked out.

'Let's explore outside a bit,' Harvey suggested.

'Which way shall we go? It seems more or less the same each way,' Isobel replied, walking into the middle of the empty road in an effort to see any interesting features.

'I have a notion that the village is to the right,' Harvey replied.

'You mean Tomberwater, of course,' Isobel replied. 'That's another part of all this which Hillary and I haven't explored since we've been here. Or, at least, I haven't. She probably has on a previous visit.'

Across the road was a seemingly unbroken line of indifferent bushes and small trees, but after walking for a few minutes they came across a break in the foliage through which they saw rough meadow, beyond which was the river. There's something magnetic about a river, and they set out across the meadowland towards the riverbank. The bank was irregular and several feet deep at that point, down to the river, which was brown and quite wide.

'I'd forgotten that there's a river here,' Isobel said. 'But of course there is. That's how the village got its name.'

'It's very wide just here, isn't it?' Harvey remarked. 'Almost as if the river has been artificially widened for a short stretch.' He paused before understanding came. 'Of course! That's it! Look there, Izzy, to the right; you can see a narrowboat. I remember, now, Gerald telling me of how the river is connected to the canal system a mile or so upstream from here, so apart from navigating the river, there's the whole of the English canal system to be explored as well – or a big portion of it, anyway. At some time, someone has widened the river here so as to allow narrowboats to turn around. I know they're called narrowboats, but they are long too, so they do need a lot of water to go about.'

'My, my, you are the sailor boy, aren't you?' laughed Isobel.

'Let's walk further along to the right. My bet is that we'll come to the village,' Harvey enthused.

Indeed they did, for after some four hundred yards – maybe less, Harvey thought – they came across a long quay, moored to which were two very well cared-for narrowboats. One was named *Happy!* And the other *Maisy Pot*. The mooring quay was no more than three feet above the water level. Behind the wharf, some fifty feet back, was an embankment on top of which was a railing, and behind that the road they had left some way back. Behind the road were some cottages, and behind them again, more signs of a thriving village.

'So we've found Tomberwater,' Harvey murmured.

'I'd like to explore this some more… but not now. It would be nice to get back for lunch,' Isobel replied.

'Yes, I agree. Let's walk briskly back, eh?'

Once they were back inside the grounds, Harvey began looking for a way through the rhododendron bushes so as to make a diagonal route back to the hall, which would take in the gardeners' complex and avoid the hassle of retracing their steps to the circle at the head of the Grand Avenue. That turned out to be somewhat more difficult than he had expected, for the density of planting was very high adjacent to the approach road. They fought their way through, however, eventually coming to the sort of woodland they had experienced on the other side of the Grand Avenue earlier that morning. In due course, they came across a large clearing in which three large sheds of differing size had been erected. They were of utilitarian construction, a modicum of nosey inspection revealing their contents: two tractors, a range of tractor-associated cutting and scratching tools, a selection of tree-pruning and macerating equipment and, of course, a wide range of handheld gardening tools. Those filled two of the sheds. The third housed wood cutting, drilling and planing tools as well as metal-working equipment, including welders and lathes. In short, everything required for the maintenance of the house and the estate in general was there in ample supply. Harvey was impressed. Isobel was a tad bored with it all and amused at Harvey's obvious interest.

'Do you work with tools yourself, Harvey?' she enquired.

'I did as a kid and in my teens, but I haven't picked up a chisel in years,' he replied, 'but I am ever curious about workshops. Just a habit, I suppose.'

'Lunch!' she replied and led Harvey out of the complex by the hand.

Harvey thought it a most romantic gesture.

She saw the expression on his face and laughed. 'Now don't go getting any ideas. Don't forget we have work to do on the others.'

Lunch hours at *The Hut* were fairly elastic. Although they were rather late, the running buffet of both hot and cold dishes was still available.

'I'm hungry,' Harvey enthused. 'I'll begin with that pepper-pot soup, I think.'

7

Marks to take a few days off, probably starting two days' time. Harvey screwed up the note and the envelope it had come in and pushed them into the waistband pocket of his trousers. He'd burn them later. He had to try and provoke a response, he knew, but he had to be careful not to blow it. He began by calling Isobel.

'Izzy, I forgot something I must do this afternoon. Could I take a raincheck of that croquet lesson you promised me? I'll see you again in time for dinner – probably in the bar. I won't forget to give Gerald a nudge.'

'Okay, and I'll tackle Hillary,' Isobel chuckled.

Harvey left his room and headed first for the main lounge. It was empty, so he moved on. He poked his head into the games lounge, saw two men in whom he had no interest, playing chess, and moved on. He knew the layout of the hall in fair detail for he had been well-briefed by Michael over a week ago, and he began to wonder where they might be. One possibility, of course, was that they were in one or other of their rooms, in which case, he would have to wait for a public opportunity to arise. Another, he thought suddenly, might be the library. After all, it would be a good place to pretend to be putting together a deal or something.

Harvey opened the library door without any effort to disguise his presence, walked up to a table which was roughly centrally placed in the large, double-story room, upon which card boxes were on obvious display, and began searching for the first title he could think of – he knew he must have one in mind, just in case – acted frustrated and looked around the library, as if to gain inspiration. At first he thought his play-acting was unnecessary, but then he spotted two figures sitting together in a far corner of the library, half hidden from any casual inspection. It was the two uncommunicative men he and Isobel had ineffectively ambushed after dinner the previous night. Harvey continued to look around the library. One wall of the room was glazed to ceiling height from halfway up, the lower half being filled with book stacks whose top shelves were reachable with the use of a sliding ladder. The windows faced north, more or less, and were extensively set with old, delicately stained glass, so that even harmful north light would not threaten susceptible paper or bindings. The opposite wall was covered with a double array of book stacks, the top one being accessed from a narrow balcony running full-length along it. There were two spiral staircases, one at each end, the bottoms of which were surrounded by low shelving for outsize volumes. Though hardly the Codrington Library at All Souls in Oxford or the Science Museum Library at the Imperial College in London – both of which Harvey had visited some years earlier – it was an impressive collection. It must have taken some time to catalogue so many books, let alone to accumulate them.

Jutting out from the single tier of shelving under the window were four minor stacks. It was between two of these, at the far end of the room from the entrance door, that Harvey had spotted the two reticent men. He looked around for their two younger female associates but could not see them anywhere.

There was a small map or chart of the library on the table with the card indexes to make searches for books easier. Harvey therefore established that his quarries were sitting near books with authors names beginning with D. He found that a copy of Dante's Inferno – or that's how he translated the title, for it appeared that the book was in the original Italian – was on the shelves, so he had his excuse for walking right up to the men. As he turned into the alcove where they were sitting, he quietly exclaimed in surprise while acutely, but ever so briefly, glancing at some papers lying on a small table between them.

'Sorry to disturb you, gentlemen. I hadn't realised that there was anyone in the library.'

They didn't reply but did turn one sheet over so as to cover their work. Harvey rummaged around on the shelving until he found Dante's great work.

'Damn! It's in Italian,' he exclaimed. 'I was looking for an English translation. I wonder if there's one on another shelf.' He rummaged some more before continuing. 'Will you all be at dinner this evening? I feel I upset you yesterday evening, and I wouldn't want to do that for the world.' Harvey had an ability to assume meekness at the drop of a hat.

He got more or less the same response as last time. That was fine with him. It saved the effort of making pointless conversation. He had managed to get a glimpse of their paperwork and that's what he wanted. He excused himself with a cheery wave and left the library. Although he had been unable to read anything in his brief glance, he had seen photographs of the Spanish couple, one of which showed them dressed in extremely formal clothes: tails for Carlos and a lovely, magenta gown for Valentina who was wearing many gorgeous jewels. It was clear that these people were spying on the Spanish couple. Harvey had known they were spies, but he hadn't been sure of their marks. Now he was. Michael had insisted that Harvey do everything in his power to maintain as low a profile for *The Hut* as possible. His job now, therefore, was to see to it that these busybodies were distracted at the critical time.

He sent an SMS to Michael asking him if he could spare the time this afternoon to show him around the kitchen garden. Back came the message – "Twenty minutes."

Harvey's choice of the kitchen garden for a meeting wasn't at all arbitrary, any more than his love of good food was a pretence. Harvey always tried to do two or more things at the same time – 'Life is too short to muck about,' he insisted to anybody who would listen – so here was an opportunity to study further the possibilities offered by *The Hut*; maybe for him to formulate a suggestion or request to the chef. Apart from that, should he be watched by the foursome (*Why four of them?* he mused), nothing could be more natural for a gourmet on holiday than to rummage around in the veggie patch.

Without rushing, therefore, Harvey strolled out of the back of the central building, close to the lift shaft there, turned left and walked on until he saw some carefully tilled and weeded rows of leafy vegetables growing in many rectangular raised beds. In the nearest bed, asparagus, both green and white, were both out of the ground. Some appeared to have been harvested already. Elsewhere, spring cabbages were fully developed. Broccoli, kohlrabi, lettuce, broad beans, salad onions, peas, some early potatoes, radish spinach and chard were all coming along very well. Harvey became distracted by one bed which seemed to be promising several varieties of beans in due course, when a middle-aged gardener wandered up.

'Can I help you, sir?' he asked Harvey.

'Hello, I'm a guest here and extraordinarily interested in food. I've only been at *The Hut* for one day – one dinner, so far, which was splendid, by the way – and it was obvious that all the vegetables were as fresh as could be hoped for, so I thought I'd have a look around and spy on your produce department.'

He smiled broadly at the gardener who was on the point of replying when Michael turned up.

'Hello, Harvey. I see you've met Gordon, our assistant head gardener with especial responsibilities for the vegetables here – amongst much else, let me say – including, Harvey, the conveyance of any special guest off the premises in security and secrecy. You may safely talk about such matters with Gordon. He is an integral cog in our machine. What have you found out about our quartet of spies?'

Harvey suddenly remembered where he had met Gordon before. 'I'm sorry, Gordon, I didn't recognise you in your other role. Forgive me.' Turning to Michael, he replied, 'They have successfully pinpointed the Spaniards for their surveillance, I'm afraid. I caught the two men together in the library having a discussion, and there were papers identifying the Spaniards on a table in front of them. I'm disinclined to search for any innocent reason for their meeting under the circumstances. I haven't seen the two young women today, however. I assume that they have been described, quite correctly, as research assistants – or gofers, I would say – but where they are and what they're doing right now, I have no idea. My reason for asking for this meeting, Michael, was to learn as much about the time and manner of the Spaniards' departure as you feel appropriate for me to know, so that I might frustrate any spying ploys which the naughty foursome may have in mind. I realise that I need not know everything about this case, but I would be grateful for any titbits you can throw my way. It always surprises me just how apparently unimportant details can help a project.'

'Some things are not difficult for you to find out anyway, so I'll certainly save you that labour. Our Spanish friends are Spanish nobles. I think that's so obvious, frankly, that there would be little point in trying to keep that fact from you, or anyone else. Carlos and Valentina are not their real names, and I don't see the need to tell you those, if you don't mind.

Suffice to say, they have been involved in some rather bleak political shenanigans at home. Depending upon your affiliations, it seems to me, their behaviour does or does not border on the illegal. As ever, this is a political matter which, to me, at any rate, is quite opaque. If you've spoken to them…'

'Isobel and I did, last night.'

'Then you will have discovered how urbane and civilised they are. For me, that counts very highly. Anyway, they are simply having a holiday away from all the intrigue over there. As you know, we insist that guests address each other only by Christian names – or other forenames – but that these may be false if they so wish. The staff here address them as sir or madam, even if count and countess might be more appropriate. We provide good food and wine and comfortable rooms and suites, so that even if our standards fail to match theirs, they will certainly be comfortable enough. Our reputation has spread by word of mouth over the years. In addition to what you, yourself, have already learned, we can provide small trips away from *The Hut*, and when we do, we keep the destinations and means of escape, shall we say, completely secret. The only way that information about our little "away days or weeks" can be discovered is from disloyal staff – and I am confident that we have none of those – or from the beneficiaries themselves. We try to choose our guests very carefully, so that is also unlikely.'

'Ah, yes! But the present quartet of spies can hardly come into that group of guests!' Harvey exclaimed.

'Oh course, but they persuaded a third party to introduce them into *The Hut*, and that party is a very good friend of ours. So they come well-recommended for their mendacity! By allowing the spies within our nest, we hope to misdirect them from suspecting anything unsavoury – from their point of view, of course. We shall move our Spanish friends at ten o'clock this evening.'

8

Carlos and Valentina had been warned to pack a small case – "enough for a few days' or, perhaps, a week's trip without any significant external interactions" – and to leave the dining room or bar for their suite in time for departure by ten o'clock.

Right on time, came a knock at their door. Their visitor introduced himself as Barry. That was the name they had expected, and he was invited in.

'We'll take the lift.' Barry said. 'I'll take your bags, if that's all right.'

The Spaniards made for their front door, but Barry stopped them.

'No, not that way. There's another way to the lift from behind. Please follow me.'

A large panel in a completely unobvious part of the side wall of their dressing room slid back in response to Barry's mobile phone instruction, and, moments later, an inner pair of doors slid open to reveal a lift.

'This lift is next to the one you would normally take but can only be used at special levels and by special means. Please be quiet for the next few minutes so that we can't be overheard,' Barry explained, and they entered the lift together.

Barry used his phone once more to close the lift doors and to direct its descent. In short order, they arrived at their destination and the doors opened. Barry left first with their luggage and beckoned his charges to follow. They walked a few metres along a curved passage until they came across a vehicle: a sort of car without windows.

'We can talk freely now,' Barry told his guests. 'We are about ten feet below ground. I shall drive you in this almost silent, electric car – you see it has large tyres for so small a vehicle, and that helps to keep it quiet. Please take your seats while I put your luggage in the back.'

There were four comfortable seats behind the driver. Carlos and Valentina sat side by side immediately behind Barry who, after climbing in, closed a sliding door which pulled in tight to the car body so that everyone was closely sealed inside. There were no windows, but some clever electronics provided a make-believe view from non-existent windows along the sides, a view which moved synchronously with the movement of the vehicle.

'Off we go!' Gordon announced. 'Our journey will take about ten minutes, for we won't drive particularly fast. Silence is more important than speed.'

After three or four minutes they slowed, and the travellers could sense a right turn, after which they accelerated again until, after a similar time, they slowed to manoeuvre a slight chicane and shortly afterwards to come to a complete halt. The side panel of their vehicle slid back while Barry came round to help them from their transport. The Spaniards were impressed with how slick everything seemed, and they told Barry so.

'Thank you, but wait for the next bit!' he replied. 'Please follow me,' he continued.

He led them along a short passageway (its curved roof made clear that it was part of a tunnel, in fact), until they found themselves standing on a small river wharf, alongside of which was moored a narrowboat. The innocuous name, *Tickle Me* was painted on the prow. From the outside, *Tickle Me* looked to be a pretty average narrowboat with rather little to commend it.

Carlos looked at Valentina with a look of some dismay.

Barry caught the glance. 'It pays to be inconspicuous. You'll find it much posher inside,' he smiled, as he spoke softly. 'Sorry to be a nuisance, but could you not speak, or at most, whisper, for the next half hour or so. I'll let you know when it's all right to speak normally. We have someone keeping watch outside and he reports that there seems to be nobody around, but you never can be sure, of course. As you can see,' he continued, in a very quiet voice, 'we are at the river. You may have seen the village wharf on another day. Well, this is a private wharf, separate from the larger public wharf, and is set into the bank, and it's curtained off so it's almost invisible from the outside. Of course, we show no lights in here. Once we're all on board, we'll cast off and use our special, very quiet electric motor as we leave upstream. The net curtain disguising this wharf will be pulled aside just as we are leaving and pulled back immediately afterwards. As I have said, there seems to be nobody around, but we always play it safe.' Barry paused while he helped his guests aboard.

As they stepped into the small aft cockpit, a cheery, chubby, blonde lady took their hands and whispered a very warm, 'Welcome.'

'This is my wife, May,' whispered Barry. 'Proper introductions later.'

He passed the Spaniards' bags over to his wife, untethered the boat, tossing the fore and aft mooring lines into the canal boat, fiddled with his phone once more to initiate the drawing back of the net curtain covering the exit of the boat, turned a switch and the boat began, almost silently, to move forward and away from the wharf. It was showing no lights, which was, of course, quite illegal, but since there was (hopefully) nobody – apart from their unseen assistant some yards away – around to see, there was no one to complain. In moments, the narrowboat had slipped its moorings and was in the middle of the river, gliding silently past the public wharves of *Tomberwater*, and in just a few moments more was lost in the darkness of the empty river beyond. Barry waited for another five minutes before switching on his navigation lights, so that he could be readily seen by any other river users. He could see where *he* was going perfectly well, for the boat was equipped with night-vision navigation aids.

Meanwhile, May had guided her charges down into the body of the boat. She closed the second pair of small double doors behind her and turned a switch to illuminate the inside of this most deceptive vessel. The outside of this narrowboat had looked somewhat dishevelled to the Spaniards. It was intended to be. It was meant not to draw attention. Inside, the contrast could not have been greater. While constrained by the basic geometry of a narrowboat, of course, every other detail could not have been more different or more surprising. The fit-out was reminiscent of that of high-end, contemporary yachts – as like as not, not at all unfamiliar to these Spanish aristocrats. Trim exploited the most beautiful woods – sycamore, mahogany and ebony, straight grains and burrs. Clever but subtle use of mirrors created a wider space than reality was able to provide. The lighting was warm and subtle, and the plentiful seating was lush. They were standing in the lounge-cum-bar-cum-dining area of the boat. Ahead was a slick galley area and beyond that a toilet.

May led her guests forward to a well-soundproofed door which slid open to reveal a private suite comprising a bedroom, a small sitting area and a shower-room with another toilet.

'These are your private quarters,' she told them. 'You can hang your clothes in this wardrobe, and other things can be tucked away in these drawers and that cupboard. That narrow door in the middle leads to the foredeck, but we suggest that you don't explore that until morning. Please settle yourselves and join me and Barry aft when you are ready. Welcome to *Tickle Me*!'

The Spaniards smiled warmly as she departed, and they dropped down on the bed.

'What a surprise!' Carlos said to Valentina in their native tongue. 'You would have no idea how pleasant this place was from the outside. I think we might enjoy our little escape, my dear.'

'You are quite right, darling, but I think we should speak English, even in private. Unless, of course, we have something really serious to conceal!'

They unpacked their few belongings and tidied them away as May had suggested, tried out the plumbing which they found to work efficiently and almost silently, and opened the door to the other half of the boat.

'We can speak openly now,' Barry said. 'I hope everything is to your liking? Please find comfortable seats. Meanwhile, can we offer you a drink or two for the night? Shall we open a bottle of champagne by way of welcome, or would you prefer something harder? We have a reasonable selection.'

The Spaniards chose to celebrate the beginning of their adventure with champagne, and, in moments, a *Taittinger Brut* found its way onto a central table in front of them all.

'I have moored alongside a bare stretch of riverbank here for the night. We will not be overlooked, and we have a small, discreet radar set continually checking our surroundings. So we can enjoy our drinks and, I hope, conversation in peace and confidence. I am Barry, and this is my wife, May, and we have been told that your names for *The Hut* are Carlos and Valentina. However, just in case someone should overhear any of our conversation during the next few days, we would prefer you to use different names. Carlos, could you please use the name, Merton, and Valentina, could you be Maggie? We realise it will be confusing to learn yet another set of names, but we are just trying to take every possible precaution. Okay, Merton and Maggie? Will it be all right for us to address each other by these names for the duration of your stay with us on this boat?'

'It most certainly will, Barry,' Carlos replied, 'and may I say right away how impressed Valentina and I are with everything you have done for us in the last hour or so. Thank you very much indeed. I propose the health of our hosts!'

And so, with many smiles, many raisings of glasses and warm words all round, these privileged refugees whiled away the dog hours of the first day of their exciting adventure.

As they rose to go to bed, Valentina suddenly looked most concerned. 'Where will you two sleep?' she asked.

'Thanks for your concern, but there's no need. These seats fold away like a miracle to produce very comfortable beds. We'll be fine! Goodnight!'

9

Valentina awoke with a start and adjusted the blinds in their bedroom to let in sunshine from a beautiful morning. Her moving awakened Carlos.

'What's the time?'

'Half past seven, more or less. How did you sleep?'

'Like a top, as the English say,' he replied. 'It is so peaceful here, and the bed is delightfully comfortable, don't you think?'

Later, they found and pressed an electric button at their bedside.

'Good morning!' they heard May say from the galley. 'When would you like to join us for breakfast in the galley?'

Ten minutes later, Carlos and his wife, dressed in casual – but ever so smart – clothes, wandered aft. The smell of fresh coffee assailed them on the instant.

'What a beautiful morning!' Valentina said. 'Surely we must be especially lucky?'

'For the sunshine, a little, maybe, but for the peace and quiet, this is pretty typical,' May replied. 'We are safe from prying eyes outside, so do go out at any time, if you wish. We provide a bar-style breakfast, so please, good friends, do help yourselves. We hope you don't mind the informality.'

Years of practise had taught May and Barry how to speak, albeit a tad nervously, to Michael's guests.

'Not at all,' Carlos replied. 'Let us please keep things that way.'

'Oh! One more thing,' Barry said. 'Whenever you do decide to go outside – even just on to the decks fore and aft – would you please wear these wigs? They are well-made, so they're not too hot or uncomfortable. We are pretty well clued up about whether there's anyone around, but we must be careful. Apart from this simple precaution, please just relax and enjoy yourselves. We have a few simple entertainments in mind for your little holiday, but basically the idea is for you to relax while you vanish.'

Carlos and his wife did indeed decide to sample the cool, morning air outside after breakfast, and donning their wigs, with smirks and good humour, they left their cabin through the double doors at the front of the boat, finding themselves in a small foredeck. They were taken aback once more by the utter contrast in sophistication between the outside and the inside of the canal boat. It was all part of a wonderful disguise, and they understood that completely.

Barry called from the aft deck that they would cast off in a moment and that there was nothing to do. 'Just relax and enjoy the scenery.'

Barry and May did everything between them. They were totally professional. They had no need to speak as they each did their part, and in no time, the *Tickle Me* was chugging along mid-stream. It was indeed still cool outside but deliciously so. Everyone had chosen to wear light jumpers for the moment, but it was obvious that these would be discarded within the hour.

Some thirty or so minutes later, they came across a narrower waterway joining the river from the left. Barry explained – loudly enough for his guests to hear but softly enough to avoid any raucous shouting – that this was the beginning of the local canal system and that they would be taking this route. He swung the tiller and manoeuvred the boat into this straight waterway.

As they continued their slow journey, Carlos suddenly realised that their engine sounded different to the sound it had made as they had slipped away from the wharf at *Tomberwater* yesterday. He made his way through the narrowboat so that he could interrogate Barry at the "back end", as he referred to the aft deck. Barry explained that what they could now hear was the sound of a conventional diesel engine, such as would be found on most narrowboats and so drawing no unwanted attention. Yesterday, they had used an electric engine which was both very powerful and nearly totally silent which, of course, was what they wanted at that moment.

'We only use the electric engine when we've really got to be silent or if, for some reason, we really need extra speed. On an ordinary run, like we're doing right now, a silent engine could draw unnecessary attention to ourselves,' Barry explained.

'Do you have any reading material aboard the boat, Barry? Novels. That sort of thing,' Carlos enquired.

'We do. If you look in that small cupboard behind the casual seating area at this end of the boat, you will find a dozen or so trashy and more posh novels. I hope you will find something that appeals. All in English, I'm afraid,' he finished.

Carlos had a rummage and found two small volumes. 'I think these will do nicely,' he remarked, and took his catch to Valentina on the foredeck.

Disguised in their simple wigs, they settled down to a relaxing read. They were interrupted less than an hour later, however, as Barry set off a small drone from on top of the cabin. Using a small, hand-held controller, he took the drone up a fair way and out to the right. After a very short time, he brought his miracle machine back to the boat.

'I've had a look around. There are no other boats for several miles. We are coming up to our first lock. We shall not need to share it with anyone, and if you are interested, you can climb out of the boat to watch proceedings.'

Carlos and Valentina were both keen to watch and learn and followed Barry up a short ladder within the lock to watch every move. May stayed on board to take care of anything which might transpire aboard. The Spaniards were more than interested in every little thing that took place during the elevation of the *Tickle Me*.

'This is rather like a childhood holiday for us,' enthused Carlos. 'You couldn't have chosen a more appealing break.'

'That's down to Michael, of course,' Barry replied. 'I'm so pleased you are enjoying your time with us. I just hope we can keep up the standard, 'cos honestly, there ain't many fings you can do on a longboat. Leastways, nothing fast or exciting.'

'There are other things than fast or exciting in the world, Barry,' Carlos replied, with a little of the so-called wisdom of old age.

They left the lock about forty minutes after entering it. Valentina and Carlos took their books to the foredeck and settled down into slow, casual reads until, about an hour later, May called out that lunch was available in the galley.

Barry had casually moored the canal boat to a tree. His guests hadn't noticed. May had provided a delightful lunch of cold cuts: turkey, ham and beef. This was served with a surprisingly good potato salad which offered far more than potato: thinly sliced raw celery, a mere spoonful of finely sliced shallot, broad beans, butter beans, cold, cooked green beans, deliciously soft, hard-boiled eggs broken into and through the salad as a whole, and the whole dish was brought together with a freshly-made egg mayonnaise. All that and a simple, freshly dressed green salad.

The four boaties gathered for their lunch, and Carlos complimented May on her offering. 'We are used to the high standards of cuisine in *The Hut*,' he said, 'but hadn't expected them to be maintained on a small boat. I do congratulate you, May.'

Barry offered his guests a choice of a light *Grenache* or a *Sauvignon Blanc*.

'Barry, do you have any beer on board?' Carlos enquired.

'Certainly do, Merton. English, Irish, Dutch, Italian...'

Carlos interrupted him: 'Goodness, you are well-stocked! I would like a bottle of Peroni, I think.'

Valentina decided on the same.

While they enjoyed their meal, Carlos asked what, if anything, Barry and May had in mind for the afternoon.

'Basically nothing,' Barry replied. 'I'd like to put a reasonable distance between us and *Tomberwater*. We have one more lock to get through today, and we can settle down for dinner and a little light entertainment after that. But, as far as this afternoon is concerned, I suggest sitting in the pleasant sunshine which we organised for you, of course, or maybe seeing what more goodies you can find in our little library.'

To Carlos' evident surprise, Valentina offered to help May tidy up after their meal. May was delighted with the offer, but, apart from asking Valentina to pass over a couple of dishes from one hand to the other, told her that everything was virtually automatic. The Spanish nobles retired to, and through, their cabin to the foredeck for some quiet contemplation.

'That was most domesticated of you, my dear,' Carlos told Valentina.

'It's nice to be nice, don't you think? These people are so courteous and caring. It is well to recognise their hard work, I think.'

Carlos nodded his agreement, put on his wig and opened his book.

'What are you reading?' Valentina enquired.

'It's a British crime novel by Reginald Hill. I believe it was made into a TV program. It's well written and very funny in places. It's fun,' he replied.

It wasn't too long before both of them were snoozing. Boating can be like that.

They were awakened by Barry's shout. 'Please come aft,' he said, briefly but firmly.

When they met him in the galley, Barry explained that they were soon to navigate another lock, but that as they moved up, another boat would be moving down so that the boats would pass close together. Although the encounter was expected to be completely innocent, Barry preferred his guests to stay on board and out of sight.

'Would you care for a cup of tea?' asked May.

Carlos was about to refuse, but Valentina thought that that would be lovely.

'Apart from – what do you English say? Oh yes! – wetting our whistles, the sound of domesticity from inside our craft will surely add a feeling of normality, don't you think?' She turned to Carlos and added, 'I think I'm getting rather used to all this cloak and dagger business. Have I said that correctly?'

Carlos grinned and assured her that she "had all her marbles in place."

Tickle Me arrived at the lock in good time to enter first, the water level inside being that of the lower part of the canal in which *Tickle Me* was chugging along. Barry manoeuvred the boat gently into the lock itself. He closed the lower gate and opened the sluice of the upper gate. Water from the higher part of the canal came rushing in and *Tickle Me* rose slowly, while May and her guests enjoyed a cuppa. Once the water level inside the lock reached that of the higher part of the canal, Barry was able to open the upper gate fully and gently move his boat ahead into the upper canal where the other narrowboat was waiting to take his place in the lock and head off down water. Barry waved to the people in the other boat, they exchanged a few brief pleasantries, and everyone was on his way.

Carlos and Valentina returned to the foredeck and their reading. At this point in their journey, the countryside around was flat and uninspiring. There were a few trees, or rather, large bushes, on one side or other of the canal, but that was just about all. The sun was beginning to wane, and a change to cool clearly indicated that afternoon was becoming evening. Barry obviously agreed, for he began the process of finding a good mooring. The Spaniards left the foredeck and freshened up in their cabin before heading aft to see what might be going on there. Barry and May were chatting as they approached.

'I think the sun is over the yardarm by now,' Barry said (he was proud of his idiom). 'What can I get you? Champagne, cocktails? We can probably satisfy most requests.'

They settled on champagne again, and an immaculately chilled *Bollinger* appeared as if by magic.

'Had you read our minds?' Carlos asked May.

She laughed. 'Just a lucky guess,' she replied.

'Were there any problems with that other boat, Barry?' Carlos asked.

'No, none, but it pays to take precautions, we think. Would you like some music in the background? We have different sorts of stuff. Do you like jazz, at all?'

'We do indeed. Have you any Mulligan or MJQ? That sort of thing?'

'Oh yes!' Barry exclaimed. 'We like that sort of thing ourselves. Have done for years. I shared that particular bug with Michael when we were teenagers.'

He pushed a few buttons on a console to the left of the rear doors, and the characteristic, breathy sound of Gerry Mulligan's baritone sax emanated from several discreetly positioned speakers around the boat. There was a palpable sense of relaxation from everyone in the boat, glasses clinked once more and gossip began.

'I think we are going to enjoy ourselves this evening,' Barry opined quietly.

Valentina smiled her agreement.

A little while later, May announced that she would prepare their evening meal if their guests would excuse Barry and herself briefly. Carlos and Valentina tried hard to be polite and not gawp at every move going on in the galley, but their curiosity won out somewhat. Barry erected a small but cosy table between the bench seats towards the galley section of the boat and quickly and expertly laid it with cutlery, glassware, crockery and napkins. Meanwhile, May had switched on a special oven. She also placed another dish from the fridge on a counter to come near to room temperature.

'Tonight,' she announced, 'we offer no choice, I'm afraid, but we think that you will enjoy what we have. Please come and sit round our little table.'

With that, May brought from her oven a gently steaming dish with a heavenly aroma. She gave everyone a portion while Barry poured each a glass of a deep ruby-coloured wine. In answer to their guests' enquiring looks, May announced that she was serving a pheasant and rabbit cobbler.

Barry immediately added, 'Tonight, I am serving a new-world red wine: a *Cabernet Sauvignon* from the Barossa Valley in South Australia.'

A large bowl of simply-dressed green salad had been placed in the middle of the table, together with a board upon which was laid a crusty loaf of bread.

'Please help yourselves. There is more cobbler if you want,' May urged one and all.

The music played on. The wine was heady and the cobbler was divine – the meat was mouth-wateringly tender and utterly delicious.

'May, when did you cook this? It is wonderful,' Valentina enthused.

May laughed. 'I wish I could say that I had cooked it, Valentina, but it was prepared in the kitchens back at *The Hut*. I merely warmed it up and did a small assembly job. But I do agree with you. It is a lovely dish, isn't it?'

'I am enjoying this wine, Barry. I confess, I am unfamiliar with it. Australian, you say?'

'I think that they like their wines to be very fruity. All that sunshine, I think. But their *Cabernet Sauvignon*s are quite heavy, or maybe I mean heady! I think it goes well with the cobbler, though.'

Rather later, after several more glasses and much tittle-tattle, May collected the dirty plates and brought back a simple cold trifle. 'Something to cool us down,' she announced.

Barry opened a bottle of *Barsac*.

Carlos raised his eyebrow.

Barry said, 'We can start this now and see it off during the evening. I'm not trying to get anyone drunk.'

They were pleasantly relaxed when Valentina thanked their hosts once more for a splendid meal. 'Can I help you with anything, May?'

'I have it all under control, but thank you very much, Maggie,' she replied.

'Why don't you take in a moment or two of the evening air while May and me tidy fings up a bit?' Barry suggested. 'Go out into the cockpit, maybe?'

When the Spaniards returned, everything was cleared away except for the table at which they had eaten.

Barry urged them to gather round the table once more. 'Please don't feel obliged, but I thought we could play a silly board game together while we listen to some MJQ. What do you think?'

'I think that might be fun, but we aren't familiar with many board games, I'm afraid – at least not English ones.'

'How about Monopoly?' Barry asked his guests.

'Now that is one we do know. At least, we did years ago. Is it in the original form?'

'I think so,' Barry replied. 'Anyway, that's good; we can give it a go.'

As he brought out the board and opened it on the table, Carlos said, 'Oh yes! That is the board we are familiar with. Do you remember, my dear, playing this game when we were little?'

'You realise that it can be played with a bit of ruthlessness between adults?' Barry noted. 'Okay, please choose your tokens.'

Valentina chose the car; Carlos, the top hat; May, the boot; and Barry, the iron. And so their evening began: the occasional drink, opportunity chest, chance, going to jail, the purchasing of houses and hotels and the collection of rents. Inevitably, the game became skewed as wealth attracted wealth, so that a small advantage early on became an enormous monopoly later on. The game was well named. Barry proposed a partnership with Valentina in an attempt to stop Carlos' ever-increasing gluttony. For a time, their partnership flourished and they became the big guys, but some time later, Barry suddenly, and seemingly arbitrarily, dissolved his partnership with Valentina, announcing that, henceforth, they would go their own ways. Within twenty minutes more, Barry had cleaned everybody out, including his former partner. Valentina was not amused. Barry made a half-hearted apology but insisted that Monopoly was a well-named game and that one had to learn to be a rat to succeed.

'Play again?' he asked.

Valentina hesitated but agreed after receiving an unseen nudge from Carlos. More drinks, a change of music (this time to Bobby Brookmeyer) and off they went again. In due course, Carlos proposed a merger between Barry and himself, which later blossomed into an immensely rewarding partnership. Out of the blue, Carlos reneged on his partnership, paid Barry off with some useless property and went his own way, only to take up with Valentina a little while later to form a new partnership. They soon wiped the board with Barry, May being an unfortunate innocent casualty on the side. The Carlos-Valentina partnership withstood the test of time – well, about half an hour, anyway – until they finally conquered all opposition and owned just about every property London had to offer.

'How do you like them apples?' Valentina asked Barry.

'Fair enough,' he grinned, 'and I like that American phrase. I remember first hearing it when Paul Newman used it – in Hud, I think.'

There was much laughter all round and a little more chit-chat before the Spaniards thanked their hosts again and departed for bed.

'It really has been a lovely day. Thank you both very much indeed,' Valentina said as they departed.

<h1 style="text-align:center">10</h1>

Next morning was even more pleasant than the previous day, though still cool while everyone enjoyed breakfast, and with an almost cloudless sky.

'The weather forecast for today is blue sky and sunshine, wall to wall,' Barry announced, 'which is good, because we have a picnic planned for later on. Now, because we shall be leaving the boat for a while, please wear your wigs, and we must use your boat names. In case you've forgotten them, Valentina is Maggie, and Carlos is Merton. I'm sorry this is all such a pain, but it would be silly of us to spoil all our efforts at this stage. This evening it will be even more important to use these names, but I'll keep that as a special surprise for later.' Barry paused. 'Oh, I do like playing Father Christmas!'

Later, as they were quietly chugging along the canal and all four were gathered together in the aft well, Carlos remarked upon the change in landscape. He noted that up to now it had been a bit boring and flat, but that it had changed – overnight, as it were – into gently rolling countryside with farmed fields, hedges and the occasional wood.

'So delightfully English,' he remarked.

'That's why we'll go for a walk and take a picnic lunch,' replied Barry. 'We know a local beauty spot which really shows off this part of the world to perfection, I think.'

Another canal boat approached them later. There was waving and some greetings called out across the water as they passed by, but then a silence broken only by the gentle chug-chug of their unlaboured engine.

'This journey is simply magical,' Valentina breathed. 'We could be in another world.'

'It's curious how far away the canal banks seem, even though we know they're not,' Carlos remarked.

By this time, the Spaniards had returned to the foredeck and privacy.

'A pity we can't hide for ever,' Carlos observed.

'I wonder what they are hiding from,' May asked Barry, but he was quite unable to provide an answer.

'Not our business, luv. Michael keeps things like that very close to his chest. I trust him to keep people like you and me clean, though.'

'They seem to be enjoying their holiday break, anyway,' May observed.

An hour later, Barry called out, 'Lunch soon!' and made moves to moor *Tickle Me* alongside the right-hand canal bank. May had already packed a large hamper. Barry was the last to leave the boat, and his final act was to carefully check that all doors were securely locked.

'We have some quite clever locks on this boat. We'll know immediately if anyone tries to force an entry, and, for that matter, the excruciatingly loud alarms would almost certainly get rid of them, anyway.'

He led the party along a narrow path beside a hedge. It was dry underfoot. Poking out from under the hedge was a variety of dainty wildflowers, all insisting upon their place in the sun. The path ran alongside a field of rapeseed which fortunately, as far as Barry was concerned, was way off flowering. He thought it pretty enough but, unfortunately, had a strong allergic reaction to the stuff.

After snaking along their way for another twenty minutes, they came to a small wood – a copse, really – of some quite tall and well-established trees, mostly oak but with occasional birch in between. Though not really dark in there, they found themselves in the shade, and the day was not yet so hot that they felt altogether comfortable. However, after just a few yards more, they came across a significant clearing carpeted in soft, green grass dotted with a splendid addition of bluebells here and there. It formed a delightful stage on which to hold their picnic.

'I like this place,' Barry said, 'and I hope you do, too. We'll set out our picnic here.'

He and May spread out a large rug upon which May began to unpack her hamper while Barry unfolded four light but strong chairs. He had a hamper of his own which unfolded to make a small table and from which he withdrew chilled bottles of New Zealand *Sauvignon Blanc* and *Pinot Noir*.

'You never cease to amaze me, Barry,' Carlos said. 'You and May are perfect hosts.'

May brought forth a plate of warm quail with a small side dish of quince paste, and a plate of salmon gravlax with a delicate dill and mustard sauce. There was also a basket of quite delicious warm, crusty bread with unsalted butter. A fruit basket and cheese plate completed their mini feast.

'I think we'll be all right,' Barry grinned, as they settled down to a leisurely lunch –designed to sit in the memory for ever.

They chatted about inconsequential things, fell silent for a long time and even dozed in the warmth of the sun. A couple of small birds came up to their picnic and pinched a crumb or two. Why not? They were very welcome.

As they were packing up, a long time later, Carlos quietly remarked to Barry, 'You have never asked why we should be hiding like this, Barry. Are you forbidden to?'

'No, we're not, Merton, but it's not our business to know those sorts of fings. May and I are very well paid to look after you – and we have really enjoyed doing that, by the way, for you are really nice guests – but for reasons of security, it's best we don't know. We trust Michael totally. He would never offer these trips to people he didn't respect.'

Carlos nodded slowly in acknowledgement and said no more.

Once everything was packed up, the party made its way contentedly back to the boat. Climbing back onto the *Tickle Me* was rather like coming home.

Two hours' worth of chugging along in *Tickle Me* took them to their next lock. Carlos helped Barry with the gates, and they moored some fifty metres or so further on alongside a strongly built wharf in front of a pub whose lights were all ablaze by this time in the early evening. There was another narrowboat similarly moored a little way along the same wharf. Barry popped into the pub to check that everything was as it should be.

'This evening,' Barry announced, 'we have something a little different to entertain you. We have booked into *The Watering Hole* for our dinner and entertainment. The pub is owned by *The Hut,* so there's already been a lot of scrut'ny to check for over-inquisitive guests. I've been told that there seem to be none of those around and that we can all relax and enjoy ourselves. Even so, please wear your wigs.'

They climbed out of the *Tickle Me*, Barry carefully locking the doors. They strolled into the welcoming and subtly lit pub and found a table which already had a "reserved" sign on it. Clearly there had been smooth and efficient planning behind the scenes for this evening. Carlos murmured something to that effect to Valentina as they all sat down.

Barry asked what everyone would like to drink and went off to the bar. There were several other people already in the place, happily talking and laughing. Nobody seemed to take any notice of the newcomers. Barry returned with his round of drinks and a menu.

'Cheers!' he said, raising his glass. 'Here's to our super guests. May your future be safe and happy!' After a moment of clinking glasses, he continued, 'The food here is no more than pub food but is well prepared. I suggest you each choose a main course, and a dessert if you want. Meantime, I'll arrange for a sharing plate of what might p'raps seem like an English kinda tapas to begin. Is that okay?'

And so their evening began —leisurely, for there was no hurry. There were more drinks. There were reminiscences of their last couple of days. There were reminiscences from Barry and May of happenings in *Tomberwater*. There was laughter. There was louder laughter.

It was after their main courses, while they were allowing their food to settle a little, that someone shouted from the middle of the room that it was time for the band. Four young men ran from the side of the room, took a bow and sat down on seats arranged around a drum kit and piano. Neither Carlos nor Valentina had noticed these items before, probably because people had been standing around them while drinking, but it all came together so naturally. The line-up comprised a pianist, drummer, trumpeter and clarinettist. A signboard behind them announced their name as *The Tomberwater Five*.

'Did you arrange this as well, Barry?' asked Carlos.

'Sort of,' Barry replied, but any further conversation was drowned out by the vigour of the band as it broke into the first of its old favourites from long ago.

The audience appreciated the performance very much. There was a great deal of applause with some laughter in between. *When the Saints Go Marchin' In* was followed by the jokey number, *Mamma Ain't Got No...* played with a fair degree of play-acting.

Carlos suddenly noted the name of the band. 'Why are they called the *Tomberwater Five*?' he asked. 'There are only four of them!'

As the applause died down, the trumpeter came up to the Spaniard's table and took hold of Barry by one hand while presenting him with a shiny trombone in the other. Carlos and Valentina looked on in amazement as Barry followed the trumpeter "onstage". The band broke into *St. James Infirmary Blues*. That slow, steady graveyard rhythm gave marvellous opportunities for Barry to show off his trombone playing. The pub audience loved it, but nobody more than Carlos who stood up as he clapped his hands vigorously, while May tried to pull him back into his seat by tugging on his shirt.

'Don't draw attention to yourself!' she whispered loudly, but in vain.

Carlos was lost in admiration for his host. At least he had the presence of mind not to shout out in an accent everyone would be drawn to.

The *Tomberwater Five* played four more numbers before taking a drinking break. Barry came back to their table looking rather pleased with himself.

'Barry, that was wonderful. I knew you liked jazz, of course, but had no idea that you played!' Carlos enthused. 'Do you play cool jazz as well?'

''Fraid not, Merton', Barry replied, using Carlos's public name and so showing a considerable propriety and presence of mind, at the same time making clear that Carlos was not to let his guard down. 'The trumpeter is my brother, Gordon. We both like bebop but find it rather too difficult to play well, and our band is just an amateur group 'cos we all have proper jobs. We play for fun, that's all.'

'Well, you were splendid, Barry. Congratulations,' Carlos beamed at him.

Later that evening the band played a second set, and the whole pub audience enthused and became merrier as the evening drew on. Afterwards, Gordon joined Barry, May and their guests for a few minutes. Carlos complimented him as well.

Gordon thanked Carlos and then, speaking softly, said, 'It's time to take you back to *The Hut*. All danger there has gone, so I will drive you both back this evening. We are quite near *Tomberwater* here. I know it may not seem that way, but boats travel slowly, while we can drive cross-country in the car and be home in a little over an hour. If you and Valentina could please pack your belongings now, I will arrange for them to be collected.'

The Spaniards were taken by surprise at the sudden end to their trip and were at pains to spend a little while thanking May and Barry for having looked after them so well.

'It was a wonderful trip. So interesting and varied. You have been wonderful hosts. I shall tell Michael so. Thank you again.'

May was so pleased with this little speech that she forgot herself and reached up to give Carlos a hug and a peck on the cheek. She hugged Valentina equally warmly who not only returned the compliment but gave Barry a hug, too. They said their final goodbyes and climbed into Gordon's car which was a large and comfortable vehicle without being excessively ostentatious. As ever, nobody wished to draw attention to themselves.

As promised, they were back in *Tomberwater* in just over an hour, having passed no other vehicle on the road, and drove into the grounds of *The Hut* by the back gate which gave onto the kitchen garden where Gordon worked – not that the Spaniards knew that, of course. Gordon took their bags, led them to the public entrance of the lift, and in minutes they were back in their old suite where everything had been prepared for their return. A dainty bunch of fresh flowers had been placed in a small vase on their dressing table, and a rather larger show welcomed them in their sitting room.

As they turned in that night, Valentina remarked, 'You know, darling, this is almost surrealistic. I am missing the sound of water lapping against the boat, already.'

11

Harvey had spent the evening of the Spaniard's departure watching the *Suspicious Four*, as he had come to think of them. Not that that had been especially easy, for they split up from time to time, and even super Harvey could not be in two places at once. He wasn't too worried by these difficulties, however, for there was little to suggest that any of the four were trying to make contact with the Spaniards. No, their movements were either subtle in the extreme or simply innocent. Harvey thought the latter. Indeed, it seemed to him that, for once, the Germans – if that's what they were – were trying to blend into the milieu of *The Hut* and to enjoy themselves. Harvey decided to test out his theory by joining his marks and raising a glass or two.

'Good evening!' he greeted the four. 'What do you think of this place? Wasn't that a splendid meal!'

It seemed that the four had conferred and decided to blend in more than they had earlier, for they greeted Harvey with smiles – well, they were a little forced, but they showed willing – and with the raising of their glasses. Certainly, there was a degree of play-acting in all this, Harvey saw immediately, but he sensed a degree of genuine pleasure in their gestures, too.

One of the men said, 'I am thinking that we have, at last, become – how does it go? – part of the place. Is that correct?'

'Yes, indeed,' Harvey replied. 'I am so pleased that you are enjoying *The Hut* like the rest of us; and, yes, your idiom is correct.'

That was an interesting little exchange as far as Harvey was concerned, for he realised immediately that his earlier supposition about these Germans had been wrong. That wasn't a German accent, it was Dutch.

There followed a few more pleasantries, a few more smiles and a little more half-forced gaiety before Harvey became convinced of his revised conclusion and that it applied to all four members of their group.

Harvey continued his explorations like a fisherman. 'Isobel and I explored some of the grounds in front of the mansion yesterday morning,' he began. 'We came across a hide.'

The Dutchmen all looked puzzled.

Harvey explained. 'You know, one of those huts in which birdwatchers can stare at little birds for hours without being seen.'

His frivolity was totally lost on his audience, but more to the point, was their total disinterest in his remarks. Harvey looked at each of them, closely but fleetingly, and was completely sure that they couldn't have cared less about Isobel, his exploration with her, or the hide.

Harvey braved a different tack. 'Isn't the library here quite wonderful? I hadn't expected to find such a large and well-organised affair in a private house like this. What do *you* think?'

This brought forth an embarrassed response.

'Oh yes,' replied one of the men. 'We also found the library most convenient.'

That rings true, thought Harvey, *though maybe they didn't intend it to be so*. He thought it best not to pursue that line and so lightly, and with an assumed butterfly mind, returned to trivial commentary on the other facilities offered by *The Hut*. When one of the young women excused herself from the group, Harvey also left.

'Call of nature,' he explained.

He had decided that those remaining probably intended to stay put, so it seemed worthwhile to check on the young lady. It turned out that she had left for the same reason, however, returning to her associates after an appropriate interval. After a while, Harvey excused himself totally from the Dutch group for he didn't want to spook them by too much attention and bonhomie. He moved around the room, making brief conversation with several other guests enjoying their postprandial drinks. From time to time, however, he looked across at the Dutch group. They were still there, and other guests fleetingly joined them. It all seemed so innocent and genuine. They certainly did not seem to constitute any kind of threat to the Spaniards.

A little before eleven o'clock, the four stood, looked around at their fellow guests for a brief moment and left the lounge. Harvey watched them as they approached the grand staircase. He rushed to the lift and managed to emerge on the Dutchmen's floor before they got there, and to conceal himself in an alcove, or small recess, really, so that he could watch without being seen. It was all very dramatic, but it turned out, Harvey decided later, to be quite unnecessary, for his marks each entered their own rooms – which were adjacent, but then, so what?

Harvey stayed there till sometime after midnight when he decided to quit and go to bed himself. *Maybe they're not politically connected to the Spaniards, after all?* he mused. He decided to sleep on it.

After breakfast, he sent an SMS to Michael requesting a brief meeting. Michael replied, choosing the kitchen garden once more, in a quarter of an hour. This time, Gordon wasn't around. Michael and Harvey took a slow stroll while inspecting the herb garden, which was a treat in its own right.

Harvey began with a question: 'Did the Spaniards get away safely?'

Michael assured him that they had, that there were no problems and, as far as it was possible to say, nobody saw anything.

'Well, I stayed with, or in sight of, our marks from about nine o'clock onwards, indeed up till past midnight. I would swear that none of them showed any interest in the hour or in any disappearing act all evening. I am also of the opinion that these four guests are Dutch rather than German. My observations a couple of days ago certainly suggest that they have an interest in the Spaniards, but it seems unlikely to be at a level of knowing their whereabouts at all times. I will try to find out if they're at all dismayed by their absence today. How long will the Spaniards be away?'

'That's not been decided yet, Harvey. I'll let you know when I can,' Michael replied. 'I agree that it is still worth keeping a watch over these people, so please keep on it.'

'You have some wonderful herbs here, Michael. I suppose that's all down to Gordon.'

'Actually, no. Certainly Gordon sees to them these days, but the original planting was down to my wife and, before that, to my mother when she was alive.'

They parted, and Harvey strolled into the house in as casual a way as he could, in search of the Dutchmen. That took no time at all, however, for he came across them in the bar, enjoying coffee. Isobel, Hillary and Gerald were there, too. Harvey collected a coffee and sauntered across to join them.

'What a wonderful morning again!' he exclaimed. 'What's on everyone's agenda?'

'Well, if you have nothing better to do, I wonder if we might explore the village together?' Isobel replied. 'We can leave these oldies to their tennis.' She grinned openly at Harvey who pursed his lips in reply.

'I think that's an excellent idea,' he said. 'Old uncle Gerald needs the exercise.'

'Cheeky young pup!' Gerald replied, but looked at Hillary with some pleasure in his eyes and his hand briefly touched hers.

This was not lost on Isobel, nor on Harvey. Isobel smiled at her cousin in a dreamy but utterly sweet way. Hillary's response was to make a barely visible pout: she did not appear put out, apart, perhaps, for a slight colouring of her cheeks.

Isobel and Harvey met up ten minutes later at the main entrance to the hall.

'I thought that went quite well, didn't you?' Isobel asked Harvey, with just the tiniest of smirks.

'I must say, I thought you were a bit obvious, but it seemed to go down well, anyway. Maybe they're halfway there,' Harvey replied.

Isobel giggled. 'I think they might be.'

They took a path to the right, which led around one of the "new" wings of the hall, on past the kitchen gardens and to a small postern gate adjacent to the entrance through which most *Hut* traffic passed. Harvey had picked up a small map of the village and of the hall's relative position, from the main desk, while renewing his *Hut* app and waiting for Isobel to join him. He pointed to a side road to the left just ahead.

'The main road – if main is an appropriate word for a B-road – carries on and curves right and then left as it circumnavigates the village. This little road to the left takes us into the village centre. I suggest that we turn left here.'

In due course, the smooth tarmac gave way to a section of very old cobbles.

'Goodness,' Isobel exclaimed. 'I thought cobbles had been removed or paved over everywhere years ago.'

'I think there's an element of local pride and sentiment alive in Tomberwater,' Harvey suggested, 'or maybe Michael has insisted upon this preservation of olde worlde charm.'

'Surely Michael doesn't own the village as well, does he?' she replied.

'I'm just kidding. Maybe your research nose can find out, Izzy? If you're interested enough, that is.'

'Not especially,' Isobel replied, 'but talking about research, I have the impression that you've been involved in some research of your own.'

Harvey was more than a little startled by this remark. 'How do you mean?' he asked, or rather, tried to ask, in a casual manner.

'Don't look so worried, Harvey,' Isobel laughed. 'Your secret is safe with me, whatever it is. But you deserted us for much of yesterday evening, and I was at a loss to know what you might find more exciting than our company.'

Harvey relaxed at her response, but then she continued, 'If you find those Germans more exciting than us, that is, of course, your prerogative.'

She was smiling broadly but her sharp eyes were probing closely, and Harvey knew it full well.

'Well, I was disappointed that we had not been able to make better progress with them earlier, so I thought I'd try again,' he replied.

'Pretty lame,' Isobel replied, still smiling broadly.

Harvey continued, 'They seemed to be trying to be much more sociable yesterday evening, I thought. Really putting on an effort,' he continued.

'As are you!' Isobel grinned.

She's like a dog with a bone, dammit, thought Harvey, wincing slightly under her relentless joking.

'I'll tell you one thing I found out from my conversation,' he said, hoping to evince a measure of interest from his tormentor. 'I am sure from their accents – all four of them – that they're Dutch, not German.'

Isobel let him off the hook at that point, but only a little. 'You found out all that from so short an encounter,' she teased.

'Dammit, Izzy, these things take time. I didn't want to upset them in any way. One has to be careful.'

'You mean, like a spy?' she enquired, this time with a deliberately sly, sideways look.

'Oh, give it a rest. I was merely being polite,' he protested.

'Yes, Harvey, that's what I thought,' she said, but, after a significant pause, continued, 'until your over-casual explanation just now.'

'I have no idea what you mean, my dear girl,' Harvey came back, trying a different bullying trick.

'Don't you "my girl" me, Harvey,' Isobel replied, 'it won't wash. The more you bluster, the worse you get. I do believe you *are* a spy, my dear.'

'Now you are "my dearing" me,' Harvey rejoined, 'and that won't wash either.'

Isobel laughed gleefully. 'Shall we call it quits, Harvey? I'll call you a spy and you'll continue to deny it, and we can live with that, surely?' She paused as another thought came to her. 'Until your next slip-up, anyway.'

Harvey looked serious and then glum for a few moments. 'I had a dog like you once. She loved chewing on a worn-out bone as well.'

They walked along in silence for a while until they came to the village pub.

'That's a good name for the village pub: *Tomber Pot*,' Isobel exclaimed. Let's pop in there for a drink when we come back.'

'Oh, you're prepared to stay that long in the company of a spy, then?' Harvey replied.

'I had a dog like you once', Isobel replied. 'He growled a lot while chewing on an old bone but always to little effect.'

Harvey laughed now. 'Okay, okay. You win. Let's call it quits.'

' All right, let's do that,' Isobel replied. 'I can live with a spy for a day, I guess.'

'Bloody hell! Harvey exclaimed. 'You can't let go, can you?'

'Woof, woof,' she replied, quick as a flash.

Harvey, lost for words, shook his head slowly. They continued their exploration of the village and even took time off from their quarrel to admire some of the old buildings in it.

'I wonder how old that neo-Elizabethan house really is,' Isobel remarked. 'I mean, this village was founded around the beginning of the seventeenth century, as far as my research has uncovered. If that house was built then – and it could well have been, simply because of its central position within the village – its style was already one or two hundred years out of date, which means that whoever decided upon its style was not much different from people today wanting an "olde worlde" style of building. So, not too much changes, eh?'

'I hadn't realised that you had done research on Tomberwater,' Harvey remarked. 'Are you on a project, by any chance?'

'In a half-hearted way, I am,' Isobel replied. 'My bank is retained by a company which is interested in wide-ranging investments. Tomberwater came up in my investigations but only in a peripheral way. I am genuinely here on holiday with Hillary, but, of course, one stone… two birds, and all that.'

'A part-time spy, then?' chided Harvey.

'You don't give up, do you?' Isobel grinned. 'I'll tell you what, though. Your discovery that the sulky four are Dutch rather than German is spot on. Sorry to put it like this, but I could have told you that already, for I spotted the Dutch tones the moment they uttered their first word on your first evening here.'

'Oh, all right. You were quick off the mark, then.'

'Only because I spent a lot of time in the Netherlands – in Holland and Amsterdam, in particular – on one of my projects a year or so ago. I was investigating the diamond trade there. Quite interesting, really, but I'm sorry to say that I got no samples for my pains!'

Harvey dropped his guard for a moment. 'Of course!' he almost shouted. 'Not politics; diamonds!'

'Now what are you talking about, Harvey? Do say. You're becoming more intriguing by the minute!'

Harvey fell silent for a moment while he almost made his decision. 'Did your work involve any study of famous diamond jewellery or anything like that?' he asked.

'Not directly, though I came across experts in that area,' Isobel replied. 'Why do you ask?'

Time to take the plunge, he thought.

' All right, Isobel,' he said. His voice had assumed a rather more serious tone than earlier in the morning. 'I am going to follow my instinct about you. I hope I am right in that I believe I can trust you with my secrets. I do hope so, for I am making this decision based upon the very short time we have known each other. Is my judgement right, do you think?' He was still thrashing around, trying to firm up his decision.

'Harvey, you can trust me. I don't lie, and I am faithful to my friends. I consider you to be my friend, even after so short an acquaintance.'

Harvey nodded, to himself as much as to Isobel. 'I *am* a spy of sorts. I am working for Michael. Those Spaniards, Carlos and Valentina, who we both took a shine to, are indeed Spanish nobles. They are in some sort of strife – I don't know exactly what, and I'm not sure really that I need or want to know – something political back in their own neck of the woods in Spain. They are here at *The Hut* to gain time and a bit of peace from whatever those political shenanigans are and most certainly to keep out of sight of any newshounds who may be around. You may have noticed that they aren't around today. They have been spirited away somewhere by Michael and his team. I don't know where or for how long, but Michael thought that the Dutchmen – Germans, as I first imagined – might be emissaries from Spain trying to get some dirt on our friends, or worse, and he has asked me to try and find out what they are doing at *The Hut*. They have been vouched for by a third party whom Michael trusts, but that might not be sufficient for safety. Anyway, I came across the Dutchmen – just the men without their female gofers, on this occasion – skulking in the library here. It's a beautiful library, by the way. Have you seen it? Anyway, they were obviously embarrassed to be seen there. I was given no explanation… but then, why should I be told? I couldn't ask, of course, but I did notice several photographs in front of them which they tried to cover up as I arrived. They more or less succeeded, but I caught a glimpse of one. It was of Valentina at some function or other. At the time, it served to convince me that they were guilty of the kind of thing that Michael was so worried about – the privacy of his treasured guests. But now, especially in view of their seeming indifference to the minute-by-minute whereabouts of their quarries – and hence, of their secret departure yesterday evening – I'm not at all sure about that. You see, that photograph of Valentina I saw in the library showed her dolled up to the nines for some formal occasion or other. Again, so what, you may ask? But right in the centre of that picture was a view of a stunning piece of jewellery hanging round her neck. Again, normally, I would have thought little of that, but now, and for little more than a sniff following your remarks about one of your earlier projects, I am wondering if their interest in the Spaniards is in their jewellery rather than in their politics. And so, my dear Isobel, I wonder if you might be able to help me find out some more about that jewellery and about our Dutchmen. What do you think?'

'Gosh!' Hillary replied, her face free of laughter now. 'Well, well! What a story. I really did think that you had been doing a bit of sleuthing, but only in a casual and amateur capacity. This is altogether more serious and important, and yes! I am more than willing to help.'

They had continued their stroll while Harvey had made his confession and had reached the embankment immediately behind the main Tomberwater wharf. Harvey broke into their conversation for a moment by observing that this was almost where they had reached on their long walk the other morning.

'Things are beginning to connect,' he observed, without, it seemed, seeing the double entendre. 'Let's have a drop of lunch in the pub today and work out a strategy.'

By now, he was totally given to his partnership with Isobel. As they turned about and made their way back to the *Tomber Pot*, Harvey put his arm around Isobel's shoulders. It was an innocent enough gesture from someone who was moving along a romantic road.

Isobel gently removed his arm, looked at him directly but without rancour, and said, 'Harvey, I think it's only fair to us both if we do not confuse trust with anything more personal. It would come as a shock to Hillary and Gerald, I'm sure, and to you now, no doubt, to learn that I am gay. I like you very much, Harvey, and I trust you, but I'm afraid we can be no more than friends. I hope I haven't embarrassed you.'

Harvey looked very confused for some moments before replying, 'Thank you for telling me at this early stage, Isobel. Certainly, I would never have guessed, and I promise to keep your secret – I assume that you would wish that – but I do not feel that it will impact adversely upon our partnership. Indeed, the reverse, probably, for we can both concentrate on the main course, so to speak. I do hope, however, that we can maintain and enjoy our newfound friendship.'

'Absolutely, my dear, let us be firm friends. I also hope that we can continue our plot to entangle your uncle and my cousin!'

Harvey took hold of Isobel's hand and placed a gentle kiss upon it. 'To friendship,' he said, as they reached the pub.

12

'Well, now, oldie, how did that go for you?' Hillary smirked at Gerald, after thrashing him yet again.

'It's only gentlemanly to let the lady win,' Gerald managed to say between gasps for air. 'In any case, I think it's time for a drink.'

'See you in the bar in ten minutes,' Hillary replied and, quite provocatively, Gerald thought, literally ran off to change, with a skip in her step.

Later, while sipping their cocktails, Hillary was recalling the conversation from earlier in the morning. 'That little minx, Isobel, is being rather naughty, don't you think? You know, the way she's playing Puck around the place.'

'I must say, I don't mind one little bit,' Gerald replied. 'They seem to be hitting it off rather well, so why shouldn't we?'

He looked closely at Hillary but saw no objection; indeed, he only noticed a tiny, dancing smile.

'I say, Hillary, why don't you and I take the afternoon off from *The Hut*, genteel though it is, and go for a drive in the countryside?'

'What a lovely idea, Gerald,' she replied, 'and how old-fashioned. We could stop somewhere for tea and cakes.'

And so it was that, after a light lunch and a brief perusal of the newspapers, they set out for their afternoon exploration. Hillary admired Gerald's graceful and almost-silent Jaguar as they pulled out from the back gate of *The Hut*.

'Tell you what; let's just drive at random, switch off the maps, get lost and maybe get surprised,' he suggested.

They turned left and circumnavigated the village, passed the Tomberwater wharf on their right, the main gate of the hall on their left, until they reached a right turn leading to a bridge over the river. They crossed over.

'I think this bit of the countryside is boring. It's too flat. Why don't you head for the hills where we can get some views?' Hillary suggested.

It took half an hour or so of many left turns and right turns and crossing over the canal before the countryside began to roll a little.

'That's better, don't you think?' she said. 'Now we have some views at last. And they are pretty.'

'I'll see if we can reach the top of that hill over there,' Gerald proposed.

In typical English style, there was no direct road, it seemed, and they were obliged to navigate around farmer Jones' fields, but they eventually found a narrow road which seemed to be heading to the top. However, after only a couple of hundred yards, it petered out into a walking path.

'Let's leave the car here and walk the rest of the way, Gerald,' Hillary suggested. 'It doesn't seem to be muddy or anything.'

The path curved a little but it did reach the top of the modest hill, and they stopped to take in the view. It was well worth it, for they could see for miles. The straight canal was clear – there were two narrow boats on it going in opposite directions; in the other direction they could clearly pick out the river as it wound its way through the countryside.

'Can you see the hall from here?' Hillary asked.

They searched for some time before Gerald pointed to their left. 'I think it's over there behind those trees. It's almost as if it has been built deliberately out of sight. It fits in with the countryside so well, don't you think?'

'Let's sit down for a while and enjoy the flowers here,' she suggested, and sat down in amongst some narcissi.

'A flower amongst flowers,' Gerald remarked. He thought about it and added, 'Corny, but still valid!'

Hillary patted the ground beside her. Gerald sat down – very close. There were acres of ground on which to sit, but he chose a spot as close as possible to her. It did not go unnoticed. It did go unremarked. They didn't speak for some time but pretended to gaze at the views before them. Hillary sensed that Gerald was looking at her, and she turned her head toward him. He leaned forward by the length of a breath and kissed her lightly. She put her hands on his face and held him gently.

'Let's find that afternoon tea somewhere,' she suggested, softly.

It took nearly an hour before they found a likely-looking pub with a tea garden. It seemed worth a punt. They were rewarded with a splendid cuppa and some absolutely wonderful, freshly-baked scones; a cream tea to have pleased any Cornish or Devonian man or woman.

Are they really that good, or does everything just seem that way? Gerald wondered. *Are Hillary's cheeks usually this rosy?*

'I wonder what the little people are up to?' Gerald asked. 'Do I recall that they went to explore the village this morning? Like as not they found the pub on their way.'

'I also wonder how well they're getting on. They seem to have responded to our manoeuvres rather well, I think.'

'Perhaps we'll be able to form a better view by dinner time,' Gerald suggested. He took hold of Hillary's hand for a moment. 'I never thought I'd enjoy playing cupid so much. I don't feel guilty, for they do seem to be a good match.'

'Yes. You can just sense these things, can't you?' she murmured.

They enjoyed a long silence together in the sunshine until Gerald laughed and remarked, 'I think we should be able to get back to the hall in time for a wee drink before dinner. You know, we'll wear ourselves out at this rate.'

Hillary laughed. 'Don't do that, my dear.'

It took nearly an hour of twists and turns before they reached Tomberwater again.

'Let's go in via the main entrance,' Gerald suggested.

'You mean, to make a grand entrance?' Hillary laughed.

Gerald turned the Jaguar in toward the main gates, used his hall app to open them and, with all due ceremony, drove slowly along that back drive, through the second chicane and left onto the Grand Avenue.

'I have been here several times, darling,' he said, 'but that view knocks me out every time.

His almost unconscious endearment did not go unnoticed by either of them.

Later in the bar, Gerald had ordered a couple of their favourite cocktails as Hillary entered. They clinked their glasses and looked deeply at one another for a moment; maybe a moment too long, for, at that point, Isobel and Harvey appeared. Isobel caught the scene in a trice and wasn't in the mood to let it go.

'Hello, you old lovebirds,' she laughed. 'And where have you two been all afternoon? We looked for you on the croquet lawn, on the tennis court, even at the chess boards. But no! You were nowhere to be seen!'

It was true that she and Harvey had glanced at those locations, but most of their afternoon had been spent head-to-head in the library, planning their next moves. Hillary and Gerald had no means of knowing that, of course, and attempted to stifle their blushes. This only added to Isobel's delight.

'Well, it's been a fine afternoon for it, anyway,' she added, pursing her lips in obvious amusement.

There was clearly no way that the older couple could win, and Gerald broke the spell by offering the youngsters a drink.

'How did your trip into the depths of Tomberwater go this morning?' he asked.

Harvey, with almost too much alacrity, replied, 'Very well and very informative,' he said. 'After seeing the wharf and several of the quaint, old houses in the village, we ended up in the pub for lunch.'

'There you are, d…' Gerald corrected himself, but his attempt failed utterly to convince either Harvey or Isobel.

'I told you that's what they'd do.' Hillary smiled broadly.

Isobel grinned. Harvey pretended not to smile.

'Stop it, you two,' Gerald said, and hastily continued. 'What did you think of the *Tomber Pot*?'

'What's that?' asked Harvey.

'The name of the pub, darling,' interjected Isobel, who was clearly in the mood to be very naughty; or, at any rate, deceitful.

'Yes, it has a nice atmosphere, I think,' he conceded.

'What did you have for lunch?' Hillary asked, in all innocence.

Harvey faltered. He couldn't remember, for he and Isobel had been too deep in conversation and plotting.

'Oh, just scampi and a salad,' he replied, hoping that his confusion had escaped notice.

It hadn't, and Hillary understood completely that Harvey and Isobel were too engrossed in each other to remember. She smiled and let them off.

As they went into dinner, Harvey remarked that there were a couple of new guests around.

'A youngish couple,' he noted, 'but I don't know anything about them, yet.'

Dinner that evening was all cold, "in honour of the lovely day", Rachael announced. *Vichyssoise*; very rare, thickly-sliced beef fillet with three salads – potato, bean and green; and, as a complement to the new guests who were Australian, a *Pavlova*. These and, as they had by now come to expect, fruits, nuts and a cheese plate. As usual, a variety of splendid wines appeared for each course.

Conversation bubbled. Rachael introduced her new guests as Judi and Barnes, which could have been real or fake names, as, by now, everyone was well aware. They seemed to be a pleasant enough couple, but Barnes seemed a bit too pushy for Hillary's taste, although she took to his wife (or so she presumed their relationship to be). Barnes talked a lot about mining, a subject which didn't excite too many round the table.

Harvey saw a chance and gave Isobel a nudge. 'Does your mining interest include diamond mining?' he asked Barnes, and glanced very briefly across at the Dutch group.

'No, 'fraid not,' Barnes replied. 'Strictly metals in my game.'

Harvey nodded and turned away. Barnes had served his purpose for the moment.

In due course, the dinner party broke up and people went this way and that.

'Fancy a game of chess?' Harvey asked Isobel.

'Sure,' she replied, without pause.

'See you guys at breakfast,' Harvey said to Hillary and Gerald, who were heading to the bar once more.

'That's a lame excuse, I must say,' observed Hillary to Gerald, with a broad grin. 'Isobel doesn't play chess – or, at least, doesn't care for it.'

They sat down and Gerald asked Hillary what drink he might tempt her with. She patted the chair beside her.

When Gerald had seated himself with a questioning look, she said, clearly but quietly, 'I think I'll turn in early this evening. Why don't you bring a bottle of bubbles up to my room – B4? Don't forget to bring your toothbrush.'

She left Gerald sitting there for a moment before he took himself off to his room, bottle in hand. No one, really, would have noticed the slight tremor in his hand as he reached for the lift call-button.

13

Harvey led Isobel through the games room with its chess, bridge and backgammon tables, into the cool night air and to one of the tables set up there.

'Did you catch the Dutchmen's reaction to my question about diamonds?' he asked.

'I certainly did. They had a virtually involuntary reaction. All four of them, to different degrees, for sure, reacted and focussed on Barnes and, to some extent, you. There was a fair degree of alarm in their glances and a collective rush to cover up and assume indifference.'

'I agree completely,' Harvey said. 'I am just more than ever convinced that they are interested in jewellery rather than politics, so far as the Spaniards are concerned. So, would you go ahead as we discussed at lunch today and see what you can find out about Valentina's jewels? I'll try and find out where these Dutch people have been in the past months and exactly who they are.' He looked at Isobel for a moment before continuing. 'I think I should tell Michael that we have teamed up over this. Okay?'

Isobel agreed immediately. 'I think I might retire now and get out my computer. There is a lot to do. Goodnight, Harvey. I'm glad to be working with you. Let's enjoy it, partner! Now, for the sake of any onlooker,' she broke off, and gave Harvey a peck on the cheek, and, as she left, added, 'Please don't get confused!'

Harvey, too, turned to his computer. His first impulse was to ask Michael to break his cardinal rule and reveal the real names of the Spaniards, but he wondered if he might be able to solve that problem in a different way. He began by googling society pages, famous jewels, parties for the rich… that sort of thing. He was not at all surprised to unearth an awful lot of boredom and junk on his way, but eventually he came up with a newspaper photograph of Valentina and Carlos at a reception in New York eighteen months earlier. It was certainly them, but their names were not mentioned. He messaged Isobel that he was sending her a link via email and that he was trying to find their names from there; all help would be gratefully received. He realised that he could try more conventional means, like trying to call the newspaper or photographer on the phone, but he thought he'd just continue with his first search, in case he struck lucky again. Yet again, he had to wade through mountains of irrelevant material.

He took a short break and made himself a strong coffee. He recommenced his search but with a somewhat fatalistic attitude. Then up came another photograph that excited his eye. This time, it showed the Spaniards together with another couple, glasses in hand and in what appeared to be serious but animated conversation. Maybe he was dreaming this last bit; maybe they were simply straining to hear what was being said over general party noise. But their expressions did suggest something serious in the air. Once more, there was no caption naming the subjects, but the occasion was identified. It was an art gallery opening in Paris, or the opening of an exhibition there – Harvey was unsure about which. He did notice, however, something in common between the two photographs he had found: namely, a beautiful necklace worn by Valentina. Then he remembered. It was the same diamond necklace he had seen her wear as she went into dinner on Harvey's first evening at *The Hut*. He sent the link through to Isobel without comment before he continued his master search, for he had decided that this avenue was worth pursuing further. Very soon afterwards he got an email from Isobel.

"That's the same necklace she wore at dinner the other evening!"

Harvey merely replied, "Yup!" and continued picking through the weeds. Half an hour later he found another picture of Valentina, now cropped to her alone, with a caption drawing attention to her gorgeous necklace. This time, there was some text provided with the picture:

"…Count and Countess de Lara from the province of La Rioja were attending an exhibition of ancient Egyptian artefacts in Coimbra, Portugal…"

Harvey almost poured himself a drink but thought better of it; another coffee seemed more appropriate right now. He emailed Isobel again with his news.

She replied: "Well done! Now I can get down to my part. Thank you!"

Harvey's next search was instinctive: "De Lara appearances." Uncle Google redirected him, and in short order, he discovered that the Spaniards had been reported as appearing in at least ten venues which included the three he had already found. He painstakingly looked at each, searching especially for any photographs of Valentina (or Luciana, as he had now discovered; and Carlos was really Nicolás) wearing expensive-looking jewellery. He found several. The couple had been photographed in New York, Paris and Coimbra, as he had already discovered, but also in London, Edinburgh, Bonn and Milan. Harvey supposed that further work on his part might reveal other locations as well, but he decided that he should quit while he was ahead and go to bed.

He signed off with Isobel: "Tired. Going to bed. A good night's work!"

It was one o'clock in the morning.

Harvey liked his sleep. It was well past eight o'clock when he woke. He quickly shaved and showered and hurried down to the breakfast room. He didn't want Gerald and Hillary to tease him about being in bed early and out of it late. Isobel was already halfway through her breakfast, but there was no sign of his uncle or of her cousin.

'Morning!' he murmured to Isobel. 'Been here long?'

'Just arrived, really. I kept at it for another hour after you signed off. I've made some progress, too. We can discuss it after breakfast, maybe?'

Harvey nodded, yawned and made a manly effort to eat a hearty breakfast.

'Better now?' Isobel teased.

'Much, thank you. Seen anything of the oldies this morning?'

'No. They probably beat us to it,' she replied. 'I see we have another nice day ahead of us. How about a walk to clear our cobwebs?'

They headed, without haste, towards the bird with two heads and thence onto the hide.

'What have you found so far?' asked Harvey.

'I won't bore you with how I got there, but I went in search of information about that necklace which Val… sorry, Luciana, was wearing in several of the photographs you forwarded to me. It turns out to be part of a modestly famous collection which has been in the de Lara family for generations. The whole collection is probably worth a couple of million dollars American. That particular piece, on its own, would likely fetch four hundred thousand dollars, I would guess. I think it's rather pretty, don't you?'

'Certainly, at that price,' Harvey replied.

'Philistine!' she pouted.

'Any further progress?' asked Harvey.

'No, dear Harvey, that was my extra hour's work after you went bye byes.'

'Okay, I want to see if there's some connection between our Spanish friends and the Dutchmen. Maybe we can both work on that angle. Perhaps you can try and find out who they are. What do you think?'

'Yes, fine. Back to our computers. I'll see you at lunch.'

Isobel hurried back to her room. As she was about to open her door, Hillary's door opened, and her cousin appeared in her nightdress.

'Hello, fair cousin,' Isobel greeted her. 'Overslept? Too much to drink with your friend?' she teased.

'Something like that, Izzy. My head is rather sore this morning. I think I'll take it easy for a while. I'll see you at lunch, maybe?'

As Hillary closed her bedroom door, Isobel half-thought she heard a cough from inside; maybe it was just the sound of her cousin's nightdress catching on the door?

Meanwhile, Harvey had begun to see if he could find out who had attended the various functions at which the de Laras had appeared in his searches. It immediately became apparent that Google had no listings. He would have to work harder and began looking instead for the names of persons or organisations which had arranged those functions. That was slow enough, but he managed to get somewhere. Then he sought the addresses of these persons and groups; more, of their head people, where he could.

By a quarter to one, he had found what he wanted, for five of the occasions. He thought that would do to earn him some lunch. Harvey enjoyed his food and would let almost nothing get in the way of a feed.

When he reached the dining room, he found Hillary and Gerald already there with Isobel, though it was clear that they had all arrived only shortly before him. He noted straight away that Hillary seemed a little flustered and slightly flushed. Gerald was beaming at everyone and talking fifty to the dozen. Isobel had obviously observed the symptoms already. She grinned openly at Harvey as he approached.

'Isn't it nice to get together again? I'm sorry if you've missed us, Hillary, but we've been a tad busy with our project.'

Harvey shot Isobel a nervous glance, but she continued, 'Harvey and I are collaborating on a spot of local history. Tomberwater is a most interesting place, and we are gleaning so much about it from Uncle Google.' She smiled charmingly at her cousin and Gerald and, with a look of total innocence, continued, 'What have you two been doing?'

Hillary's mouth opened and closed for a moment before Gerald jumped in with a shortened, truthful account of their movements. 'I took Hillary out and about in the Jag yesterday to explore some of the lesser-known byways around here. We had a most pleasant afternoon.' *There*, he imagined saying to Hillary, *close but not too close*.

'Yes, it was a lovely break,' Hillary hastened to add, remembering, rather late in the piece, the old adage: *Don't talk too much; never explain!*

Isobel was on the point of asking them exactly where they had been but decided in favour of a little mercy. 'Let's eat,' she said. 'I'm famished.'

During their lunch, Hillary suggested that they might all indulge in a game of croquet later on in the afternoon.

Harvey saw Isobel's confusion and jumped in very quickly to say, 'That would be lovely. Izzy and I want to finish up a couple of things. We could meet after that, say four o'clock?'

To Isobel, after their lunch, Harvey explained, 'I reckon that we'll both be heartily sick of our project by then and have become jaded, so we might as well be sociable for a few hours. It will give us a breather before we continue later this evening. Are you happy with that, Izzy?'

'You're right. Let's put in a couple of hours right now before we relax – if such is possible with Hillary playing croquet!'

*

Harvey set about contacting the organisers he had found that morning. He knew he would need help, and he contacted his office where he was able to call on the services of at least one researcher. They agreed upon a division of the labour and set about their work.

By half past three, Harvey had lists of attendees at three of the venues attended by the de Laras. There were two common denominators: a French lady and a Dutch gentleman. The Dutchman's name was Erik van Reiden, a citizen of Amsterdam and a dealer in precious stones by profession. The French lady appeared to be a society lady of some not insignificant age – Harvey had been unable to find more about her thus far. He had similarly been unable to obtain any photographs of van Reiden.

He quickly emailed Isobel with his findings, arranging to meet her on the croquet lawn in ten minutes. She replied immediately that she had been searching for other world gatherings where very precious jewellery was on display. At first, she had been led up several blind alleys before finding a likely grouping of such meetings. Like Harvey, she had sought lists of attendees at these functions and looked for commonalities. So far, she told him, she had garnered data on only two such gatherings. There were two guests in common: a French lady whose name she had so far been unable to determine, and a Dutch diamond dealer called Erik van Reiden. She added that she could positively identify van Reiden from his photograph as one of their target Dutchmen.

Harvey quickly sent back: "Bingo! See you in five!"

When they met on the croquet lawn, Hillary and Gerald had not yet appeared.

Harvey breathlessly told Isobel, 'We've certainly found our Dutchman. I had discounted the French woman, but now I'm not too sure. I wonder if she is somehow connected; maybe as some sort of financier for the Dutchman's enterprise, whatever that actually is.'

'Okay,' she replied. 'I'll look into that after dinner. I suggest that you look into jewel robberies. It's a long shot, but you never know. Oh look! Here come Hillary and Gerald. They do seem to be a little tired. I wonder if they slept well last night.' Isobel giggled. 'I think we won, Harvey.'

'Hello, you two,' Gerald called out, with somewhat exaggerated bonhomie. 'We two against you two?'

Harvey's concentration was somewhat lacking – he was still excited by what Isobel and he had discovered – and his strokes were far below par. The same was true for Hillary, though for what reason Harvey neither knew nor, in his preoccupation with the Dutchman, did he care. Isobel, however, seemed to have an ability to switch on or off at will. She repeatedly struck well, making roquets on most shots and, on many occasions, several in a row. She was murderous when she croqueted, sending Gerald's and

Hillary's balls way off. Occasionally, however, she played her croquets gently, in order to position her opponent's ball in an ideal position for another roquet. Harvey had played the game several times before but had nothing like the touch of his partner. He was quite lost in admiration of her skill. Gerald made a roquet and placed his ball against Isobel's, ready to send her off court. He then put his foot on his own ball and was about to make a grand swipe when Isobel cried out.

'Oh, no you don't, Gerald. We don't play dirty croquet here. Foot off, please. That kind of thing is just for urchins!'

'Really?' Gerald queried. 'I wasn't aware of that.'

'Ah, well, Gerald. Sometimes we young 'uns can teach you old 'uns a thing or three! You don't use your foot when making a croquet shot. You placed your ball against mine correctly, but you must allow yours to move, as well as mine. Of course, if you are skilled,' she said, now in a schoolmarmish voice, 'you can control how far your ball will move.' Reverting to more teasing tones, she continued, 'But if you want more information on that topic, it will cost you rather a lot – in time, as well as whatever else I can extract from you!'

'She's right dar… Gerald,' Hillary said, and blushed at her mistake.

Isobel was feeling a little wicked. 'I'd give it up, if I were you, cousin. You're caught. Enjoy it.' She giggled and her eyes lit up like torches.

'Oh, all right,' Hillary said. 'Let's get on with this game and go for a drink.'

They finished the game, agreed that nobody had their mind properly on it, except perhaps for Isobel, that they would leave the match there and make for the bar. Hillary and Gerald chose cocktails, as was their wont, while Isobel and Harvey both decided on spritzers.

'You seem to be taking your researches very seriously,' Hillary observed, with more than a fleeting smirk.

Isobel smiled broadly and sweetly at her cousin but didn't bite. Conversation settled into chit-chat and wonderings about what would appear on the menu that evening. After a quarter of an hour or so, Isobel asked Harvey to accompany her on a little stroll round the tennis courts.

'That's a new way of putting it,' Hillary remarked.

Isobel beamed at her, stuck her tongue out a little way, took hold of Harvey's hand and the two young ones moved off.

'That should confuse them,' Harvey remarked. 'It almost confuses me.'

'Play the game, Harvey,' Isobel said, smiling sweetly.

It's hard to believe, Harvey thought, but disciplined himself to ponder no further along those lines.

'Let's get back to our computers,' Isobel said. 'I think I will enjoy dinner so much more if we just get a bit further with our project.'

They hurried back to their rooms. Just as Isobel closed her room door, Hillary walked up to hers. She stopped, put her ear to Isobel's door for a moment or two, heard some indistinct speech and discreetly left for her own place, smiling with a Cheshire cat's grin as she did.

Isobel often talked to herself while working on her computer. She had the idea of searching public police files and charge sheets in the cities of most acute interest to Harvey's search. Another long shot, for sure, but you never know…

She found nothing with the van Reiden name attached. That would have been too much to hope for. On second thoughts, she reasoned, maybe they were thieves but had never been caught. She did, however, come across two cases involving significant jewellery theft: one in London and the other in Milan. In both cases, the van Reidens had been present at some glittering function or other. So had the unknown French woman.

That's enough for now, Isobel thought, as her attention turned to dinner, for it was nearly time. She sent a short summary of her findings to Harvey and left for dinner. So preoccupied was she that she had almost reached the bar when she realised that she was still dressed for croquet. She hurried back to change into her favourite little black number, a touch-up to her lipstick, and back downstairs.

Harvey was arriving at the same time. He came up to congratulate Isobel on her find, so the two of them were in what would appear to onlookers as a close huddle, as they entered the room. Hillary and Gerald were already there – probably on their fourth cocktail, Isobel surmised.

'Lovely dress, darling! Hillary said. 'Pity about the shoes.'

Isobel looked down at her shoes. She still had on her white flats from playing croquet.

'I'll just be a moment,' she said, and rushed off.

'My, my,' Hillary said to anyone who cared to listen, but her eyes were firmly upon Harvey. 'How absent-minded the young are these days.'

Her eyes glowed with fun, especially at Harvey's confusion. He, of course, was confused, because he had no idea why Isobel had put on the wrong shoes, any more than he was aware that Hillary had heard a voice at Isobel's door. And thus, conclusions are made. And they are very hard to unmake.

In due course, dinner was served, and everybody strolled into the dining hall. Michael made a point of sitting close to Isobel.

'Saw you playing croquet this afternoon,' he said. 'It's so nice to find the time for these elegant pursuits, I always think.'

He was smiling widely, but Isobel couldn't shake off the notion that she was being criticised. She wasn't a girl to let things go.

'Harvey and I have been collaborating…'

Michael's brows knotted a little in alarm.

Isobel continued, '… on our proposed history of Tomberwater.'

Michael relaxed.

Isobel smiled at him, especially sweetly. 'We have discovered so many interesting things. You'd be amazed, Michael.'

'I would love to hear of your progress, my dear,' he replied, rather patronisingly, Isobel thought, but she let it go. 'Tell me, how do you like game?'

Isobel misheard him and began talking about croquet.

'No, no,' Michael said. 'I meant game, as in pheasants or venison, for example. Because that's what this evening's meal is all about. That and offal. It's rather rich, but we have some suitable wines to help it all go down.'

'Your cuisine here is just wonderful, Michael. I do congratulate you,' Isobel said.

Michael beamed, but added, 'It's as much due to Rachael as to me. We spend hours together dreaming up these dinners. I think we enjoy the conception almost as much as the consumption.'

And so it was that dinner began with three small slices of sautéed *foie gras* surrounded by small slices of apple sautéed in butter, the whole being accompanied, interestingly, Gerald thought, with a white *Saint Joseph*. As usual, for *The Hut*, portions were modest, but that only made them savour each mouthful the more. Gerald gently took a modest piece of his *foie gras* between his tongue and his palette and squashed the morsel so that it oozed over much of his mouth. He was unaware of Hillary looking at him.

'You enjoyed that, didn't you?' she said, with a smile hovering over her mouth.

'Almost as much as sex,' he replied. 'Close call.'

Hillary smiled widely but said nothing. The *foie gras* was so rich. For their quite disparate reasons in fact, if not in their different perceptions, our four lovebirds were somewhat more ravenous than usual. Harvey kept nibbling at his bread, which was, in truth, an excellent sourdough. But he needn't have worried. There was a lot to come.

The main course offered loin of venison served with both a white and a black pepper sauce and adorned by crumbed potato noodles, poached apple with cranberries, and small, blanched celery rolls stuffed with puréed celeriac. Once more, Michael's guests took their time to savour each subtle and delicious morsel. It was all helped down by a heavy red from the Rhone valley.

A Sussex pond pudding brought up the rear – well, almost, for one was not to forget the seemingly obligatory fruit and cheese platters which ended all hall meals – and it was apparent that the smaller portions offered hitherto were not only chosen to encourage deep appreciation of the earlier dishes, but also for that most old-fashioned of sentiments: to leave room for the pud. The waiters cut into the suet shells of each pudding so that luscious, sweet, liquid butter flowed out, revealing within the suet cover a whole, soft, tart lemon – skin and all. A most British sweet, for sure.

There was no way that Harvey or Isobel were going to rush back to their rooms to work on their computers immediately after all that. They accepted the situation with grace and enjoyed some post-prandial drinks and conversation with their fellow guests. The new couple joined them at one point. He turned out to be a miner, and his partner, a surgeon.

'Barnes digs 'em up and I cut 'em up,' joked Judi.

It was obviously a well-worn introduction for them. They were, in any case, a jokey couple and provided Isobel and Harvey with some much-appreciated light relief.

Later, Harvey and Isobel joined up with Gerald and Hillary in the bar but left them for "an early night" after half an hour or so. Of course, they had to run the gauntlet of some self-satisfied taunts from the older couple, but they were a small price to pay.

As Isobel and Harvey climbed the main staircase, Harvey said, 'I'm going to try my luck with a senior cop I know. I may get nowhere, but I think it's worth a try. If I do get anything, I'll let you know. Otherwise, I'll see you at breakfast.'

'And I shall try to find out anything I can about the gems in that stolen jewellery,' Isobel replied, as they waved goodnight.

Back in his room in Gerald's and his suite, Harvey settled into an armchair and called Martin Prinn, an old school friend of his from years back. They had remained close friends for years. He got through immediately, and, after some pleasantries, Harvey told Martin of his and Isobel's project. It was a long conversation.

Eventually, he asked, 'Martin, I would be most grateful for anything you might be able to find out and relay to me about that Dutchman, Erik van Reiden. And, for that matter, about those mysterious robberies we've discovered.'

Martin promised to do what he could and call back. Harvey undressed and got into bed but sat up in the hope of a call-back. After an hour, he decided to call it a day, slid down under the sheets and fell soundly asleep.

At seven o'clock next morning, his phone rang.

'Sorry to wake you, old chap, but you're young enough to take it.'

It was Martin Prinn, eager to help his old mate. Or so Harvey hoped.

Martin continued, 'I have found out quite a lot about your mark, Harvey, but I'm afraid I cannot tell you too much. That's because I'm not allowed to.'

Harvey expressed some surprise but was immediately interrupted by Martin. 'Yes, I know, I'm a superintendent these days and you might expect that I can do what I like, but you know how it is – life's not like that. I have my superiors like anyone else, and I have been given very clear instructions about what I can tell you. That, in itself, should tell you quite a lot, but, to be explicit, Mr. van Reiden is known to several police forces around Europe – and beyond, actually – in connection with jewel robberies. We have our suspicions but insufficient evidence. He is being watched – intermittently – as is that French lady you mentioned. I cannot give you her name, I'm afraid. That's it, my friend. I hope my report is of some use to you. If not, I apologise.'

'Do not apologise, Martin. It is very useful indeed. If I find out anything new, I shall let you know, of course. You must have worked long to get all that. I appreciate it very much.'

'I had help,' Martin replied.

Later, at breakfast, Harvey told Isobel about the call. She, in turn, was able to report that there was some evidence that at least one of the stolen jewels appeared to have been cut and reset before being offered for sale. The evidence was slim but suggestive.

'I think we should have a meeting with Michael after breakfast. Okay with you?' Harvey asked.

*

They were invited into Michael's office. The door was locked behind them.

'I think it's best not to advertise any possible collaboration between us, if you don't mind,' Michael began.

'Agreed,' Harvey replied. 'Well, Michael, we have both worked very hard on our computers and putting the hard word on some friends – don't worry, neither you nor *The Hut* have been mentioned – and we are as near sure as can be that the Dutchman, whose name we have ascertained as Erik van Reiden – is that the name you know him by, by the way? – is most likely associated with jewellery thefts around the world. He is known to several police forces but, as yet, there is insufficient hard evidence for them to make an arrest. It seems that he and a mysterious French lady have been stalking our Spanish friends, whose names we have determined as Nicolás and Luciana de Lara, by the way...' Harvey paused to watch for any reaction from Michael but saw none, so he continued. 'So, all in all, Michael, Isobel and I are convinced that robbery is the connection between the Dutch couple and the Spaniards. We have unearthed absolutely no smell of any political connection such as you hinted at originally.'

Michael looked pleased as he thanked them for their work. 'The names you have unearthed are quite correct but, once more, I beseech you not to reveal them to anyone outside this room. I am so relieved by your conclusions.'

'So, what will you do now, Michael? I mean, bearing in mind that we can offer no legal proof of wrong-doing?'

'Well, I'm pleased that you have no such proof, otherwise we'd have to call in the police and suffer everything that goes with that. No, I shall call in the Dutch couple, make clear that their intentions are obvious and request – a suitable euphemism, don't you agree? – their immediate departure. After I'm satisfied that they are well away from here, I'll arrange for the return of Carlos and Valentina. Once again, I am so grateful for all your work together.

'May I urge you both now to relax and enjoy *The Hut* as it should be enjoyed.'

14

Mid-summer was upon *The Hut*, Harvey and Isobel, Gerald and Hillary, and Carlos and Valentina had all moved back to their lives outside, and, of course, the same was true for the four Dutch troublemakers. The Australians were still around, for they were clearly enjoying an extended holiday away from the heat of Western Australia, or wherever Barnes' centre of operations was. Curiously, neither Barnes nor Judi Normand ever imposed upon their audiences anything about their work – apart from their party-piece introduction, of course.

Meanwhile, a new group had arrived, a trio of clerics: clearly well-heeled clerics to be staying at *The Hut*. One was a black-haired, rather handsome man in his early-forties. He was obviously and certainly a cleric, for he wore a very dark charcoal-grey – almost black – suit over a black shirt with a white clerical collar. He spoke with a deep, pronounced, honied and lyrical Irish brogue with more than a hint of the six counties. Neither of his two friends – for that, they certainly were – wore clerical dress. They were clearly some ten years older than the priest. One was a tall man with sandy hair and had quite lovely long fingers which he entwined together from time to time as if unsure quite what to do with them. He seemed a little unsure of himself generally and gave the impression of being the guest of the third man, a short, somewhat portly, balding fellow who was manifestly both gay and self-confident. The latter's accent was English, rounded and home-counties, while that of his timorous friend was strongly Irish, soft and, one could gather after a little study, from the south. They were a talkative group, amongst themselves and with others at *The Hut*, also. That these last two were also clerics – of a sort, so far as the tubby chap was concerned, perhaps – quickly became evident when in conversation with the trio. For the most part, the three men seemed inseparable, as if – and it might well have been so – they had been saving up their time, and maybe money, to make this holiday together. Their point of contact with Michael, it seemed, was through the quiet fellow, but exactly how they had come to know each other was not clear to any casually-interested, fellow guest. Despite their disparate faiths, these three men of religion had one thing firmly in common. They all loved their drink. The short one, Martin David, favoured gin while the other two, Tim Allen – the timid-seeming fellow – and Chris Niles, the priest, preferred whiskey – with an 'e'. That is not to say that they didn't enjoy a nice glass or three of wine with their meals, merely that that is where they came home to roost. They could sink a lot, but one is grateful to report – and, no doubt, Michael would not have invited them had it been otherwise – that they belonged to that fellowship which the world might describe as 'good' drunks. They did not become loud or argumentative – which is not to say that they didn't enjoy some animated discussions from time to time – but simply fell asleep. And if they snored a little, it was but a quiet purr. Neither Martin nor Tim had any problem with having surnames which sounded like forenames; although, perhaps in order to confuse others, Martin always addressed Tim as Allen, which the world and his wife always heard as Alan, of course. Therefore, on this occasion, house rules for *The Hut* were broken, the three men of God going around as Chris, Allen and Martin, although other guests thought they were Chris, Alan and Martin.

Before these three came on the scene – but after the Australians – a Yorkshire couple had joined Michael's nest: Alan and Wendy Pensonby, a pair of lawyers from Bridlington, a small fishing town and local holiday destination on the Yorkshire coast. They invariably referred to their home in "Brid", and newcomers were left to work it out for themselves.

Alan was a bloke of average height and build, seemingly around fifty years old and sporting a bushy moustache under a fine but long, thin nose. He had a head of mousy-coloured, curly hair. His eyes curiously seemed incapable of deciding to be blue or green, but they were as clear as day about one thing: Alan was a sharp cookie. Not only sharp but, as an obvious twinkle made clear, a sharp cookie with a sense of humour. Mind you, being a lawyer and having a sense of humour is far from uncommon.

Wendy was probably of a similar age to her husband and, quite obviously, his intellectual match as suggested by the lively twitches her mouth was given to. She had gorgeous pepper-and-salt coloured hair, yet with more than a hint of red in it. It hung in waves from her head, asking to be caressed. She dressed very smartly but in "sensible" clothes, which in no way, however, detracted from her bubbly character.

For more than ten days, this pair had been dallying with the Aussie couple. They clearly found traits in each other to make their visit to *The Hut* enjoyable.

It was on their third day at *The Hut* when Martin and friends found the music room. More to the point, they found the piano. Martin and Tim both had experience as players of their church organs, as their conversation frequently attested. They would diapason this and tremulant that; the bourdon was hearty, and the chimney flute sent them into hysterics. Sadly, there was no organ in this music room, but the Bechstein piano would more than do, it seemed. Martin sat down at the keyboard of this wonderful instrument in its beautiful walnut case, opened the keyboard and launched into a mangled menage of songs from Rodgers' and Hammerstein's best-known musicals. Most of the notes seemed correct, if not exactly in place, but the rhythms were relentlessly intact from beginning to end.

'Been a long time since I played those,' Martin announced afterwards, 'but you never forget. It's the intervals, you know. It's all in the intervals.'

Before either of his friends – or even a straggle of other guests who had heard the strains of *Oh, what a beautiful mornin'* through the open door of the hallowed music room – could compose themselves, let alone form a question or even a comment, Martin recommenced playing; this time, a selection – from memory, of course – of those beautiful old favourites, like *I do like to be beside the seaside* and even *Any old iron, any old iron…*

He stopped playing eventually, probably because he came to the end of his repertoire but maybe just because he reached a certain level of breathless inebriation. He laughed heartily at himself, closed the lid of that abused but forgiving instrument and, with his more-than-a-little-amused compatriots, moved on to the lounge where soft seating and gin and tonic – or Jameson and Bushmills whiskey, as was their wont – awaited them.

Wendy and Alan joined them at that point. Alan noticed that Allen and Chris chose different whiskeys.

'Why do you guys drink different makes of Scotch?' Alan asked them.

Martin jumped in immediately: 'They don't, dear boy, they drink Irish.'

'What's the difference?' Alan persisted.

'Chalk and cheese, dear boy,' Martin replied, in what any Englishman would have called a very posh voice. 'They are made in different countries. An Irish blended whiskey is infinitely superior to a Scottish blended whisky and, furthermore, they're spelt differently; the Scots forget the e.'

'Well, thank you for that important item of education, Martin,' Alan replied. 'Please don't think me rude or anything, but I think I might check you out,' whereupon he ordered a snifter of each.

'Nothing like the A/B test,' he observed, took a sip of his Scotch and took his time savouring it as he manoeuvred it around his palette. He then did the same for the Irish.

The trio of priests held their collective breaths while awaiting his verdict.

'I think you might be right, Martin,' Alan announced, well aware of his audience, of course. 'But...'

There was a perceptible group intake of breath.

'...maybe I should sample a few different makes before coming to a firm conclusion. What do you think?'

'You may do that, of course,' intoned Martin, in his most mellifluous tones, 'and I dare say your experience will be enjoyable. Alternatively, you might simply put your trust in those before you.'

Wendy burst her bubble and actually snorted as her laughter welled up uncontrollably.

'That's you told, Alan,' she said.

But Alan wasn't finished yet. 'Okay,' he continued, totally indifferent to his chastisement. 'Why do you drink Bushmills Irish whiskey, Chris, while Allen seems to prefer Jameson's?'

Chris replied in an almost unconsciously guarded manner: 'I just prefer the flavour,' he said.

Martin had no embarrassment in explaining what was going on.

'You see, Alan, Chris champions the left-footed brigade, and Bushmills is made by a Catholic family. Allen, on the other hand, is a Protestant, and Jamesons is made by a Protestant family. And thus, the age-old religious demarcation of the six counties is maintained.'

'You can't be serious,' Alan replied, genuinely stunned. 'This is the twenty-first century, for goodness' sake!'

'Ah, well, at least the three of us have learned to live in peace with it all,' Martin replied. 'And just to add to your confusion, Alan, Chris is a Roman Catholic priest, born in Belfast in the north – that is, in the Six Counties – while Allen is a Protestant curate, born in Dublin in southern Ireland – that is, in Eire. I trust that all is now as clear as my glass of gin?'

'And what about you, Martin?' Alan asked. 'I'd guess you're English, born in the Home Counties?'

'Ah, dear boy,' Martin replied, pushing his treacled tones to the max. 'Amongst other things, I'm a Protestant lay preacher in the Midlands but born and bred near Belfast in Northern Ireland.'

'Jesus!' exclaimed Alan. 'How do you account for your accent, Martin?'

'Ah, Jaysus indeed,' Martin replied, laying on a Northern Irish accent nice and thick for his Yorkshire audience. 'You must never assume too much from the way a fellow speaks. Ain't that so, lad?' This last, he pronounced in a fair imitation of a Yorkshire accent, albeit not one from around Bridlington.

Barnes and Judi had joined the group somewhere in the middle of these exchanges. They struggled to keep up with the nuances of this niche conversation, but Barnes was game to try.

'Ee by gum, lass,' he said to Judi, in a passably acceptable imitation of some kind of Northern English accent. 'The Poms do go on about how best to speak to one another, don't they.'

Alan replied with a warning, 'I think you're likely out of your depth here, Barnes. This is probably something best left to those with an ear for this kind of thing.'

'You're probably right, Alan. They all sound pretty much the same to me.'

Martin looked at Barnes with a mixture of incredulity and pity. Perhaps he had wasted all those years of perfecting his mellifluous tones, you might think. One might think so, but not Martin. His self-confidence was impregnable.

The evening wore on for quite some time yet and, in due course, the Yorkshire couple and the antipodeans drifted away, Alan and Wendy to bed, and Judi and Barnes to get a breath of air from the cool evening outside. As these two re-entered the building to go to bed in their turn, they passed the three Irishmen sprawled out over their low, comfortable lounge chairs. All three were asleep with their heads lolling to one side or the other. Martin's mouth hung open and he emitted a quiet purr.

'Oh, look!' Barnes said quietly to his wife, Judi. 'A piss-up of priests!'

She couldn't repress a giggle. 'There's an alliterative collective!'

'Shhh!' Barnes said, his finger raised in the air.

15

The Aussies and the Yorkshire couple were enjoying their breakfasts quite early the following morning. They were all pretty frisky and raring to go, as they had agreed two days earlier on a short golfing holiday. They had learned that *The Hut* owned a well-regarded golfing hotel not far away and, being nuts about the game, all four enthused about their upcoming few days away from the hall.

They were on the point of quitting the breakfast room as the three Irishmen appeared. Chris was as neat as ever, hair brushed neatly back, walking with almost a spring in his step. Tim walked a little slowly and cautiously, but fully upright. His complexion seemed a touch pallid this morning, Wendy noted. Bringing up the rear and looking, it simply had to be said, as if he had slept in yesterday's clothes – and maybe he had – came Martin, whose complexion was anything but pallid. His rosy face (not cheeks) clearly shouted for milk or water, but above all, for coffee. His eye colour neatly matched that of his face.

'Morning!' greeted Alan.

Some might have interpreted the grunt from the priests as "Good morning" also, but only with Christian charity.

'We're off for a few day's golfing,' Barnes informed the trio.

'Enjoy!' Martin managed to say as he flopped down on a chair, and, after the others had departed, added, 'Bloody silly pastime, golf.'

Meanwhile, the four golfers were gathering together their golf bags and all other things golf, ready for the off. Alan had elected to drive the four in his Merc. They hadn't far to go: a little over an hour and they were there, checking into the hotel. Their rooms weren't yet available, but the hotel staff were used to this sort of situation and put their travel bags and golfing gear in a holding room, while the new guests familiarised themselves with the hotel lounge and coffee bar. They enjoyed another coffee and gazed out at the panoramic view offered by the extensive windows in the room which gave out onto the eighteenth. However, they were able to see far beyond that.

None of the four had been to this place before. It had quite a high reputation in golfing circles, the course having been designed by a British champion in the forties. Whatever the merits of the holes themselves, the whole layout of the course and hotel were surrounded by gently rolling hills, some of which were very well-wooded. There was a sense of being enclosed, of being cradled within the landscape.

The more Wendy looked at it, the more she came to appreciate how clever was the siting of this wonderful facility.

There were a few other patrons in the coffee lounge but, to nobody's surprise, most seemed to be distributed around the course itself. The four escapees from *The Hut* decided to play as a foursome straight after an early lunch. Barnes took himself off for an exploratory stroll, while Judi picked up a magazine and settled into one of the many reclining armchairs littered around the place. The weather was set fair for the next day and a half, so there was a relaxed anticipation of the rounds to come. The general ambiance of the hotel was pleasant and expensive but lacked the subtlety of *The Hut*, as was only to be expected.

When lunch came around, the same qualitative differences between the two places was evident. The hotel food was excellent rather than inspired. On the other hand, *a la carte* was provided here, and patrons dined at separate tables. Nevertheless, it was all completely acceptable.

The afternoon game began with the Yorkshire couple teeing off first – or, at least, Wendy did – and the four came to grips with the peculiarities of the course. Her handicap was an excellent nine, Alan's sixteen was more than respectable, as was Judi's at eighteen. Barnes was the champion at four. Their pairings could be expected to produce a well-balanced game all round, they thought. Of course, it didn't quite go like that. The women had an excellent game, but the men badly fluffed a couple of holes and ended up some four shots each behind their spouses. All in all, though, everyone expressed pleasure in their first game together and were more than happy to make their way into the bar after depositing their bags in the lock-up. The sun had been quite strong, but they had barely noticed it because of a light breeze all afternoon.

'The sun was pretty warm out there,' Wendy remarked, as they settled down at the bar.

'Have you ever been to Australia, Wendy?' Barnes asked. 'We get temperatures like those in the middle of the night.'

'I'm not sure I would like that,' Wendy replied. 'Surely it isn't that hot all over Australia?'

'No, it's not,' Judi interrupted. 'Barnes is just doing his macho bit. Pay no attention. Any minute now, he'll tell you about clearing the greens of brown snakes with his putter before finishing the hole.'

'And aren't there dangerous spiders in the holes?' Wendy continued.

After a while, Judi realised that she was being taken for a ride. 'Okay, okay. How often have you been out to Oz?' she asked.

'Two or three times, but the last was for several months and we made sure to move around, so we've seen quite a bit. We loved it,' she grinned. 'We also learned to drink Aussie beer.'

'I still prefer a proper pint of wallop,' Alan interrupted.

'Don't know how you can drink that warm piss,' Barnes said.

'Character-forming,' was Alan's reply.

'So tell me, mate, what do you think of the course? How did you enjoy you's arvo?' Barnes was testing the Pom's grasp of his own language.

'Oh yeah,' Alan replied. 'She was beaut, mite. Let's crack a tube or two before tucker.'

'A mite old-fashioned, old boy,' replied Barnes, in a fair imitation of the upper crust. 'What say we call it a draw, old bean?'

'I think that's a bloody good idea,' Judi laughed. 'Give it a rest, boys.'

It was while our friends were on their third bevvy that Barnes' face suddenly froze. Judi noticed immediately.

'Whatever's the matter, love?' she asked, her face full of concern.

'I'll tell you later,' Barnes replied, making an effort to return to his former gaiety. He seemed to succeed, for it was only when they got round to dessert that his mask dropped and he told everyone what the problem had been.

'I saw a bloke, back of the bar in there, who I knew; well, who I know. An Australian, originally from Perth, name of Paul Hutchinson. I don't want to know him. I don't want to meet him again. And why is he here, miles from anywhere, and certainly miles from any of the places you would normally associate with that bastard?'

'What's the problem, love? Is he a threat or something? A thief? What?' Judi was obviously very concerned.

'Alan and Wendy don't want to hear my problems, Judi, especially when we're all enjoying a golfing break. I'm sorry to have put a spanner in the works. Let's just get on with our holiday,' Barnes said, and seemed to make a great effort to put his concerns behind him.

Later that night, Alan and Wendy were changing for bed.

'Did you notice how Barnes' Aussie accent almost disappeared when he was telling – or rather, not telling – us about that bloke?' Wendy remarked.

'You mean he's not actually Australian?' Alan asked.

'No, I didn't mean that. I'm sure he is, but what he is not, is ill-educated,' she replied. 'He likes to put on a blokey face, I think. Probably to disarm any strangers he meets.'

'Like us.'

'Like us, but God knows why. We're no threat to the guy.'

'And he knows that, I'm sure. I imagine that, like far more people than are prepared to admit it, he is still, to some extent, shy.'

'Doesn't explain how rattled he was about that bloke from Perth, though.'

'No. That's something different, certainly.'

'None of our business, Wendy.'

'No, but you can't help wondering.'

*

They had arranged to fight another round after breakfast. The morning was sunny and the views lovely, but the air had a nip in it. They dressed accordingly. Barnes seemed to have forgotten his problems of the day before. Certainly, he was thrashing everyone else.

'My God, you're on song this morning,' Alan commented, as they were teeing off on the seventeenth.

'Good night's sleep,' Barnes replied, full of concentration as he made a two-hundred-and-twenty-yard drive.

'I must try that,' Alan replied, blinking at Barnes' performance.

Later, in the bar, while sipping some beers, Judi observed that the weather outside was turning a bit sour.

'The forecast for this afternoon is for steady rain after about half past two,' she said. 'I don't think we have any hope of another round today.'

'Pity,' observed Alan. 'Barnes needs some practice.'

Wendy giggled. Judi smiled. Barnes either didn't get it or, more likely, judging by his distant gaze, hadn't heard it.

'What do we do in this place when golf is off the menu?' Judi asked to no one in particular.

'I'll read the papers, I think,' Alan replied, as they made their way into the dining room, 'and maybe I'll over-indulge a little at lunch.'

The rain came on cue. There were a few minutes of tiny showers before a sudden downpour began. The sky was leaden, and they knew they were in for it. After the curtain call, the rain settled in for a steady, strong soaking. If it were to continue like that for the rest of the afternoon, it would almost certainly follow that the next morning's golf would be a literal washout.

Like other hotel guests gathered in the bar and lounge, the four from *The Hut* watched and wondered. Alan's head was buried in his newspaper, Judi was reading a book and Wendy was checking emails or something on her smartphone. Barnes' head was well back in his seat and his eyes were closed. Actually, half-closed might be a better description, for Wendy observed them to be wide open from time to time when she looked up from her phone. Suddenly Barnes stiffened, and his eyes narrowed to slits as he obviously pretended to be asleep.

'What's the matter, darling?' asked Judi in alarm.

'Shhh!' Barnes said and kept quite still. 'Please, everyone; just keep doing whatever you were doing and ignore me.'

Barnes' gaze (can it still be called a gaze when it is performed through nearly shut eyes?) was fixed upon something or someone in the far corner of the lounge.

'Bloody hell!' he breathed after some minutes, but did not elaborate. His feigned sleep continued for some further five minutes or so, before he sat up with fully open eyes and said, 'I need to think. I'm going up to our room. It's likely that Judi and I will leave this place this evening.'

'Can we help?' Alan asked with great concern. 'Do you want to talk about it?'

Barnes looked at the three puzzled, sympathetic and concerned faces around him and paused a moment as he made a decision.

'Come and join us upstairs,' he said. 'Order some drinks, Judi. I, for one, will certainly need more than one.'

Fortunately their hotel was fancy enough for there to be four comfortable chairs around a coffee table in the Australians' room. Once they had settled and poured themselves some drinks, Barnes began his tale.

'Look, I'm sorry to have spoiled our holiday, people. I have been taken completely by surprise. Yesterday, I caught a glimpse of Paul Hutchinson, as I told you all at the time. I must explain who he is, but first you'll need some background. My father is the founder of our mining company. He discovered significant deposits of rare earths in South Australia some twenty-five years ago. Of course, by far the largest deposits of rare earths in Oz are in Western Australia, but Dad's find was large enough to be well worth extracting. I'm the boss of Normand Mining, now that Dad is semi-retired. However, before he did settle into a part-time role, Dad had worked closely with Paul Hutchinson, treating him almost like another son, as he built the business. I don't know if you guys will know this – it depends on how much chemistry you've done...'

Alan shook his head. Wendy pulled a face.

'Doesn't matter. The thing about the rare earths is that there are fourteen of them, but each has subtly different physical properties that they feature in the electronics world in many different ways, depending upon which rare earth you are dealing with. From our point of view – because, believe me, you are not the only guys to struggle with all this – all we know is that some are used in television sets, some in computers, some in a myriad of other electronic devices, but, these days, the greatest demand is for neodymium in electric vehicles. The point of all this for us, as miners, is that, *chemically*, the rare earths are very similar to one another, which makes them difficult to separate. You can't just stir a mixture of rare earths with some acid or base or other reagent and expect them all to do different things, so that you can separate them out just by filtration or evaporation, or something easy like that. That's why rare earths all occur naturally together: even nature has difficulty in telling them apart. Trouble is, their *physical* properties are sufficiently different, in that one is good for computers, another for magnets, a third for some clever electronic device. So, the market wants them separated.

'Of course, the simplest thing was for Dad's company just to dig up – it's not that easy, but there's no need for me to elaborate, I hope?'

There came an eager round of head-shaking.

Barnes continued, '…dig it up and flog it. We got a fair price and made money. But if we could separate the different metals rather than leave that step to the Americans, for example, then we could sell pure samples of the particular rare earth that a manufacturer of permanent magnets for electric vehicles, for example, would require. Then we could charge very much more for our product. Obviously, a win. Actually, a very big win. That is where Paul Hutchinson comes into the story. Hutchinson and Dad developed a process that allowed us to separate some of the rare earths more cleanly and more quickly – which translates into more cheaply, of course – than those processes elsewhere that were known to us. I have to put that caveat in, because, in this game, there's a great deal of secrecy; although patents are safer in the long run than trying to keep secrets. Anyway, they found a way to do what we wanted, and it was decided to apply for a patent – actually, several patents – to protect our intellectual property. It turned out that Dad was too trusting, because Hutchinson had the patent worded in such a way that he, and he alone, became the owner. I know it all sounds very sloppy, but Dad trusted Hutchinson as a son. I told you that already, didn't I? He had given every encouragement to Paul from the beginning and then he was rewarded by this piece of absolute treachery – bastardry. When we found out what had happened, Hutchinson tried to bluff his way round it but refused absolutely to pass over the ownership to Dad – or even to share it, which might have been equitable, actually. There was a God-almighty row, and Dad threw him out of the company. I think "Let him go" was the phrase used at the time.'

'How long ago was this?' asked Alan, who was paying rather more attention than Barnes had expected.

'About eight months ago,' Barnes said. 'Anyway, here are Judi and I, taking a bit of a break from our troubles – not that she knew about all this, mind you –trying to come to terms with the whole mess and to see if we can dream up some way to recover at least some of our property, when, as you saw, Hutchinson appears from the other side of the world in the same, very unlikely, venue. One hell of a coincidence, I reckon. But why would he be seeking me out? He could have done that at any time back in Adelaide, had he wanted.'

'But something else happened today, Barnes?' Alan suggested.

'Exactly. What I saw just now explains everything, and I don't like it one little bit. Hutchinson met a guy whose face is familiar to me. I've forgotten his name for the moment, although I'm sure I know it, but I know his business. He's from the American company which does most of the world's separation of rare earths. The bastard is selling out! It's obvious. He'll get a lump sum, plus a percentage, and he can then swan off to any playpen in the world. All at Normand Mining's expense!'

'But why here?' asked Judi.

Wendy put her oar in. 'That's obvious,' she said. 'They wanted to meet in neutral territory miles away from home. Who would think to look for them, or overhear them, in a golfing hotel in a quiet backwater of the English midlands?'

'Yes,' Alan said. 'I agree.'

' All right, Barnes,' Judi asked – she didn't use his name that often – 'What can you do about it? Apart from fume? Or murder?'

There was silence for some time while everyone sipped their drinks. They had hardly touched them earlier, rapt as they had been by Barnes' tale.

'What kinds of patents were they, Barnes?' asked Alan quietly. 'Provisional, design, innovation, standard…'

'No idea, Alan. I'm afraid I know nothing at all about the subject. That sort of thing has always left me cold.'

'I understand that completely, Barnes, for, let's face it, that attitude – and I'm not blaming you, my friend – is what makes lawyers rich. The machinations of religious philosophers in the middle ages had nothing on what you will find in any good set of law books.'

Barnes harrumphed his agreement, paused as enlightenment dawned, and asked very slowly, 'What kind of lawyer are you, Alan? You didn't say.'

'No, you're right, I didn't. I specialise in patent law. And while we're on this topic, Wendy's forte is in international law. Maybe, between us, we can help you, Barnes.'

'My God, if you could, that would be wonderful. I'd be forever grateful. Just name your price.'

'No, my friend. Anything we can do for you – and I promise nothing at this stage – will be *pro bono*.'

He looked at Wendy who nodded quietly. It was not missed by either Barnes or Judi.

'My god. What a piece of luck,' Barnes said. 'I really am lost for words.'

'As I said, Barnes, we cannot know if we can help without first studying your papers and much else, so please don't get your hopes up too high right now.'

'Had I known this earlier this morning, I would have let you win the golf!' Barnes said, grinning.

There followed some lengthy and lubricated conversation about how and where to get started on all this before Wendy suggested, 'The weather forecast for tomorrow, at least, is not good. Why don't we call it quits on our little holiday and go back to *The Hut* where we'll be better able to relax while we work; where we'll be able to swing a cat, in other words.'

'And we'll be away from Hutchinson and Mr. X at the same time,' observed Judi. 'Look, if we get a wriggle on, we can be back in time for dinner!'

It was agreed, and not too long later, the four slipped very quietly away in Alan's Mercedes. The comforts of *The Hut* yet again seduced its visitors.

16

The three amigos had arranged to hire a sleep-on launch, which *The Hut* was able to offer from time to time, and to take an adventure trip upriver, in which they planned to include a visit to a special village church not too far distant. The launch, which was a very fancy affair, was moored to the village wharf. It was to be crewed by Ken Gaston from the *Tomber Pot*, and his wife, Jill. One of the cars owned by *The Hut* organisation conveyed the Irishmen there mid-morning after they had enjoyed a leisurely breakfast. They had each packed just one bag, as requested by *The Hut* management.

Once aboard, introductions made, and having shown their guests their cabins, Jill cast off, jumping back on board as Ken took the helm. The launch, if that was a fair name for this rather snazzy motor vessel, was rather like some of those desirable yachts one sees around the Greek Islands – smaller, certainly, but no less chic inside. Vessels were speed-limited on the river, of course, so there was no question of zipping off and leaving a foot-high wake. In any case, there was absolutely no hurry. This was to be a leisurely holiday, and everyone aboard knew it. It was a nice day, sunny with a light breeze, so our heroes sat on a well-cushioned bench seat forward. Unlike the canals, the river was a natural waterway, of course, meandering this way and that, wider here, narrower there. The land through which they passed for the first couple of hours was rather flat and, the Irishmen complained, "Nothing like the Mountains of Mourne", which was a rather silly remark, seeing that they were in the west midlands of England.

Their complaint was heard by Jill who was preparing their midday meal. She rushed out – after a busy moment or two – with three gin and tonics. Word had got about. The Irishmen, astonished and delighted, graciously accepted the offering without demur. As if it had heard the earlier complaint, the scenery gradually changed, and the trees on the riverbanks began to look taller, grander and more graceful.

Ken knew of a good mooring a little further on. He reduced power and gently slid the boat into place alongside a small pontoon at the side of the river. He had obviously done this before.

'Gentlemen,' he said, 'please make your way back into the rear cabin where lunch will be served.'

Martin and friends found that the forecabin was fitted out as a lounge. Barely separated from it was a dining area with seating for eight. Everything was light, airy and supremely comfortable.

A short staircase led down to the galley from which food preparation noises emanated. Jill appeared, carrying two large trays from which she distributed platters of cold cuts, salmon and some delightful salads. She retreated but reappeared moments later with a plate of cheeses and a basket of several breads. Ken opened a miniature fridge adjacent to the staircase and brought forth a *Sancerre*. From a cupboard on the other side of the stairs, he removed a *Pinot Noir* from New Zealand.

'I hope it's all right for Jill and me to join you for lunch,' he said. 'The management feels guests feel more comfortable this way. We hope you agree.'

'By "the management", I presume you mean Michael,' Martin remarked. 'In any case, he's quite right. We're all communists here! It's a pleasure to meet you both. And we do appreciate your choice of lubrication.'

'We thought you would. Have you tried the *Tomber Pot* yet?' asked Ken.

'What's the *Tomber Pot*?' asked Martin.

'Ah, it's the village pub. Jill and I hold the licence. We serve a mean jug of ale, if you don't mind me saying so.'

'Who's running the place while you're here with us?'

'We employ a locum – a temp. – who we trust completely.'

The lunch was good. The guests appreciated everything, and Jill was pleased. Ken suggested that the three Irishmen might retire to the lounge or the deck, or even take a walk, while he and Jill cleared everything away.

Allen opted for a short walk. Chris joined him. Martin thought he might take to the lounge and have a quiet think. His eyes closed the moment his bum hit the seat.

Allen had known Chris for some ten years by now. He had been introduced to him by Martin. Come to think of it, Martin was a bit of a fixer. Martin had known Chris when he was a lad – ten or so years Martin's junior – for he walked the same streets. While Martin pursued a career in education – his wealth did not, of course, come from that activity, but by inheritance from his father – he had always had a keen interest in the Church of England. To say he walked the same streets as the young Christopher is hardly accurate, of course, for the segregational practices of those days meant that pavement curbs painted with the tricolour defined a different space to those painted with William's orange. But nothing is set in stone, and these two men became firm friends despite all that incredible idiocy. Martin seemed to know everyone and was ever eager to make new friends.

On the other hand, Allen was the member of this trio who had known Michael. They had been at University in Bristol together and had come together through a common interest in music. Tim was studying philosophy and religion, while Michael had always had a wide appreciation of music and went to as many concerts in Bristol as he could at that time. He never lost his love for jazz but saw no reason not to enjoy classical music at the same time. Allen was a more than competent pianist, though not to concert standard. He had obtained a good second-class degree at Bristol but then took up his first calling which was the church; in his case, as an Anglican in the Church in Ireland. Martin and Allen also became acquainted through music, as we shall learn in due course. It has been noted already that Allen gave the impression of being Laurel, in the Laurel and Hardy pairing with Martin. He seemed timorous and retiring. To some extent, such was the case with many of Martin's friends, which speaks, however, to Martin's boisterous nature rather than to his friends' shyness. Allen was a well-educated man and could hold his own in discussions and arguments. When he didn't, it was down to his preference for a little peace and quiet.

As he and Chris took their stroll that afternoon, they reminisced about old times and compared their respective training for the priesthood. Each admired the other's qualities which were, however, somewhat different. Allen was easily Chris' superior intellectually, although Chris was given to initiate philosophical discussions at the drop of a hat, but Chris had moved higher up the priestly ladder than had Allen. Allen was, quite simply, far less pushy. Chris was a practical man, while Allen was a bit of a dreamer and idealist. However, with Martin, they both loved their tipple and all three had a hearty sense of humour. Their unlikely liaison was, however, good and firm.

Anyway, after chewing the fat for half an hour or so, Chris and Allen turned back to the boat for whatever Ken had in mind for them for the remainder of the afternoon.

As they climbed on board, Martin was waking up. He smiled and asked them if they had enjoyed a good chinwag, for he knew that would have been their pastime. Ken joined them in the lounge to announce that they would cast off and make their way further up-river to find a mooring for the launch where they would stay for the night.

Their journey began to get more interesting now, in that the scenery became rather more lush: taller trees in larger copses and woods on ever more rolling countryside.

By six o'clock they reached Ken's desired mooring, and Jill joined her guests to enquire what they would care to drink before dinner. Should she open a bottle of bubbly, or would they prefer to stick with their G&Ts?

'Let's have some bubbles,' Martin suggested, 'and celebrate our boating holiday in proper style.'

A bottle of Moët was brought forth. Martin observed that it wasn't "your average Moët" but clearly upmarket and actually worthy of the name Champagne. He tried to persuade both Ken and Jill to partake, but they declined.

'We'll join you in a drink after dinner perhaps,' Ken replied, 'but right now, we have to prepare a dinner we'll all enjoy – but especially you, our guests.'

While the three clerics settled into the comfortable lounge chairs in the saloon, their hosts busied themselves in the dining area, in the galley and, to the confusion of their guests, on the wharf to which their boat was tethered. Breaking into their conversation, Martin suddenly realised what was going on outside.

'I do believe we're going to have a barbeque,' he interrupted. 'Why not? It's summer and a lovely, warm evening.'

'We thought it best to incinerate your steaks outside rather than to fill the boat with fumes,' joked Ken. 'How do you like your steaks in general? Rare or very rare?'

'Well done,' replied Martin.

'Not on this barbeque, I'm afraid, sir,' Ken replied, smiling broadly. 'It's not equipped for "ruined".'

Allen enjoyed the exchange enormously and, after Ken had gone to further his endeavours, remarked, 'Not often someone gets one over Martin, eh, Chris?'

Shortly afterwards, indeed as their champagne ran out, they were summoned to the dining saloon. Jill brought up five plates from the galley, while Ken extracted a bottle of clear liquid from beside the staircase.

'Oh, marvellous!' Allen said. 'I do so like gravlax.'

'With schnapps, too,' Chris added. 'I think this promises to be a good evening.'

When they had consumed their fish, Ken explained that there would be a small delay while Jill and he engaged in a ritual panic dance between wharf and galley. Their guests were welcome to applaud or jeer, as they preferred, as a way of filling in the time 'twixt courses.

'This guy's a comedian,' observed Martin.

Indeed, there was a lot of coming and going, but one had no special need to be particularly sharp to realise that their dance was a piece of ballet. They understood each other's moves, and the whole thing came together as a work of art. Once more it fell to Jill to bring five plates to table, while Ken, having forsaken his manly barbeque, transformed into a wine-waiter. There appeared before each of the diners a cylinder of perfectly cooked fillet steak, about five centimetres in diameter and the same in thickness. The top surface of each steak was scorched to perfection, crusty and with deep cracks extending into the interior. Another cylinder on each plate was a timbale of *Gratin Dauphinois* of similar dimensions to the meat. A third such cylinder was in the form of a parcel of lettuce leaf wrapped around something or other.

'This is no barbeque!' Martin said. 'This is a feast!'

'We hope so, gentlemen,' Ken beamed, 'and I think this might help it all go down.'

He brought out a bottle of an excellent *Chateauneuf du Pape*, which he had obviously tended earlier.

As Martin placed his knife onto his fillet, he found that he needed to apply only the gentlest of pressure to pierce the meat. The crusty, caramelised surface gave way to such tender red beef that he could make no complaint about its rareness.

'Yours is rare, Martin; the others are *bleu*. I hope you approve.' Ken smiled, knowing that he had done the right thing.

Martin cut into the lettuce parcel with the curiosity of a little boy opening his Christmas presents. Out fell a small, tender onion and tiny garden peas with the occasional little baton of bacon.

'Clever!' said Chris.

'Subtle!' said Allen. 'Indeed, the whole dish is not only delicious, but a work of culinary art.'

'Not a barbeque!' Martin repeated, still overcome with the tenderness of his steak.

The meal was rounded off with a cold almond soufflé. There was no alcohol served with it. Ken explained, without any hint of an apology, that he thought it best for his guests to savour the delicacy of the soufflé unimpeded, as it were, by any more booze – he clearly enjoyed mixing up the delicacy of his language – especially as he anticipated his guests relaxing into further misdeeds after dinner. His remarks were met with applause from the three clergymen who were nothing if not self-aware.

As the three moved off into the lounge area of the top deck, where their first drink was to be coffee – so they were informed by Jill with a twinkle in her eye – Martin was still mumbling, 'Not a barbeque at all.' Ken and his wife then left the three happy Irishmen alone, while they cleared up and made everything shipshape as their guests settled down for the evening.

Some while later, Ken appeared with a tray upon which were bottles of Tanqueray gin, Bushmills and Jameson whiskey, bottles of tonic and an appropriate selection of glasses.

'Gentlemen, we shall now leave you to your own devices – you know your way to your beds, of course – and will see you in the morning. Probably more clearly than you will see us,' he added with a grin.

'Cheeky bugger, but I like his grin,' Martin commented as Ken departed.

The evening progressed, and conversation came and went as these old friends fell in and out of sleep, comfortable in each other's company. Martin, however, had an issue he wanted to push. Allen had obviously heard Martin on the subject before, so he left it to him. It was all a bit silly, really, but Martin was trying to extract some fancy clerical attire – and, for the layman, dress is probably the exact word – from Chris. Martin, you will recall, was a lay preacher in his village in the Midlands. He managed to get his chance to conduct services when the proper vicar was away for some reason. Occasionally, Martin was in a position to enact some special service or other, with the local choir in procession. Martin loved the theatre of it all, and, truth to tell, he was a show-off. Chris, the Roman Catholic priest in Northern Ireland, lived in a comfortable bungalow, courtesy of his church, close by a small but homely chapel wherein he preached every day to his faithful parishioners. Every day. Religious sentiment was strong in those parts, and Chris would hold forth to some two hundred people every day.

'I let them off lightly on weekdays in the early mornings,' he would explain. 'They have to go to work afterwards. They have to earn their bread and look after their families, so ten minutes is all I take.'

Chris was greatly loved by these churchgoers. He never let them down. He always fronted up at their weddings and other celebrations, and he always appeared in their houses in times of strife or sorrow, because of illness or death, for example. He was a great comforter – a most human man.

'At the weekends, however, I give 'em hell and keep them there for a good hour and a half!'

Poor old Martin, on the other hand, was lucky if he got six parishioners in church at the same time. Such, of course, is the lot of most vicars in the Church of England. It wasn't Martin's fault. If anything, he might have seen one or two more at his "special" services, if only because of the hours of cajoling in which he indulged, advertising in person, during the week or weeks beforehand.

Anyway, his project that evening on the boat, after that splendid meal, was to persuade Chris to lend or give him one or two of his (to the protestant mind, ostentatious) lacy surplices, that he might, thereby, appear ever more resplendent to his congregation. All six of them.

Martin had been rabbiting on in his mellifluous tones about these damn vestments for half an hour or more before Chris exclaimed, in his very broad Northern Ireland accent, 'You can have lace up to your nipples, but it won't get the bums on the seats!'

It is appropriate at this point to help any reader not familiar with the sonics, shall we say, of the Northern Ireland speech. First, one must mention a feature common to all Irish accents, namely the diphthong. An Englishman once described Ireland as "The Land of the Wandering Diphthong", without appreciating the superfluity of his remark, for a diphthong describes how, in a word with adjacent vowels, the sound may begin as one of them but finish as the other – the sound wanders about, if you like. Many, maybe most, languages have diphthongs: even English, which often comes as a surprise to Englishmen who believe in the simplicity and honesty of their mother tongue. For example, the sound of "Oh" or "over", for example: words which don't actually contain two adjacent vowels (yet another way of confusing foreigners) can be pronounced in a multitude of ways, all of which use the structure of the diphthong. Contrast to the way a German might pronounce those words, using a dead-flat tone, one might say, through rounded and pursed lips for the "o".

Well, enough of all this formality. Suffice to say that Chris' vowels were all over the shop. When he said "lace", it came out a bit like "layiece", and his "seats" as "sayiets". And while we're at it, although diphthongs have nothing to do with it, his "nipples" sounded like "nuppuls", with a firm emphasis on the "pp". Altogether, therefore, "You can have layiece up to your nuppuls, but it won't get the bums on the sayiets!"

The reader may well wonder why so much is being made of Chris' accent. After all, we all have funny ways of talking, to someone else's ears. Of course, we don't hear our own speech as out of the ordinary, in any way. That was as true for Chris himself as for any of us.

Later on in the evening, the subject got around to the Australian couple the three had met at *The Hut* in the days before their boat trip. Allen was saying how he liked Alan and Wendy, and Martin was remarking on the confusion between Alan's forename and Allen's surname.

'I think I'd quite like to visit Australia one day,' Allen remarked.

'I wouldn't,' Chris replied, rather more firmly than one might expect in a casual conversation.

'Why not?' asked Allen. 'They seem fun people to me.'

'I can't stand the accent!' Chris replied with force.

Tim's mouth hung open. Martin exploded in laughter. Chris was utterly nonplussed.

'Time for bed,' Martin announced, and everyone disappeared into the bowels of the boat.

17

They made a moderately early start in the morning. At least, Ken and Jill did. The clerics were slow in recovery. Anyway, this was the day for their planned exploration of the Church of St. John the Baptist in Healdsmill, a village which lay close to the river some miles further on, which was why Ken had cast off at seven o'clock. The plan was for his three guests to find a spot of lunch in Healdsmill before their pilgrimage to St John's. That pilgrimage stemmed from a piece of research which Allen had done before their grand holiday at *The Hut*. He had discovered that the Church of St. John the Baptist in Healdsmill possessed a very fine organ. To someone unacquainted with this subject, it might well come as a surprise to learn that some of Britain's finest organs are to be found in out-of-the-way parish churches. Of course, the very best are in the various cathedrals around the country, but the second-rank – but still very good – instruments, shall we say, are spread far and wide.

Anyway, Allen had discovered this one at Healdsmill. It had a thirty-two-foot diapason. Even if you are not an afficionado of organ architecture – and that is very likely, for sure – you will appreciate the grandeur of a group of pipes (several, of course, because there has to be one pipe for each note) with a fundamental which is thirty-two feet long. There are sixty-four-foot pipes in existence, but they belong to the very few, very grand organs which are to be found in great cathedrals or concert halls distributed round the privileged world.

The organ at Healdsmill was quite famous amongst the cognoscenti, and both Allen and Martin wanted to see and to hear it. They were unlikely to hear it, however, unless it was being played while they were there, but at least they could hope to see it. Chris was happy enough to go along for the ride but made no bones about his overall disinterest in the topic.

They arrived at Healdsmill wharf – well, it called itself a wharf, but, in truth, it was no more than a pontoon – around half past eleven. Ken was pleased with their progress. His guests said their farewells, leaving Ken and Jill with a few hours respite, and followed a path marked as leading directly to the village centre.

Before going very far, the path led them around a handsome-looking mill, a substantial brick building with a timbered upper story and a large waterwheel at one side. A narrow canal leading from the river in a loop provided the waterpower for the millwheel. There was no indication outside the mill as to whether waterpower was still in use for anything, but there was a sign indicating that the building was now a museum.

The three friends walked on, passed through a kissing gate and arrived at a short road adorned with leafy chestnuts giving way at each end to long streets running parallel to each other and at right angles to the short road they had first entered. To the right lay the church they were to visit. However, they had taken the left of the two roads without initially realising the overall geometry of the village layout.

'Let's look for a pub,' Martin suggested. 'We should be able to find a spot of lunch there, I would guess.'

It wasn't long before *The Lion* came into view. As Martin, who was leading the trio into the premises, got two feet past the door, he reversed, pushing his friends back outside. In his fruity, rounded home-counties tones and with his face contorted in disgust, he pronounced:

'Oh! I don't think so. It smells of stale sweat, and the benches are upholstered in torn plastic. Let's look elsewhere.'

Three youths in studded bomber jackets pushed past the three Irishmen on their way into the pub.

'And there's another reason for you,' Martin said, with a look of absolute disgust on his face which was not entirely missed by the largest of the youths.

He gave Martin the finger but carried on into the pub.

Years of experience gave the other clerics total confidence in Martin's assessment of the interior, but they hardly needed that on seeing the local clientele. They continued their quest. The street was quite long and, finding no other watering hole, our heroes were beginning to feel anxious. The road petered out but not before offering another short street to the right, in the middle of which they found, illuminated by a garish sign, *The Hollies*. Martin looked at the others with a sinking feeling as he pushed open the door. There were two doors to negotiate before he gained full entry, which was just as well, all decided, as the volume of God-awful musak assailed their ears. Martin reported back that, noise aside, there was no food on offer and the place was as dark as the grave. They walked on.

'We should have brought a picnic,' Allen opined.

'Fine time to think of that,' Chris replied.

At the end of that short street, they had to turn right once more and, in this way, came to understand the overall geometry of the village. They walked on yet again, getting glummer by the minute. By the time they were within hailing distance of the end of this street, they spied a third pub, *The Oak*, which had an old-fashioned sign outside and looked, for all the world, like what the three travellers called a real pub. Marin hastened inside and was gone a few moments before returning, his face wreathed in smiles.

'Bingo!' he told the others. 'Bright, clean, nice, delicate smell of fresh beer and a good-looking menu. This is the place for us.'

Indeed, it was. Martin ordered three pints of their best bitter and took menus to a table which Allen had selected under a window with a window box outside, filled with carnations or something – he was unable to be sure what flowers they were, through the frosted glass. Allen chose scampi and a green salad; Chris, crumbed fish and chips, and Martin went for a steak pie.

'That's a funny choice,' observed Chris, after they had given their order. 'After that wonderful steak last night, your steak pie will seem rather downmarket, don't you think?'

'Yesterday was yesterday. Today is all new and fresh,' Martin observed.

They spent a happy hour in there. Only one other table was occupied, this by a smart-looking couple in their sixties, who nodded at the three clerics, at the end of their stay. As they left the pub, happy now that their hunger was assuaged, the Irishmen observed what they could not have missed before but for their eagerness to find a watering hole, namely the Church of John the Baptist opposite, admittedly set back quite a way from the street front.

'If we'd turned right instead of left as we left the kissing gate, we'd have found the right pub straight away!' Allen exclaimed.

'More to the point, we'd have found it immediately if we had obeyed the cardinal rule of village life,' Martin observed.

'What's the cardinal rule?' Allen asked.

'There is always a good pub immediately opposite any village church. The faithful require stroking after long, boring sermons,' Martin explained.

'Not mine!' Chris observed.

They crossed the road and found an open door into the church.

Even before they tried the door, they heard the organ. Allen and Martin looked at each other with wider eyes than before.

'We are in luck!' Martin said, in an urgent but quiet voice.

As they entered the nave, even Chris was impressed with the beauty of the church. It had a serenity about it. The walls and columns were of a very pale cream-coloured stone and were in the cleanest of conditions. Indeed, the condition of the whole building was immaculate. Clearly a great deal of care, love and money had been lavished upon it. Behind the altar, a gloriously colourful stained-glass window cast a predominantly golden glow over the church. Unusually, perhaps, it illustrated harvest time, so that much of the colour derived from its depiction of sheaves of corn. The windows elsewhere, along the sides of the nave and to each side of the altar window itself, were of plain glass. Well, old, plain glass, striated and full of small air bubbles, imperfections which only gave warmth and life to these old panes. Any disappointment that the paucity of coloured glass might evoke was amply compensated by the degree of pure light in the building. Everything was so light and fresh. The pews were of honey-coloured oak and appeared to have been refurbished recently: either that, or lavish and regular care was taken of them. Here and there someone had composed beautiful flower arrangements – not over-large or overdone; simply tasteful.

Chris began a slow examination of the various wall plaques and busts, while Allen and Martin looked for a staircase leading to the organ loft. There was a gate across it which was no doubt locked at most times but which they found open because the organ was in use. They waited quietly until the organist had finished the piece of music he was playing, and then knocked loudly on the gate frame and called, asking if they might come up. A cheery voice invited them forward, in as friendly a manner as one could wish for. They introduced themselves to the organist, a slight man with little hair but a wide smile, explaining that they had made this pilgrimage to St. Johns in the hope of seeing but, above all, hearing its famous organ. They also told him that they were organists themselves, part-time in Allen's case, but merely intermittently in Martin's. There followed a quite technical discussion of the organ's characteristics: of its voicing, stops and couplers, of the contents of its swell-box. Down below, Chris could hear their excited conversation perfectly clearly – itself a reflection of the church's fine acoustic – and was amused to hear from a stranger's mouth all the same words he had been obliged to listen to from his friends for years.

'Would you care to try it out?' asked the organist.

Would they ever! Martin grabbed the opportunity with his customary force, while Allen, though equally keen, held back. Martin's repertoire was rather less than his ambition, shall we say. He quickly found the music for Bach's *Toccata and Fugue* in D minor and, with head held back – for it was more than likely that he was playing from (imperfect) memory than from the page – and body erect, he launched into that all-too-famous toccata: da, da, da, diddle-de-dumdum. It was certainly an enthusiastic performance, even if it did raise the eyebrows of the organist of St. John's.

As Martin reached the end, with a somewhat overdone rallentando and crescendo, he turned to Allen and said, 'Why don't you take over from here, Allen?'

It was more a cry for help than some gracious offer to share.

Allen slid along the organist's bench, adjusted many stops so as to produce a more restrained, delicate tonality, and began to play the long fugue. As the organist of St. John's noted immediately, this was a horse of an entirely different colour. Of course, Allen had played the piece many times before but obviously not on this instrument, so he was giving it his full concentration and care. Martin knew full well that he was completely outclassed by Allen – which was why he had given over the instrument to him anyway – but he had no jealousy of his friend – only admiration. Even Chris downstairs, sitting in a pew now, kept very quiet as Allen played. When he finished, both of his friends joined the organist of St. John's in gentle applause.

'I so enjoyed that,' said the latter. 'Please look through my music and see if there is anything else you might care to play.'

Allen riffled through the first pile of manuscripts until he snorted, always wanting to exercise his wicked sense of humour, and placed his choice of music onto the organ desk.

'Do you remember this, Martin?' he asked and began to play.

'Oh, yes!' Martin replied, after just a couple of bars. '*BWV 881*, I do believe.'

'Ah!' Allen replied, continuing his playing without pause, 'but do you remember any other connection?'

Martin was nonplussed. After some moments, the organist of St. John's, who had quickly picked up on Allen's sense of humour, said, 'I do believe that the Swingle Singers made hay with that one.'

BWV 881 was the *Prelude and Fugue, Number XII* from Bach's *Well-Tempered Klavier*, and the Swingle Singers had indeed made something of that particular piece.

'Of course!' Martin conceded. 'You're quite right.'

Chris continued playing to the end of the prelude. He then made ready to go on to the fugue, changing from his customary preference for delicate voicing to a more suitably dominant soundbox. As ever, he played the fugue without hitch, for he had played it many times before, and as he reached the closing bars, he let rip with the thirty-two-foot diapason which he and Martin had been raving about like schoolboys the previous day. Martin's chest enlarged as he breathed in time with these final bars. He was in seventh heaven. In fairness, so was Allen himself, for he had not been able to employ so fine a set of pipes for a very long time.

'You enjoyed that, didn't you?' smiled the organist of St. John's.

'You bet!' agreed Martin.

'Thank you very much for allowing us to play your instrument,' Allen said. 'I shall remember this afternoon with great pleasure, and for a long time.'

He vacated the bench for his host, and the Irishmen left the church with joy in their hearts.

*

They strolled slowly out of the churchyard and back into the village, making their way to the kissing gate through which they had first entered

Healdsmill. They were completely preoccupied, chatting about the sound quality of the organ and the acoustic of the church. Even Chris was enthusiastic about their performances. They had barely passed through the kissing gate when three youths – the same youths, Martin realised, who had been so rude to them as they had left *The Lion* some hours earlier – accosted them with jeers and threatening gestures.

'Wot yer doin' in our village, yer poofters?' jeered one – at Martin especially. Yer bin kiddie-fiddlin'?'

'Oh, go away,' Martin replied, even as he knew he shouldn't have spoken. 'Behave yourselves.' Even worse, he turned to his friends and said, 'What can one expect?'

The boys didn't give Allen or Chris time to reply.

'What can one expect?' they mimicked, and continued, 'Ain't we posh?'

Martin, especially, was getting concerned and was losing control.

'Go away, stupid boys!' he cried.

They were looking for a fight, of course. Indeed, they were looking for an excuse and, in their eyes, Martin had just given them one.

One of them pushed Martin and yelled, 'Who are yer callin' stoopid, pufter?'

Martin totally lost control of his tongue. 'You probably can't even spell the word, you ignorant whelp!'

The big youth who had been leading the verbal barrage hit Martin full in his face. Martin, who was nearing his sixty-third year and was, in any case, in no physical shape for fisticuffs, even if he had had the courage for it, staggered back, clutching his bloodied nose.

Chris immediately placed himself between Martin and his assailant.

'Listen, sonny,' he said in measured tones. 'Don't go around hitting people, especially older people like my friend.'

The bully tried to imitate Chris's Northern Irish tones.

Chris replied, in full control of himself, 'Now go away while you can, and take your friends with you.'

But the youth was having none of it. He had run out of words from his all-too-limited vocabulary and made the fateful decision to attack Chris. He swung at the youngest Irishman of the group, telegraphing his immature move by a mile. Chris, who wasn't a particularly big man, was, however, both fit and skilled in a way none there suspected. He had been a very useful fighter in his youth, having learned several techniques from boxing and other self-defence arts, and was not afraid of a little squirt like this one. Quick as lightening, he grabbed the boy's wrist and gave it a forceful twist. The boy yelled in pain and found himself flat on his back. His mates, not yet understanding that they had met their match, made to join the attack on Chris at this point.

'Any more?' Chris asked. 'One at a time or two at a time. It's all the same to me.'

One of the boys left standing, lunged at Chris who adroitly stepped aside. The boy staggered as he missed his mark.

'I'm sure you can do better than that,' Chris chided him.

The boy made to try again, but the third youth pulled him back.

'Let's go, Mick,' he said.

The three youths ran off, showing, as ever, that bullies are cowards first.

Allen, who was very shaken, attended to Martin's nosebleed. After some while, the three men of God continued on their way, silent now, their pleasure from the church organ lost. It was to return later, and they knew it would, but the incident with the local yobs had shaken them all up quite badly. Chris was the hero, certainly, but even he was quite disturbed by the whole thing. They walked on in silence, each trying to muster a degree of control for the moment they would meet up with Ken and Jill again.

'Hi!' Ken greeted them. 'Did you see the organ, then?'

The three friends found their voice.

'Oh, yes!' Martin replied, 'and we played it too! It's a wonderful instrument. I'm so glad we came.'

'Have you eaten?' asked Jill.

'We eventually found *The Oak*,' Chris replied, 'and enjoyed our lunch very much.'

'Mind you, we tried *The Lion* and *The Hollies* first. They were awful,' Martin said, carefully omitting any mention of the bullies.

'It was surprising to find three pubs in so small a village,' Allen remarked.

'Healdsmill is known for that,' Ken said. 'Sorry, I should have told you.'

'Well, make yourselves comfortable,' Jill said, 'and I'll bring some drinks. You probably need one after all your excitement.'

The three clerics looked at one another but said nothing.

Some time later, Jill and Ken provided their guests with another delightful meal and, once more, left them to their own devices with post-prandial drinks in the saloon lounge. The conversation meandered for a while between this and that, that and this. Eventually it turned to what was really uppermost in their minds: the attack from those boys.

'Why did those youths call us poofters?' Martin asked the others.

'That's easy,' Chris replied. 'It's your accent.'

'But my accent is a good, rounded English accent,' Martin protested.

'Maybe I shouldn't have said "accent", exactly. But it's the way you talk, Martin. It's obvious you're a poof. We all know that and we love you for it, but you do lay it on a bit, you know.'

'Well,' Martin replied, holding his head up in protest, 'I'm sure I don't know what you mean, dear boy.' He pouted for some moments before another thought came to him. 'And why did he accuse us of kiddie fiddling? I've never done any such disgusting thing in my whole life!'

'That isn't difficult to understand, either,' Allen said. 'With all the anti-Roman rhetoric going about these days, people of their – how shall I say it? – limited intelligence, easily latch on to such notions.'

'You mean it was levelled at *me*?' Chris protested. 'That's disgusting. Had I realised that at the time, I'd have broken his arm!'

'I'm sure you wouldn't have done that, Chris, but maybe it was just as well that you hadn't understood his jibe,' Allen replied.

Now it was Chris' turn to ask, 'But why me? How did he know I'm a Roman Catholic priest?'

'Well, of course he didn't, but it's your accent,' Martin replied.

'Bugger off, Martin,' was all Chris could find in reply. But he said it in such mellifluous tones.

His remark served to puncture their collective angst. They relaxed and poured themselves another drink.

Martin said: 'Talking about accents, I must tell you a story about a couple of Irish working women – I don't mean tarts – chatting together in Drury Lane several years ago. They had stopped outside the theatre where "My Fair Lady" was playing.'

'What's all dat about?' asked Siobhan of her friend Mavis.

There was an attribution to George Bernard Shaw in the poster on display. The ladies had read every last word on the poster.

Von said: 'Oh, I'd love to go and see dat filum, Maeve. I'd just love to see dem pigmy loyons!'

Chris picked up a small cushion from the sofa on which he sat and threw it at Martin.

'Stop taking the piss, Martin. You're the one who changed!'

18

Rachael and Michael were having breakfast in their private quarters. They occasionally did that, rather than mix in with guests from the hall, who were, in any case, coming and going as they saw fit.

'Michael,' Rachael asked, 'would you mind if I asked Maureen to stay with us for a couple of weeks? I mean, with us in our private apartment?'

'Not at all, darling,' Michael replied and, without pause, continued, 'Who's Maureen? Have I met her?'

'No, you haven't, but I have told you about her. She and I were at the same primary school years ago. We haven't been particularly close over the years. Not because we don't get on or anything like that – I wouldn't want to invite her otherwise, anyway – but really because our paths haven't crossed very often. But I have seen her occasionally, usually when I have gone up to London for a couple of days, and we have spent time together. And every time we have met, I have thought how nice she is and how I would like to spend real time with her. I have no idea whether she or her husband can afford to stay at *The Hut* officially – judging by her clothes style, I suspect that they're not well off – so I thought that a short, private visit might be nice. What do you think?'

'I've already said, my love. If *you* like her, that's all it takes. Do you want me to ask her, or should I leave it to you?'

'No, I'll do it. After all, you don't know her. But thank you.'

And so it was that three weeks later, Maureen pulled up at the side entrance of *The Hut* in her little Volvo. Rachael was there to meet her and let her into the grounds, and she guided her the short distance to the garages where a place had been reserved for her.

As a little girl in primary school, Maureen had been a petite child with fair-to-blond curly hair, blue eyes and a giggle which she employed often but not incessantly. Now in her mid-fifties, Maureen was still petite with curly, fair hair and blue eyes. And she still giggled often. The only change in her, really, was that she had thickened out. It wouldn't be fair to say that she was fat. No: she was chubby. And chubby went with her lovely personality perfectly. Rachael had seen the changes before from when they had met up on one of her jaunts into the capital, so there was no shock at their meeting. Maureen was still dressed in a simple, floral dress with a white lapel. It probably cost just twenty quid, Rachael supposed, but it suited Maureen to a T. In any case, it was probably all she could afford.

Rachael welcomed her, hugged her, relieved her of her suitcase and led her into the rear entrance of the hall, close to the lift. They ascended to the fourth floor, using Rachael's private key, where Rachael ushered her guest into a large vestibule from which many doors led. Maureen looked about her with interest but without anguish or embarrassment. Rachael noticed this with a little surprise but said nothing as she showed Maureen into her room. As were all rooms at *The Hut*, but especially so for these private quarters, it was large and beautifully decorated and appointed. Its style was modern but without shrieking.

'Please make yourself at home, Maureen. I'll come back for you in ten minutes, if that's all right,' and she left her guest to adjust.

Maureen was sitting on her bed, skimming one of the books she had found in a small bookcase on one wall, when Rachael reappeared.

'Do come through, Maureen. I apologise for leaving you on your own, but you might have become confused by the array of doors outside in the lobby. Let me give you the guided tour.'

She led her guest back into the grand lobby and began to open every door for her, saying a few words about the rooms beyond each one. Finally, they ended up in the lounge where Rachael asked Maureen if she'd like a cup of tea or something stronger.

'Oh! Tea for now, I think. I know the sun is over the yardarm somewhere in the world, but I feel it's a bit early for me,' she replied, with an ease which Rachael hadn't expected.

Rachael went off into the kitchen to collect tea and cakes which she had already arranged in the certain anticipation of Maureen's choice. Maureen had followed her, saw the pre-ordered afternoon tea on the counter, but ignored it completely.

'This is a lovely kitchen, Rachael. What sort of ovens do you have? We have Miele.'

Now Rachael was a most talented lady, as we know, and was most active in the gardens, consulting with Gordon and his merry men. Furthermore, she joined with Michael in designing menus for their *Hut* guests. And she had continued with her love of history ever since leaving university all those years ago. She was *not*, however, a cook. She made no pretence of it, least of all to Michael, relying instead on the magical services of *The Hut's* kitchen staff. Now, all of a sudden, she felt a little embarrassed as she admitted that she had no idea what make her ovens were, let alone how to switch them on. Maureen giggled and helped her host out.

'That's all right, Rachael. To tell you the truth, I'm rather glad you're no cook. I mean, after all, you are so clever at your history and that sort of thing. It wouldn't be fair if you were good at everything!'

Rachael beamed at her and said, 'Let's go and enjoy the afternoon tea. I know I didn't make the cakes, but I can assure you they are very good. So please enjoy!'

While they were forcing each other to take second helpings, Rachael looked again at Maureen's dress. She decided that it wasn't a twenty quid job off the hanger. It was too well made, and the material hung beautifully.

Rachael became more and more interested in Maureen's presentation. Her hair was much as she remembered it, but it was so very well done. So were her nails and her makeup. She wore a simple pearl necklace and pearl earrings. Rachael was no expert in such matters, for she really didn't care too much about such things, but she knew enough, she suspected, to recognise quality when she saw it. Those pearls were real and good quality, she thought.

'I love your pearls, Maureen,' she said. She couldn't really help herself at this point in her examination.

'Oh! Thank you, Rachael. Yes, Bill got them for me several years ago. He's very good like that.'

'What does Bill do, Maureen?' Rachael asked. 'I can't remember if you told me already – sorry.'

'Rachael, you don't know about ovens, and I don't know about finance. Bill does something in the city, but I have no idea what. I believe he's very good at it but, honestly, I don't understand these things.'

'Do you still teach, Maureen?' Rachael asked.

Maureen had been a primary-school teacher for most of her life. She never rose to principal, but then, she never wanted to. She just loved kids. Indeed, she had three of her own: two boys and one girl.

'We thought we'd stop there,' she had told Rachael some while ago.

Rachael and Michael had no children, and Rachael protested that they had never wanted any.

'In answer to your question, Rachael: I gave up teaching nearly five years ago. The job was becoming more and more controlled by whatever the Department of Education wanted, rather than by what I enjoyed teaching and the kids enjoyed learning about. In any case, we're empty nesters these days, and Bill wanted me to go out with him to more and more functions, so it all came together, and I decided to hang up my chalk.' Maureen giggled at her little joke. It was a lovely giggle.

Suddenly Michael strode into the room. 'Hello! I'm Michael. You must be Maureen. Welcome to *The Hut*.'

'What's *The Hut*?' Maureen asked.

'Oh, I'm sorry, Maureen,' Rachael said. 'I haven't shown you the set-up yet. I will later, but for the moment, please understand Michael's remark as we all do around here, as his little joke. You'll understand it later, I promise.'

'I see you've had some afternoon tea. Might I suggest a wee tipple now? How about you, Maureen? What say we crack open a bottle of bubbly? It would be nice to welcome you properly,' Michael said, as he cleared the tea things.

Maureen giggled and said, 'I just knew you'd find yourself a good man, Rachael!'

The three of them spent a jolly hour together. Michael told a lot of jokes which Rachael applauded, having only heard them fifty times before. Maureen enjoyed their company enormously and giggled a lot.

Dinner was served at seven o'clock. They had moved to a small but elegant dining room, and Charles, the waiter who usually attended to needs in the private quarters, brought in some dishes. The evening meal, however, was anything but formal. After a simple but subtle tomato soup, a choice of dishes was placed centrally on the table and the "family" were left to help themselves. Today: a simple steak and kidney pie under a superb puff pastry, a boiled ham, and Pease pudding. Afterwards, there was a choice of an apple strudel or a cheese plate. Maureen was offered a *Beaujolais* or a *Chablis*: she chose the red.

Michael apologised for the simplicity or ordinariness of the meal, explaining that official guests were treated with greater splendour. He realised immediately that his remarks could be taken to suggest that Maureen was not regarded as special, and he hastened to correct any wrong impressions he may have given. He carried on like that for a moment. It was quite unlike him to stumble, but he was trying so hard to make Maureen's visit a success. Maureen, bless her, understood his dilemma completely and sought to reassure him instead.

'Michael,' she said, in a thoroughly motherly way, 'Please don't go on. The dinner was a delight. Please congratulate your cooks for me. That pastry was to die for. Fancy meals are all well and good in their place, but it takes a lot to beat a good steak and kidney pie, especially when the chef has added something – I can't tell what exactly – to the mix, which really lifts a humble dish to a gourmet delight.'

Michael took hold of Maureen's hand and placed a feather-light kiss upon it. 'Why don't we take Maureen on a tour of the facilities downstairs and introduce her to some of *The Hut's* guests?'

'Yes, let's do that,' Rachael agreed, 'and tomorrow I'll take her for a look at our gardens and, indeed, the outside of the hall generally.'

They took the lift down to the ground floor and moved toward the lounge bar where Rachael and Michael knew most of their guests would congregate at this time in the evening.

'So this is a hotel,' Maureen said. Reasonably so.

'Sort of,' Rachael replied. 'It isn't completely open to the public, as only those of whom we approve may stay here. We think of them as friends as well as guests – and, indeed, they truly are – but they don't come for free. Indeed, our charges are very high, but we try to give them the very best service, food, wine and entertainment money can buy. We also offer a general guarantee, as far as we are able, of privacy while they are here. Everyone goes by a name of his or her choice. These may be real or not – we don't care. Some guests may be very much in the public eye and subject to the indignities of the paparazzi. Should they wish to leave *The Hut* without being seen, for good or for just a few days, we have secret ways of arranging that.'

'Sounds very cloak and dagger!' Maureen replied. 'Even exciting!'

Michael spoke to one of his guests as they passed. A man replied with obvious pleasure.

Another, a tall lady with dark hair and a most striking face, waved and called out: 'You were right, the other evening, Michael. Clever you!'

Michael laughed and moved on.

'What was that about, darling?' Rachael asked him.

'I haven't a clue! I remember chatting with Melinda two evenings ago, but I'm damned if I can remember what about!'

Rachael turned to Maureen again and told her about the library. 'Come. I'll show you. Catch you in a moment, darling,' she said to Michael.

They moved out of the lounge and into the grand library. It was late in the evening now, so it appeared to be quite dark outside, notwithstanding the extended dusk, so that the coloured-glass windows couldn't be shown off.

'This place is well worth a visit in daylight. We're very proud of it.'

'I can see already that it is not the sort of room to be found in the average hotel,' Maureen observed.

They nosed around the library briefly, and Maureen agreed to look more closely at it tomorrow. Rachael then took her to see the breakfast room.

'We'll take breakfast in here tomorrow,' she said. 'We run a rolling breakfast. Help yourself from side tables to more or less whenever you want. We occasionally use our private quarters for this meal, but rarely for lunch.'

'What about evening meals?' asked Maureen. 'Would you normally eat down here with *The Hut's* guests?'

'About fifty-fifty,' Rachael told her. 'Michael likes to keep faith with our guests – and so do I, actually – so we regularly dine with them. Look, here's the dining hall. As you see, there is just one large table. Unlike a regular hotel, dinner is a communal affair and, apart from catering to some individuals' allergies and such, everyone has the same meal. Mind you, we try to make each meal memorable. Michael and I spend hours planning menus way ahead of time. Not all meals are *haute cuisine*, shall I say, but all are as well-cooked as possible.'

'Like that steak and kidney pie,' Maureen interrupted. 'That was made with real love.'

'I'm so glad you liked that. And yes! We sometimes serve that down here, too. Anyway, let's go back upstairs. I'll show you the rest in the morning.'

As they passed Michael, who was engrossed with his guests again, she pointed her finger upwards. He nodded as the two old school-friends made their way back to the lift.

Some while later, Michael joined the ladies in the private lounge. They were sipping something or other, so Michael helped himself to a small malt.

'It must be difficult keeping sober in this place,' Maureen observed. 'Oh! I don't mean to be rude,' she hastened to add, with a giggle. 'It's just that there are so many occasions to wet one's whistle that I would have thought that a fair degree of self-restraint was called for.'

Michael laughed warmly at this poke. 'You've hit the nail on the head, Maureen,' he said. 'I try very hard, and one day I'm going to say, "Not hard enough", but it really is difficult, not least because all our booze is so good! You know, I was brought up to this sort of life. My family owned this place outright for centuries – death duties put paid to that, of course – and I and my parents ate and drank pretty much as our guests do now.'

'A life of privilege then,' Maureen said. 'Oh! I'm sorry. I didn't mean to be rude, especially after all the kindness you and Rachael have shown me.'

'Don't worry, Maureen. It's a perfectly reasonable remark. I am privileged and I'm spoiled. It wasn't my fault, though, for I was brought up to believe that my way of life was perfectly normal. But my father was something of a liberal – I don't mean with a big L – and encouraged me to mix with the village folk – we must show you our village while you're here, too – at every opportunity. Okay, I went to the same public school my father and grandfather had attended, but in the holidays I helped paint a canal boat owned by the publican, and I became close friends with two boys from the village who had beaten me up once – and no! I hadn't deserved it. Those boys played, and still play, in their own jazz band in our village and elsewhere, by the way. One of them became our assistant head gardener. He liaised with my mother when she was alive, and now with Rachael, who is very enthusiastic indeed about the grounds here. So, we can't really help what world we were born into. What matters, I think, is how one treats people. It's a simple matter of decency, really. I don't mean that in a patronising way, though. Mind you, we pay our workers very well. Way above the going rate. They do us proud and are very loyal, so we are obliged, in my mind, to reciprocate. And we do.'

'Gosh, that was some speech, Michael, and I apologise again. However, I understand better than you, or Rachael even, for, as Rachael knows, I was born into a humble environment with loving parents who wanted the best for me. They voted Labour on every occasion, quite simply because they believed that Labour's policies were the ones to provide the opportunities in life that every child needs. I went to the local primary school in our village – which is where I met Rachael, whose family was, I quickly realised, much wealthier than mine. That didn't stop Rachael being my best friend, so, like you, I count personal traits more highly than almost anything else. Rachael was always cleverer than me – yes, Rachael, I always knew it – but that was no more her fault than mine. It was just the case. She went on later to university and all that. I went to a teacher training college and became a schoolteacher. I remained a schoolteacher until only a few years ago when Bill, my husband, began to spend so much time in Westminster. I have had a very happy life. I have always voted Labour. My husband always voted Labour, which is just as well, nowadays, I suppose. But like you, Michael, it's the people you meet who matter. It's how you interact with them. Bill and I were pretty poor at one time, but now he's probably worth nearly a million pounds, I should think. We have a nice mock-Tudor house in Hampstead, something that my parents could never have imagined. But they would have been pleased for me and continued to vote Labour. So, Michael, we obviously began very differently and are clearly in very different financial circles even now, but it's clear to me that you are a very kind and hospitable man – I observed how you interact with your guests downstairs – and that is what matters in my mind. End of speech!'

Some while later, everyone decided to go to bed.

'Let me know if you need anything, Maureen,' Rachael called out, as her guest departed.

'I'm sure I won't,' Maureen replied with a giggle.

19

Michael stopped dead in the middle of shaving and called out to Rachael who was watching some early-morning television.

What's Maureen's surname, darling?'

'Land. Maureen Land. An unusual name, I guess,' she replied.

Michael came into the bedroom with his face still half-lathered up, picked up his smart phone and began googling.

'My god!' he said. 'Have you any idea who her husband is, Rachael?'

Rachael noted that Michael had called her by her name rather than by his usual endearment. This must be serious.

'No idea, at all, beyond his being something in the city. That's what Maureen told me yesterday afternoon.'

'Yes, and last night she mentioned his spending a lot of time in Westminster. Do you remember?'

'Yes. I just assumed she was confusing places in London.'

'I don't think so. I agree that Land is an unusual surname. I think Bill Land is Baron Land, a Labour peer of this realm. Bill Land is chairman and CEO of Land Enterprises, a newish player in the specialist telecommunications world. I would guess that Maureen's guestimate of Bill's wealth as "nearly a million" is probably an underestimate by a factor of ten.'

'Good heavens! Doesn't make him less likable in my eyes, however,' Rachael replied, and then, remembering, she added, 'I'll bet those pearls are the genuine article! My goodness. Oh! I am *so* pleased for Maureen, darling.'

'I'd like to meet Bill. Why don't you suggest that Maureen ask Bill to join her here at *The Hut*?'

' All right. I'll do that while I show her around outside after breakfast. By the way, your face is still lathered up.'

Maureen was waiting for them in the lounge when they surfaced, and all three took the lift down for breakfast. After their meal, Michael excused himself, saying (correctly) that he had to check his mail and do all his housekeeping jobs. Maureen wondered what those might be but was in no doubt that dusting and hoovering were not on Michael's list.

'Fancy a bit of a walk?' Rachael asked, after Michael had disappeared. 'The view of *The Hut* along the Grand Avenue never ceases to amaze me. I remember the first time when Michael showed it to me. This way.'

Rachael stopped Maureen from looking back until they were halfway between the bird with two heads and the circle at the far end of the avenue.

' All right, Maureen, turn round,' she said with obvious pride.

Maureen gasped at the view before her. 'My goodness,' she said, after a pause. 'This is all yours?'

'No, no. You have forgotten what Michael told you last night. It was in his family for several generations, but death duties did for that. It's now totally owned by *Marchant Enterprises* in which Michael owns a good, but far from controlling, share. The arrangement upon surrendering the property to that company was, in part, that Michael and I have the use of our large apartment for the rest of our lives. As you know, we have no children, so that arrangement will cease upon the death of the last of us still standing. In return for that accommodation, Michael and I get to arrange the concern Michael amusingly calls *The Hut*, as we will, with paying guests of our choosing until we are no more. The arrangement was hammered out between Michael and his father on the Montayne side, and Geoffrey – who was our best man, by the way, and who we both got to know at Bristol University – and *his* father, for the Etheringtons who owned *Marchant Voyages*. *Marchant Voyages* became *Marchant Enterprises* as part of the amalgamation of the two family concerns. So you see, Maureen, all this looks very grand – and, of course, it is – but it's not actually ours!'

'Rachael, I don't really care who owns it. It is truly magnificent, and I do envy your being able to call it home,' Maureen replied. Then she giggled and said, 'Who would have thought you and I would end up as we have?'

'Well, you haven't done too badly either, Maureen. Or should I call you Lady Land?' Rachael asked.

'Ah! So you've found out. I find it all very strange, I must tell you. I was so proud of Bill when he was ennobled, but I don't really understand it all. He says that Callaghan put him there because he wanted to increase the Labour count in the Lords. I must say I don't understand how these things work, but there it is. I still can't get used to it, and I very rarely use the handle. Certainly not with old friends who might be embarrassed.'

'Please don't think that we're in the least embarrassed, Maureen. We have friends in both British and Continental nobility and even Royalty, and Michael continues to make friends of other rich or famous or titled people all round the world. He enjoys making new friends anyway, but, truth to tell, it helps build our guest base for *The Hut*. No one has their arms twisted to come here, of course. It's just that through Michael's ever-widening circle of contacts, *The Hut* becomes a home from home to so many interesting people. And the real bonus, so far as we're concerned, is that we gain an ever-widening circle of really interesting friends. The point here, you realise, is that we don't invite people we don't like or find interesting. That is a great luxury for us, of course, but it was built into the agreement which is part of *Marchant Enterprises*. Let me show you more of the grounds now.'

Maureen was shown the croquet lawn, the tennis courts and eventually Rachael's great pride: the kitchen garden. Now Maureen enthused, for she had been interested in growing her own produce for years. When she was little, she had helped her dad in the vegetable garden. In those days there was a great need to save every penny, and Maureen's family hardly ever paid a penny for their vegetables. Even when growing their own produce was no longer essential, after Maureen had married Bill, she kept the habit because her vegetables were in better condition than anything she could buy in the shops, and also because she could grow what she wanted rather than be obliged to accept the commercial imperatives of the supermarket.

When she saw what Rachael had in her extensive vegetable plots, Maureen was in seventh heaven. And then she spotted the herb garden. She went from one row to the next, identifying each one.

'You have borage,' she exclaimed.

'We mostly use that for its flowers,' Rachael said. 'Our chef designs some fascinating dishes where borage flowers are included.'

'I would like to bring Bill here so that we could be official guests. Bill can afford to do that, and he would love to meet you and Michael, I'm sure,'

'Maureen, consider yourselves invited. I'll give you an official invitation this afternoon, which explains all the details,' Rachael replied, beaming at her old friend. 'It's a nice day for a stroll, so why don't you and I go and explore the village now? Actually, we could pop into the village pub for a spot of lunch. The *Tomber Pot* will do us proud.'

As they went on their way, Rachael explained the (public) history of the Montaigne/Montayne family, the creation of *Tomberwater*, and something of the central role of *The Pot* (but not its secrets, of course), by which time they had reached the river and the wharf. Maureen was fascinated by the narrowboats moored there, so they walked down onto the wharf itself so that she could get a close view. As luck would have it, Ken popped his head out from the *Maisy Pot* while Maureen was excitedly examining every little detail of the boat.

'Morning, Rachael,' he said gaily. 'Lovely day for it.'

Rachael introduced Maureen who giggled as she complimented Ken on his boat.

'Would you like to look inside?' he offered.

Would she ever! He took her hand and guided her in through the double back doors.

'Please go through. Go anywhere you like.' And then, 'Please feel free. I mean it; look in anything that interests you,' he insisted.

Rachael explained that Maureen was a friend of many years and that they had been at the same primary school. Eventually Maureen reappeared, thanking Ken repeatedly. She had really enjoyed herself; it was so interesting. She had wanted to go on a canal boat for years, she said. They waved goodbye to Ken as they made their way back up to the road and from there to the pub.

'I'm ready for a drop of lunch now,' Maureen said, as they passed through the door of *The Pot*. 'What will you have, Rachael?'

'I fancy a white wine, but let's get a bottle and take it to the table where we can eat. But first,' she said, as Jill appeared behind the bar, 'let me introduce you to Jill. Jill is Ken's wife.'

Maureen looked puzzled for a moment.

'Ken, who you met on the boat,' she explained.

'Oh, I did so enjoy that, Jill,' Maureen said with a giggle. 'I've wanted to go on a canal boat for years.'

'Jill and Ken will take *Hut* guests on a trip upriver and into the canal system for a few days, by arrangement. It's rather like taking your own pub with you on the water,' laughed Rachael.

They settled into their seats by the window.

Maureen said to Rachael, 'This is a marvellous place. Not just the pub, I mean, but the hall and all its grounds, the village, the river and, so far at least, the people. You have a piece of heaven here, Rachael.' This time, Maureen didn't giggle.

Rachael took her hand and squeezed it in reply. 'We think so, too,' she said. 'Now, let's order.'

*

'I'm still in the mood for seeing more of this place, Rachael,' Maureen said, after they had arrived back at the hall. 'But please don't feel obliged to chaperon me everywhere. You go in and do whatever you would normally do, and I'll take myself off and explore your enormous park.'

Maureen set forth, as so many guests had done before her, along the Grand Avenue where she examined the bird with two heads before taking herself into the wooded area leading to the hide. She examined the hide in detail and spent some time there to see if she could spot any interesting birds. From there, she found the circle at the end of the Grand Avenue and climbed the steep, winding road up to the gate where Gerald had first taken Harvey some months earlier. She tried to leave the grounds there but found the gate locked. Not having been supplied with *The Hut* app meant that she couldn't open the security gate. She decided to stroll back to the hall now, for after all, she had been on her feet for most of the day. Mind you, she was a fit lady, but everyone deserves a rest sometime in the day.

'My goodness!' she thought. 'This is a mighty enterprise.'

She recognised how hard Rachael and Michael worked to make the place such a success, for it had been clear yesterday evening how much the other guests appreciated Michael's and Rachael's efforts. Nevertheless, they had a fabulous life, she thought. Maureen, being the sort of person she was, the sort of person Rachael fully recognised her to be, was in no degree envious of her hosts. Her thoughts were of admiration and pleasure, but also of wonder at their construct.

When she got back to the hall, she decided to take a nap in her room for an hour. Rachael had told her of a treat coming up that evening but had refused to be drawn on what it was. Maureen thought it best to refresh herself for it. Whatever it was, it was to be preceded by dinner downstairs, so she decided to wear the best dress she had brought with her.

In due course, she walked into Rachael and Michael's private lounge in her teal-coloured satin number and wearing a simple gold necklace with yellow diamond earrings which Bill had given her for her last birthday.

'You look stunning!' Rachael enthused. 'Shall we be wicked and have a wee cocktail before dinner?'

'Could I have a *Gin-Gin Mule*?' asked Maureen.

'I'm sure our barman can provide one,' Rachael said, 'whatever that is!'

'Oh! I don't know. I just like gin and I remember being served one in New York, so I thought I'd try and be sophisticated,' Maureen said with a giggle.

'I'll join you with that,' Rachael said. 'Education is a wonderful thing!'

It seemed that the barman was in no way fazed by the order, for two of these dynamite hits appeared in no time.

Rachael spluttered as she took her first sip. 'My god, Maureen,' she said through her coughs. 'This is a real discovery. I'll be sure to offer it to all my stronger guests!'

Michael appeared and Rachael suggested he try one of their cocktails.

'What is it?' he asked.

' *Gin-Gin Mule*,' Rachael replied.

'No thanks,' Michael laughed. 'I'll save myself for a time when suicide becomes the norm.'

Maureen giggled.

They went down to dinner together, arriving just as the butler was announcing it.

'Come and sit between us, Maureen. When you get fed up with our conversation, you can talk across the table.'

Maureen giggled.

Her giggle was heard and appreciated by an American sitting opposite.

'That's a happy laugh, ma'am,' he said. 'My wife used to giggle in exactly that way. You remind me of her. Thank you very much. Sorry, I'm Noah, by the way, and that's my real name.'

'It couldn't be anything else!' Michael said with a grin. 'Noah, meet Maureen, an old friend of Rachael's and now, I hope, of mine. And that is her real name, too! Maureen, Noah is from The United States of America.' Michael pronounced the "You-nided" in a slow, deliberate drawl.

'…in case you hadn't caught on, Maureen,' Noah said, smiling broadly.

'We take people from anywhere here,' Rachael said, joining in the fun, 'even from parvenue countries.'

Noah laughed again and replied, 'It's hilarious how those from very old countries tell very old jokes!'

Maureen giggled.

'Oh! Do that again… please,' Noah urged Maureen.

'I can't do it to order,' she said. 'You have to say something funny to get me to do that.'

'How about, Micky Mouse for President?' Noah replied.

Maureen gave him a thin smile.

'How about Trump for President?'

Maureen giggled. And again.

'Ah, so we've learned what side of the great divide you are on,' Noah said, and then, as an afterthought, 'Thank god.'

'I'm on the side of the truthsayer,' Maureen replied.

'I'll drink to that,' Noah enthused, 'or I would if there was anything in my glass. Where's the wine waiter?'

'Oh dear, Noah, are you dry for a moment?' Rachael taunted.

Michael had turned to talk to the guest on his right, and Rachael to Divit Deshpande sitting on her left, an extraordinarily handsome Indian fellow of truly, gigantic physical stature. He had a deep, resonant voice which Maureen couldn't hear because it was so soft. So much of a surprise from so large a man. Maybe.

Noah was talking. 'I've been here for about a week now, Maureen. I've been before. I always enjoy myself at this table. How long will you be staying, Maureen?'

In typical American style, he was hammering her name into his memory by repetition, something the English find so hard to do.

'Just a week,' she replied, 'but I intend to return, next time with my husband. Like you, I'm here alone.' She smiled and continued, 'Where abouts in the States are you from, Noah?'

'I was born and raised in Montana, which is where we still live. And, by the way, I'm here with my son, Lucas. He's sitting at the far end of the table.' Noah paused, then, 'I spent some time at the university in Chapel Hill in North Carolina.'

'I know Chapel Hill very well. At least, as a visitor,' Maureen replied. 'It's a lovely town, and it has lots to see. My husband visited the University of North Carolina once and took me along for the ride, so I got to know the area near the university quite well. I shall always remember a little café – or was it what you'd call a diner? – which had a large, pink, plastic pig fastened to its roof.'

'It's still there!' Noah replied.

'It also had a large bookshop which specialised in the resale of student's books. I found some wonderful novels there – from the freshman and sophomore classes, I think – nothing technical, mind. I'm self-taught, so novels by good authors is as far as I get. I remember the bookshop was imaginatively called *The Bookshop*!'

'Still there!' Noah replied. 'I've bought many second-hand books in that shop, too'.

Maureen and Noah went off into a comparison of the books which they had bought there, what sort of books they liked best, by which authors, and how their tastes had changed over the years. Before they knew it, they were into the fruit and cheese course which *The Hut* served at every dinner.

Looking back, Maureen was able to relate what each course had been to Bill when she got home, but it was an effort.

'He was such a nice bloke!' she insisted.

'Me thinks the lady protests too much,' Bill replied, with a kiss on her forehead.

'I want to take you to meet Rachael and Michael and to see the set-up they have. You'll be amazed,' she insisted.

'Yes, okay,' he replied, without his mind on what he was saying.

Maureen insisted. More than once.

' All right, dear,' he conceded. 'You arrange it with my secretary, and we'll go.'

'For three days at least', Maureen replied, pushing her luck while she had the chance.

'You'll be lucky to find three days free in my calendar,' he laughed. Maureen insisted.

' All right, all right. See what you can carve out.'

That was enough. Maureen knew when to accept victory.

'You'd have loved the cabaret, darling,' she said, continuing with her account of her visit.

'Humm,' was all she got on that.

It had been a great cabaret. After dinner, she had been taken by Rachael and Michael, with Noah in attendance too, downstairs to the cabaret theatre. It had seating for up to forty people, at a pinch, but no pinch was required that evening. There were about twenty-eight in the audience, and the first half hour was taken up getting drinks from the bar and making up tables of two, three or four around the place. The entertainers were left with the very tight space of the small stage there in which to perform, so that a most intimate experience was guaranteed.

The evening began with an emcee introducing himself as host and, with any luck – he placed his hands together, as in prayer – as a comedian. Having received a smile, he announced that that was his first joke. That got a nervous titter from those who feared that he meant what he said. They needn't have feared. Walter knew his stuff. He could work a small, intimate audience like this. He had obviously done it many times before. He held his audience in the palm of his hand. He was applauded wildly when he finished and took an exaggerated bow. He followed his act by introducing the next act, with extreme courtesy and gravitas.

Walter introduced Rita who was to sing excerpts from the shows. He failed to specify which shows. Rita was a beautiful redhead with large, green eyes and a full, well-painted mouth. Her other attributes clearly came as a matching set. She briefly introduced her accompanist on the piano as Ron, who immediately broke into the theme of an aria from Pagliacci. The aria belonged to the male lead rather than the female. It told of how the hero of the piece intends to do for his wife and her lover.

Rita began in a suitable contralto voice with all the solemnity and vigour of a would-be murderer. The audience is made to understand all this, not by the lyrics which Rita sang – and, let it be said, sang beautifully – in Italian, but by her stopping mid-way through to translate. Her translation was spoken very clearly. The audience didn't know which to applaud most: her beautiful voice or her hilarious gestures, while she mimed murder by stabbing, with all the enthusiasm she could muster, while giving her translations in a bell-like cockney voice. Her foray into opera would end there, the audience were happy to learn. Her pianist then broke into a rendering, as these folk are wont to say, of *I do like to be beside the seaside*, whereupon Rita performed the ditty, while contriving – very successfully, for sure – to look like the typical girl on the dirty seaside postcard.

Rita advanced on one of the older men in the audience, who had no means of escape, and beguiled him with her most adequate charms. The man's wife, if that is who she was – for who can tell at these functions? – was beside herself with laughter. Mind you, one suspects that the fella enjoyed himself thoroughly. Which was the point, after all.

Having displayed the end-points of her act, that is, from the sublime to the gor' blimey, Rita turned to a somewhat more sophisticated form of cabaret; to none other but Noël Coward. Her first song was a simple piece of exquisite beauty. She sang *London Pride*. She sang it straight, gently and beautifully. It's a lovely song and she did it proud. The audience were absolutely hushed right through and wild with their applause afterwards.

Rita was unable to behave herself for too long, however. She followed her beautiful self with her wicked self: *Alice is at it Again*. If ever there was a lyric which lent itself to naughtiness, that is it, surely. At one point, Rita draped herself over the shiny, closed lid of the grand piano, tummy down for some of the time, up for the rest, as she helped herself to a cigarette in an exquisite, long, black holder offered mid-tune by her accompanist. She draped herself, she rolled about, and she showed just enough to excite her audience – probably the ladies as much as the men, for they certainly appreciated the skill and style of little Rita.

Her last choice was *The Stately Homes of England*. She preceded it by walking up to Michael, taking his hand and holding it daintily aloft as she said in the sweetest of voices, 'For you, Michael.'

When she came to the lines about the impoverished son of the family inheriting a stately pile which he could not afford to keep up, Michael grinned and shouted, 'True, my dear.'

Rita mock-marched forward towards her audience in the final bars, found Michael again, and the two of them took a bow together. The house was in hysterics, not least Rachael, who had probably arranged the whole thing with Rita beforehand.

Walter returned and kept his audience amused for another ten minutes when the show came to an end. Everyone was happy, conversation was somewhat louder than usually heard at *The Hut*, and the evening drifted lazily and alcoholically – but never rudely – on beyond midnight.

'It was a marvellous evening, darling,' Maureen repeated to Bill, as they went to bed on her return home that evening.

20

Noah Calhoon was visiting *The Hut* with his son, Lucas, as he had informed Maureen a week earlier. He had brought his son, not just to see *The Hut*, but to see Britain in general. Lucas was nearly nineteen, boisterous as some teenagers can still be at that age, although he was just about out of that phase now and eager to find out as much as he could on this, his first trip with the old man to the old country. He referred to Britain that way, because Lucas's great grandfather had come from Scotland. Noah always bracketed Scotland and the rest of Britain together in his mind, so a stay in this quaint old English pile was totally natural to his way of thinking.

The Calhoons were far from poor themselves – any visitor to *The Hut* had to have a fair income, anyway, or be sponsored – and the size of their spread in Montana easily exceeded that of *The Hut*, but, to appeal to a well-worn phrase, size isn't everything.

Lucas's eyes were out like organ stops (another well-worn phrase) from what he had seen on this visit. In truth, his father was equally gob-smacked (yet another over-used phrase, but it does so cover the point) but as a man with some years under his belt (see previous asides), he had learned to mask his feelings to a degree. The Calhoons' wealth had been said to have been made in less than two generations and so did not qualify as "old money". Noah was in no way ignorant or ill-educated, even though his time at Chapel Hill had been brief. Nor was he a red neck, a political liar, as so many in the United States seem to be. He was no socialist either – that doesn't get you very far in the States. Even being a Democrat with a big D didn't properly describe Noah. He was certainly a democrat with a small d, but he was, above all, a Decent man with a Big D.

His father had taken advantage of what America offers, worked hard with what *his* father had left him, and made a pile in agriculture. Noah had taken over and increased that pile again, having diversified within the food sector. Yet he remained a decent person. There are many people in the

States like that. Unfortunately, there are many more who take advantage, not only of the system but of people too, and such magnates are often loud so that their presence seems greatly over-represented. It's a great shame, Michael thought, for you will find, in America, everything from the sublime to the gor' blimey; from some truly subtle souls to the loudest of brash swanks. Michael never, ever, let the latter obscure the former.

Michael had liked Noah from the moment when they first met on one of Michael's many trips to America when still in his twenties and had formed a strong bond of mutual affection and trust with him. Now was Noah's second visit to *The Hut*. He had lost his wife to breast cancer four years earlier when she was still in her forties. Rachael and Michael had met Noah again in Montana a few short months after that tragic event and had done their best to assuage some of the huge hurt to Noah and Lucas. So it was that the friendship had grown, and the English couple were particularly proud to have earned the trust of Lucas, especially in view of his being only fifteen at that time.

Rachael and Lucas were chatting together over the fruit bowl after dinner that evening, a little more than a week after Maureen had returned home to Bill.

'I seem to remember that your great grandfather was a Scot, Lucas,' Rachael was saying. 'Did he migrate directly to Montana or go there via Canada?'

'As far as I know, it was direct. Actually, to be honest, I know very little about him,' he replied.

'I understand from your father that your grandfather made the family money from farming and that your dad increased that by diversifying into a wider range of foodstuffs. Are you interested in the family business, Lucas? Are you going to continue the tradition?'

'I probably will, but the plan is for me to take a bachelor's degree first – in agribusiness, so I should be well prepared. This trip is for me to enjoy a touch of freedom before I get on with it.'

'Have you been to Scotland yet? You know, by way of tracing your roots?'

'To tell you the truth, I have always thought of England and Scotland as being the same thing, Aunt Rachael. I guess I shouldn't say such a thing, but from the other side of the Atlantic, and Britain being so small and all, it kinda seems only natural to me.'

'Do you think of Montana and Oregon as being the same, Lucas?' Rachael asked, with a laugh.

'Okay, I deserved that,' Lucas laughed.

'That's all right, but I'm interested to know if you are curious about where your great grandfather came from. What did he do in Scotland before he emigrated? Do you know?'

'I heard once that he fled the old country to escape the cops. Something to do with illicit hooch, I think,' Lucas said, grinning, 'but I never heard any details. Say, Aunt Rachael, you're a historian, aren't you? Would you be able to find out for me, do you think? I mean, don't feel obliged or anything, but I guess it might be nice to find out something about the old guy.'

'I'll see what I can find. Mind you, I would like to begin by asking your dad if he knows anything. Word of mouth can give a great start to these things.'

Later that evening, Rachael told Noah about her new project, asking if he had any objection and, if not, whether he could expand on the little she had learned from Lucas.

'I suppose I ought to be able to help,' he said, 'but the subject never came up between my dad and me. In fact, I seem to recall him deliberately avoiding all mention of his father's background. I now wish I'd been more curious, I gotta tell you, but I wasn't. We spent most of our speaking time together talking business. Dad was a damn good businessman. I learned a lot from him. He just mentioned one day – he kinda let it just slip out, you know – that his old man had jumped ship from the cops back in Scotland. Something to do with illicit distilling. I suppose that was serious back then.'

'I doubt it, Noah. My impression is that half of Scotland were at it!' Rachael replied. 'But I'll see what I can find. There's been no name change, has there? Your family name has always been Calhoon, so far as you know?'

'I do believe so, Rachael,' he replied. 'But look now, don't you go putting too much effort into our family history. I mean, I don't mind or anything. It's just that I'm sure you have other things to do!'

'Don't worry, Noah. I'll give it a few hours. If nothing exciting turns up, I'll drop it.'

The Calhoons were planning to stay at *The Hut* for another two weeks, so Rachael felt that would define a stopping point for her. Of course, being a professional historian, albeit not normally interested in *local* history, meant that she could work fast. She knew how to search the literature, and these days Google can help with that, even if it didn't go too deep – it would be a good place to begin, at least.

Indeed, it was. Calhoon, she found, was common in the US where it was a derivative, or simplification, of Colquhoun, which was the preferred name in Scotland. She had been told that Noah's grandfather had appeared in the States around 1890, although there were doubts about the exact date. Rachael began searching newspapers in the Scottish west, because Lucas had a vague feeling that his forebear hailed from that neck of the woods. She was loath to begin with Glasgow, for there was bound to be an awful lot of material to get through from that large city. On the other hand, there were no other cities of any great size in the west, so she thought she would probably have to study Glasgow papers eventually. Rachael was always keen to take a punt, however, and thought a couple of hours searching papers from Oban might give something. If not, she would only have wasted a short time.

She soon found references to illegal distilling. None were attached to the name Colquhoun or to Calhoon, Colhoon, Colhoun or other similar names. At least none for the years 1885 to 1890, which was as far as she got in her first hour. She was tempted to quit and move on to Glasgow straight away but thought that she should see through on her promise to herself.

Talk about luck! In 1892, there was a report of a police raid on some premises owned by a Mr. Finlay Colquhoun, which were being used to distil alcohol for whisky-making. It was a sizable installation, apparently, and the raid found ten dozen cases of the illicit hooch. Rachael continued her search into papers for the rest of that year and then into the next. Oh, what a find! It seemed that three other places in and around Oban yielded similar finds, all down to this Mr. Finlay Colquhoun. The police had not, however, apprehended Mr. Colquhoun or even seen the man anywhere near these sites. His name only came into it because his was the name on the premises.

Then, in late 1894, there appeared a report of a police raid on the Isle of Mull near Lochbuie. Once again, the property was in the name of Finlay Colquhoun, but, on this occasion, the haul was huge. They weren't talking of dozens of cases of illicit booze, but thousands, and those thousands were being loaded onto a small vessel which was on the point of leaving the loch and putting out to sea. It seemed that Mr. Colquhoun wasn't a small-time spiv on the make but a fully-fledged bootlegger.

Rachael was getting very interested – she had been at all this for three days, by now – and decided that a scoundrel of this daring might well have made it into the big city papers. So off to Glasgow newspapers she went. Thank goodness that, by this time, all those records were available via the internet. Time was, when she would have been obliged to travel up to look through the records of the various newspaper offices in their old store of hard copy or, more likely, via microfiche readers located only on the premises.

Anyway, blessings of the modern era aside, Rachael struck lucky. The Colquhoun case had indeed been taken up by *The Glasgow Herald*. Mr. Colquhoun was a star, it seemed. Or to be more exact, he was what modern parlance would call a "person of interest". The parlance of *The Glasgow Herald* in 1894, however, made no bones about Mr. Colquhoun. He was a major crook, a dastardly bootlegger who had been seen on his various properties from time to time – but was never there long enough for the police to catch him, it seemed – and, as the paper put it, "the net was closing in". Rachael continued her search into several years' worth of both the Glasgow paper and the one in Oban but found only two further mentions of Mr. Colquhoun. They both said the same thing: Mr. Colquhoun could not be found; he had vanished. Furthermore, no cash relating to his disgraceful doings had been recovered. The trail had obviously gone stone cold.

Her first thoughts for her next step were to delve into records in Montana, but, only moments before setting out on that path, Rachael had a thought. Where was all that illicit hooch going? Where was that vessel, which had been stopped in Lochbuie, headed? Did the police ever find out? How was she to get to grips with that question? It was late in the afternoon when these questions surfaced, so she decided to sleep on it. She was very pleased with her discoveries so far, and she planned to tell Lucas and Noah all about them soon, but it would be nice if she could just follow the trail a bit. Wouldn't it?

One hears so much about the theories of sleep. The brain is recovering from the day's excesses. Memories are being sifted and set in stone. All that kind of thing. Theories are wonderful things. Designing experiments to validate the theories – or not, as the case may be – is very much more difficult than inventing the theories. But the expertise of the average punter is truly marvellous. "Sleep on it" goes the phrase. The brain, it seems, isn't too fussed about its reputation. The brain doesn't defer to peer review: it reviews itself. And when it gets an idea, it just knows it's right. Until it knows it isn't, but why spoil a good yarn?

Rachael had a good night. Actually, she usually did sleep very well. Her good night, however, was good until it wasn't, which is to say, that she slept like a log until she woke with a start around five thirty the next morning. That wonderful, magical piece of inspiration had not so much welled up to the surface but verily exploded into the daylight. Was Finlay Colquhoun a supplier of hooch to the Montayne family when they were the Montaignes? What a coincidence that would be! How might she check out her idea?

Breakfast provided an answer. Once fed, the brain is able to concentrate. Another good theory. She should look in the hall library. It was full of dusty, old books. Some were the standard sort of novel or geography or other factual tome which you might find almost anywhere. But some there were which she had once glanced at but found to be hand-written. Ledgers going on for page after page. Records. Records of what? Might they be records of the goings-on of the Montaigne booze-running enterprise of three generations ago? *Oh, come on!* she thought. *I couldn't get that lucky – could I?*

I'll give it a couple of hours, she decided. That had worked before – maybe it would work again. It took well over an hour in there before she was able to understand what was written in those very dusty, old books. They were, indeed, ledgers, and they did record purchases and sales of gin, brandy and whisky in the late nineteenth century. It was also abundantly clear that those transactions were between the Montaigne family and others. She was tempted to ask Lucas to help her now; help to find his great grandfather's name, if it were there. But then she thought about whether

Michael would want to have his family history broadcast, even to good friends like the Calhoons. No, she must do the work herself, and if her guess turned out to be true, then she would consult Michael before anyone else.

Michael had noticed that Rachael seemed rather preoccupied of late and eventually asked her if all was well. In the privacy of their own quarters, Rachael explained what she was doing and why. Michael was very surprised to discover that his friend's forebears were bootleggers (like his own!) and was astounded when he heard of Rachael's central query, namely: were their families connected three generations back?

'If so, is that something you wish them to learn about, Michael? I mean, for them to learn not only about their history, but yours too?'

'I'll think about that,' he said. 'Let me know what you find first, please.'

And so it was that Rachael spent the next three days pouring over the family records. Reading in libraries was a minority sport at *The Hut*, so she wasn't disturbed once in all that time. She wasn't much concerned with being overly secretive, but she just didn't want to be interrupted in her search.

On the third day, she found it. Colquhoun. That was about a purchase of seven hundred cases of "Special C Whisky" from Finlay Colquhoun from Oban, Scotland. Rachael took note of the price paid and immediately went in search of excise duties charged at that time. That didn't take too long, and it was abundantly clear that no excise had been prepaid. The entry in the ledger she had found also tabled the price the whisky was sold at. There was a healthy profit of twenty percent and no mention whatsoever of excise duty. The sale had taken place just two weeks after the purchase. If the rest of the Montaigne business was like that, it was clearly a well-run, smooth operation. Then she remembered, of course, that the transportation of the liquor from Tomberwater was down to the Etherington organisation.

Rachael called Michael in to show him her evidence.

'What kind of family have I married into?' she teased him.

'Don't act so surprised, my love. You have known about this for years. What amazes me is that written records of all that have been sitting in plain sight, as it were, in our library for generations!'

'What am I going to tell Lucas and Noah?' Rachael asked.

'I think you should tell them everything but with me present, if you don't mind, so that I can impress upon them that we don't want all this broadcast to the world. I mean, we haven't done anything wrong ourselves, but I'm just a little unsure about our historical legal position, so let's just play safe. I trust Noah totally, and I also trust him to have brought up his son as we would all like. I know that is presumptuous of me, but the sharing of mutual secrets should really only bind us all the more. I suggest that we invite them both to our private quarters this evening.'

Later that evening, Rachael told her story to the incredulous Americans. What exercised Noah more than anything else was the probability that his grandfather had seeded the Calhoon business in Montana from bootlegging in Scotland and that he might have continued in his wicked ways on arrival in the US.

'I'm not sure which I like less,' he complained. 'Those two possibilities, or my father failing to tell me anything about *his* father, for he must have known, surely.'

'Not necessarily,' Rachael said. 'Some families hold their secrets very close to their chests.'

'I'm not at all sure that I am happy to have my family history broadcast, either,' Michael said. 'I am hoping that you two will hold our secret tightly.'

Noah looked long and hard at Michael and said, with as much sincerity as he could muster, 'Michael, I promise you that neither of us will ever breathe a word about this,' and then, turning to Rachael, 'Thank you very much indeed for your work – it must have taken hours, I'm sure.'

'Noah, Lucas,' Rachael said, 'the one avenue I have not yet pursued is searching sources in Montana to try and trace the arrival of Finlay Colquhoun and, of course, to try and find out if he continued his former profession. If you don't mind, I'll leave that to you. If you do find anything, though, I would be pleased to hear about it from you in due course.

'By the way, Lucas, if you have the time while you are over here, a visit to Oban and the Isle of Mull would be a lovely thing to do. It's very beautiful there.'

Not all guests at *The Hut* become so involved with their hosts. This was a most special set of circumstances for Michael and Rachael. Coincidences are funny things. Sometimes, it is said, they come in threes.

21

Divit Deshpande must have been a large baby, seeing as his parents named him Divit, a name which suggested that he reached for the sky. But maybe that was just a coincidence. Regardless, Divit was an enormous man, probably six foot eight in old money. Everything else about him was in proportion. He wasn't at all obese, simply huge. His hands were easily twice the size of those of a "normal" man, for example, but he never crushed anyone else's when shaking. He was the archetypical "gentle giant". The same was true of his lovely but gentle voice. No one knew if he actually had an especially loud voice, though. All that other guests at *The Hut* had ever heard were gentle tones.

Michael had first met Divit in Mumbai when a guest of a high court judge there, a son of a close friend of Michael's father, Arthur, from way back. Divit's family were reputed to be seriously wealthy. Divit had rounded off his education at Oxford. He spoke immaculate English.

The source of the Deshpande wealth was not old money from some maharaja or other. It was from business. Divit's dad was big in Bollywood. Those Indian musicals which made millions at home but, as yet, barely registered in the west, were produced in their hundreds. Divit himself was not especially interested in the film industry. He was proud of his father's achievements, naturally, and obviously benefitted greatly from them, but the business didn't stir his soul. His father was somewhat disappointed but, being a supreme realist, accepted that Divit had to plot his own course in life. He spoiled him rotten, of course, so that Divit was not, as they say, short of a bob. Nevertheless, the old man did keep on with a gentle needling, for he wanted his son to establish himself in *something*. Divit understood his father's concern and even the increasing worry – and, indeed, he shared that concern himself – but so far nothing had caught his fancy.

Nothing, that is, until the day he questioned Michael about how the concept of *The Hut* came into being.

'Michael, I am enjoying myself very much at what you quaintly call *The Hut*. In many ways, your creation reminds me of collegiate life in Oxford, although I never sat at High Table, of course. But I imagine that there are similarities. Did you plan it that way, or has it just developed like that over time?'

Michael began to tell Divit about how *The Hut* came about, omitting anything about the murky family history, of course.

'Death duties meant that I could no longer own this estate outright as had my father and his before him,' he explained. 'The best thing we could think of was to amalgamate this property with that of old family friends who ran a very successful cruise business. We agreed on various practicalities, amongst which was that Rachael and I would carve out an apartment for ourselves, that we would employ a manager for day-to-day stuff, but that I would have complete authority on how the place is run, who may come as guests, and so on. I travel quite a bit, often with Rachael, which provides us with many opportunities to make new friends who might fetch up here as *Hut* guests in due course. We don't advertise, we try to provide very good food and wine at all times, and we offer one or two different forms of entertainment. Mostly, however, we have created a collegiate style, or monastic if you turn a blind eye to our excesses, shall I say, in the victuals department. In truth, that style applies mostly to dinner each day. The rest of any guest's time here is not very different from staying at *The Savoy* or some top hotel like that. And you've experienced some of the entertainment we offer, Divit: occasional cabaret, a music room where professional musicians sometimes perform, our quiet games room for bridge, chess and backgammon and, of course, the ever-popular bar and lounges. Outside, we offer croquet and tennis as well as simply ambling through the woods. Oh! And there's a hide for anyone who goes in for birdwatching. In addition to all that, the company of which *The Hut* is but a small part, owns and runs a golfing hotel and a couple of pubs not too far away, for those guests who might like to escape our confines for a day or a week. *The Hut* also owns a river launch for trips lasting days or weeks and has access to a narrowboat for those who would like to spend a similar time away in the local canal system. For the river and canal trips, we provide a cook and a sailor, shall I say, so that guests do not need to do anything but sit back and relax. We're working on a rocket to Mars, but that might be some way off yet!'

Davit's eyes widened as Michael told him all this. Michael presumed that he had made an unexpectedly fine sales-pitch and gave himself a pat on the back. The subject changed to other matters, none of which was important to either man, and the evening ended with drinks in the bar, as usual.

Next morning after breakfast, Rachael spied Divit setting out in a purposeful manner along the Grand Avenue. Over lunch, he told her that he had walked the full length of the Grand Avenue and even as far as the main entrance to the estate, and that he had encountered a pair of small deer on his return through the woods. Later on, she heard him challenge another guest to a game or two of tennis. She wondered how that would go, bearing in mind Divit's size and reach, but then she thought that the advantages of reach might be offset by the disadvantages of moving so big a man at speed. Divit's opponent, a medium-built man in his thirties (as was Divit, by the way) called Marcus, had probably made a similar calculation. As they went into dinner that evening, Rachael asked Divit how the tennis had gone.

'It was fun,' he replied happily. 'I let him win in the end, but he had to do an awful lot of running.'

Interestingly, Michael thought, Divit made strenuous efforts to collar him after the meal, as many guests were moving through to the lounge and bar.

'Michael,' he said, very politely but equally firmly. 'I do apologise to you for monopolising you for two evenings on the trot, for I do understand that you have many other guests to entertain – and I promise not to do the same tomorrow – but I would greatly appreciate your ear this evening.'

Michael, ever patient, ever polite, replied, 'Divit, that is no problem at all. What can I do for you?'

Divit steered them to a quiet corner of the room and a pair of soft armchairs. Michael sensed a long session coming and initiated proceedings by suggesting that they order some drinks.

When they had settled, Divit began a speech which was, for him, one of the more important ones of his life. The rest of the world mightn't find it so riveting, but Divit clearly did.

'Michael, you know that my father is forever chiding me to get a job. Naturally, he doesn't put it like that, but he does wish me to carve out some sort of career or occupation for myself. I don't need the money, of course, because he provides a generous allowance, but he always makes the point that an empty life is an empty life. I feel bad about it, but I haven't found anything to tempt me. Until, that is, yesterday evening when you told me all about *The Hut*. Michael, I have a great favour to ask. Could I steal your idea? I would like to create a *Hut* of my own back in India.'

Michael was astounded. 'First of all, Divit, you may *not* steal my idea. You may copy it! I am honoured that you feel so strongly about it. However, you must realise that *The Hut* was born of necessity and, it seems to me, that you have no such exigency. Furthermore, Rachael and I live on the job, so to speak. Do you want to do that? Finally, we have built up a clientele by years of patient work, as well as fortuitous chance, much of which had been accumulated well before the idea of *The Hut* came up. In short, I met many of our guests or their parents and other relatives by extension through my father. So you see, Divit, there are aspects of *The Hut* which are not easily copied.'

'Our lives are very different in detail, Michael – that is true – but there are many qualitative similarities. We both come from wealthy homes, mine made by my father; yours, I understand, from a long line of forebears. We have both been introduced to many interesting people throughout our childhoods and have continued to make many varied friends. You came to have money at your disposal, as it were; I have always had money at my disposal. You already had this estate; I can afford, I think, to buy one. I'm sure that I could persuade my father to indulge my little whim and to expand his empire into hostelry – you are not the only one to invent whimsical names for your creation, Michael! As you can appreciate, I have been thinking about this idea all night, and throughout the day while I walked around your estate. I wouldn't do it in exactly the same way as you. I don't think I could, to be honest. But I think I could create something similar to *The Hut* in a different way – something in the spirit of *The Hut*. I would buy an established estate somewhere in India. There are a great many of them in my country, many in need of a great deal of cash for refurbishment. I am absolutely sure that I could find one – several actually come to mind immediately – which would replicate *The Hut*, but in an Indian idiom, of course. I could set up a wildlife park nearby to provide one form of entertainment for international guests. I would not manage the place personally as you do, and I do understand your distinction between manager and overseer, if I may call you that. I do not think I have the necessary skills for that job – nor would I be content to stay too long in the place myself, anyway! I would seek out someone to do both jobs. Obviously, such a person would be worth his weight in gold to the enterprise, so I wouldn't hesitate to pay the right person, or preferably couple, very handsomely. I am sure I could do a great deal in the way of introducing guests to my establishment, as you do, for the reasons I have already given. It goes without saying that I would employ excellent chefs and sommeliers. What do you think, Michael? May I copy your business plan?'

'My goodness, Divit, you really have thought hard about all this. Your plan seems fine to me. If you can raise the cash – and, by God, you'll need lots of it – and if you can persuade your father and get hold of that sort of money, I think you might well succeed.'

'Michael, assuming all that, could I call on you as an occasional consultant to help me through difficult corners as they arise? Paid, of course.'

'I think you can, Divit,' Michael replied, 'but may I suggest that we both sleep on this for a while to see if we can see if there's anything you've forgotten?'

Part II

22

Isobel Dance always enjoyed visiting Copenhagen. She saw there a clean, well-ordered city where care for everyone appeared to be its clearest characteristic. Mind you, she had heard that the social ideals of the nineteen seventies had been whittled away somewhat by the time the second decade of the twenty-first century came around.

She had landed at Kastrup airport just before nine o'clock that morning, and the air outside was clear and the weather sunny, albeit cool, for this was still (just) formally the winter season. A car had been arranged to take her to her hotel downtown. She left the secure zone and looked for a card bearing her surname. There it was. A courteous man, by no means obsequious, led her to a large, black Lexus. As they drove along the dead-straight Amager Landevej into Copenhagen, Isobel saw, on her left in the distance, the dense conglomeration of Copenhagen's business district where she was scheduled to visit next day. For now, however, she was bound for the older and far prettier centre and, in particular, for the *Hotel D'Angleterre* in the old square of Kongens Nytorv. She smiled at the thought that Kongens Nytorv meant King's New Square in the seventeenth century: everything old was once new, of course.

Isobel had blossomed in the past four years. Her reputation as a financial assessor or detective had grown steadily. She now worked freelance, her services and skill being sought out by clients from all over the globe. Now in her late thirties and even more striking to behold, she had acquired an air of great confidence about her. To those who didn't know her, she appeared as assured and formidable; to those who did, she still chuckled a little as her eyes flashed at the sheer fun of living. Isobel seemed to have it all. And why not? Someone has to maintain the average.

Her room downtown was everything one could expect of one of the best hotels in Copenhagen; indeed more, because she had been assigned a room at the front of that beautiful building overlooking the square itself with its resplendent circle of trees. She only had the rest of this day to enjoy the city, for she anticipated having to concentrate on work after that. That being the case, she was determined to revisit some of her favourite haunts while she could. In particular, Copenhagen's famous "walking street", Støget.

Having planned her day way before even leaving home, she had dressed appropriately for a long stroll: designer jeans and flats. Strøget is a succession of something like nine old streets, which between them lead from Kongens Nytorv at one end to the Radhuspladsen, or City Hall Square, at the other. That is quite a long walk and there is much to distract the visitor along the way.

In earlier days, she had first visited *Illums Bolighus,* an upmarket furnishings store. Since those days, she had seen what stores in Florence could offer and which had taken the shine off the *Bolighus* somewhat. There was also Jensen's jewellers which seemed to concentrate on all things silver, linked with stylish Danish design. Nearer the Radhuspladsen end of this long pedestrian thoroughfare was a jeweller who specialised in amber. There were many cafés, of course, and restaurants, too. Isobel was not looking for anything in particular on this occasion. This was more by way of a homecoming for her.

By the time that she had walked from one end of Strøget to the other and back, it was time for lunch. Again, she had planned her day in some detail, for she had decided that rather than have lunch at the hotel – excellent, though, she knew it would be – she would eat at Gorm's, a restaurant at low-level along the south side of Nyhavn, the old harbour comprising one of the fingers of water projecting right into the old central square of Copenhagen, Kongens Nytorv itself. Low-level merely refers to the place being a semi-basement, rather than there being any sort of pejorative aspects such as being associated with dubious sexual establishments. She had even booked a table for herself, well in advance. She had chosen the south side – where as far as she was able to ascertain, there was only one restaurant to choose from, while there were maybe ten on the north side – partly because one could see the more interesting side of the harbour from there. It specialised in simple but well-cooked Italian food, for Isobel knew that there would be opportunities to sample Scandinavian fish dishes during the rest of her stay.

After lunch, she meandered along the quayside for a while, looking at the small fishing boats moored there and generally absorbing, once more, the atmosphere of one of her favourite cities. She had planned a treat for her evening, so she decided then to return to her hotel to relax and, for the umpteenth time, to remind herself about Chen Hong Tao, a man styling himself in the west as Jim Chen.

Mr. Chen was a fabulously wealthy entrepreneur, reputed to be worth tens of billions of pounds, who was thought to have made his money basically from anything that moved plus anything that didn't. No one, apparently, could pin down Chen's main line of business. He must have had an enormous number of fingers, because he seemed to have the proverbial finger in every pie. Many of these pies were easy enough to define, locate, and probably, to quantify. Others were far less clear and might have been of dubious legality. Not that Chen had ever been charged with anything wrong. But with his money, maybe that is no surprise.

In any case, Isobel had no direct reason to suppose that Chen actually dealt in anything murky, not even in his gaming and casino enterprises. It seemed that Chen's forays into that area of human folly were but modest, in line with his, to Isobel's mind, very careful choices of business enterprise. It was natural that Isobel should have put some work into finding out as much as she could about her new client, of course, if only to protect herself and, in any case, information of that sort all went into her accumulated wisdom. You can never know when such knowledge will come in handy. All she knew about Jim Chen one week earlier was that he had asked her to carry out some financial investigations for him. He had offered a very good fee and all expenses paid. *Why be churlish?* Isobel had asked herself.

By late afternoon, she had showered, changed into a slinky evening dress and was to be seen in the hotel bar, martini in hand. *Michael would be proud of me*, she thought suddenly.

Why she had suddenly thought of Michael was completely unclear. It had been four years since she and Harvey had helped him at *The Hut*. Harvey was another name which hadn't crossed her memory in all that time, for she had been so busy building her success. She raised her glass a little to her memories of him as she watched the passersby outside.

Shortly afterwards, she wandered through into the dining room. She had opted for an early dinner to allow her time for her upcoming evening's treat. The menu of this Michelin-Guide-starred restaurant was almost enough to tempt her to overindulge, but that would have spoiled her evening. Therefore, with the steely discipline learned from years of overindulgence, Isobel held herself to half a dozen oysters, accompanied by bleak roe and horseradish; a pigeon "royal" with sweet onions, aged balsamic vinegar, and *albufera* with madeira sauce; and a panna cotta with burned meringue, honey tuille and citrus. With considerable restraint, she took recommended wines for each course – but only one glass in each case! Oh! What it is to be young! What it is to have steely self-restraint!

The weather was acceptably mild outside as, in her shawl, she crossed the square to The Royal Danish Theatre. She was headed to a performance of, amongst other pieces, *The Miraculous Mandarin*, the ballet by Béla Bartók.

Ballet had been a passion of Isobel's ever since visiting this city for the first time, fifteen or so years earlier. There is something magical about the Danish ballet style (quite apart, by the way, from the cheapness of the seats in The Royal Theatre, which are subsidised incredibly well by Danish taxes), a style owed to the pioneering work of August Bournoville – who the Danes pronounce Bonn-ville, by the way – a nineteenth-century dancer and ballet master who established a uniquely Danish style of ballet. There is a quality in Danish ballet dancing that defies gravity. Dancers appear to stay in the air longer than is actually possible. They float and they jump very high, often returning to earth with a soft plié. It is quite magical.

Isobel found her seat in the middle of the auditorium and settled down to an evening which she already knew would be wonderful. Typically, at that theatre, the programme was divided into two unequal parts in which the last item in part one is the main feature, so to speak – on this occasion, Barók's *Miraculous Mandarin*. The second, and usually shorter, half is given over to lighter pieces, which this evening, were collectively called *Aimez vous Bach?*

What on earth is that going to be about? Isobel wondered.

The program was opened by a balletic interpretation of an old, Danish folk story which was not known to Isobel. It was clearly a beautiful story, but, at first, Isobel wondered if the lead ballerina was not up to snuff, for she danced in a faltering way which was really quite embarrassing. However, as the story unfolded, she became a little more competent. It took quite some time before Isobel realised that the changes in dancing skill were all deliberate, such that the development of the ballerina's technique was a metaphor for the development of a young girl into a fully aware young woman. It was danced so gently, with such tenderness, that, opener though it might be, it could have satisfied anyone as the *plat du jour*. It was quite long, certainly taking up an equal share of the first half of the evening's performance. That ballet was clearly well-known to the local audience who applauded rapturously as the principals and then the whole company, took their bows.

There followed a five-minute pause while the stage was being reset behind the fire curtain. And then Bartók's masterpiece began. Exciting music depicted the chaos of the city in this pantomimic and, in its early days, shocking and immoral story.

The audience were introduced to three poverty-stricken tramps who force a girl to entice passersby into their room so they can rob them. Her first two attempts succeed, only to yield first an old rake who seeks to slake his lust and refuses to consider money, and then an impoverished student. After delightful dances depicting the sentiments and the action, both are thrown out by the tramps. Finally, they see the bizarre figure of a wealthy Chinese mandarin who they manoeuvre inside and onto the balcony of their room. The girl inflames the lust of the mandarin who takes centre stage at that point.

The set itself generally depicted the street scene in rather diminished light. The balcony, running part-way across the back of the stage, was in near-total darkness. Some ten or fifteen minutes into the action, the shadowy figure of the mandarin appeared in the middle of this balcony. He was hard to see but, nevertheless, the audience was made fully aware of him. There came a point of great excitement in the dancing below, depicting the rising passion of the mandarin as the girl increased her enticements, when without warning, the musical intensity rose to a tremendous crescendo and crash from the brass, so much so, that Isobel's and probably everyone else's hair stood up on end. At the same time – and the timing of the choreography at this point was incredibly precise – the shadowy figure on the balcony leapt down onto the stage, landing miraculously exactly as the brass section made its shattering crash. With equally precise timing, a bright spotlight picked up the face of the mandarin who had just jumped to the stage and was briefly in a sort of squat posture with his arms outstretched. He was wearing an iridescent lime-green mask. The moment was electric, and the audience – every single person there – was stunned.

Afterwards, the tramps rob the mandarin and try to kill him. After vacillation from the girl, which was represented by some beautifully choreographed dancing, the mandarin is finally allowed to live, and he falls passionately upon the girl who ultimately does not resist.

When Isobel recalled the ballet much later, it was the moment of the electric entrance of the mandarin which had burned itself into her memory more than any other.

There followed a good twenty minutes to half an hour interval, as is typical of The Royal Theatre, in which patrons may stretch their legs walking upon a wide balcony or, of course, indulging in some liquid refreshment. This was all brought to an end by a discreet bell, and the audience piled back into the theatre for what everyone anticipated as the "fun" half of the evening. The only clue given to *Aimez vous Bach?* was a short note stating that the piece was to be performed by the full company of junior ballet dancers – by the trainees, in effect. That, and a list of about eight separate pieces, labelled as solos or *pas de deux, pas de trois, pas de quatre* and so on.

The collection began with two solos danced by female, and then, male dancers. As the young dancers did their thing – and did it very nicely indeed, it had to be said – an older male dancer strode up and down before them and to the side, making dramatic gestures with his arms as he did so. He was the only fully-fledged member of the company to be seen and was clearly to be regarded as the young ones' teacher. Each piece was enthusiastically applauded by the audience as the whole set progressed.

Then came a *pas de deux* danced by a fresh-faced youth and his delicate partner. There were a couple of those. What had all this got to do with Johann Sebastian? one might well ask. Well, the music chosen to accompany all these dances were all well-known pieces by the Master.

Who, Isobel wondered, *had the cheek to couple ballet with JSB?*

It all worked superbly well. Several pieces were preludes from *The Well-Tempered Klavier* but played, not by a solo piano or harpsichord, but by the ballet orchestra. However, when it was the turn of the *pas de trois*, and the orchestra broke into that most famous organ piece, *The Toccata and Fugue in D minor*, the audience broke into spontaneous applause at the sheer audacity of the idea. By the time the fugue began, the ballet grouping enlarged to four and then more. That piece of music is quite long, of course, and after a while, the audience became aware that the senior, dancing the part of instructor, had wandered offstage. It was so cleverly done, because the juniors managed to let the audience know that this had happened simply by surreptitious glances amongst themselves. Some little time later, the juniors made clear that, by now, they too had all become aware of their teacher's absence, whereupon they discontinued their beautiful, classical dancing and broke into jive, without breaking the musical pulse, however, and which they did very well, by the way, as one would have expected, of course. That continued for some time. In due course the teacher returned, feigned shock and anger, and the juniors immediately snapped straight back into the classical idiom.

The audience loved it and the applause continued for some time. All in all, enough pieces were chosen so as to provide opportunities for all of the juniors – some, obviously very green indeed – to have an opportunity to perform. The whole thing was so charming.

Isobel, like everyone else there, was enthralled and delighted, and all showed their appreciation as the evening came to its close.

'I have never been disappointed by the Danish Ballet,' she told a woman who had joined her for a drink back at *The Hotel D'Angleterre* afterwards.

They spent a happy half hour or so comparing their days in the city, before Isobel, with an eye on her important meeting on the morrow, bid her drinking partner goodnight.

<h1 style="text-align:center">23</h1>

At ten o'clock next morning, the same shiny, black Lexus arrived to whisk Isobel away for her interview with Chen.

'Call me Jim. All right if I call you Isobel? Hotel all right? Please take a seat.'

Jim Chen obviously didn't waste much time on pleasantries. That was not to say he was at all unpleasant, just a man always in a hurry. He probably thought that he knew everything worth knowing about Isobel, anyway. He had certainly done his homework on her. Isobel liked this way of working. Get to the point straight away. Don't mess about.

'You come highly recommended, Isobel, so I'll get to the point straight away. I am a very wealthy man. To be exact, those who know of me, know me as a very wealthy man, but only by repute. You will not have been able to find anything more specific. I invest in just about anything. I buy and sell. I lend money and collect interest. I invest. I have a reputation in some quarters as a bit of an easy touch. I am not.'

Chen smiled broadly at Isobel at this point. She believed him completely. This man was no push-over.

He continued: 'What do you think of my office here in Copenhagen, Isobel? Pretty modest, eh? I have offices all over the world and they're all like this. Functional. After all, the rent is pretty high in premises like these. Not that that's a problem, of course, because I own the whole building. On the other hand, I am losing that rent from someone else. Modesty is good.' He grinned even more broadly at his guest. 'Have you heard of *Marchant Enterprises*, Isobel?'

Isobel could not hide her surprise completely. Although she knew a little more, her previous interaction with that company had been through Michael at *The Hut* when she was helping Harvey. *I wonder how Harvey is now?* she mused. A muse like that can last but one second. There is always time for one of those.

'Actually, I have,' she replied. 'I once stayed at a semi-private estate which is part of the *Marchant Enterprises* business. However, most of their operation is concerned with cruise ships, I believe.'

Jim Chen's smile widened to a grin. 'You get around, don't you Isobel?' he said.

'You take your luck as it comes, Jim,' she replied.

Chen's smile broadened even more. 'Okay. This is why am hiring you – I hope you are happy with my terms, by the way.'

A high per diem rate with a generous minimum, plus expenses equivalent to her stay at *The Hotel D'Angeterre*. She was more than happy.

'Thank you, yes,' she said. It would be silly to over-enthuse.

'The CEO of *Marchant Enterprises*, Geoffrey Etherington, has approached me for a large loan. Two hundred and fifty million pounds, to be exact. Yes,' Chen said, as Isobel's eyes widened. 'Not an insignificant sum. The interesting aspect of his request is, of course, that such a sum might normally be sought from one or other of the world's great banking institutions. The question, therefore, is why does he come to me? I make no secret of the fact that I charge significantly more than the banks. I do so because, when people come to me, they are having trouble finding support from the banks. In other words, they are a riskier proposition than the average bank is game to take on. Jim Chen, that spiv Chinaman who plays risky games with casinos might well be their saviour. Well, Ms. Dance, let me tell you; I didn't get where I am today by being a soft-touch spiv.'

Mr. Chen is getting a little worked up, Isobel thought, but held her tongue.

'So, what I'd like you to do, Isobel,' Jim said, in a calmer voice now, 'is to find out what sort of trouble Etherington is in. I am prepared to lend money to – how shall I say – less secure ventures, but I need to know the nature and extent of the applicant's troubles. Does your knowing this Michael Montayne fellow make for any difficulties with the task I have set you?'

'Not at all,' Isobel replied immediately.

Was she professional or what, for goodness' sake? Only later, when recalling every little detail of her interview, did she realise that she hadn't mentioned Michael's name in her earlier admission to having been at *The Hut*. It was then that she realised that Jim Chen had already found the answers to his questions. Isobel's part in all this was clearly to confirm what Jim already knew. Once again, Jim Chen was clearly no fool. And he was certainly loath to waste time. He hadn't even offered Isobel a coffee that morning. Her task had been set. He had seen her in the flesh. Job done.

She had been driven back to her hotel, and her chauffeur had given her a number to ring when she was ready to be taken to the airport. Clearly, it had been up to her how many days she stayed in Copenhagen.

*

She decided to leave later that day. Business is business. She was sitting in one of the smaller hotel lounges, on the point of booking her return flight, when out of the blue, she heard, 'Izzy, darling! Fancy meeting you here!'

Hillary's voice was unmistakable.

'Hillary! Likewise. When did you arrive?'

'Two days ago. You know how much I love Copenhagen. And the ballet, of course.'

'Oh, I so wish I had known you were around. I arrived yesterday and mooched around on my own, killing time, in a way, before the main event. I went to the ballet yesterday evening,' Isobel told her cousin.

'So did I! Wasn't it marvellous?'

Isobel had a thought. 'Are you here alone?'

'Yes.'

'Damn. We could have watched the ballet together. Anyway, what did you think of it? Wasn't it marvellous!'

'It was. I'd seen the *Miraculous Mandarin* once before, although we saw a stunning performance last night,' Hillary enthused. 'Wasn't the entry of the mandarin extraordinarily well done?'

'And timed to perfection,' Isobel agreed, and then, 'Changing the subject for a moment, how long are you staying in Copenhagen?'

'Three more days,' Hillary told her, paused for an almost undetectable moment, and then coloured up a shade as she continued, 'Gerald is joining me tomorrow.'

Isobel grinned widely at her cousin. 'So, Harvey and I won, then,' she said.

'What on earth do you mean?' Hillary bridled.

'Well, you and Gerald were trying to pair me off with Harvey four years ago at *The Hut*. We knew full well what your game was and decided to return the compliment. It seems that we succeeded!'

'What is the situation between you and Harvey?' asked Hillary, crudely eliding Isobel's question.

'We're friends,' Isobel replied, and like a dog with a bone, 'And what's the situation between you and Gerald?'

'We're friends,' Hillary replied, adopting a distant gaze.

Isobel wasn't having any of that. 'Good friends?' she persisted.

'Good friends,' Hillary agreed.

'Very good friends? Isobel clearly didn't know when to stop.

'Yes, darling. We're lovers. Happy now?'

'Completely, cousin dear.'

'Are you here alone?' asked Hillary, suddenly having an obvious thought.

'Yes, I am. I'm here on business, actually,' Isobel replied.

'How long are you staying in Copenhagen?' Now it was Hillary's turn to ask.

Isobel was on the point of saying that she was off today, when her business mind switched in. 'I thought I'd stay till the day after tomorrow.'

'Oh, lovely, we can all go out somewhere together.'

'Yes, and it will be lovely to catch up with things,' Isobel said.

'Where shall we dine this evening? Here in the hotel?'

'Why not?' said Isobel. 'I'm sure that Jim won't mind too much.'

As they settled into a preprandial drink or two, the cousins were rarely silent for even a moment. They hadn't seen each other for a year or so – and even then, only briefly – and there was so much to catch up on. Their dinner was as excellent as one would expect of *The Hotel D'Angeterre*, and by the time they took off for their beds, they were just a little squiffy.

*

Gerald arrived early next morning. *He probably caught the same plane as I did two days ago*, Isobel mused.

Isobel had met up with Hillary and Gerald for lunch at the *Sejlklubbernes* restaurant, north of Hellerup and overlooking the Sound, that stretch of water which separates Denmark from Sweden. Gerald had found this place on an earlier visit to the city and wanted to revisit it and to share his memory with Hillary. It was lovely to sit close to water and watch the comings and goings of the many small yachts around.

Their lunch was simple but delicious: oysters followed by a variety of smørrebrød and finished off with a lemon tart and coffee. That, and a couple of bottles of pleasant Chilean wines, made for a long, leisurely catchup. There was so much to talk about and, of course, much of it was between Hillary and Gerald. That is not to say that Isobel felt in any way to be a gooseberry. Indeed, Gerald seemed particularly pleased to see Isobel; probably, she intuited, on behalf of his nephew, although his name, which did come up, was not to the fore.

Isobel waited until the conversation cooled a little before she remarked, with expert and subtle control, 'I was saying to Hillary yesterday, Gerald, that it was four years since we all met at *The Hut*. That was a delightful time and so different from other breaks I have taken. Tell me, how did the whole concept of *The Hut* come about?' She hoped that her question seemed casual.

It seemed so, for Gerald was only too happy to launch into everything he knew about how Michael had created the concept, how it had been forced upon him by death duties, how it was all part of the travel and leisure business called *Marchant Enterprises*, and even as much as Gerald knew about the agreement made between Michael and his father with Geoffrey Etherington and his.

'I first met Michael at university in Bristol,' Gerald told her. 'That's where Michael met Geoffrey and, for that matter, Rachael. Geoffrey was Michael's best man when he married Rachael. Those three have been bosom pals ever since.'

'Is the financial status of *The Hut* sound, do you think?' Isobel asked. 'I mean, the place treats its guests almost like royalty but, unlike pretty-well any of the world's great hotels, its overheads have to be met by, not hundreds of guests at any one time, but by – what? – forty at most, I would think; probably less. I assume that *The Hut* is not some kind of loss-leader for *Marchant*, but its margin must be very small: maybe just three percent. What do you think?'

'I've often wondered about that myself, to tell you the truth. Yes, I think your estimate of the margin is probably right. I presume that it was a matter discussed at the time *Marchant Voyages* became *Marchant Enterprises*. Anyway, the thing has been going now for the best part of twenty-five years, so I guess it all works out.'

'Why do you think *Marchant Voyages* agreed to – what do I say? – amalgamate with Michael's ancestral home? Or maybe a better question is why did they agree to letting him have a permanent home there? I presume it is permanent, by the way?'

Gerald could not really answer questions like that. He simply did not know why. Isobel pursued the matter a little further before deciding to leave it alone. She had probably learned as much as she could from Gerald, and any more nosing on her part might arouse suspicions.

She excused herself from her friends for five minutes while she fixed up her return flight and her chauffeur. When she returned, she announced that she would leave Copenhagen late that afternoon.

'Why so soon?' asked Hillary.

'My business has become rather urgent, I'm afraid,' Isobel explained. 'It's been wonderful to meet up like this. I'm sure you two will find plenty to do without me.'

She looked at Hillary with such a sweet smile and with such a twinkle in her eye that her cousin coloured up. *Why can't I control myself?* thought Hillary.

Isobel was back in her own apartment in London by a little after eight thirty.

24

Geoffrey Etherington was relaxing at home one evening some ten years earlier, enjoying what he – deservedly, it should immediately be said – considered a well-earned whisky. His father had died some years ago and Geoffrey, his heir and, in many ways, creator of *Marchant Enterprises*, had been CEO of the company for seven years even before his dad's passing. His father had been proud of his son and approved very much of his handling of the company, and he had told him so on several occasions.

Geoffrey had been a bright spark at university and had fulfilled his early promise in spades. He was proud of himself, but far from complacent. Building a company was one thing; maintaining it was another; expanding it was even more taxing. And Geoffrey desperately wanted to grow his company. His father had done so, and now it was his turn, his responsibility.

So, that evening found him in a mellow mood, thinking back over his years as boss and those of his father before him when *Marchant Enterprises* was called *Marchant Voyages*.

He had learned, even before his good friend, Michael Montayne, about the – Geoffrey paused and smiled in his reminiscing to find a more delicate word than had immediately come to mind – dubious history of the Etherington-Montaigne collaboration, which had amassed the fortunes of both families, and to the business which grew from that in time, under the guidance of Geoffrey's dad, to be *Marchant Voyages*. For it was, indeed, Geoffrey's dad, Bob, who had realised that the world was changing rapidly and that there was neither honour nor safety in continuing the bootlegging of the earlier years; of the earlier century. He had begun to ship coal in his little fleet of tugboats and lighters: coal and potatoes and an increasing variety of other goods around Britain, via the rivers and canal system which was rapidly expanding at that time. Initially, there hadn't been much money in that business – certainly not compared with the old bootlegging days – but it was legal, safe and respectable. Bob had worked very hard growing his firm, using the illicit capital he inherited, very wisely, to build a solid enterprise. A tax-paying enterprise! Not that he paid much tax in the early days, if only because his profits were small and rather little since then – his accountant was well-paid.

Over several years, Bob's firm grew. At first, this growth was to be seen in terms of the steadily increasing number of narrowboats plying the canals, and later, in the purchase of an increasing number of small ships delivering goods to and from ports around the coast of Britain. So, the narrowboat and lighter trade began to be amalgamated with that around the coastal waters of Britain. In due course, Bob began to invest in cargo-handling equipment: hoppers, cranes and powered conveyor belts, for example, at one or two of the ports his vessels regularly patronised.

Bob's greatest triumph, especially in the eyes of his successor and son Geoffrey, was to expand beyond the confines of his mother island. Bob gradually, and with all due care and caution, bought first one, then two larger cargo ships and began trading across the North Sea, initially to Amsterdam and Rotterdam and later into Scandinavia. He made sure to employ Dutch, Norwegian, Swedish and Danish seamen on his ships, as appropriate, so that his property was treated properly and safely in foreign ports. Etherington shipping became well regarded wherever he traded, an esteem which Bob greatly treasured. He used to say that it marked out his company as a serious player in shipping circles.

One day, not long after his first forays into the continent, something happened which turned the business tide for Bob Etherington, something which changed the focus and the direction. In itself, it was a simple thing, which another man might not have thought much about.

On that day in 1951, a man called Erik Hansen – a name which was to lodge in Bob's mind for ever – approached the master of one of Bob's cargo ships, asking whether he might take a couple of paying passengers across the water to Oslo. Many a master might have simply agreed, pocketed the fare and said nothing. This master contacted his boss and asked for his opinion on the matter. Bob Etherington gave his permission for Hansen – and his wife, as it turned out – to berth in whatever space the ship's master could find, and to take twenty percent of the fare for his own pocket. The passengers were delighted, the ship's master was delighted, and Bob had a new idea. He would go into the passenger business. Of course, it didn't happen just like that. As with everything else to do with his business, Bob put in the homework, looked into how big the market for passenger travel was and might become, and what costs and profit margins attached to that trade. Bob spent several months examining the travel business, speaking to as many knowledgeable people – owners, in particular – as he could find. His conclusion was that there would be many, many more Erik Hansens, their wives, and other relatives willing to pay for travel across the sea and, indeed, many, many of them willing to pay for a round trip during which they would be able to explore sights and places they had formerly only read about. Holidaymakers. That was what it was about, and Bob Etherington's research strongly suggested that he would make a bomb from providing such people with comfortable passenger-only ships in which to sail.

Of course, other shipping companies were already in the game. Where else had Bob gleaned his information, for goodness' sake? But Bob's enthusiasm and business nous convinced him that there was room in that business for one more at least. Room for him. He knew, of course, that he couldn't compete with the likes of *P&O*. No, he would find a niche in the smaller end of town, by taking modest numbers of passengers on two, three and four-week holidays around fjords of Norway, to the many famous ports in the Baltic, along the continental coast of the North Sea. He would begin his new life as owner of one or two small passenger ships, with maybe one hundred or fewer berths, he thought. He would change the name of his company. Henceforth, it was to be called *Marchant Voyages*. The more he thought about his new venture, the more he became convinced to begin it with two vessels, so that there might be some savings that way – economies of scale, he said – and so he set about finding some second-hand ships – used, rather than old, which he thought would involve him in less financial risk than the exorbitant price of new vessels. And in any case, he argued, new ships take quite some time to build, so it might be a couple of years before he could get cracking. Bob was a careful man and could be patient, but not that patient.

Once again, Bob did his homework, eventually finding two reasonably similar ships, one with eighty berths, the other with one hundred, for forty-one million pounds between them. The larger one was fifteen years old, the smaller thirteen. Both were in excellent condition, the former having recently had a modest refit. Bob had already been to his bank to negotiate a ten-year loan for about that sum and had been more than gratified to find that they were willing to play. Naturally, he had employed a team of ship's engineers to examine both ships very carefully. Everything was fine, not to say shipshape. The deal was struck, the new company name was registered, and Bob had moved into a new business. He had every intention of keeping the old business going, meanwhile, for there was nothing wrong with it. It had got him this far and would always be good for a quid.

Bob took over the crews of both vessels, of course, but looked very carefully into what he had inherited, for he realised from the beginning that the crews could make or break him in this new venture. All crew members were sacked on the spot but told to reapply immediately. He wanted them to know who their new boss was. He tried hard not to embarrass any of the old crews, but he was firm about who he wanted in charge. As far as possible, he moved a man sideways rather than demote him and gave him every opportunity to maintain his wages in the process. Once the new business was under way and stable, Bob was quick to reward effort as soon as he saw it. He earned his crews' respect and built loyalty, for that way, he insisted, lies success.

Bob Etherington played his customers in much the same way. They were well-fed, albeit with no more than the fashion of the day, and the crew were instructed to accede to every little whim so far as they were able. Initially, Bob chose the routes himself, but, even from the beginning, he made considerable efforts to find out what customers wanted. Where did they want to go? Did they wish to disembark anywhere? If so, for how long? Were any of them prepared to pay more for superior accommodation? How long a trip did they prefer? He could not, of course, accommodate all the requests he received, but he built a picture of customer demand, and as time went by, he gradually began to change the style of his company and move up a notch.

He also began to recognise that he wasn't running a shipping company which just happened to carry passengers, but rather one which satisfied long-held dreams. He was selling holidays. He was in people management. It was inevitable, therefore, that he expanded his enterprise into land-based hotels as well as water-borne ones.

He bought two hotels on the coasts of Britain: one in Southampton, the other in Blackpool. The latter resort was, of course, a long-standing favourite destination for holidaymakers from all over Britain but especially from the North of England, while the former provided a useful take-off point for those wishing to holiday on the South Coast. Southampton was also useful, in some respects, for passengers going out to or coming in from international destinations via the great ships of the *P&O, Cunard* and other grand lines. Bob's first thoughts about hotels had simply been those of a hotelier, of a provider of holidays. His second, which followed hard on the heels of the first – in fact, he was hard-pressed to separate them in the end – was that he might couple his land-based and water-based hotels: stay at our hotel for a few days, take a trip around the coast for a few days more, and stay at another of our hotels after that. All right, that was rather ambitious, he knew full well, but it might be an idea worth exploring.

By the time that Geoffrey entered Bristol University in the late '60s, all these things were reasonably well established, and *Marchant Voyages* was probably worth about three hundred million pounds. That was a lot of money. Geoffrey was keen to go to university, and he intended to do well there, but he had already made up his mind to follow his father into the business. He thundered home with the top first in Economics. He was a star! He was pleased with himself, his mother was crying with joy and his father was beside himself with pride. Geoffrey was bound to be a wonderful asset to the family business. Great things were expected; great things would undoubtedly happen.

As we know, it was while up at Bristol that Geoffrey met Michael and, through him, Rachael. However, what was not made clear earlier is that Geoffrey introduced Michael to his father on one occasion when Bob had come to visit his son early in his third year at Bristol. Bob had recognised the name Montayne immediately, of course, from the "bad old days" of his and Arthur's fathers, when the latter's surname was Montaigne, but he made no mention of the fact at that time. It was the Etherington's and the Montaigne's past goings-on together, of course, which made Bob sit up when Geoffrey proposed Michael's scheme to solve his death duty problem back in 1970. And it had been then, rather than days later, when Arthur Montagne delivered his denouement of the family histories, that Bob appraised his only son of the murky family past. Geoffrey had been amazed but not unduly worried, a reaction which had rather surprised his father. It was perhaps a first inkling of Geoffrey's future single-mindedness when it came to the matter of his father's business.

Anyway, Geoffrey and his father hammered out an arrangement which suited them in the first instance. Certainly, Geoffrey wanted to help Michael, but he also wanted to make a good deal for *Marchant Voyages*. As Bob pointed out so strongly to his son, the construct which was to become *The Hut* would be working on the thinnest of margins. Certainly, there were many fine hotels throughout the world which served food and wine equal to that proposed for *The Hut*, and even with comparable entertainments, but they worked off a customer base of several hundred. Several hundred paying customers, that is, whose steep charges were able to offset the standing army of servants above and below deck, as Bob put it, or front and back of house, as a hotelier might say. *The Hut* was likely to have forty paying guests at most. If it could be made to provide a return of three percent, they would be lucky.

Bob's instinct was to walk away from such a deal. But they were talking about friends; indeed, of past allies. Bob was perfectly well aware of how much, from the beginning, his company had gained by its intimate association with the old Montaigne family. He recognised that he owed them. He also felt strongly that he owed himself and his son. By the time that Bob and Michael came back together to address both families, the Etheringtons had set the terms.

Those terms were that the shares which the old Montaigne family had in the old Etherington business, worth some sixteen million pounds at that time, would continue to be held by the Montayne family and would accrue value according to the fortunes of the new company, *Marchant Enterprises*. The complete estate of Tomber Hall and its grounds was to become part of the new company which would, in due course, be responsible for the death duties which had brought on this crisis for the Montayne family in the first place. The Montaynes were allowed to live on in a new apartment within the hall and enjoy all amenities of the whole estate. Michael would run the construct, henceforth to be called *The Hut*, as he saw fit, always recognising that he would bear responsibility for its commercial success. Michael would have a seat on the Board of *Marchant Enterprises*, control over which business would be in the hands of its CEO and the board, with voting rights apportioned according to the holdings at the time.

When *Marchant Enterprises* was established, the Montayne estate was valued at thirty million pounds after those death duties had been paid. It was also proposed by Michael, and agreed in due course by the Etheringtons, that the properties within *The Hut* enterprise should comprise the old Montaigne estate in its entirety, together with two specified nearby hotels, one of which was a golfing hotel complete with its own course, and three named public houses, in addition, of course, to the *Tomber Pot* which had always been part of the family estate.

Michael and his father, Arthur, had been delighted with this deal, but Bob was at pains to emphasise that the Etheringtons were only agreeing to this scheme out of their long association and friendship with the Montaignes, now Montaynes, and that they had doubts about the business efficacy of *The Hut* concept. He emphasised repeatedly that they expected *The Hut,* in toto, to return a profit, however meagre that was likely to be. The Montayne family understood that perfectly, and it's worth recording even at the early stage of this account, that *The Hut* actually did make money for the parent company; never very much, but a profit, nevertheless.

25

The following two decades were successful and busy times for *The Hut*. They were also busy and even more successful for *Marchant Enterprises* as a whole. Geoffrey had shadowed his father for the first five years, learning everything he could, not only about the family firm itself, but also about the travel and leisure business in general, which had begun to expand around the world. When Bob retired, feeling utterly confident that his son would do him proud, *ME* had bought a major golfing hotel near Aberdeen in Scotland and had begun to ship passengers to that port from others on the English coast and from the continent.

By now, Geoffrey had grown sufficiently confident to begin scratching his itches. He wanted, not merely to see his dad's ideas through – and he had – but to initiate some ideas of his own. He wanted to expand the company on the continent. He promoted one of his more able assistants, a bright, young woman called Elise Walker, who spoke Spanish, Italian and French, as well as having a degree in business management, to oversee that expansion. He set her the task of seeking out suitable hotels which he might buy on the Mediterranean and the Adriatic. In particular, he was interested in hotels in Spain, Italy and Croatia. While Elise set about that task, which took the best part of a year, Geoffrey began scouting for two more ships, and this time he was looking for two-hundred- and three-hundred-berth vessels.

Elise struck gold first, finding a delightful, fifty-room hotel in Alghero in Sardinia. Alghero had so much to offer the tourist, from the old town itself within the province of Catalan on the northwest coast of Sardinia, which had been under Spanish domination for four centuries, to the many bays and beaches, the beautiful *Caves of Neptune*, an old lighthouse on a rocky promontory, and various archaeological sites in the surrounding countryside. She had previously visited Alghero as a student and fallen in love with the place. She had retained a particularly clear and fond memory of those wonderful caves, recalling large formations of beautiful stalactites hanging from all over the roof of that awesome grotto. The entrance to the main cave is only a metre or so above sea level at the foot of that high promontory, accessed, however, by climbing down hundreds of steps from a car park at the top. This was most certainly a tourist attraction for the young and fit. The same was true of the rapidly expanding sport of scuba diving in that part of the world, for other nearby caves, which were permanently submerged, offered a marvellous opportunity for those with a love of beauty and exercise at the same time. She could foresee an important role for the *Hotel Catalan* in *ME's* future.

From her room there, where she stayed for several days to explore the possibilities of the locale, she had a clear view of the old harbour and of its many small fishing and touring vessels. She envisaged *ME* owning a small vessel for transporting passengers from an *ME* cruise ship to the harbour wharf, and a larger and swankier boat for day excursions along the immediate coast. The hotel was in need of some love and care but seemed basically sound.

When she presented her case to Geoffrey, she urged her boss to accompany her on a short holiday to see the place for himself. He did, and he was delighted. He was so delighted that he and Elise got married five months later. Rachael and Michael attended the ceremony, as did some sixty-odd close friends of the happy couple.

Elise stayed in her job. Geoffrey bought the hotel and had it refurbished. He also bought the two small vessels which Elise had suggested. Three months later, he found and bought an upmarket cruise ship with two hundred and twenty berths. Though eight years old, it was in mint condition and required no refit.

Geoffrey immediately set it touring the Med, specifically calling at Alghero, so coupling the fortunes of *ME's* two newest acquisitions. Geoffrey continued to specialise in the shipping part of the business, leaving his most-capable wife to oversee the land hotels.

She began by smartening up the staff inherited with the *Hotel Catalan*. In particular, she hired a new *chef de maison*. In due course, she and Geoffrey visited the hotel unannounced and were more than a little impressed with what they saw and ate. The staff wages were raised immediately afterwards, for Geoffrey had always believed that, while words of appreciation are good, cash in the hand shows how sincere such words may be.

Geoffrey also asked Elise to oversee the catering on *ME's* newest ship, the *Robert Marchant*. The name *Marchant* had always been an invented one, but the choice of *Robert* was in honour of Geoffrey's dad.

Bob was as pleased as punch. It was good that he felt that way, for it was almost the last thing he got to approve, because he died quite suddenly of a stroke seven months later. Geoffrey was devastated.

Rachael and Michael were amongst the hundred-odd mourners at Bob's funeral. As if the gods were in sympathy, it rained buckets that day. Geoffrey was now well and truly on his own at the helm of *Marchant Enterprises*, albeit ably assisted by Elise.

It must be made clear that Elise was very able at her job. That is to say, she executed quite demanding tasks cleanly and with considerable skill. She did not, however, have the imagination and sheer daring of her husband. In fairness, few people had.

As though to prove her worth at a time when Geoffrey was still stinging from his father's death, Elise found another possible hotel purchase, this time in the Balearic Islands off the coast of Spain, at Mahón on Menorca. This was a ninety-bed establishment, once again in need of some money being spent on it. Basically, however, it was a fine property with moderately large grounds. It gave onto a fine view of Mahón harbour, which is one of the longest harbours in the world, and the old town of Mahón lying at the end of the three-mile long and nearly one-mile-wide inlet from the Mediterranean near the southeast corner of the island. Most significant was that the water was deep – deep enough for *ME's* vessels to sail right into. The port had been in the possession of the British for over forty years in the eighteenth century for precisely that reason, and there remain many signs of that time; in particular, and somewhat incongruously, Georgian-style buildings with sash windows. Access to the other islands of the Balearic archipelago was, of course, a great attraction for this location, and the *Robert Marchant* would not be the only visiting ship to disgorge passengers.

Again, Geoffrey was taken to see her find. He signed off on it and left the details to Elise. Another detail he left for Elise – after his initial involvement, of course – was her becoming a mother to a daughter they called Mahón. Rachael and Michael, who never had any children, in part because of a medical condition of Rachael's but also because they never really felt the desire to be parents, were present at the Christening. There was a degree of amusement about the child's name, but the babe didn't seem to care.

Some while after that momentous event, Geoffrey hired a man to replace Elise in the business. She, however, insisted that Peter Marsh was to be her assistant while she retained a supervisorial roll. There was some truth in both descriptions. For example, it was Elise who found *ME's* next hotel, this time in Croatia on the Adriatic coast. It was a hundred-bed hotel at Makarska, which lies about one third of the way from Split to Dubrovnik on the Dalmatian Coast. From its front-facing rooms was to be had a wide and uninterrupted view of the Adriatic. There were beaches and rocky coves to the left and to the right for miles. Dubrovnik, about two-and-a-half hours away, was an almost impossibly lovely ancient place to visit. The hotel had been refurbished in the old days of the communist conglomeration of those Balkan states called Yugoslavia. Communist they may have been but commercially minded they certainly were, the British, in particular, being extremely fond of holidaymaking in that region.

The hotel which Elise found on this occasion was, without doubt, in need of considerable modernisation but, once again, was basically sound. Elise also suggested that they might build a large swimming pool on the site, one with high diving boards which might also be used for a weekly display by professional divers to entertain the hotel guests. She had seen such displays in England, in which very skilful divers were dressed up as clown-like characters, playing the fool on the high board before being mock-attacked, when they would fall, somersaulting on their way down to the pool below. Elise argued that it would be a wonderful attraction for their hotel guests.

Geoffrey thought the hotel was a "steal" and signed on the dotted line. It might not have been as financially attractive a choice as her earlier finds, for holidaymaking in that part of the world had long been particularly selected because of its affordability. From the provider's point of view, of course, cheapness can mean smaller profits. However, Geoffrey suggested that Elise look around the east coast of Italy as well, arguing that a find there would make for a sensible round trip at sea in due course.

His enthusiasm at this point was becoming ever greater, and he began to look for another cruise ship. This time, however, he was after a new ship with up to fifteen hundred berths. It was to be *ME's* flagship. Geoffrey recognised full well that *Marchant Enterprises* was no *Cunard* or *P&O*, but he saw no reason not to aim for dominance in the mid-size sector of the market. Ambition had served his father well in his day and, so far, at any rate, under Geoffrey's stewardship also. But there's a funny thing about ambition. It seems to grow exponentially. Certainly, it has a tendency to outpace ability. However, Geoffrey was a very able businessman, and great things only come from great ambition. He saw nothing but logic in his decision at that time to expand *ME's* portfolio of hotels around the Mediterranean. Actually, he was holding himself back a little, for in the back of his mind, but straining to get to the fore, was the notion of expansion out of the Med and into the Americas. Perhaps Geoffrey actually did have *P&O* in his sights. Who knows? *One thing at a time*, he reasoned, as he set his mind to the simultaneous purchase of several hotels around the Mediterranean and of a new flagship. His dreams whirled and twirled around these two projects every night, as he woke tired in the morning and became increasingly ratty during the day. Ambition is a wonderful thing.

26

Geoffrey's new ship, with emphasis on the word "new", was going to cost him a few quid short of four hundred and fifty million pounds. That was a breathtaking sum, and Geoffrey lost plenty of sleep over his life-changing decision to order that vessel. He had been to *ME's* bank for the cash, of course, a loan to be repaid over fifteen years at their standard interest rate for such large loans. He had explained that the travel business was generally on the up world-wide – that more people were finding themselves able to buy the treat of a lifetime and sail the Med. Indeed, he had argued, there was an increasing number of people who were beginning to take their holidays as ship cruises every year. His bank agreed with his assessment, for they had their experts, too. More importantly, the bank officials saw *Marchant Enterprises* in general, and Geoffrey Etherington in particular, as very well established in that field, as a business showing every sign of continued and, moreover, increasing success. They felt that their money would be in safe hands. Their earlier – albeit smaller – loans to *ME* had all been repaid in full, with interest and on time. In short, Geoffrey Etherington was a good bet. Delighted, and now thoroughly excited, Geoffrey placed the order the same day.

Of course, he could not maintain that level of excitement until delivery, for that was promised as one year from the laying of the keel. And that didn't happen overnight. For one thing, a dry dock had to become vacant first. Geoffrey jumped up and down in front of the builders and on the phone. They were pleased to have his firm order, of course, but he was a new customer. In one way, that worked for him, for the shipbuilders were keen, not only to expand their order book but also to expand their customer base. On the other hand, they had existing customers to satisfy; customers who were bigger than *Marchant Enterprises*.

So bloody what? argued Geoffrey. All their customers were once first-time buyers.

He felt that if he had persuaded his bankers that he was a safe bet, then his builders should respond in kind. All these thoughts were a waste of energy, however, for the builders had heard it all before. They wanted his business, and they did their utmost to satisfy his impatience, anyway. They suggested that *ME* might have its new ship in fourteen months. "Might" is a mighty word.

Meanwhile, Elise was doing her best to find new hotels around the Mediterranean. This time, partly because he had nothing else to do in the creative side of the business – and the day-to-day stuff was, fortunately, going along very smoothly – Geoffrey stuck his oar into that side of the business. There were a number of territorial arguments between husband and wife, but eventually they treated each other as adults and formed a powerful alliance.

They formed a plan of integration between the water- and land-based hotels. They argued that such an integration could be manifested in two different ways. In one, making special use of *ME's* smaller ships, holidaymakers would be offered a voyage to one particular location – and *ME* hotel, of course – being dropped off at the beginning and picked up at the end of their stay. In between, the ship would sail on to another *ME* location and deliver any passengers wishing to disembark there by prior arrangement. With notice and more than a little organisational skill, they should be able to satisfy their customers as if the whole trip had been arranged solely for their benefit. That might require some special advertising skills as well, they admitted, but it was worth a try. The alternative grand plan, when the big ship was delivered, would be for the flagship to sail a round trip, calling at all places where *ME* had hotels – and maybe elsewhere, too – drop anchor for three or four days while passengers could disembark, stay at the company hotel, use a company launch or other small vessel to explore the neighbouring shore, and generally increase the reputation of the locale for tourists, for longer-term gains of that kind would surely be expected to come good in time.

And thus, Elise's next task was to find hotels which would complete the Mediterranean circle. They already had a hotel in Menorca, in Sardinia and in Makarska. What about one on Malta, one on the east coast of Italy, one on one of the Greek Islands, one on Crete? How about one on the north coast of Africa? Go for it, Elise! Five more hotels. It was rather like a game of Monopoly! There was a difference, of course. These hotels had to be paid for with real money and, once more, that would have to come from the bank.

So it was, that Peter Marsh and Elise spent a busy year scooting about the Med. in search of hotels for sale – or to be more exact, for sale in reasonable condition, in superb locations and at sensible prices.

The first to come up was a seventy-room hotel in Nafplion, a sizeable and ancient city which was once the capital of Greece. Though not strictly on an island, it lies on a large area of land which is connected only by an isthmus to the largest part of the country. Nafplion is about two hours by car from Athens, so the visitor to Nafplion enjoys the benefits of clear waters and clean air in what has been called the "most romantic city in the world", while having the wonders of the Acropolis within easy reach. The hotel was very much in need of work to bring it up to contemporary standards, but the sellers obviously recognised that fact, as reflected in the price. Nevertheless, Geoffrey began to haggle while he approached the bank once again.

His task now was particularly difficult, because he was uncertain how much he wanted to borrow. He was after five hotels – here, there and everywhere – and he would only know how much he wanted to borrow when he had found them all. He therefore made an estimate of the total cost by the time-honoured method of holding a wet finger in the air. The bank was less than amused. But Geoffrey argued that he was saving them time by coming to them once rather than five times. They argued that they were perfectly happy to have him apply five separate times. Geoffrey knew, of course, that each application would be harder than the one before, if only because his total indebtedness to the bank would be that much greater. They understood his argument and sympathised with his predicament but wouldn't budge. He came away with a loan which would cover the cost and refurbishment of the hotel in Nafplion.

Almost immediately, Peter found a place in Chania on Crete, a smaller hotel with some forty bedrooms but requiring no remodelling. This very pretty seaside resort on the north coast of the island was quite idyllic. The price was fair, once more. It was such a pity, Geoffrey thought, that he hadn't waited, or been able to wait, to apply to the bank for the two Greek hotels together. He was tempted to wait, this time, for the next one to come up, but he heard of a sniff of interest from another party. That rumour may or may not have been true, but he didn't want to take the risk. Armed with a portfolio of gorgeous photographs of the hotel and of the coast nearby, together with a pricing analysis for the area, including voluminous historical data, Geoffrey approached *ME*'s bank once more. To his great surprise, there was hardly a murmur. He signed the loan papers three days later. He was at quite a loss to understand why it was so easy this time, but one doesn't look a gift horse in the mouth.

It took rather longer for Elise to find a hotel in Cyprus, but she located a grand place in one of the best resorts on that island – in Ayia Napa on the southeast coast. It was rather larger than she normally looked for, offering one hundred and fifty bedrooms, and situated in an ideal spot with a splendid view over the bay and Pantachou beach. The hotel was in excellent condition and had been on sale for some time. Elise suspected that the price was too high. Her homework suggested the same thing. She began to negotiate but made little headway, so she called in Geoffrey to play hardball, but he did little better. They made clear that they were interested but not at that price, and they left the island.

Meanwhile, they sent in Peter to make an offer a little higher than their last bid. He was refused, but he left his card and vanished. They decided to sit it out and begin looking at possibilities on the North African coast.

Nothing came up which excited Elise's attention, and she really had looked hard. They would come back to this in time, she decided, and turned her attention to Malta and the Italian coast on the Adriatic. The latter rather quickly offered up a medium-sized hotel of eighty rooms near Ancona, an incredibly beautiful part of the country. As far as position was concerned, Ancona suited *ME* to a T, for it was just across the water from Makarska in Croatia – about an eight-hour trip. The local position for this hotel was equally attractive, being set up high above the green, translucent waters in the area. There was so much to see in the surrounding countryside that a holidaymaker could make this hotel a superb centre from which to explore. A little money could be spent on the hotel with advantage, but that wasn't necessary absolutely immediately.

The price seemed sensible to Elise, and she recommended the place to Geoffrey. He sent Peter to confer and to add his opinion. He was in total agreement, which did no harm to his promotional prospects in the company.

Geoffrey took their find to the bank. Yet again, he hadn't to work too hard to convince them to cough up.

Meanwhile, Peter found a possible buy at St. Julian's in Malta. Just a short distance north of Valetta, the capital, it was a place with lively nightlife, access to beaches and, because Malta isn't large anyway, could serve as a central point to explore much of the whole island. Malta, of course, lies more or less smack in the middle of the Mediterranean, a short distance south of Sicily. Peter's find was only small – forty bedrooms – but was in tip-top condition. The owners had run into financial difficulties and wanted a quick sale. The price was low because of that. Geoffrey set Peter the task of finding out what those financial difficulties were. Obviously, if they were associated with the hotel as a going concern, *ME* wouldn't proceed.

The answer wasn't hard to find. The owner was into gambling in a big way and he was bust. Apparently, this wasn't the first time he had done something like this. Peter, ever careful, did due diligence on the hotel business itself and was able to report back to his boss that the hotel did very well and had a good reputation amongst the locals also. Geoffrey put in an offer immediately, even before consulting his bank, which was accepted after no more than a little wrangling. Geoffrey took his new project to the bank, omitting to mention that he had already signed the contract.

The bank took ages to respond, and Geoffrey began to think that his request had become lost somewhere in the vaults of that large organisation. Eventually, he called the manager for loans to enquire. He assumed a jaunty tone, for he was confident that after what had happened earlier with his other applications, the bank would see just what a bargain *ME* had found.

A meeting was convened shortly afterwards. There had been a reassignment of personnel at the bank – a shake-up, as Geoffrey called it afterwards – and the new guy, a fellow called Adrian Fellows, was decidedly unimpressed with Geoffrey's application. He wanted to know when all this hotel buying would stop. He took the view that Geoffrey was running too fast and that he should take a stroll for a while. If all went well with the new assets he had purchased in recent months – say, for a year or three – then that might be a good time to reapply. Geoffrey was utterly amazed at the bank's attitude. Did they not understand that this hotel in Malta was a snip? Snips don't come up every day. This snip would not be there in one- or three-years' time. He then reminded his lenders of his original plan which was, he said, nearly complete. He was on the point of putting in an offer on a wonderful hotel in Alexandria, which would round off the circuit he had planned. *That* was when it was appropriate for him to take a breather, he said. Geoffrey spoke, not as a supplicant, but as someone who was graciously offering the bank an opportunity. Mr. Fellows was not impressed, and *ME*'s application was refused.

Geoffrey was only short of nineteen million pounds which, in the scheme of things, was small beer. The trouble was that he had signed the contract, and he didn't have nineteen million pounds hanging around. He did have three million, or rather, he had had three million, but he had used that as a deposit on the Malta hotel. It was not a good thing to be without a float, anyway. Any little problem could arise and cause endless difficulties. He had to find a way of getting hold of nineteen million quid fast.

Apart from that, while all this waiting for the bank to respond had been going on, Geoffrey's fib about having found a wonderful hotel in Alexandria actually came true. Elise had found a fabulous place and had summoned Peter to join her in Egypt to investigate her find carefully.

They had found no problems. The hotel – a large, one hundred-and-ten-room establishment – was in good condition, and the present owners were aging and had decided to cash in their chips. The price was a little high, but Elise and Peter both felt that a little bargaining, Egyptian style, would bring it down to something palatable to Geoffrey and *ME*. And, of course, its purchase would complete the circle of properties in the Med., which Geoffrey had set his heart on. He needed nearly forty million pounds for the place in the end. Well, he argued to anyone who would listen, they got it down from fifty-two million!

The point remained, however, that Geoffrey was now short of sixty million pounds in round figures. Geoffrey was always fond of round figures which left a little spare in the kitty.

It was around this time – almost to the day, actually – that news came through that the people at Ayia Napa hotel were beginning to bite at Peter Marsh's offer. Geoffrey instructed Peter to withdraw his offer, making an excuse that he had lost interest in Cyprus altogether. Geoffrey sat back with crossed fingers and waited. A few days passed before the Cypriots came back with an asking price just a couple of percent lower than their original demand. Geoffrey offered ten per cent lower yet. They struck a deal at seven percent below their original ask. Gung ho by now, Geoffrey signed on the dotted line for fifty-five million pounds. He now wanted to borrow one hundred and fifteen million.

Geoffrey returned to the bank. This time, however, he put extra effort into his proposal, making the point that his ambitions for more hotels was at an end for the foreseeable future, that this chain, or circle, of hotels made abundant commercial sense, that his track record for running the leisure trade was immaculate, that everything was in place and, finally, that he had the personnel to oversee the expanded *ME* venture. The presentation was abundantly glossy with pull-outs all over the place. No one could argue that *ME* hadn't done its homework.

Mr. Adrian Fellows, however, was not for turning. Once more, he charged Geoffrey with having eyes bigger than his stomach. He was in too much of a hurry. There would be other opportunities for expansion in a few years, once *ME* had shown proof of its ability to run so large an empire.

"Come back then and the bank will be pleased to help you once more."

Geoffrey pleaded and cajoled – something which didn't come easily to him – but eventually reverted to bluster. It was all to no avail. Fellows wouldn't budge. He expressed his regret. There were almost tears in his eyes. But he wouldn't budge. No more money. Geoffrey left the meeting in a rage. He was also scared.

27

There was, of course, no point in Geoffrey trying his luck at another bank. They would find out in no time that his usual bank had refused to help, and they would follow suit. He could have sold one of his ships but that thought never even crossed his mind, not even for a second. He did think of approaching a friendly bookie, but he reckoned that one hundred and fifteen million might be out of such peoples' reach. But then the big thought came to him. Could he find a private source of finance? Some might call such people loan sharks, but that would depend, surely, upon what terms might be agreed. Money-lending, like anything else, has a continuum of its own. There are sources which one would place somewhere between banks and loan sharks. Furthermore, the more you borrow, the more respectable the lender. No? Geoffrey set about finding a new source. A change of engine oil, he called it to his colleagues who were nervous about such a venture, having lived completely with the angels so far in their careers. Nervous or not, their task was set, and Geoffrey was in a hurry.

Thus, Geoffrey came to learn about a Singaporean Chinese businessman by the name of Jim Chen, a man with fingers in more pies than even Geoffrey's mind could contemplate, a man who bought and sold, who managed large companies operating in disparate fields, a man who was prepared to lend money in large amounts. The question for Geoffrey, of course, was how much would such loans cost him? Obviously, something more than his bank would charge, but how much more? And even before he was prepared to apply to this Chen fellow, Geoffrey wanted some evidence of his straight dealing. He wanted to talk to someone who had borrowed from Chen already. How was he going to find that someone? You can hardly put an advert in the paper: Wanted: "Borrower of millions from Jim Chen". Geoffrey thought a little more about this and decided that the thing he really wanted to know was the character of Jim Chen. He needed a specialist detective. After only a couple of days, one man's name came up: Harvey Trentham.

Geoffrey explained to Harvey just enough for him to understand the task he was commissioned to undertake – that Geoffrey's company was looking to borrow one hundred and fifteen million pounds or so, from this man, Chen. How reliable a lender was he? To cut to the chase: was he straight? Would Harvey take the commission?

Harvey was more than pleased to accept the job. For one thing, he had already heard of Chen and knew where he might find out more about him. Harvey had his contacts. After all, that was Harvey's job. He hadn't gained his reputation as bloodhound for the wealthy from nothing. His long experience of this sort of thing meant that he had built up a considerable dossier on all manner of people around the world. You never know when something might come in useful, he argued, and he had been vindicated time after time.

Geoffrey had emphasised to Harvey that speed was of the essence, so Harvey had no need to strain his mental faculties too far to surmise that Geoffrey was in dire need of a lot of cash. Harvey was not, in any case, dim-witted.

Harvey Trentham reported back to his employer in six days. His message was strong and clear. Chen lent large sums of money to people all over the globe, he charged two percent more than the average bank, he was as careful with borrowers' privacy as he was with his own, he was scrupulously careful with his own money, lending only to people he thought were safe – and he worked hard to convince himself of that – and he made decisions to lend as quickly as his investigations would allow. Harvey further noted that he had not heard one word against Jim Chen but conceded that there could always be a first time for anything. He explained that, within the short time he had been given to report back, he had found the name of only one borrower of substantial sums from Mr. Chen, a man in Australia in the mining business. He provided contact details for Geoffrey should he decide to learn details for himself.

Geoffrey was more than pleased with Harvey's report and closed business with him, but not before assuring him that he would be happy to recommend him to others. Harvey was pleased with himself and could now eat for a while. Such was the nature of his business.

Geoffrey lost no time after that in contacting Jim Chen, initially by email. Chen requested a concise application for a loan in the first place, promising a prompt reply for an in-principle judgement. Geoffrey furnished Chen with a two-page summary for a loan of one hundred and fifteen million pounds with which to purchase the hotels on Malta, on Cyprus, and in Egypt. He also provided a thumbnail sketch of *Marchant Enterprises'* business. He knew, of course, that Chen would check everything out for himself, anyway. As requested, he sent his request by encrypted email.

As promised, Chen replied in like fashion within three days, saying that he was prepared to consider lending *ME* that kind of money and would therefore like Geoffrey to prepare a detailed application, as for a lending bank (obviously, he would have known that Geoffrey had been there first), and to present it in person to Chen in Copenhagen. Geoffrey called him back, on the phone this time, to thank him and to tell him that he had already submitted his request to his bank but without success, as he surmised that Mr. Chen would have expected, and that his detailed submission was already available. Chen asked that it be sent to him by courier, after which he would study Geoffrey's submission and get back to him as quickly as possible thereafter.

'I know that time is money,' he said graciously, for it was obvious that Geoffrey was in a hurry.

There was nothing more to do. Geoffrey just had to sit it out. How long would Chen take to make his decision? More to the point, how long would it take for Chen to make his enquiries, for he would obviously do that? *How long is a piece of string?* Geoffrey mused ruefully.

Before the week was out, he knew that Chen was at work, for rumours came to him that someone was making enquiries about the business. He had no idea who was asking questions, and in any case, it was pointless for him to find out. Nor was he bothered about what questions were being asked. He had nothing to hide. He was proud of his business. He was proud of his management skills. Indeed, he had told his bank all that many times over. Their rejection of his last request did not diminish his reputation in his own eyes one jot. He couldn't see why it would do so in others' eyes either. Geoffrey was a confident man. He just hated having to wait for other people to do whatever they had to do.

He got a call two weeks later. Could he come over to meet Chen at his office in Copenhagen? He could. A date was fixed for two days later.

Geoffrey was in Chen's bland office very shortly after ten o'clock. They had each seen photographs of each other but somehow photos don't quite do it. Chen looked a little older and wiser than he had appeared in the media, and Geoffrey looked more relaxed and confident than his images suggested. So all that was good. They were off to a good start. Chen explained that he liked to meet applicants face-to-face before making a final decision.

'There's something about the look in one's eyes, isn't there?' he asked. 'I'm not impressed with a person's handshake, mind you. It tells you nothing useful, in my opinion. Please, let's talk about your hopes and plans for your company, for a while. May I offer you a drink? Coffee, or something stronger?'

They took coffee while Geoffrey began to describe how he had planned to grow *Marchant Enterprises*. He was careful and deliberate at first, but Chen was a marvellous listener and a crafty man who had assessed bigger men than Geoffrey many times over. Soon, Geoffrey became a little excited as his obviously genuine enthusiasm showed itself. As far as Chen was concerned, enthusiasm was good.

After half an hour's talking, Chen said in his beautiful English accent, an accent more polished than Geoffrey's own, 'Mr. Etherington, I am prepared to lend you the sum you requested. You already know my terms, and I assume by your presence here that they are acceptable to you. We can sign a contract right here and now, if you wish, although it might be more proper for you to take it home for your legal department to look over. Yes, do that. I can make the funds available to you virtually immediately after receipt of your signature. I wish your business enterprise well.'

That was it. Geoffrey was both surprised and delighted. Chen brought the meeting to an abrupt close. He was perfectly polite, but it was clear that, from his point of view – the only one he really cared about – their business was concluded, and time was money. Geoffrey had had his half hour, although really it had been Jim Chen who had had his.

Chen had already done his research, of course. Isobel had furnished him with a most comprehensive report on Marchant Enterprises, with her final conclusion being that Geoffrey Etherington was an utterly honest businessman but was in a great hurry. In her opinion, he was able to handle the fast rate of expansion he proposed. Jim Chen had already formed the same view and was pleased to have it confirmed by Isobel's independent enquiries. Her contract with him had finished at that point. He had added ten percent to his agreed fee in recognition of her careful work. She was very pleased.

And the bottom line, as the over-used epithet goes, is that Geoffrey got his three hotels.

The fortunes of *Marchant Voyages* didn't end there, of course. Life moves on. Problems and opportunities arise. A manager's job is to deal with each and every one as it arises. Most of the problems were small, of the kind any business is subject to from time to time. Geoffrey and Elise were putting together attractive tours for their future customers, and everything looked as it was supposed to look, at this most exciting time. *Marchant Enterprises* was in hock for seven hotels and three ships, one of them being the monster fifteen-hundred-berth vessel to be delivered now in less than five months, but Geoffrey was confident that the business could meet its repayment schedule.

And then Geoffrey caught the whiff of a rumour.

A passenger shipping company, small but well-enough known in the trade, was coming up for sale. It possessed two medium-sized ships, one with five hundred and the other with six hundred berths, and had been in business for many decades. Geoffrey knew of the Estonian owner, Stefan Kukk, by repute, but they had never met. Kukk's business was concentrated in the Baltic and, occasionally, along the northwest Norwegian coast. Why the sale? Had they gone bust? Geoffrey made some enquiries.

It turned out that old Kukk had done nothing wrong at all. He had retired, but without descendants. He was hanging up his uniform or whatever and calling it a day. He was already a rich man and it seemed that he was not worried about getting the last cent out of his business. What he did care about was that it be sold to someone who wouldn't break it up but who would continue to employ its workforce. *My God*, Geoffrey thought, *a ready-made shipping line for sale at a more than reasonable price*. He just couldn't walk away from this opportunity. Chances like this simply don't happen every day. In fact, they almost never happen. He just needed six hundred million pounds. *Walk away*, a voice deep inside his head told him. *No way*, another voice, rather more to the fore, replied.

This was such a good opportunity, at such a fair price, that Geoffrey thought it worth trying his bank once more. He put in his business plan with great care. Adrian Fellows was still in place and Adrian Fellows was of the same opinion, an opinion which was not going to change simply because some ships had been substituted for some hotels. And that was that. Geoffrey was mad but, this time, didn't show it. He wondered if Fellows knew he had persuaded Chen to lend him one hundred and fifteen million pounds a few months ago, but he couldn't see how that would help his case at the bank. *Well, I tried*, he thought, as he walked out of the meeting. *Now I'll try Chen again.*

'Please send me your full business plan, and I will look into it.' Chen was remarkably calm over the phone, Geoffrey thought. Perhaps he lends out billions every day.

He sent his plan and full details of the company he was hoping to buy by courier, and waited. Chen asked Isobel to investigate the financial and personal side of Kukk's company. He put his own watchdogs onto it as well. These things take time, of course, which meant that Geoffrey was obliged to wait for some weeks. However, Chen agreed to lend *Marchant Enterprises* the six hundred million pounds at the same interest rate as before. He knew, of course, that he could take the shipping line should *ME* default. So did Geoffrey.

In a few short years, Geoffrey had grown *Marchant Enterprises* probably five-fold. *Maybe more*, Geoffrey told himself. Even Geoffrey now thought that he should take a breather and concentrate on making everything he had, work. What was needed now was the steady income stream he had predicted. What could go wrong? The times were right. More and more people were taking to cruising. It seemed that everyone's ships were full. Geoffrey gave way, perhaps, to a little smugness, but he was no fool. He knew that he would have to work hard and so would all his employees. He passed the message.

28

The two ships in the old Kukk line – Geoffrey hadn't really got into the swing of referring to them as part of *Marchant Enterprises* yet – would be modernised when the company could afford it. For the moment, Geoffrey decided to run the line more or less as Kukk himself had run it, keeping the same staff but looking carefully at its business plan to see if worthwhile improvements could be made. In truth, Geoffrey wanted to learn more about the Baltic, its ports and holiday resorts before making changes. *ME* already ran a couple of small passenger ships in the area, but Geoffrey had put so much thought and effort into the Mediterranean that he had neglected this earlier part of the business. The time had come, therefore, to knuckle down to some serious research. He asked Peter Marsh to head up this segment of the business.

It was but two weeks into Peter's new responsibilities when disaster struck. Peter had rushed to Geoffrey's home while he was still at breakfast – Geoffrey always believed in a hearty breakfast – to break the news in person. The *Sally Vee*, the larger of Kukk's fleet, was putting into Tallin dock, a manoeuvre the ship's master, Endrik Pärn, had made many times, when, for God knows what reason, she ploughed hard into the concrete wharf and tore a huge section – in Peter's possibly panicky report – from its hull. No, he replied to Geoffrey's immediate first question, she was not sunk. The damage was above the water line. And nobody was killed, in answer to Geoffrey's second. Nor seriously injured. However, judging by Pärn's report – by telephone and in great haste and anguish – the damage was very bad indeed. Photographs, which were only snapshots at this stage, confirmed Pärn's description. At this point, there was no independent commentary on Pärn's seamanship. The fact remained that he sailed his ship hard into the dock.

Geoffrey asked for a full report as soon as possible and began to look into how he might salvage the holidays of the passengers on the ship and those booked on her for the coming months. It was already clear to Geoffrey, and Peter too, that repairs were going to take a long time and were likely to be costly. Peter was instructed to get onto the insurers to warn them of the upcoming costs. Insurance had been taken out by Kukk with an Estonian company. Geoffrey had seen the insurance policy before his purchase of the company, of course. He had not studied it very carefully, however, a mistake he was never likely to make again. It turned out that the policy covered total loss of the vessel, by sinking, for example, but not for any significant amount to cover damage. Geoffrey checked Peter's assessment very carefully and agreed with his terrible news. *How could I have made such a stupid mistake?* he fumed. Of course, he sent the papers to *ME*'s legal department, a grand name for a part-time solicitor in Bristol, and was rewarded with a note in full agreement. Geoffrey had never heard of such an insurance policy before.

'Ridiculous!' he cried, and asked the legal eagle whether it could be challenged.

'Doubtful,' was the reply, 'but you need the services of an Estonian lawyer.'

'Get on it!' Geoffrey had shouted to his legal team. 'Now's the time to earn your retainer.'

None of this venting aided Geoffrey's panic that day. More pictures of the accident came in on the following day, together with a preliminary engineer's report on the damage. It was clearly very bad indeed and was going to cost a bomb to fix. And, of course, there would be the loss of business while the *Sally Vee* was being repaired.

Geoffrey, however, was nothing if not gritty, and he immediately got cracking on all that needed to be done, the first being to instruct Peter to get on with it all. While waiting for a report from an Estonian solicitor – *And who knows how long that might take?* he thought – he began enquiries into repair costs and timing from the local Tallin shipyard where, it turned out, the *Sally Vee* was originally built. He asked the shipyard for an initial estimate for insurance purposes. Soon. Yesterday would be best. The yard promised a rough and ready estimate within the month.

Geoffrey used more expletives around that time than at any other in his life. None of them did him any good. However, the Tallin shipyard were as good as their word. After twenty-eight days, they made an interim assessment with enough caveats to sink the bloody ship. Geoffrey wished the *Sally Vee* had sunk. The figure he didn't want to hear was close on forty million pounds. Had it been one hundred and forty million, Geoffrey's choice would have been clear: sell the ship for scrap. Ruminations of that kind weren't helpful. Scrapping the ship would entail one hell of a loss, quite possibly the thick end of two hundred and fifty million pounds. No! He needed forty million or so for the repair. Was he going to get anything from those damn insurers?

He chivvied his legal chappie who passed on his concern to the Estonian chappies. He asked for a preliminary assessment. Time was of the essence. Two weeks later the Estonians replied, using very long legal words, the essence of which was that he had absolutely no chance of getting any money whatsoever from that insurance company for that ship repair. Where on earth was he to find forty million quid?

When he put his case to Jim Chen, he received a prompt reply. Sorry, no dice. He thought he might improve his chances by following up his written request with a phone call. The answer was still no.

'Why don't you sell something?' Chen had asked.

Geoffrey reminded him that much of what *Marchant Enterprises* owned was actually owned by Jim Chen. Selling one of his older, smaller ships or one of his hotels would be bad business because they were bringing in the mortgage repayments for Chen.

'Why not sell *The Hut?*' was Chen's next question.

Geoffrey was thunderstruck. He had never contemplated that, even for a moment. *The Hut* was part of the founding agreement of *Marchant Enterprises* with Michael all those years ago.

'It doesn't earn much money, does it?' Chen remarked.

Geoffrey ended the call no better off. He was well and truly deep in it. Rather than have hysterics as he really felt he wanted to, he took a firm grip on himself and began to think things through. While he was at it, he took a firm grip on a very large whisky as well. He began to think back over all the earlier acquisitions which he had steered through *Marchant Enterprises*. Without doubt, they had all been sound. The disaster over *Sally Vee's* insurance was his first mistake, he felt. Mortgaging the company up to the hilt and beyond showed spunk and bravery, not foolishness, he assured himself. He couldn't sell one of *ME*'s smaller ships or hotels. He had been

right when he told Chen that they were paying for everyone's wages –
Chen's included. He couldn't sell off the family silver. Chen was right. *The
Hut* wasn't really earning its keep. If it were to be sold, though, it would
have to be sold as a money-making concern – as a golfing hotel, maybe. It
would still offer high-class accommodation and cuisine but not to the
indulgent standards Michael had maintained.

Get real, Michael, Geoffrey thought. Two percent return, which was
all that *The Hut* had actually achieved, he insisted, was simply bad business.
How much was The Hut worth on the open market? he wondered. *There
was the Tomber Hall estate plus two hotels and three pubs – or four pubs,
if you included the Tomber Pot*, he remembered. He ruminated for a while.
I reckon we could get near to two hundred million for all that, he thought.
That would solve ME's problems, for sure. He did not admit that they were
his problems before they were *ME*'s. He decided to sleep on it all.

He told Elise about his thoughts next morning. She was aghast, for she
liked Rachael very much. Rachael – and Michael, she admitted to herself –
had been very welcoming to her when she joined the "clan", as she referred
to the original group of university friends.

'That would mean their having to move out. To lose their ancestral
home.'

'They've already lost it in reality,' Geoffrey replied. 'The hall and all
that estate is actually owned by *Marchant Enterprises*.'

Even so, Geoffrey felt quite sick at the thought of turfing his friends of
twenty-five years out. *Mind you, their shares in ME are worth millions, so
they won't starve*, he rationalised. He decided to sleep on it all.

He tried explaining the circumstances of *Marchant Enterprises* in full
again to Elise the next morning.

'I really cannot see an alternative,' he insisted. 'We're in a complete
bind.'

'You mean *you* are!' she retorted. 'But I do see what you mean. It really
does make business sense.'

'I think I must put out some feelers at this stage. Let's see if there might
be any interest out there in purchasing *The Hut*.'

Feelers are like rumours. They tend to spread abroad. They tend to end
up in the ears of the most unlikely people. Maybe not so unlikely if they're
in the business, however.

*

Isobel had heard a whisper. *The Hut* might be up for sale. *Surely Michael wouldn't want that*, was her first thought. *Who is trying to sell it?* was her next. She was curious. After all, things like these were her business. She had the need to keep abreast of all rumours. *You never know when you might be asked for your professional opinion. In any case, I'm curious*. It didn't take her long to sort it out. *The question now*, she thought, *is, does Michael know about it?* She was fond of Michael. Everybody who had ever stayed at *The Hut* was fond of Michael. She simply had to find out if he knew or whether the place was being sold from under him. She thought she'd pay Rachael a visit. Girls together.

Rachael was delighted to hear from her. She asked about Cousin Hillary. Asked about Gerald. Asked about Harvey. There was a degree of coyness, and there was a degree of hilarity. Isobel slid in a question of whether Rachael and Michael still enjoyed entertaining as they did. They did.

'Doesn't it all get rather harder as time goes by?' she asked.

'Not really. If anything, it gets easier.'

Isobel opined that she would begin to find the whole thing too much after so many years and would like to give the whole thing up. Rachael disagreed.

Isobel formed the strong opinion that Rachael, at least, and therefore probably Michael as well, had no idea of the impending sale of *The Hut*. It so happened that Michael appeared at that moment.

'Any tea left?' he asked. 'I fancy a nice cuppa if it's not gone cold.' He picked up a small cake from a plate on the table between the two women. 'How are you, Isobel? Lovely to see you again. How's your cousin?'

Isobel didn't quite know how to begin her tale of woe. She was helped out by luck as Rachael said, 'Izzy was asking if we still enjoyed our life here in *The Hut* – all the entertaining and so on.'

'Why wouldn't we?' Michael said. 'We enjoy every moment. I wouldn't want to change a thing.'

Well, there it was. Clear as day. Michael and Rachael had no idea of the axe hanging over their heads. Isobel clenched her hands for a moment before she did what she had to do.

'I take it, then, that you have heard nothing of a rumour going around that *The Hut* might be up for sale?'

'I don't listen to rumours,' Michael replied, obviously not taking Isobel's message on board.

'Please take me seriously, you two,' Isobel replied. 'I think you are in trouble.'

She proceeded to lay out all she had heard. At last, Michael began to believe her.

'My god,' was all he could say, and then, 'Are you absolutely sure, Isobel? Could you find out for me? Professionally, I mean. I'll pay you, of course.'

'I'd be happy to, Michael, but I won't accept a penny from you. This will be for friendship's sake. I suggest that you keep all this to yourselves until I report back. Okay?'

That might have been the moment when Camelot died.

29

Isobel worked especially hard over the next two days. She was very careful not to leave signs that anyone was enquiring on behalf of Michael and Rachael. It wasn't too hard, however, to find out what was going on, for Geoffrey hadn't been as careful as he should have been, under the circumstances. She was able to give Michael and Rachael a pretty fulsome account of affairs within that time.

'I'm afraid that the rumours are true,' she began. 'May I begin by telling you that I know quite a lot about *Marchant Enterprises* from my professional life. Please don't ask me about that, for I am obliged to keep secret those things which I must keep secret. It is enough, however, to tell you with complete certainty that *Marchant Enterprises* has been expanding its travel business enormously in the past few years. I will also tell you that it is in hock to the tune of more than a billion pounds. That's billion, not million. I don't propose to tell you any more details of the mortgages and loans that have led to that situation. It is clear, however, that Geoffrey Etherington is a frantically ambitious man and that I, for one, would estimate that he has every chance of succeeding in his ambitions. However – and here's the nub of the story – one of the ships he recently purchased was involved in a bad accident some weeks ago. As far as I can ascertain, no one was hurt or killed, but the ship suffered very, very expensive damage and the insurance company will not pay. Exactly why that is, I have been unable to find out, but I am assured that it is so. Geoffrey has borrowed up to the hilt, and he's now short of some forty million pounds. It could well be more. He sees *The Hut* as the way out of his difficulties. As far as I can ascertain, he is serious about finding a buyer – and soon. I am so sorry, Michael and Rachael, for I understand perfectly, I think, how devastating this news must be. I must add that I doubt if Geoffrey Etherington has much choice at this stage. I think he has made a classic mistake of over-extending himself, having left nothing in the kitty for unforeseen circumstances. I see nothing vicious in his decision – or should I say, half-taken decision. At least, you have a heads-up. If I can help further, please ask.'

Michael took Isobel's news very quietly. He had, of course, already acclimatised himself to her news from their earlier meeting and made some special enquiries of his own. His main concern now was that *The Hut* might be sold from under him and the sale presented to him as a *fait accompli*. He saw no option but to initiate further proceedings himself. He asked Rachael to phone Elise with an invitation to her and Geoffrey for dinner.

'Soon!' he told Rachael.

Rachael could be most persuasive when she wanted, and she needed to be this time, for Elise began to prevaricate, being embarrassed with the supposedly secret knowledge she possessed. However, a date for twelve days hence was fixed, friendly noises were made all round, and that was that.

The Etheringtons duly arrived, prompt, as was their custom, and were greeted by Rachael who ushered them into the Montayne's private quarters where a bottle of good bubbly was opened to celebrate this quite rare occasion. Rare, because work had kept the Etheringtons generally too busy to have fun. They hadn't deliberately shunned the Montaynes. Things had just turned out that way. All four understood the situation without rancour. Elise and Rachael had met occasionally in the past but even those meetings had become infrequent. So, in principle, this meeting deserved a little ceremony. In any case, Rachael, especially, was fond of a glass or two of champagne.

There followed a good half-hour of general and insignificant chat before the butler popped in to announce dinner. Michael and Rachael had chosen the menu with all their customary care, and the chef had produced a simple but lovely meal: a lobster bisque, followed by a squab in lattice pastry with seasonal vegetables, in turn followed by a delicate almond soufflé. Michael had chosen a *Sancerre* with the soup, and a *Beaujolais* with the pigeon.

Their casual and meaningless conversation had continued throughout the meal. The Etheringtons were offered fruit and cheese to follow but refused.

'Thanks, Michael,' Geoffrey said, 'but we have had more than enough. That was a lovely dinner. Thank you very much.'

Michael suggested they all return to the comfort of the lounge seating for a whisky or whatever.

'Cheers!' Michael raised his glass of Dalwhinnie. 'Here's to friendship.'

Elise looked away, raising her glass in an automatic but completely embarrassed way. Geoffrey took a sip of his rum but said nothing. Michael paused and allowed the silence that followed to seep into everyone's bones. Geoffrey was being given every chance to speak, but he didn't. Michael had no choice.

'Geoffrey!' he began. 'I understand that you plan to put *The Hut* up for sale.'

Michael had never been in the armed forces, but he knew how to lob a grenade!

'Oh, Geoffrey!' Elise wailed. 'I told you to tell Michael straight away.'

'Geoffrey?' Michael said, and waited.

Geoffrey took a large swig of his rum before he began his little speech. 'Michael, I have been intending to contact you for weeks. I am a coward. I just didn't know how to begin. *Marchant Enterprises* has been growing at a tremendous rate over the past few years. Please excuse my hubris when I tell you how proud I am of what has been achieved in the business. I won't bore you with all the details, but suffice to say, the business is over-extended, and I left nothing in my purse for unforeseen events. That was a stupid mistake for which I take complete responsibility. Now one of the ships we bought recently sailed hard into a concrete dock and suffered enormous damage. The insurance won't cover it. That is where I made my second mistake. I had been in too much of a hurry to check the fine print on a foreign insurance policy. The bottom line is that I need forty million pounds in a hurry. I have borrowed up to the hilt, and I cannot raise that sort of money other than by selling *The Hut*. I have been wanting to tell you about it ever since I made my decision, Michael. I just didn't know how to. I am so terribly sorry. I should at least have told you straight away.'

Geoffrey took another large swig. Elise was embarrassed beyond words.

Michael then spoke very calmly. 'Have you actually put *The Hut* up for sale yet, Geoffrey?'

'No, I am finalising *ME*'s end of the deal, but I intend to make the first formal move early next week.'

My God! thought Michael. *I've cut this close!* 'What will you raise from the sale, Geoffrey?'

Geoffrey began to bluster a little.

'Geoffrey, we are in private, and, for the sake of our past friendship, you owe me the courtesy of some straight answers. I am, after all, a shareholder in *Marchant Enterprises*. I understand completely that my vote cannot prevail over yours, but you can, at the very least, give me the chance to do something about the thing that means more to me than anything, except Rachael.'

Rachael took hold of Michael's hand but said nothing.

'I will willingly give you that chance. But what can you do, Michael?' Geoffrey replied. 'I mean, do you have forty-odd million quid in your back pocket? In any case,' he hurried on, 'I need a lot more than that repair money. I need to insulate myself from the next disaster whenever it comes along. Selling *The Hut* will do that for me.'

'You haven't answered my question, Geoffrey. What do you hope – realistically, mind – to raise from the sale of *The Hut*?'

'Well, by *The Hut*, we still mean Tomber Estate plus the two hotels and three pubs, don't we?'

'Four pubs, if you include the *Tomber Pot*,' replied Michael.

'Yes, four. I was lumping that in with the Tomber Estate,' Geoffrey replied.

'So, how much?' Michael repeated.

Geoffrey fell silent for a moment while making up his mind whether to tell Michael, for he probably wasn't obliged to do so in law, he thought. Maybe he was, though.

'I am looking for one hundred and ninety million pounds for the lot,' he announced. 'You see how big this matter is? I am so sorry, Michael,' he said yet again.

Now it was Michael's turn to stay silent for a moment. He wasn't exactly savouring the moment but acknowledging to himself that it was a defining moment. He gave Rachael's hand, which was still in his, a gentle squeeze.

'Very well, Geoffrey, I'll pay you one hundred and ninety million pounds for *The Hut*.'

Geoffrey looked at Michael with incredulity. His mouth hung open. Not completely, but open, nonetheless. Elise simply gasped. Only when Geoffrey saw the calmness in Michael's face and, above all – yes, above all – the matching peace in Rachael's, did he comprehend that Michael was making a serious offer.

'Where the hell are you getting that sort of money from, Michael?' he blurted out.

'Well, strictly, it's none of your business, Geoffrey,' Michael replied, 'but I'll give you half an answer. My shares in *Marchant Enterprises* should easily fetch seventy million pounds. After your magnificent efforts to grow your company, they will certainly fetch that much. Yes,' he added, seeing Geoffrey's growing understanding, 'I am well aware of what you have been doing over the past few years – and I sincerely congratulate you – and, of course, thank you for increasing the value of my holding.'

'Do you have a buyer for them?' Geoffrey asked.

'I think so, Geoffrey…'

'And what about the remainder? That's about one hundred and twenty million pounds,' Geoffrey interrupted.

'Thank you, Geoffrey, I can manage simple arithmetic,' Michael snapped.

Michael was clearly mad. Geoffrey got the message.

'Sorry. But can you find the rest?' Geoffrey persisted.

'Yes, I can, Geoffrey. Would you please get your lawyers to draw up a bill of sale? I can sign that immediately. Do we have a deal?'

Geoffrey nodded, and the two men shook hands on it. The ladies took due note.

Michael refused to comment any further. It wasn't in his nature to be nasty or evil, but he was very hurt by Geoffrey's actions. Not only by his cowardice, but by his refusal to consult with Michael in the first place, and to throw him to the wolves. Saying sorry over and over again just didn't cut it.

The Etheringtons left soon afterwards. Elise was close to tears. Neither Michael nor Rachael did anything to help them in their brief moment of distress.

30

Immediately after Isobel had delivered her findings to Michael nearly a fortnight earlier, he had begun to think of a possible way out of his problem. He sent out invitations – urgent, almost pleading, invitations – to three of his good friends; friends who admired *The Hut*: Bill Land a. k. a. Lord Land, Noah Calhoon and Divit Deshpande. He got what he wanted within the week.

Maureen Land had been most insistent that Bill should accompany her as bona fide visitors to *The Hut*. Bill retained his working-class accent but only to a small degree. Now it was overlain with those nebulous tones and semi-drawls which highly successful people – men, in particular – frequently acquire. One is tempted to say that the two aspects to those sorts of accents are there, or were put there, so as to appeal, at one and the same time, to two quite different groups of people. However, despite his lordship's way of speaking, Bill was both objective and kind. He, too, recognised that it was no more Michael's fault to have been born into a wealthy family than it was his own to have been raised in near poverty. He also acknowledged Michael's innate kindness and, best of all, he had enjoyed his first experience at *The Hut* enormously. Bill was easily honest enough to admit that he adored being spoilt, even when he was paying handsomely for it. Conversations around the communal dining table provided Bill with yet another platform to show off. Bill hadn't got where he was without a great deal of showing off.

For his part, Michael learned more of Bill's business enterprises.

'I'm sure Maureen has no idea just how wealthy Bill is, you know,' he told Rachael around the time of Bill's first visit to *The Hut*.

Rachael concurred, but then asked, 'Actually, how much *is* he worth? Do you know?'

Michael felt sure he was worth close to a billion pounds.

'What!' Rachael gasped. 'Are you sure?'

'Pretty much. I've done my homework.'

'No, I'm sure Maureen has absolutely no idea what Bill's worth. I'll bet he's scared to tell her. Her socialist bent is pretty strong, you know.'

Since then, the Lands had been guests at *The Hut* four or five times – for brief visits only because of the pressure of Bill's work – and they had enjoyed themselves enormously. Michael and Bill got on together like brothers.

As for Noah Calhoon, well what can one say? He was absolutely delighted with Rachael's discoveries years before. He found the whole bootlegging saga hilarious, but most of all, he felt bonded to Michael's family by it. He had never told a soul about his grandfather's murky past and had sworn Lucas to secrecy, too. Michael and Rachael were the only people he could talk to about it, and he did so whenever he came over to *The Hut*. If Noah's fortune was founded on illicit money, he didn't care. He was in just the same boat as Michael. There was one difference, however. Michael wasn't exactly poor, but Noah was filthy rich, a fact which did not lessen Michael's affection for the man one little bit.

Meanwhile, over the past eight years, Divit Deshpande had done what he said he would. He had set up a "*Hut*" of his own in India. His Bollywood-derived wealth made the financial side of his venture easy. His good taste and gentility did the rest. Michael and Rachael had visited his establishment on two occasions and were most impressed. Of course, the cuisine was different from that of *The Hut*, although international dishes were served, but unsurprisingly there were many Indian dishes too. The difference between these and even the best Indian dishes on offer throughout Britain was quite staggering. Divit had obtained the services of some of the best chefs in India.

The music permeating the place was different too. Of course it was. Divit liked classical Indian music in particular, and ragas were to be heard quite regularly. He had, however, set up a small theatre in his establishment. It was extremely well soundproofed. It needed to be, for there, musicians let rip, allowing their Indian exuberance full rein. Bollywood with earplugs, Rachael had called it, but like so many others, was intoxicated by its life and glamour.

The grounds were magnificent, with palm trees everywhere, beautifully manicured lawns, and Divit had even set up a croquet lawn.

What was so amazing about the *Indian Hut*, as Michael called it, was that the whole thing had been established within three years. Of course, that was down to money. Divit had absolutely enormous amounts of it available to him. His *Hut* was by way of being a hobby. Unlike Michael, he didn't live on site and act as host at dinner, or everything else, for that matter. He lived quite far away and only turned up to see it now and again, or when some special guests were due. Guests like Rachael and Michael, of course.

Michael had managed to get all three of these wonderful friends on site, at *The Hut*, at the same time. He convened a meeting with them all together; Rachael, too, was in attendance. Michael appraised his wonderful friends of the mess he was in.

'I don't want to spend hours telling you every last bit of news, half-news, or gossip about all this. It is possible that Geoffrey will not seek to sell *The Hut,* but I think that very unlikely. I would like to be in a position to buy *The Hut* myself, but I don't have enough money. I believe I can come up with sixty million pounds. I think *The Hut* might raise one hundred and ninety million pounds on the open market. With vacant possession, of course.'

Rachael's eyes became very wet. Her reaction was not lost on Michael's audience.

'I am therefore looking to you good people to see if you would care to join with me in purchasing *The Hut*, with a view to maintaining it exactly as it is now. The return on your investments would be very low, I'm afraid: three percent at best. By the way, *The Hut* comprises the Tomber Estate plus two hotels and three pubs. I think you know that already, and in any case, if there is even half a chance that you would say yes, I should, of course, furnish you with a detailed prospectus and contract. My own share would be the largest, but we would write into any contract, appropriate escape clauses. Your opinions would be sought at that point. Right now, I am asking only for your first reaction. Of course, I don't expect you to reply on the spot.'

Divit took hold of Michael's hand and said, simply and with overwhelming sincerity, 'Michael, give me a paper to sign, and I will do so – here and now. *The Hut* must go on, my friend. I'm in.'

Noah was not far behind him. 'Michael, your news is appalling. Of course, I am more than willing to play my part. Let me see your proposal on paper, and I will surely join you both.'

Bill Land was a little more cautious. 'You're asking for a lot of money, Michael. I will want to see a complete prospectus, of course. Let me say, immediately, that I am more than inclined to join you all. Michael, you know how much I admire what you and Rachael have accomplished here. Time was when I wouldn't have contemplated supporting a life of privilege like this, but I have grown a little since then. I wouldn't vote for government support of an institution like *The Hut*, but I think I might well support you in private, with my own money. Just let me see the details, my friend.'

Michael looked at Rachael and then at his three friends. 'I cannot say much right now,' he began. 'I will not pretend that I am surprised by your reactions, but to see them in reality – in the flesh, as it were – is overwhelming. I will get back to you all with full details as soon as I can, but probably not before Geoffrey tells me of the sale himself.'

Noah was probably the most hotheaded of Michael's three guests. No, that's too strong. Noah's background and upbringing allowed him to express a view which each of the others also felt.

'I'd like to horsewhip the bugger,' he said.

Michael raised his hand to stop Noah in his tracks. 'Noah, I think it very likely that Geoffrey has no choice. I believe he has been a tad too ambitious and very unlucky. I think he has made a mistake and has no option but to take this path.'

'That's very generous of you, Michael,' Noah replied. 'But everyone must accept responsibility for their actions. Geoffrey may not have meant to put you in the shit, but he did so.'

'And while we're at it, Michael,' Bill intervened, 'it is disgraceful that you only found out about his plans by following a rumour. His secrecy is not the action of a friend.'

'Maybe he just didn't know how to tell me,' Michael replied.

'You are being incredibly stoic about this, my friend,' Divit replied. 'I'm not sure I could be so forgiving.'

'Oh, I'm not at all sure I shall be forgiving,' Michael replied. 'At this stage, I am trying to keep my mind as open as I can until I hear the full story. Let us stop conjecture at this point. I promise to let you know everything just as soon as I know it. For the moment, you have provided me with the security I sought. I am in a position to negotiate. I do understand, *of course*, that the whole plan may come apart if the details don't meet your standards. That is only right. It was your agreement in principle that I was after today, and you wonderful, wonderful friends have given me that. Let's have a drink!'

A bottle of *Bollinger* had done the trick.

*

After Michael and Geoffrey had shaken hands, Michael moved very quickly to make sure he could live up to it. He contacted Bill, Noah and Divit, asking them to confirm their promises. They all did. Michael now needed to find someone to buy his shares in *Marchant Voyages*. He turned to Isobel once more. Could she find somebody to buy them? He wanted seventy million pounds at least, he told her. Isobel didn't hesitate. She went straight – by videophone, that is – to Jim Chen. *Was he interested?* she asked. Even Isobel was impressed by Jim's reaction. His eyebrows shot up, he grinned from ear to ear and replied within the second.

'Yes, I'll buy them, Isobel. I'll give him seventy-five million pounds for them. That okay, do you think?'

Now it was down to Isobel not to let her astonishment show. 'I'm sure I can prevail on Michael to accept that, Jim,' she said, not too quickly, not too slowly, with just a sweet smile on her face. She felt sure that she had pulled it off.

Chen smiled back. 'Send me the bill of sale. By the way, there's no need to keep my name secret,' he added, before cutting the link.

Isobel was altogether less guarded when she told Michael about her customer. Michael had never heard of Jim Chen. Why should he have? That was not Michael's world.

'Is he good for it?' he asked Isobel.

'Oh, yes! He could buy the whole of *Marchant Enterprises*.'

Isobel quite professionally refrained from telling Michael that it was Chen who had bailed Geoffrey out with many hundred million pounds not so long ago. No, some things were for Isobel's ears alone.

Michael told his backers the news. He would contribute fifty-two million pounds from his shares and requested that Bill, Noah and Divit each cough up forty-six million pounds. He felt it only right, he told them, that he should risk the most. Were they all perfectly content with the arrangement? Everyone knew what was going on. Everyone was clear about his own part in the deal.

In due course, the whole thing happened. Michael was as bored as everyone else in the nuts and bolts of getting appropriate bills of sale drawn up and all the other legal niceties, but their solicitors claimed to be happy with everything. There was one moment which shone out in all this, however. When Geoffrey learned – because Michael saw no reason to conceal the information – that it was Jim Chen who now owned a significant, albeit minority, share in *Marchant Enterprises*, his face turned as white as a sheet, and he nearly fell down on the spot. Well, that might be a slight exaggeration, but he most certainly staggered.

Michael and Geoffrey barely spoke to each other throughout the proceedings. It seemed easier that way.

Part III

31

Life at *The Hut* resumed. Actually, as far as anyone else was concerned – staff or guests – it never stopped. Nobody outside the immediate family knew that anything had happened. Maybe Michael seemed a little subdued, but no one *really* noticed. New guests appeared, and as was invariably the case, were delighted with what they found there. Old guests reappeared only to sing their praises for *The Hut* all over again. Rachael, however, saw a change in Michael. It was subtle but, for her, at least, as clear as day. He seemed to have lost his appetite for life, for people. Sure, his good manners and sense of responsibility determined his ever-polite and charming behaviour. People had come to *The Hut*, at considerable expense, expecting to see something of Michael, to hear some of his old jokes as well as some new ones. They came for charm as much as anything else. There was always a sprinkling of guests who were particularly concerned about their privacy, a concern which often overshadowed their other needs or desires, but *The Hut* was more than equipped to help such folk. And they were far too preoccupied to notice any changes in their host. Really, no one noticed any change. Except Rachael.

She saw a distant focus in his gaze, a slight slowness to respond to others' remarks. He seemed permanently preoccupied. When he thought no one was looking, he looked sad. There were no tears, no shouting, no moaning. Just a slight stoop in his manner, in his gait, in his happiness. Rachael understood completely that *The Hut* was now financially secure and could be maintained exactly as it always had been. But Michael was sad. Like something had died inside him. She decided not to raise the subject with him, for it might all go away. The winds may change and blow it all away.

She waited weeks and then months. The wind did not blow it away. If anything, it was all getting slowly worse.

'Talk to me about it, Michael,' she said out of the blue one day.

'About what, darling?' he replied.

She frowned at him with disapproval all over her face.

'Let's go for a walk,' he said. 'Through the woods, maybe.'

A stroll through the woods usually lasted a long time. They had trodden that path on occasions when some deep thinking had been necessary; twice when they had discussed not becoming parents from every point of view they were able to imagine. That was long ago, now.

They had reached the two-headed bird at the crossroad along the Grand Avenue.

'I've often wondered about this statue,' Michael remarked. 'Of course, it sits above the junction of the underground passages, but there is no real symmetry underground. The main passage goes either to *The Hall* or to, and beyond, the *Pot*. In the third direction, lies the escape route under the hide. The more serious bird face looks towards the hall and the softer, almost humorous one, towards *The Pot* and beyond. There's no symmetry to the statue, at all.'

'I had never noticed any difference in their expressions before,' Rachael said. She examined the sculptured heads more closely than she had done in the past – she had only given them a casual glance at best. 'Yes! You're right! Why the difference?' she asked.

'Exactly my point. I've lived with those heads all my life. I was just a kid when I first noticed the difference between them. I remember asking Father. He hadn't seen the difference either and could suggest no cogent reason for it.'

'Perhaps it's just a piece of sculptors' whimsey,' Rachael mused. 'You know, like the gargoyles high inside some of our famous churches. Some not so famous, as well. They were often portraits of the sculptor himself, or of one of his mates.'

'Yes, but there it was very difficult to see them. You needed binoculars. So those sculptors' jokes weren't really meant to be seen. They were by way of being in-jokes. But here, they're in plain sight.'

'Yes, but many people miss the point. Like me and Arthur, for example. It might be no more than the sculptor telling us to look closely at his creation. A casual glance isn't good enough – maybe insulting to its creator,' Rachael mused.

They moved on.

Michael spoke. 'That business three months ago – or is it more? I've lost track – anyway, the shock when Isobel first told us about the rumour that Geoffrey was going to sell *The Hut* was like nothing I've experienced before. It hurt me from two points of view: that we were going to lose *The Hut*, we were going to lose our home, and I was going to lose my ancestral home; and that Geoffrey, one of my – no, our – best and oldest friends, the man who had been my best man, the man who, with his father, had saved my family home for us; that this man had plotted behind our backs about the second-most-important thing in our lives.'

'Second?'

'After you and me.'

'You said at the time, that while he might have been something of a coward, he probably had little choice,' Rachael said.

'But he had, you know. He could have sold one of his hotels. I have looked into *Marchant Enterprises* quite carefully since that time. I am amazed at the expansion he has wrought. He has moved the company into the big league. His father would have been so proud of his achievement. Geoffrey's argument for not selling one of the hotels would have been that many were still very heavily mortgaged, so that he wouldn't have raised enough money. But that wasn't true for all of them. One or two of the older ones, maybe one which Bob Etherington had bought or one of those which Geoffrey had purchased early on in his stewardship of the company. Of course, if he had sold one of those, he would have suffered income loss, income which he needed to help service the vast loans he took out in recent years. Yes, it's true: it would have been a bad decision from a financial point of view to sell one of those properties. Much better to be rid of *The Hut*, an enterprise which has returned only between two and three percent over the years. It would have been bad business. And business clearly came higher up Geoffrey's list of priorities than old friendship, affection or loyalty. I felt betrayed. I still do.'

'Yes, he was a shit,' said Rachael.

Michael looked sharply at his wife. He had never heard her use such coarse language before.

He continued. 'If Isobel hadn't given me the heads-up about the sale, we'd have been thrown out of this place.'

'Well, maybe you would still have been able to form a consortium,' Rachael suggested.

'Maybe, maybe. But we were put *en prise* by Geoffrey's indifference. Betrayal from another point of view. And you know, he had given absolutely no thought to the possibility that we might have been able to raise some cash. He gave us no chance. He was careless with our happiness – betrayal in yet another way. I loved Geoffrey, you know. To be disregarded by someone you have loved for a good part of your adult life makes a deep hurt. I can't stop thinking about it, and the more I do think about it, the worse it all seems. It's like a burrowing cancer in my brain.'

'Perhaps he never felt as strongly about you as you do about him. He wasn't obliged to, after all.'

Michael slowly nodded. 'That's true.'

'I suspect that you still do love him in a way,' Rachael murmured.

'I probably do. But there will be nothing more between us. Nothing except that hurt which never seems to diminish.'

'It will in time, darling,' Rachael answered, taking his hand. 'So this is what is making you so sad these days?'

'Only in part,' Michael replied. 'There is a much bigger problem'.

Rachael was startled. Bigger? What could be bigger than Geoffrey's betrayal? She said nothing.

'I think I've lost faith in *The Hut*,' Michael said very quietly.

'What on earth do you mean?'

'I'm not exactly sure. That whole business left me feeling drained. I had been scared at one stage and then sick – I mean nauseous. But, for god's sake, Rachael, why should *The Hut* matter a damn? It's an entirely artificial concept, just a place where some incredibly over-rich people can play from time to time. Is it anything more than my indulgence? Why should I – or anyone, of course – live this over-privileged life? More particularly, why should I complain if fate tells me that it has come to an end? I could have sold my shares and bought what most people would consider to be a pretty fancy home somewhere else and still not have to lift a finger. Maintaining this pile for me, just because my dad and his dad lived in the place, is just the sort of ammunition the lefties love. And they're probably right.'

'Well, for a start, my dear, you have lifted considerably more than a finger to construct *The Hut*. *The Hut* is far more than this estate. You are right to call it a concept. You have built this concept almost single-handedly.'

Michael began to protest.

'Yes, all right, I and many others have helped you, but the real meat has been yours. You went out and found people who would like to come. You did that by the force of your personality. Sometimes I think you are quite unaware of just how much everyone cares for you, my darling. Just look at how Noah and Divit jumped to your aid; and even more than them, consider how amazing it was that sober, acute businessman, Lord Bill, joined you almost without a second thought. I'm sure that you could have elicited help from just about every single one of *The Hut*'s guests. Why do you suppose these people keep returning here? It isn't cheap! They could just as well go for a holiday at *The Savoy* or *The Ritz*.'

'They probably do,' Michael mumbled.

'Of course they do! But they keep coming back here to share your table and to hear your jokes all over again!'

'So I'm successful at providing a playpen for the wealthy,' Michael retorted.

'What is so terribly wrong with that, Michael?'

Rachael was getting exasperated and decided to leave her protests for the moment. Michael was quite obviously deep into his depression and, in her judgement, at least, needed to sulk for a while longer. They continued their stroll arm in arm but in silence.

'Let's go the long way round,' Rachael suddenly suggested. 'Out through the main gate, past the village wharf and *The Pot*.'

'Yes, all right,' Michael replied, but without much enthusiasm.

They spent some time at the wharf. *Maisy Pot* was tied up there. It still had the tribute to Braque, which Michael had painted decades earlier. Some things really do last a long time.

'Have you ever taken *Maisy Pot* on the canal by yourself, Michael?' Rachael asked. 'Or, at any rate, as captain, so to speak? I mean, apart from on our wedding night?'

'I did a long time ago,' Michael replied, without much enthusiasm.

They walked off, continuing their circular tour. As they came to *The Pot*, Rachael took Michael inside. She didn't suggest doing it, for she feared rejection. She ordered a couple of beers from Jill at the bar. Jill was in a happy mood, although she never seemed not to be, cheerfully joshing Michael and Rachael about their slumming it in *The Pot*.

'Now, now, Jill,' Rachael replied. 'None of your reverse snobbery, if you don't mind.'

They had played these games before. Nobody minded. Michael mumbled something and took his beer to a table.

Rachael felt obliged to excuse him. 'Out of sorts. Pay no attention, Jill,' she explained.

By the time they got back to the hall, Michael was as morose as he had been when they left it.

32

Michael continued to slide down into ever-blacker despair for several weeks more, and no amount of quiet hand-touching or simple acts of distraction by Rachael seemed to halt that slide.

In the end, Rachael lost it. It might have been better had she become desperate by design, but she too was feeling the strain of the increasingly leaden load of Michael's self-pity.

'For god's sake, Michael, grow up!' she burst out one morning.

Gentle Rachael, for whom nothing seemed too heavy to carry, too ugly to cringe from, too dark to run from; gentle, even-tempered Rachael who could always be depended upon to smooth over any little bump in the road; gentle, *calm* Rachael really lost it.

'You have been wallowing in self-pity long enough. And what is really the matter? Geoffrey betrayed you. Well, it happens, Michael. Shit happens! So you give up? You no longer feel that what you have created is worth nurturing? You feel over-privileged? Well, you are, Michael.'

She was getting even more worked up now, losing her self-control.

'You *are* over-privileged. Your family has been so for generations, and you, no more than they, do not deserve to live your life without all the struggles which make up the lives of ordinary people. You know what, Michael? Those struggles make their characters. They don't whine. They get on with it. For god's sake, Michael, bloody well get over it. Grow above it, Michael. Stop whining. Make *use* of the privilege you are simply lucky enough to have been given.'

Michael was astounded by the ferocity of her outburst. 'Rachael…' he began.

But Rachael couldn't stop. She hadn't finished. She hadn't vomited forth all that had been building up in her for the past months. 'If you feel so useless and unable to see how much you are loved and admired by everyone you know, if you cannot comprehend just how great was that gesture by

Divit and by Noah and by Bill three months ago – and I don't just mean their money, but their trust and their love – you might as well sell up and become a recluse. By yourself, Michael, for I'll not join you. I am sick to the back teeth with your behaviour.'

Her face was flushed, and she was breathing heavily and, by now, she had run out of steam. She looked at Michael and saw the astonishment in his face. Bewilderment and incomprehension that his beloved Rachael should talk – shout – at him like that. In all their married life and in all their time together before that, she had never raised her voice to him. He hadn't been aware that she had a loud voice; that she had it in her to shout.

His eyes began to soften and to weep. Michael adored Rachael, but he was ever master of his demeanour. Or so he had thought, for he had most certainly not been in control of it for the past few months.

Having blown her top, Rachael reverted to type, of course, and seeing the look of hurt and guilt on Michael's face, she burst into tears and held him close.

She began to say, 'I'm sorry…' just as Michael blurted, 'Oh Rachael, I am so sorry. You are right, completely right. You are, but I don't know how to get out of this hole. Please help me, darling.'

Rachael held Michael tightly and tried to soften her words.

'I will try to, but you must try too,' she said quietly. 'I must think about what can be done. Let's sleep on it.'

They left it there, for neither could see a path forward right then and there. They would indeed sleep on it; Rachael perhaps more fitfully than Michael.

Rachael saw that she had to take charge for a while. In a wifely fashion. With subtlety. By the bucket load. But with the heavy fist of authority, if needed.

'Michael,' she began after breakfast, some days later (some days later, because Rachael had been busy organising. You understand.) 'We're always sending our guests upriver or up the canal as part of their experience at *The Hut*. The time has come for us to avail ourselves of these same facilities. We are going on a mystery tour, starting early tomorrow. Oh, all right, after breakfast. Pack your bag: sloppy for on the boat, and smart casual for on a treat. Don't ask. I won't tell.'

'How long shall we be away?'

Rachael wagged her finger and left the table without a word.

Quite smartly, after breakfast next day, Barry turned up in one of the company cars to pick them up. It was one of the small cars. Michael complained that they could hardly move in it.

'We're not going far, so stop whinging,' Rachael replied.

Indeed, they weren't. Just five minutes from hall to Tomber wharf. Michael began to walk towards the smart launch, the one the three Irish priests had taken some years back.

'No, Michael. We're taking *Maisy Pot*,' Rachael informed him. 'Ah! And here's Ken to help with our bags. Good morning, Ken!'

They climbed aboard and, as their feet hit the rear deck, Jill appeared from within.

'Good morning, Michael. Good morning Rachael!' she greeted.

Ken took their bags through to the guest quarters. A delicious smell of fresh coffee permeated the whole boat. Michael began to relax a mite. Ken wasted no time before casting off. They were under way in less than five minutes since their arrival at the wharf.

'You know, I'm not sure that I've been on board *Maisy* since her last refit. It's very pleasant, isn't it?'

'*I* think so,' Rachael agreed. 'Coffee?'

She nodded at Jill who brought a carafe to the table in the cosy common area. Rachael poured for Michael, herself and Jill. Michael's expression was one of puzzlement, but he said nothing.

'I'll swap with Ken in a few moments.' Jill answered Michael's unspoken – and unintended – question.

'Do you know where we're going, Jill?' asked Michael.

Jill looked at Rachael with a soft smile and replied, 'Rachael said that you'd ask that. Yes, I know where we're going. So does Ken. So does Rachael.'

'And you're not going to tell me,' Michael said. 'I could sack you.'

Jill grinned. She was beginning to enjoy herself. 'No, you can't. You're not employing me at the moment – Rachael is.'

'And I'm not sacking anyone,' she said.

'This is a bloody conspiracy!' Michael said.

Rachael and Jill nodded their heads sombrely.

Meanwhile, Michael had failed to take note of the direction they had taken from the wharf. He realised, quite suddenly, that they were chugging downstream rather than upstream, which led to the more usual, happy hunting grounds. He didn't bother to ask. Ken tapped on the door, and Jill took over the helm so that Ken could enjoy some of her wonderful coffee.

'We don't go this way very often, Ken,' Michael said.

'True,' Ken replied, without qualification.

'I see that you're in on this conspiracy of silence, too, Ken,' Michael complained.

'What conspiracy is that, Boss?' Ken replied.

'Okay, I get it,' Michael said. 'I give in.'

'Good. Now that we've got all that over, darling, why don't you just lie back and enjoy it all?'

'Haven't had an offer like that for years,' Ken smirked.

Rachael giggled. Michael did his best harrumph.

'There are newspapers in the rack over there,' Ken said. 'It will be about an hour and a half before anything exciting in the nautical area comes up. I'll leave you two to it,' and he joined his wife on the rear deck.

'We haven't read the papers together for a long while,' Rachael said. 'This is turning out to be a proper holiday!'

Michael turned to the obituaries column in *The Times* but found nobody he knew and turned away in some disappointment. He found some more disappointment as soon as he turned to the headline news. That seemed to steady him. Rachael had observed this performance and passed Michael the lifestyle section of her paper.

'There's an article about Philip Roth in it,' she said.

That worked. Michael was intrigued by Philip Roth.

Ken poked his head in.

'Thought you'd like to know. We're about to perform a manoeuvre! Turning to port, into the Avon.'

Rachael and Michael joined Jill and Ken in the cockpit. The river was quite a bit wider here than it was at Tomberwater. Up ahead, it widened markedly as it joined the mighty Avon river. They were miles from the mouth of the Avon but, nevertheless, it was still a much larger river than theirs. Ken slowed *Maisy* to a crawl as he steered upriver into the Avon.

'I've only been here once before,' Michael announced, 'and that was easily twenty years ago. It seems much the same, though.'

'How far up did you go?' asked Ken.

'To just about here, actually. Enough to say we'd seen the Avon, and then we turned back for home. So from now on I'm in unfamiliar territory.'

'That's good,' Rachael murmured.

'How far are we going?' Michael asked.

'Nice try, darling,' laughed Rachael.

They remained in the cockpit for an hour or so. It was warm enough there, and there was quite a lot of interest in the passing scenery. Then Rachael disappeared into the cabin. By that time, Michael and Ken were well into chatting about the boat; how long between engine servicing and all that sort of really exciting stuff.

Jill ducked into the cabin for a few moments, reappearing with a couple of beers for the men. Very soon thereafter, Ken manoeuvred *Maisy Pot* into an enticing bit of riverbank where he moored the boat by tying the mooring lines to trees at either end. There were many trees around that area, which made for cosy countryside, but he had found a clear spot of grass against which to park the craft.

He and Michael were standing on the bank when Jill called to Ken to take a hamper from her. Ken spread a chequered cloth out on the grass and found some plates, glasses and cutlery. Jill joined the men, holding a bottle of champagne and four flutes.

'I'll be mother,' she said, as Rachael climbed down to join in.

'To our little adventure!' Jill toasted.

Then Rachael got up and climbed back into the boat, reappearing from the cabin after a moment, carrying two large bowls which she passed to Jill. Jill placed these on the ground in front of the men.

'Rachael has been busy,' she said.

Rachael climbed out of the boat with a large open plate in her hand.

'There we are. A cold plate with salads. That should do us for lunch.'

Michael looked at Rachael a little quizzically.

'This is a holiday for four,' Rachael explained. Everyone gets the chance to do the work. Cheers!'

It was an excellent lunch and always a winner with Michael. Everyone seemed to enjoy themselves. Even Michael took on the appearance of somebody at peace with himself. Okay, it wasn't so, but even the appearance of it was a small win for Rachael. Afterwards, Rachael took Jill by the hand, pulled her up and made to go.

'Thank you, boys. You clear up while Jill and I go and explore.'

One thing Michael was not and that was work-shy. In any case, he rather enjoyed the idea of an equal-share mystery tour. They had everything washed up and put away well before the girls got back. When they did return, Rachael announced that they would not go too much further today so that they would not overshoot somewhere she was avid to see tomorrow. They would have a short and gentle chug upriver, moor for the night and settle down to drinks, eating and a game of cribbage or two. Michael frowned.

Rachael asked, 'Don't you like cribbage, Michael? Surely it's just the thing to play when we're all sozzled.'

Michael shook his head. 'No, cribbage is fine. I was just trying to think what could possibly be of interest just a few miles further along.'

'Michael, be a good boy and give your brain cell a rest. Everything will become clear in the fullness of, well… you know.' Rachael smiled at him. He had always liked that smile. She knew it.

They climbed back onto *Maisy* and cast off. Ken chose a slow and lazy speed. They hadn't seen any other traffic on the river so far, so they weren't in anyone's way. Michael picked up the newspapers again and became moderately engrossed. Rachael relaxed a little. They moored again by five o'clock.

'Cocktails everybody?' Ken asked, to receive a mock-sombre nod. Ken was good at cocktails.

'You decide, love,' Jill chirped.

Ken passed them up to Michael from the galley. Four bamboos.

'What are these, Ken,' Michael asked, 'or is that a secret, too?'

'No,' Ken replied. 'Sherry, dry vermouth, Angostura bitters and orange bitters. Nothing could be simpler.'

'Oo! That's nice,' Rachael said. 'How many cocktails do you know by heart, Ken?'

'Probably fifty or so, but I've made several hundred over the years. And, of course, I've had to road-test them all.'

'How could you be a good barman otherwise?' encouraged Michael.

Ken did not feel at all patronised by Michael's characterisation of him. They both knew Ken was the licensee of the *Tomber Pot*. Barman was but one of Ken's many accomplishments.

After a while, Jill asked Ken to give her a hand in the galley.

'Our cook this evening,' she explained.

Michael and Rachael continued to enjoy their bamboos.

Michael remarked: 'You and the Gastons seem to have planned this trip down to the last nut and bolt.'

Rachael flashed one of her special smiles at him. 'Yes, we have,' was all she said to that.

Jill provided the party with her *coq au vin*. She often made it, but then, why not? She was very good at it and, of course, she had prepared it before their trip began, which is always a good thing on boats.

Ken turned up with a useful little *Morgon*. 'We don't want headaches, after all,' he chortled.

They finished with a cheese plate and a bottle of port and more *Morgon*, as Jill wasn't fond of the fortified wine. She and Ken cleared away, refused help from the Montaynes – 'Your turn tomorrow,' she said – and brought out the cribbage set.

'This has seen some play,' Michael observed.

'That's true,' Ken agreed.

Jill slid a box of chocolates towards Michael and Rachael. 'Low calorie,' she lied.

Ken and Jill had played cribbage for years and were considered to be rather good at it. Michael had played a few games when he was in his very early teens but, by now, had more-or-less forgotten how to proceed. Rachael had never played. Jill brought out a pack of cards and some peg boards.

'You'll soon get the hang of it,' Jill told Rachael, and began to explain how she was to move her pegs in a leap-frog fashion as each round was played.

She then began to list the various ways of gaining points. By the time she got to "one for his nob", Rachael was near to hysterics.

'It gets easier,' Jill encouraged her.

'I should hope so,' Rachael replied. 'Have you got all this written down somewhere?'

'Somewhere,' Jill replied.

'But not here,' Ken chimed in.

This was going to be difficult.

'So ace is always low, the picture cards are worth ten, and the rest take their face value?' Rachael began again. 'I'm looking for a hand which adds up to fifteen, or a pair, or three of a kind, or a flush which is four or more in the same suit, or runs of three or more in mixed suits.'

'The aim of the game is to score 121 points as indicated by the pegs in your row on the board. Once you have done that, it is said that you have pegged out...'

'Which I likely will before much longer.' Rachael turned to Michael. 'Pour me another drink, darling,' she pleaded.

'Let's just begin,' Ken suggested. 'We can point out the possibilities to you as we go along. For this learning game, let's lay our hands out face up, so that Jill and I can explain.'

'Now there, you see,' Jill barged in, as soon as they were under way. 'You can take the six and seven of diamonds in your hand with the eight of diamonds on top of the pack to form a three of a kind.'

'What's that worth?' Rachael asked, her face furrowed with concentration. She was getting progressively more flustered. She looked at Michael with a pleading look.

'You chose to play cribbage, my love,' he said.

'Let's play music instead,' she said. 'This makes my brain ache.'

Michael smiled and acceded immediately.

'I bet you can't remember how to play the game, yourself,' Rachael continued.

Michael attempted to save some face. 'I'm sure it would come back after a few minutes.'

'The three of us could play if you prefer,' Ken offered.

Michael politely declined. 'I think the booze is fogging my brain,' he said.

'Weak!' scoffed Ken, but let the idea drop.

'You two play. We can watch and see if we pick up anything,' Michael replied.

Jill and Ken began to play, explaining as they went.

'No, don't explain. It will ruin the game for you, and it's too fast for us,' Michael said.

He and Rachael watched for all of five minutes before toasting each other silently and sitting well back on the cushions. Jill and Ken seemed to play at a furious pace while Michael and Rachael played a little late jazz from the collection on board. They were enjoying themselves, so all was not lost.

*

Rachael and Michael saw to breakfast in the morning. They had slept well, and a good, strong coffee helped counteract last evening's booze. Ken cast off and took *Maisy Pot* for a forty-five-minute sail before mooring once more.

'We have a half-hour's hike to do now,' Rachael announced, after everyone had disembarked.

She led the way along a narrow, barely worn path leading away from the river, and uphill. The way was soft underfoot but not at all muddy.

'Have you heard of the "House that's a Garden", Michael?' Rachael asked, after they had been walking for a few minutes.

'Can't say I have,' he replied. 'Tell me.'

'Well, it's quite famous around these parts. The owner/architect built the place some time ago. It's been built in the spirit of an even more famous Japanese house in Tokyo. The one in Japan is many stories high, while this is a much more modest affair built over four stories. As you climb the stairs, you have the choice of remaining at that level, or to leave the side of the building and continue upwards, but on the outside. Then, you re-enter the building at the next higher level, and so on. Everywhere there are plants, mostly in beautiful planters which are part of the structure of the building and which have also been designed by the architect. Altogether, as you climb to the top of the building, you walk in, and then out, of the building, so that inside and outside become one.'

'I gather that this place is open to the public, then?' Michael asked.

'Yes and no,' Rachael replied. 'It is open for viewing to selected people just half a dozen times a year.'

'So how come we have been chosen?' Michael asked.

'I've known the architect for years. We had briefly met at a party at university some time before you and I got together. I have seen some of his creations in glossy magazines from time to time, and I remembered about this one – his own home – when Jill and I planned this trip. I called him and he agreed to show us the place. I'm quite looking forward to meeting him again. I haven't seen him since my old Bristol days. I wonder whether I'll recognise him.'

There came a bend in the path they were all treading, and the ground opened up to reveal a level area almost enclosed by lightly wooded areas. In the middle was the most amazing building that any of them had ever seen. It seemed as if its entrails had been laid bare before them. On the ground all around the house and in planters, some of which were actually part of the construction itself, and around the building at all levels were beautifully kept plants of various kinds, acers in particular. Many were meticulously trimmed in bonsai style, but not all. There was an eclectic mix of Japanese and European styles. The woods around included, once again, several different varieties of acer.

'Those maples colour up to reds and gold in the autumn,' Rachael said. 'I've seen pictures of this place. I feel I know it already.'

A slight, sandy-haired man wearing a neat, white silk shirt with a Mandarin collar, and dark-blue pants came out to greet them.

'Rachael!' he said, extending his hand. 'I wondered… but you haven't changed a bit.'

'And you are still charming, Nigel,' Rachael replied. 'May I introduce my husband, Michael. Michael…?'

Michael stared at the man for some while as he shook his hand, which he did not release. 'Are you Nigel Plater?' he asked eventually.

The man couldn't take his eyes off Michael. Rachael began to wonder if something wasn't quite right about all this.

'Are you Michael Mountain?'

Michael smiled. 'Montayne,' he said.

'I have wanted to contact you for years, but I lost your address. I wasn't quite sure even of your surname.'

The man called Nigel suddenly grasped hold of Michael's arm and hugged him closely. There were tears of joy in his eyes. Rachael, Jill and Ken looked on in amazement. And then Ken got it too.

'You're the kid Michael rescued from the lock!' he shouted.

'And you, Ken…' Nigel said. 'It is Ken, isn't it? You helped save my dad's life that day!'

'How is your father?' Michael asked.

'He died fifteen or more years gone. Peacefully. Thanks for asking.'

Ken suddenly found his manners, 'This is my wife, Jill,' he told Nigel.

Michael was still making a fair imitation of a goldfish. 'I had absolutely no idea you lived around here,' he said. 'For that matter, I didn't know you were an architect, either, let alone a famous one. Rachael has just been telling us a little about you, but she hadn't got around to mentioning your name.'

Nigel replied: 'I have been wanting to contact you for years, but I had absolutely no idea where you lived. I so wanted to write to you. I know you gave Dad and me a note with your name and address, but we lost it.'

Michael had still not yet released Nigel's hand. Rachael was flabbergasted. She couldn't have planned anything better than this had she tried.

'Come inside, everyone. This calls for a drink. I'll be back in a moment.'

Nigel rushed off, returning almost immediately with a bottle of champagne and five flutes. 'I'm so sorry that my wife isn't home to meet you all. She's spending the family fortune at the shops in London this week.' He raised his glass to his guests, but to Michael in particular. 'For my father's life and mine!' he said, and drank. 'Sit, sit,' and he ushered his guests into comfortable chairs.

It was only then that Michael noticed that all the furniture in the room was proportioned as to reflect the masses of the building itself, and that the chairs couldn't be moved, for they were all placed with precision and fastened down. He began to look around. Everything in the room had obviously been chosen with the utmost care. Every item was exquisite.

'This is beautiful, Nigel,' he said. 'You must be very proud of it. I would guess that you designed the furniture, as well as the house.'

'And chose the plants as far as your eye can see,' Nigel replied. 'Many would argue that I am the archetypical control freak, I'm afraid. Come, let me show you around.' He looked at last at Rachael once more. 'Oh!

Rachael, I am so very pleased that you contacted me the other day. What a surprise. What a coincidence.'

Drinks in hands, the party followed Nigel around the house. He didn't point to any piece of furniture or particular object, leaving it to his guests to look and find for themselves. But as they made to climb further up the house, Nigel opened doors leading to external staircases.

Michael remarked, 'It must have been quite difficult to weatherproof these doors, Nigel.'

'Yes, it was. I spent quite a time working that out. The trick is not to over-strive to prevent leaks but rather to arrange that any water caught in the closure runs away outside rather than in.'

'What if it's cold and wet outside and you want to go to bed or whatever?' Michael continued.

'Quite,' replied Nigel. 'That's okay, because there is an internal staircase, too. Even I do not take my design to the level of religion. I enjoy comfort just like anyone else!'

'Do you do the bonsai and other plant trimming yourself?' Jill asked.

'I do a little, but my wife takes on most of it. Bonsai has been a hobby of hers for years.'

They spent a long time in the house, looking at every little detail very carefully. There was barely a right angle in the whole place.

'I am lost in admiration for what you have done here, Nigel,' Michael enthused, not for the first time that morning.

'Let me show you some different views of the house from outside,' Nigel said.

He had clearly done this many times before. One or two views he enjoyed showing to his guests were from the surrounding woods but framed by overhead branches from some of the many acers around.

'In the autumn, these acers turn bright red or orange or yellow. And some just stay bright green until they shed,' he remarked. 'I helped choose some of them and their positions, but really this part is down to Lilly, my wife.'

They stayed for nearly an hour and a half before thanking their host profusely and taking the path back down to the river.

As Ken cast off, he told them that just ten minutes further on was a nice little hostelry where they would enjoy a spot of lunch.

'After all that excitement, we can leave it to someone else to provide for us,' he said.

They settled on ploughman's lunches all round, with beers and wine by the glass, as they preferred. Rachael remained more or less silent throughout lunch. She just couldn't believe their luck. She couldn't believe hers in providing so memorable an interlude for Michael, for it was obvious to everyone that he hadn't been that alive for a long time.

*

As they climbed back into *Maisy*'s cockpit, Rachael announced her plan for the rest of the day.

'As a special concession to Michael, I will now reveal – to him, at least – our destination today. We are going to Stratford where we will grab a bite to eat at a local restaurant before we go to the theatre for a performance of *A Midsummer Night's Dream*.'

'I guessed that we would go to the theatre,' Jill said, 'but I hadn't realised which play would be on. I've not seen it before. Actually, I haven't seen much Shakespeare before.'

'Or even any,' Ken confessed. 'Will we understand all that Old English?'

'You will. Don't worry. The actors see to that. The plot is a little complicated, but I'm sure you'll pick it up in no time.'

By late afternoon, they had arrived at their final mooring for the day. It was well out of Stratford itself, safely away from tourists and anyone who might get near the boat. What it was near, however, was Stannells Bridge, just off Seven Meadows Road.

While everyone changed into smarter clothes for the evening, Rachael phoned for a taxi to meet them on the bridge and to take them into town, and the restaurant she had chosen for a bite. It all went very smoothly, as did everything Rachael ever arranged, and they had time to enjoy their meal, and then to stroll into the Royal Shakespeare Theatre in good time for the evening's performance. Rachael was a little nervous on behalf of the Gastons, though. She really wanted them to enjoy their first outing to one of *The Bard*'s plays. Another one might have been easier for a beginner, but that was all that was on offer at this time.

They found their seats in the stalls and settled in. The Montaynes smiled at each other, as they enjoyed that familiar auditorium. The Gastons looked nervous as they, nevertheless, bathed in the theatre's atmosphere.

By the time the play had introduced its first half-dozen characters, Jill's face was beginning to screw up with concentration. By the time that the second plot was introduced, with the six characters playing other characters, Ken's face was a picture of utter confusion. He never looked away from the stage, however. When Puck began painting the magic potion on the wrong pair of eyes, Ken's and Jill's expressions were of calm concentration, at all times trying so hard not to lose the plot. Or a plot. At the conclusion, when Puck suggested to the audience that maybe they had all just experienced a dream, Jill and Ken were in total agreement.

The four friends left the theatre in silence, each fumbling with his own thoughts. They decided to catch a cab back to Stannells Bridge as soon as they could, so that they could drink and talk about their evening within the familiar comfort of *Maisy*'s embrace.

Ken found a light dessert wine while Jill brought forth some of her own, homemade truffles.

'Well?' Rachael asked them, once everyone was comfortable. 'What did you think of your first Shakespeare play?'

There was an embarrassed pause before Jill spoke up. 'Are they all as complicated as that?' she asked. 'I mean, much to my surprise, I caught on to the language sufficiently well, I think, to understand what was being said – and I suppose that was down to the acting abilities of the cast – but that complicated plot! Or rather, plots, all interwoven. It was so hard to follow. If the characters continually argue and get confused about who's playing who – that's like a play within a play within a play – how more difficult yet is it for a first-time observer?'

'Yes, I agree. It isn't the easiest of plays, but it does get clearer with time and repeated exposure,' Rachael replied.

'You thought cribbage was complicated! *A Midsummer Night's Dream* seems far more complicated than that!' Jill protested.

Michael laughed. 'That's a fair point, Jill. I have to admit that I struggled with *Midsummer* for a long time. I read the play afterwards and talked about it with friends before I really got the hang of it. It certainly isn't the play for beginners.'

'I'm sorry,' Rachael said. 'I agree with that, but there was no choice, and this evening was especially for you, Michael.'

'No, that's all right. Even though I didn't understand it, I want to go and see it again,' Jill replied.

'Can't say fairer than that,' Michael replied, and popped another truffle in his mouth.

Later that evening, as Michael and Rachael were settling down in bed, Michael turned to his most-loving wife and told her, 'You have really thought so hard about this trip, darling, haven't you? It has been so interesting and so varied. I have really enjoyed it. Thank you.'

*

They spent a couple more days getting back to Tomberwater. Rachael felt rather pleased with herself, and with Jill and Ken who had been such a tremendous support. She told them so.

33

It seemed that Rachael's efforts to take Michael out of himself were bearing fruit, for, some weeks after their return from their trip in *Maisy Pot*, Michael suddenly suggested that they invite Isobel and Harvey to join them at *The Hut* for a couple of weeks, as a way of thanking them for all their hard work during their troubles. Rachael was more than delighted, seeing this as a sign that Michael was beginning to take an interest in the world and people, once more.

Three weeks later, their guests appeared together in Harvey's Porsche.

Michael explained to them over cocktails that he had nothing planned for them except "good wine and diet" – and, he hoped, good conversation too – and he suggested that they should just refamiliarize themselves with everything *The Hut* had to offer, relax, and generally enjoy themselves. Rachael took them aside to explain that all this was just as much for Michael's benefit, as he had been feeling low for some time. Their presence around the place, in and out as they saw fit, however, would be a great help. Michael took them aside to explain that their presence would be a great help to Rachael and, by the way, as far as he, Michael, was concerned, either or both of his guests were free to discuss any details of what they knew about *Marchant Enterprises* and *The Hut* between them.

'Up to you, my dears.'

Everything was therefore perfectly clear!

It wasn't too long before Isobel challenged Harvey at tennis. Harvey, ever the gentleman, didn't try too hard, thinking it better to let Isobel win. Isobel saw through this in a moment and hit one ball as hard as she could right at Harvey's midriff. Her aim was good. Well, goodish. It hit low. Harvey took some time to recover. Isobel smiled sweetly at him and suggested that he should try harder. This seemed to knock the gentleman out of him, and he fought as hard as he could thereafter. He won the first set but only just. Both now saw clearly that they had a fight on their hands, and both played like demons from then on. Isobel just squeaked home to win the second set.

'One more?' suggested Harvey, breathing heavily.

'If you're up to it,' Isobel replied, disguising her own lack of puff as well as she could, 'but we can leave the decider until you're recovered, if you like.'

'Another, then,' Harvey grunted.

Play continued. They were pretty equally matched, and they knew it. Harvey, however, felt that he had Isobel on the ropes and put in a super-human effort. It was fortunate that they had agreed to play with tie-breaker rules, or they might have been at it till death. Isobel won in the end. Neither had much breath left to congratulate and commiserate.

They made it to the bar, via showers and changes, each looking so fresh that butter would have had a hard time even to soften in their mouths.

'What do you fancy?' Harvey asked Isobel.

They settled for large G&Ts.

'I hope I didn't over-tax you,' Isobel teased him.

'I only wish you would,' replied Harvey.

The ambiguity was clear to Isobel, who smiled warmly at Harvey, so warmly that he felt encouraged. Until he remembered, that is, about Isobel's preferences.

Later, over dinner, sitting opposite Michael and with Rachael within earshot, Harvey and Isobel independently both commented upon the unique nature of hospitality at *The Hut*. They had both enjoyed the superb environments, meals and drinking at some of the world's best hotels and resorts, but the thing which, in their view, raised *The Hut* above them all was the communal dining under the gentle guidance of its genial host.

'At bottom, Michael, *The Hut* is you,' Isobel said.

Harvey confirmed this view with enthusiasm.

Michael was astounded by the obvious sincerity of their opinion. He was also very pleased. Obviously. And he was warmed by it.

Embarrassment caused him to protest: 'I didn't invite you two here to be a cheer group!'

'There are not too many people who can put their stamp on an enterprise in the way you have done here, you know. There are folk who are good at making money, who become artists of distinction, scientists, writers, and the rest. But there is something quite unique about Michael Montayne.'

'I thank you most sincerely for that remark, but I must insist that beauty is only in the eye of the beholder. Naturally, I admire your eyesight, but the possibility of your wearing rose-tinted glasses to disguise your growing cataracts cannot be overlooked, I'm afraid.'

There was some laughter from those within earshot before the conversation dissolved and fragmented, and the evening progressed into familiar paths, but Michael was pleased. So was Rachael.

Harvey and Isobel made plans to walk over to *The Pot* for lunch the next day after exploring the Tomber wharf rather more closely than either of them had done on earlier visits to *The Hut*.

It was pleasant to renew old acquaintances and sights. They walked back to the hall via the main gate, as they had done together so long ago. They didn't see any deer this time. They talked a lot about what each of them had done for Michael at his time of great anguish, and how they came to be nearly on the same page so far as those events were concerned. Their business activities recently had nothing to do with any of the parties involved at that time.

As they came near to their happy hunting ground, namely the lounge bar of the hall, Harvey suddenly had an idea. 'Izzy, why don't we go off for a few days? I'm thinking of climbing in Snowdonia. We both like walking and, so far, we've not been wanting for subjects to talk about. It would make a lovely holiday within a holiday, don't you think?'

What could have been better for a couple of young(ish) people with strong limbs and open minds? Isobel agreed immediately.

'Let's have a drink while I make some phone calls,' Harvey suggested. Soon thereafter, he asked Isobel if she was game to climb Snowdon itself. 'The website says that it will take about six hours for the round trip.'

'Sounds fine. We can do that,' Isobel replied, full of confidence.

'Okay, I'll look for a place to stay,' he said, and began to fiddle with his smartphone. 'There's a very upmarket place here. We could try for that.'

'I'm happy with anything you can arrange, but don't forget, at this time of year we'll be lucky to find anything!'

Harvey got to work. After half an hour he turned to Isobel and, with a long face, agreed with her fears.

'You were dead right. Everything is full. All I've been able to find – and that's down to a last-minute cancellation – is a whole cottage. It looks clean but rather more basic.' He continued to study his smartphone. 'Damn, there's only one bedroom. But two beds. Are you game to share a bedroom, Izzy?'

'Sure,' Isobel replied brightly. 'We won't be staying long anyway, and we'll be spending most of our time on the mountain and around, won't we?'

'Yes. Oh! One double and one sofa bed. No, that's okay, I'm happy to take the sofa. Apparently the views from this cottage are to die for. It won't hurt us to rough it a bit. Shall I go for that?'

'Do it!' cried Isobel without hesitation.

By the time they had ordered, and drunk their first cocktail halfway, the cottage was booked.

'Izzy, find this website on your phone,' he said, and then, 'You see, it suggests that beginners like me – and you, I presume? Yes? –take the Llanberis path up the mountain. We're pretty fit, I know, but we shouldn't be silly, so I vote that we take the easy route. They all take about the same time, by the way. Look, we can park in Llanberis easily enough and climb from there.'

'One last problem to solve, Harvey,' Isobel said. 'Climbing clothes and any special gear. What do we need, and where can we buy it?'

'Here we are!' Harvey came back in less than a minute. 'Several shops, and at least one hires climbing gear, so we won't need to buy something we're unlikely to reuse. Problem solved. So, we'll drive to the cottage tomorrow, stop on the way for lunch and an evening meal, buy some groceries and get settled in. Next day, we go to Llanberis, get togged up and climb immediately. Then a day at the cottage with some easier walking, maybe. Next day, we return here. How does all that sound?'

'We should be the fittest people around by the time we're back at *The Hut*,' Izzy smiled. 'Yes, all of that's fine with me. You know, that must be the quickest piece of holiday-planning ever!'

'That's how we two do business!' Harvey grinned. 'Right, let's have another while we wait for the gong.'

They mixed in with some strangers at the table that evening: a couple from Croatia, and a single man from Huddersfield. All three turned out to be most interesting guests. Yet again, Michael's guests rarely failed to amuse. They told him so. Rachael was very pleased.

*

They left early the next day, for they had some distance to cover and Harvey wasn't at all clear about the kind of road, or traffic, they were likely to encounter. By the time they felt like a spot of lunch, they had gone well over half the distance, so they felt they were able to relax. They found a nice little pub just off their main track and settled for a ploughman's lunch for Isobel, and scampi and chips for Harvey.

'I love the sweetness of langoustines,' he told Isobel, 'even in this corny style.'

They got under way again. The countryside was becoming ever more gorgeous with rolling green hills and plenty of trees everywhere. As time went by, the trees got fewer, and the colours of the hills, mountains even, became ever more varied and beautiful.

'Thank god for satellite navigation,' Harvey remarked. 'No more looking feverishly at maps with tiny printing.'

They found the cottage by a little after five in the afternoon.

'Let's settle in and then go find a place to eat. Preferably nearby, so that we won't have to take the car, and I can have a proper drink.'

They were well enough pleased with the cottage. It was hardly super smart or modern or even artistic, but it was scrupulously clean and smelled fresh. They picked up the key from a neighbour, some quarter of a mile away, as instructed by the letting agent. They unpacked and freshened up. Isobel suggested that they find a shop for routine essentials. They took the car but were delighted to find that a well-stocked village shop was to be found within an easy half mile of their cottage. Couldn't be better. They also sniffed out a pub which looked clean, and the menu seemed fine.

'This is all going too well,' Harvey remarked.

'Shh…' Isobel replied. 'You'll put a jinx on it!'

They drove back to the cottage with their groceries which included a bottle or two of wine, one of which they opened immediately to toast their cottage and the scenery around it, which was exactly as described in the advertisement – gorgeous. There was a bench on a veranda outside from which to contemplate the view. It was very pleasant sitting there, side by side like any other couple. They were both conscious of the feeling and felt a little awkward. Harvey took hold of Isobel's hand for a moment. It was simply from instinct. He did it without thinking. She did not protest, nor try to remove her hand. Harvey frowned as he realised what was happening. It was not a frown of displeasure – far from it. Rather, it was a frown of puzzlement.

'Please tell me if I overstep,' he said, and then added, because he just had to, 'I seem to remember your telling me…'

Isobel interrupted Harvey. 'Such things can change,' was all she said.

They continued to hold hands like an old couple – or like a couple of kids. Harvey wasn't sure.

Isobel broke the spell. 'Let's go and explore that pub. Let's see if it's as good as it looked.'

They walked to the pub without holding hands, but gestured to each other all the time as they saw something new by the path or on the hills in the distance. Everything about that short walk seemed sharp, memorable and intense. Neither of them smiled. It was all so serious; so important.

They did smile at each other as they entered the warmth of the hostelry. The warmth derived from the lighting and the buzz of conversation in the place, rather than from any fire or central heating. There was no need for either of those just yet at this time of year.

They found a small table near a window and began to study the menu. It all seemed very tempting. Indeed, everything seemed very tempting to them that evening. A pitcher of cold water would have seemed very tempting. They were well aware of the atmosphere.

A waitress came, and they ordered meals and a bottle of wine. They looked out of the window at the fading light, knowing that it would fade slowly.

'Dusk is a wonderful feature of this country, don't you think?' Harvey said.

Isobel replied that she was about to say exactly the same thing. They looked at each other for a few moments and then back at the view outside. Their hands met momentarily on top of the table, but the moment was broken by the arrival of the wine. Harvey poured and they took a sip.

'That's okay,' he said. It wouldn't have mattered if it hadn't been, really.

Harvey wanted to ask about Isobel's "change" but didn't dare in case it broke the magic. Conversation didn't – couldn't – begin. God knows how long that silence lasted. They had no idea. The food came and they ate.

'This is quite good, don't you think?' Isobel said after some moments.

'For a pub, it's excellent,' Harvey replied. 'I suppose that's rather patronising, but I think it's fair. I'd certainly be happy to recommend the place to others. By the way, I didn't notice; what's the name of this pub? Did you see?'

'I did actually, or rather, I noticed when we did our recce earlier. It's called *The Pen Y Banc Arms*. I remember it because it might just as well be called *The Penny Bank Arms*! I've no idea how one is supposed to pronounce the name. I think it refers to a nearby hill or mountain.'

'The Yorkshire Penny Bank has a mountain of cash. Is that any help?' Harvey asked.

They laughed and turned back to their meals. They kept on toasting each other throughout their meal.

Over coffee, Isobel suddenly said, 'You asked about my sexuality.'

'I don't think I did, Izzy,' Harvey replied.

'Well, you meant to. I could see that. I told you I was gay a long time ago. I was then, but as time's gone by, I began to feel attracted to men. As well, that is.' Isobel paused.

'So you are bi?' Harvey blurted out.

'Maybe. As more time went by – that's by with a "y", not bi with an "i", by the way,' she giggled. 'Anyway, I rather think I'm more or less straight now. Just thought you should know.'

'Thank you, Izzy. That does simplify matters. You know, even all that way back when you told me you were gay, I found it difficult to believe. I rather thought that you were just getting rid of unwanted intentions I may have had.'

'No, Harvey, I was gay. I did find you attractive, but I didn't want you. Then.'

Her pause was but for a fraction of a second but they both noticed, and the air became electrified once more. They did not look away at the view this time but at each other, face to face, eyes to eyes.

'Let's go,' Harvey said.

He quickly paid the bill as they left, and the couple strode back to the cottage.

Some while later, Isobel whispered to Harvey, 'You said you were going to use the sofa bed.'

*

Next morning, they somehow managed to wake up, have breakfast and drive to Llanberis by half past seven. They soon found a shop from which they could hire all they needed for their climb up Snowdon, although they also bought a couple of warm jumpers while they were at it. The man in the shop asked them whether they had climbed Snowdon before and then approved of their choice of route.

'It's pretty easy now, but watch your step anyway. The climb should take you about six hours, round trip. Enjoy yourselves.'

The track was obvious and well marked, as was the start point. It was a little misty. Just early morning mist. The forecast had predicted a fine day. With joy in their hearts – a joy deriving from far more than the beautiful scenery and the crisp morning air – the pair set out. Very soon a gentle ascent became much steeper. Nothing to worry about, but steep enough for them to appreciate that they were going to have to work at it.

'Just a good workout,' Harvey grunted.

'We need that,' grinned Isobel.

Harvey took her hand and kissed it. Their climb resumed. At around three thousand feet above sea level, they paused, moved a little off track and broke off for what Harvey called "elevensies" – indeed, it wasn't too far off eleven, so, he argued, they were ready for a break. Just a soft drink and some biscuits. They were entitled to that, he argued. They kissed. Other climbers passed by and they kissed again.

Harvey stood and helped Isobel to her feet. 'I reckon that we'll be at Clogwyn Station within twenty minutes,' he said. 'Immediately after that, apparently, the going can get a bit slippery. In winter, it gets downright dangerous, I read.'

He was right. They reached the station as predicted, and the path for the next half hour – maybe less, but they were concentrating, like everyone else climbing there that day – was slippery and covered with loose stones and shale. That bit over, they once again moved a little off track to allow others to pass while they took another breather.

'We're going to be so fit by the end of this,' Isobel gasped.

'Or knackered!' Harvey replied between little gasps.

They took in the views which were, indeed, quite awe-inspiring. They kissed again. Several times.

'Okay,' Harvey announced. 'Once more unto the breach. I think we'll make the summit this time.'

Off they went again, with determination and joy. The rest of the way, though fairly steep in parts, was pretty much plain sailing, and they finally reached the top some three and a half hours after leaving Llanberis. Considering their two leisurely stops on the way, they felt quite pleased with themselves. While catching their breath at the height of just short of three thousand, two hundred feet above sea level, they turned to look in all directions. They could see Anglesea – even Ireland in the distance – and all the wonderfully beautiful peaks and valleys all around Snowdonia and beyond. There was a slight breeze and it was cool, so their warm jumpers had been more than necessary. They kissed to celebrate their achievement, and again to celebrate the sunny day, and again...

Time, they decided, for a spot of lunch. They had bought some sandwiches in Llanberis and sat down to enjoy them. Afterwards, they took many photographs, well aware that the professional postcards available at base would be far better. Theirs, however, had them in the picture – even a couple of "selfies".

Eventually they began their descent. They kept looking around at the views, wanting to imprint as much of this wonderful day in their memories. They were commenting now upon every view that took their fancy. After all, they were descending rather than climbing. Harvey turned to Isobel, who was a step behind him at one point, pointing as he urged her to look at one particular view. They were on the slippery stuff just above Clogwyn Station as Harvey spoke. He spoke as he turned his head round, lost concentration and slipped. He rolled down the steep slope to their left, ever faster as he failed to get a grip on anything useful. And then his head hit a half-buried rock. It brought him to a standstill, but he had been hurt badly and was bleeding profusely. Isobel had hurried, but carefully, after him.

'My god! Darling, are you all right?' she cried.

They sat while he checked his sight and anything else he thought might be hurt.

'I reckon I'm okay,' he said. 'It just looks worse than it is, I think. Do you have any plasters with you, by any chance?'

By good fortune, she did have a packet. They cleaned Harvey's head as best they could and put a couple of plasters over the nasty gash near his temple. That seemed to work well enough. Harvey made to get up.

'Let's get going and have a drink to mend this,' he said.

As he put weight on his right ankle, it gave way and he fell, nearly continuing down the mountain once more. He tried to stand again but with far greater care this time. The pain was excruciating, and he couldn't move an inch.

'This is no place to get a broken ankle,' he said.

'You'll just have to hang onto me somehow,' Isobel replied. 'See if you can walk. Hold onto me so that you don't put weight on that side.'

They were fit people and they did it, but not without a few unsuccessful trials, cries of pain, and a wide variety of language which Isobel pretended later not to have heard before. Shortly afterwards, a couple of men caught up with them and offered their help. Between them all, and with Harvey's and Isobel's enormous gratitude, they got down to base and the gentle walk back to Harvey's car. They had expected to get back to base by two or three in the afternoon. They had made it by five o'clock. They exchanged names and contacts with their rescuers, and after many more thanks, were left to manage alone. Isobel took the Porsche's keys from Harvey – to his extra consternation and a finger-wagging from Isobel – and drove them round to the hire shop so that they could return their gear and, of course, an account of Harvey's accident. They were directed to a doctors' surgery nearby where they were told there would, at least, be a nurse to check Harvey's ankle.

'I'd prefer a pub,' Harvey complained, being ever so manly.

Isobel was having none of it. The nurse checked his ankle, gently moving his foot this way and that, and stated that he should see the doctor tomorrow, but that she thought it most likely that he had done no more than sprain it. She wrapped Harvey's ankle firmly in what seemed to be a mile of gauze bandage and wished him well.

'Enjoy your evening,' she urged, 'and come back to surgery at nine o'clock tomorrow morning.'

They thanked the kind woman. As they left, Harvey, who was wincing as he walked the few steps to his car, urged Isobel to get him to a hostelry as soon as ever possible so that he could have a double whisky for medicinal purposes. She nearly suggested that they wait until they got back to the cottage, an hour or so away, so that they could walk there rather than take the car. Then she realised that they would need the car whichever pub they went to, so she began to look for somewhere in Llanberis itself. That took no time at all, and they staggered into it together. It made a change, Harvey observed, to staggering *out* of a pub. They giggled their way inside, found a table, and Isobel went off to the bar for a double scotch for her man, and a glass of alcohol-free wine for herself. Harvey was shaking a little from his exertions.

'Why don't we move over near the fire?' Isobel suggested. 'And order something to eat here. I know we were going to eat at *The Penny Bank* but, under the circumstances, why don't we eat here, get warm and you properly recovered before getting back to the cottage – and bed.' She made the pause deliberate.

Harvey smiled gratefully at her. 'I may be of little use.' He smiled a wan little smile.

'Never mind that. We'll have plenty of time back at *The Hut*!' she came back.

Things seemed rather rosier after a while. They had warmed up in front of the fire, and they had struck gold with the food: lamb shanks with mashed potatoes and lashings of gravy. And a *Spotted Dick* to follow.

'I most certainly will not be able to move anymore after that,' Harvey noted.

'No, dear,' Isobel replied, smiling sweetly at him. 'Now, if you don't mind, I'd like a proper drink, so let's go back to the cottage and settle in for the night.'

There were many consolations that night. Their plan had been to have a peaceful day afterwards anyway, so they didn't hurry unduly to get up the following morning. The doctor back at Llanberis confirmed the nurse's diagnosis and prescribed a bandage and a pack of aspirin. They spent the rest of the day driving around, lazing on the veranda of the cottage and eating at *The Pen Y Banc Arms*. Harvey was much recovered by nightfall, as they were to (partially) explain when they arrived back at *The Hut* the following evening.

*

It was no coincidence that they made it back to *The Hut* in time for a drink before dinner. Afterwards, they sat opposite Rachael and Michael again, to tell them of their adventures. They were both most concerned about Harvey's accident. However, by now, Harvey was hobbling far less than he had been, and he made light of it. Their changed circumstances, however, did not pass Rachael by for one second. As the evening drew on to everyone making their way to the lounge, bar or elsewhere, Rachael took Isobel aside and asked her the big question straight out.

'Well?' she said.

'Well, what, Rachael?' replied Isobel, not wanting this to be too easy.

Rachael was having none of it. She wagged her finger side to side and smiled sweetly at the younger woman.

'Yes, all right,' Isobel said, whereupon Rachael hugged Isobel warmly.

'Oh, good!' she said. 'Michael will be so pleased.'

'You two are like Mother and Father Hen,' Isobel replied.

'You can't have a father hen,' Rachael said, and hugged Isobel again. 'I hope it all goes as you wish, Izzy dear.'

When the four met, *en passant*, for breakfast next morning, Michael hugged Isobel warmly and kissed her cheek.

I think you can *have a father hen,* thought Isobel.

Harvey and his love spent another week at *The Hut*, relaxing, allowing Harvey's ankle to strengthen and to spread their pleasure to Michael. As they bade goodbye to their hosts, all four clucked away in their happiness.

34

Autumn that year was cooler than usual, or so it seemed, for human powers of recollection are notoriously exaggerated, but then, maybe not, because many people in the village, let alone the hall, were lighting fires in the evenings. Compensation for the chill was to be found in the blanket of cosiness.

Rachael's input into *The Hut* at this time was to suggest that they give over the cabaret room in the basement to an evening of jazz from the local, amateur jazz band. She knew how much Michael loved the genre and that Tomberwater's own group were well regarded. Michael was delighted by her idea but suggested that she expand it into four evenings of amateur jazz from bands to be drawn from all around the area.

'Are there sufficient bands good enough to perform here?' she asked.

Michael was in no doubt about that. 'You'd be surprised at how many small groups there are playing just for a pittance. If we offer just a reasonable fee, they will be overwhelmed, I'm sure. And I, for one, will go to every session!'

Rachael talked to Gordon in the gardens that very day and asked him to come up with some names. He was as pleased as punch. It didn't take him long to get back to her, and arrangements were concluded within ten days. What a difference from working with professional, famous performers and their agents!

Gordon, who coordinated the whole thing, thought it a good idea to have two bands share each evening, two of which would be devoted to traditional jazz or its immediate derivatives, one to contemporary jazz of various shades, and one to modern jazz, which was, of course, considered to be "old hat" these days, though many people still love it to death. Rachael accepted Gordon's suggestions completely. Michael wasn't consulted, for Rachael wanted some small element of surprise in the package, for his benefit. She was still working on her husband's psyche.

Both Michael and Rachael were a little nervous about the likely reactions of their *Hut* guests in general. Those who had been at *The Hut* on other occasions knew that events in the basement did not come up too often, but when they did, they had been of a sophisticated nature in the genre of cabaret. Others had no idea what to expect. Michael put it about that there was to be a *Hut* version of a jazzfest, that the bar would be running throughout each evening – he hesitated to call it a concert – as tradition would surely require. When asked about details of the kind of music to be played, Michael handed over to Rachael.

'She's the boss. Talk to her!'

Rachael, in turn, admitted only to being a go-between and that the assistant head gardener was the man to consult. She also suggested that he was going to be very busy organising the bean-feast and might, therefore, be most likely to suggest that everybody wait and see.

'Is that fair, Michael?' she asked.

Michael grinned at her as he said, in subservient tones, 'Yes, dear.'

Rachael was not to be put down, however. She was able to announce the overall plan. 'On evenings one and four, there will be Traditional Jazz, in both cases featuring, amongst others, our local *Tomber Jazzmen*. On evening number two, there will be so-called Modern Jazz, which will include bebop from the fifties…'

'Eighteen fifties?' asked one of their guests mischievously.

'I will not be put off,' Rachael insisted and continued, 'And on the third evening, we plan to have something called Contemporary Jazz, which, so far as I can ascertain, will revisit old times but with a modern twist.' She breathed in heavily. 'That will have to do.'

There followed a round of good-hearted applause.

And so it came about, this feast of strange noises from the bowels of the hall for those four nights in that chilly autumn. Furthermore, the standard of skill and artistry from the various groups was, to Rachael more than to Michael, surprisingly high. Gordon did them proud. One or two players appeared on several evenings, showing off their skills in different genres of jazz. Jonesie Morton, for example, who came from a village some eighty miles away, was one such. His instrument in the Modern Jazz, bebop evening was an alto sax, which he played breathily, a little as if it were the heavier baritone instrument – an *homage* to Gerry Mulligan, no doubt – but he also appeared in the Contemporary Jazz concert, playing soprano sax when he spent much of his time in subtle, doubling for the lead trumpeter, so producing a soft sound which everyone found both captivating and memorable – almost too memorable. Someone in the audience feigned annoyance, complaining that one of his pieces was like an earworm, which can, if you like it, be a great compliment.

Barry and Gordon Roland, still the core of the *Tomber Jazzmen*, did *The Hut* honour with their work in the opening and closing nights. Harpie Collins, who lived even further away and occasionally entertained in night clubs somewhere in London, played lyrical guitar. His pieces, barely accompanied, were exquisitely delicate and beautiful. He was applauded most enthusiastically by the audience, indeed to every last one there.

Michael, in whose honour the whole jazzfest had been made, didn't stop smiling and grinning throughout. He enjoyed himself no end. He said so when he stood up after the last concert, to thank everyone who had contributed.

'I hope we can do this on a regular basis,' he said, turning to Rachael, 'if I can persuade the boss and Gordon to organise it.'

There was much applause – genuine applause, for many of *The Hut*'s guests had never listened to jazz before and certainly had no idea of its various manifestations – which went on for a long time.

Michael had barely finished speaking when the professional manager of *The Hut* rushed up to him and whispered – well, shouted, really because of the volume of the dying applause in the room – in his ear.

The colour drained from Michael's face. 'Oh, god, no. No!' he cried.

Rachael had never seen him quite so agitated. 'Whatever is the matter?'

'There's been a fire in the village. *The Pot*'s burned down!' he shouted.

The Roland brothers immediately hurried from the room.

'What about Jill and Ken? Are they all right? Has anyone been hurt?' Rachael demanded.

'As far as I know, everyone is safe.'

They excused themselves from the jazz audience and rushed away to the village. By the time they got there, the fire brigade had begun to pack up their equipment and were preparing to protect the place.

It turned out that nobody was hurt and that *The Pot*, though badly damaged, was by no means destroyed. It seemed there had been an electrical fault in the kitchen after most of the day's cooking was over. No one was in the kitchen at the time, and it was most likely that hot oil and a spark set the whole thing off. There would be an investigation, of course.

When Rachael and Michael arrived, Jill and Ken were outside in the street, being consoled by several villagers – regular customers at *The Pot*. Rachael went up to Jill and wrapped her in her arms. Michael did the same for Ken.

Ken was saying over and over, 'I'm so sorry, I'm so sorry.'

'Ken, it was an accident. We know how much you love *The Pot*. It's not your fault.'

After a while, Rachael and Michael swapped over with their hugs and commiserations.

And later, Rachael said, 'Come and stay with us for the night.'

Michael added, 'For as long as you like. Stay with us until *The Pot* is rebuilt.' Then he emphasised with total sincerity, 'Ken; Jill: It will be rebuilt. It will.'

*

Much of the next couple of weeks were spent securing the pub's booze stock and making professional assessments of what real structural damage had been wrought. The fire had pretty well gutted the kitchen and its extension into the former outbuilding in the yard, but had then seemingly changed direction, leaving the rest of the ground floor dirty but undamaged, instead heading upstairs where the bedrooms were pretty much ruined. At first, it seemed that the basic structure upstairs was sound, but they were unsure. In due course, a specialist surveyor gave the thumbs down on that. No. Most, if not all, of *The Pot* would have to be rebuilt.

It was shortly after that, when Michael, Rachael, Jill and Ken were sharing dinner in the Montayne's private quarters at the hall, that Michael quite suddenly came up with an idea.

'Why don't we ask Nigel Plater to design a new *Tomber Pot* for us?'

Jill looked puzzled.

'You remember, love,' Ken said. 'He built that beautiful inside-outside house we saw with Rachael and Michael a few months ago.'

Jill was immediately excited. 'Do you think he would do it?' she cried. Then she had another thought. 'Would the council allow us to build in a modern style in the middle of an old village?'

Michael thought about that for a moment. 'That could be a problem, but it *is* possible to build modern but with great respect for old surroundings. If anyone can do that, I feel sure that Nigel could.'

'I agree,' said Rachael, and added, 'I wouldn't wonder if Nigel has mates in the county planning office.'

'That's a thought,' Michael agreed. 'Look, we can't do more until we have discussions with Nigel – not least to get him on board, of course – but there is one question we ought to consider even before that.'

Three faces turned toward him.

'I think that Ken and Jill should decide how many bedrooms they would like the new building to have. Before they had only one guest bedroom.'

He looked at Ken. 'My point is: how many guests would you like to be able to put up, care for and feed? The same rules will apply. Namely that all profits from the guest rooms go to you as landlord. So, more rooms, more profit. On the other hand, more rooms, more work!'

'Yes, but we wouldn't have to let all the rooms all the time. When there are other demands on our time, not least moving *Hut* guests around on boats – which we dearly love, by the way – we can just reduce the number of *Pot* guests.'

'I agree,' said Jill, 'but the old *Pot* had only one upper floor with two bedrooms and a bathroom. We lived in one of those rooms and shared the bathroom. How are we to increase the floor space?'

'Well,' Michael said, 'suppose we build over the old kitchen extension – make the new kitchen take in the old one, plus extension, of course – making use of its footprint in the pub yard. And then,' he paused, getting just a little excited, 'then we could go up a story. Three stories in all; that is, two above both kitchen and pub saloon/lounge. Plus the cellar, of course.'

'That might make three or four good-sized bedrooms with en suite, in addition to your own quarters,' Rachael said.

The enthusiasm and excitement in the room was palpable.

'We can't do more until we have Nigel on board,' Michael said eventually. 'Let's just mull it over, and tomorrow I'll give him a call.'

Nigel agreed to design a new *Pot* and to see the building through to its finish. He also knew of builders who could do a good job and who, by good fortune, would be available in three months.

'That would be the very soonest that anything could be done. Indeed, it would be a miracle. But I specialise in miracles.'

He came back to Michael with detailed drawings within five weeks.

'I told you that I do miracles,' he explained, for he understood only too well just how important it was to get the show back on the road.

The Montaynes and the Gastons were gathered around Rachael's large dinner table as Nigel showed them what he had conceived.

'I was expecting just a larger version of the old *Pot*,' Ken said.

'This is brilliant!' Michael expostulated.

Nigel had fashioned a new building which now made use of the old, quite small footprint, together with a sixty-odd percent increase by taking in part of the old pub yard. Once upon a time, a lot of space had been necessary in that yard so as to turn the dray horses around and to provide a place for their fodder as their cart was unloaded. Life with motorised vehicles was much simpler, so the business of the pub could be continued with a much smaller yard. Instead of just making elevations of brick and stone like the old building, Nigel was proposing two timbered upper stories, the timbers being of oak and protruding in and out from the building line as defined by the lowest story – which would be finished in old brick – so that no two faces were alike. The upper story window alignment, or misalignment, had been brought about by intersecting the main building and the kitchen extension, whose foundations were at about thirty degrees to one another. Some of the upper story windows extended over two stories, even though there was no unwanted contact between the second and third story bedrooms. He had even managed to squeeze in some attic space within the roof line which was well back from the front of the building.

' No one will be aware of the roof from the ground,' Nigel explained, 'and even from the few buildings around, the roof is set back from a near-flat roof right at the front, so that the pub will seem quite far away and certainly unobtrusive. The oak will be oiled but otherwise left untreated. It will age beautifully and, in no time at all, will have the appearance of having been there for decades, if not more.'

'Do you think you can get this past the planners?' Michael asked.

'I do believe so. They are more broad-minded in our county than you might imagine. In any case, the top man is a friend of mine. We get on very well.'

Jill and Ken began pouring over the plans for the inside.

'These rooms seem to be quite large,' Jill remarked, 'even with the en suite shower rooms.'

'In part, that comes from the odd few square feet provided by the angled windows. In effect, you get more space from the top stories overhanging the ground floor. The principle was established hundreds of years ago, of course. It's just that today, modern materials allow for thinner, lighter walls, so you can do more.'

'Nigel, I think your design is absolutely fabulous. I cannot thank you enough,' Michael congratulated him.

'I'll leave it with you to pour over and digest. I'm sure I can accommodate any small changes. After that, we can submit.'

They made no changes whatsoever. The plans were submitted. The design was approved within three weeks. Nigel believed that was a record. The builders were signed. Money was paid. The building work began. Only then did Michael remember the secret tunnel beneath. There were some hours of panic as he revealed the secret to Nigel. It turned out that the few extra foundations required for the new building would miss the tunnel by a good margin. Nigel swore that the old secret would not be revealed to anyone else.

*

Once again, the Gastons and the Montaynes were gathered for dinner in the private wing of *The Hut* when Rachael made an announcement about which she and Michael had been thinking for some time.

'Ken, Jill, the rebuild of *The Tomber Pot* is going to take a year, at least. You are obviously aware of that. The question therefore arises of what you might want to do with yourselves while you wait. Michael and I would like to make a suggestion for at least a part of that time.'

Jill interrupted Rachael's flow to assure their hosts that they could look after themselves. 'We thought that we might take some courses at Bath College, maybe in hotel management or something like that.'

'Sure. If you would like to do that, we'd be happy to pay all necessary expenses: accommodation and so on. However, what Michael and I had in mind was something a little different. Not as an alternative, but in addition to anything you had thought of,' Rachael continued. 'We wondered if you had any interest in touring the United States. We pay, of course.'

Ken and Jill were lost for words.

Michael helped them along. 'You could go wherever you please. For example, you might begin in Boston, hire a car and work your way down to New York and then to Washington. After that, you might want to leave the very big cities alone for a while and continue south, exploring places like Charleston and Savannah, on your way to Florida. You could pop into Disney World and then see Cape Canaveral. Then leave the Pan Handle and work your way across the Gulf to New Orleans. After that, have a look at Texas. That will take a while! See *The Alamo*! Perhaps by then you will have really got the travel bug, so you might fly over to the West Coast. Los Angeles and San Francisco. Come back inland and see the Grand Canyon. There are so many places. You don't need to plan everything beforehand. You could just play it by ear as you go. What do you think?'

Ken could hardly speak. Jill was in tears.

'I thought Rachael was talking about a couple of weeks. Anything like you suggest would take months,' Ken said.

'Easily,' Michael replied. 'Look, you have a year – probably more – to fill, so you might as well take the opportunity to explore the US properly. I've often heard you saying how you'd like to go sometime. Well, that time is now! And just to make it perfectly clear, you two – you take our credit card and pay nothing yourselves.'

'But that's so much!' Jill blurted out. 'We don't deserve that much.'

'Oh, but you do,' Rachael said. 'Michael and I have spent some time talking about this. You have both helped us so much over the years. You have never complained when we made sudden decisions about the boats, for instance, and you and your family before you, have looked after *The Pot*, the heart of the village, for years and years. Of course you deserve it. Michael and I are eternally grateful to you. Especially for our trip together a few months ago. You were a tremendous help to us. More than you can ever know.'

There were hugs all round.

Ken suddenly cried: 'God! We must burn down *The Pot* more often!'

'Can't guarantee it will work more than once,' Michael laughed.

In bed, later that night, Michael said, 'I can't tell you how pleased I am that we have been able to do something meaningful for Ken and Jill. It's a wonderful thing to be able to properly thank people who have been so good to us.'

35

Months passed, but Michael remained agitated. Rachael suggested that they invite Allen to stay a while. She knew that Michael felt very strongly about this particular old friend.

'This time without his friends. I have nothing against them. I would just like to see Tim Allen on his own,' she said.

Tim Allen and Michael had been inseparable during the year they had in common at Bristol. Tim had always been the quieter of the two men. He was shy and very sensitive. Maybe Michael wasn't so very different, though much less shy. Their great shared love was music. Michael, of course, had eclectic tastes, finding great enjoyment in jazz as well as in the classical field. Tim's love was exclusively for the classics, although, incongruously perhaps, he also had a thing for Gilbert and Sullivan's operettas. That was not something Michael shared. Tim's preferences within the classical field were broad. He adored anything at all by Schubert, arguing that that composer's great strength was his overwhelming sense of beauty. He found that quality in some operatic pieces, too. He loved Schumann's work, particularly his piano music, and he had a soft spot for Mendelssohn. Once started on such listings, however, Tim couldn't stop. By no means did he restrict his listening to the nineteenth century, for he adored just about anything by Britten, for example.

While Michael was merely a consumer of music, Tim also played. He played rather well and, for some time before entering Bristol University, he had considered pursuing a career as a professional musician. His instrument was the piano, although he was more than handy at the organ as he had demonstrated on his last visit to *The Hut* with Martin and Chris. As a student, but by now committed to entering the church after his degree in philosophy and religion, Allen regularly played for Michael in his room.

The two young men also shared a love a good food: Michael from his upbringing, and Tim from aspiration. Tim's family weren't poor, but neither were they ridiculously wealthy.

In between treating Michael to endless, beautiful and competent piano playing, Tim would debate philosophy and religion with him till the wee small hours, almost every night. Michael always had had a penchant for self-examination, so that chewing the fat with Tim about the meaning of life from all sorts of viewpoints, and over a drink or two, was just like taking a warm bath. These things are so intense during student years, of course, and Michael later confessed to Rachael that they must have talked more utter rubbish than the world's deepest sinkhole could swallow. But it was, nevertheless, pure pleasure. At least, that's what his memory suggested.

Rachael knew all about this history, for Michael had told her of it several times. In her invitation to Allen, she warned him of Michael's long depression and of her hope that Allen might be able to shake it out of him.

Tim arrived on time – for he was ever fastidious in such matters – in a small hire car. As ever, he was so polite to Rachael and never seemed to realise just how much she adored him. Most of the women he met felt that way about Tim Allen and most would complain of the "waste" when they heard of his proclivities. Michael gave him a hug, which clearly embarrassed him a little, but one just had to show one's affection somehow.

Rachael showed him to his room and suggested that he join Michael and herself in their private lounge when he was ready. Allen (he had become used to, over the years, being addressed by his surname) had his usual tipple, a long gin and tonic, while Michael and Rachael indulged in a cocktail. They spent a happy hour catching up on what had transpired in Allen's life since he was last at *The Hut* with his friends, and on books he had read meanwhile. Tim Allen, though not a voracious reader, was a pretty wide-reading man in his spare time, of which he seemed to have plenty.

Tim, now in his late fifties, though still boyish in appearance, was but a curate – or less; Michael wasn't quite sure – within the Irish Anglican Church in Dublin. Either he was unambitious or had been passed over for promotion. That was also something which Michael knew nothing about, and Allen had never volunteered anything on the subject. Nevertheless, Tim always appeared to be a contented soul. He was a quiet man, but he always had been, except when animated within a philosophical discussion – never an argument, for Tim hated arguments. He was quiet and thoughtful. Thoughtful about whatever was being discussed and thoughtful for others. He really had been a "find" for the church. None of this is to say that he couldn't hold a lively conversation on most subjects. The reciprocated affection he shared with Ken and Chris was ample evidence of that. But even at his age now, Chris still retained a preference for getting his teeth into philosophy and religion. Michael was well aware of it. And Michael needed to talk.

Ever the gentleman, however, he didn't hurry Allen into his chosen groove. Tim was encouraged to relax, enjoy the food and wine which *The Hut* always provided so beautifully, and to play the Bechstein piano in the music room. Rachael, meanwhile, asked Tim about his clerical friends who she had found so amusing. Allen, loyal to the last, insisted that they were always amusing but did admit that they were not to everyone's taste.

'But that's true of just about all of us,' Rachael retorted.

'Except me,' Michael remarked, in his mock-aggressive style.

Rachael wondered whether to refer to this as his schoolboy humour rather than undergraduate.

'A fine distinction,' she had once remarked.

On his second day at *The Hut*, Allen did indeed wander into the music room, just as Michael knew he would. On some shelves behind the piano were many piano scores, either bound into volumes or in loose sheets within folios. Allen began to rummage through them. He found a volume of Bach's great preludes and fugues and decided that he would begin there, just to loosen his fingers. He played a couple but stopped suddenly, not being in the mood for Bach, and returned to the bookcase. This time he found the complete set of Waldscenen by Schumann. He sat down at the piano once more, failing to notice that Michael had entered the room and sat down at the rear.

Allen began the first piece which instantaneously brought tears to Michael's eyes. It always had done. Michael had once tried to read a critique of the work by Charles Rosen. It was clearly a scholarly piece of work, certainly well thought of by many who knew music thoroughly, but Michael wasn't one of those. He was just an ordinary listener. He liked what he heard. In this case, the music moved him. He had heard a musicologist once sneer at the person who "knew what he liked". He also bet that

Schumann had a listener like him in his sights even while he explored ways of moving him. Sure, it was Schumann's job to understand how to make his magic. It was the average listener's job, surely, to do his, and feel it. Some argue that understanding the nuts and bolts of a piece of music serves to deepen one's appreciation of it. It is certain that without such understanding, one cannot judge such assertions. It is equally sure, Michael felt, that knowledge of how the bricks in a building were fired would not guarantee a greater love of the building. Indeed, on balance, he rather felt that such knowledge would merely provide a second knowledge; no doubt interesting in itself, providing width but maybe not depth. Then again, perhaps the width interacts with the depth to produce a fuller whole. That must be so, Michael would muse. He was excusing his ignorance or laziness. Such thoughts always entered his head shortly after falling in love one more time with a familiar piece of music. Perhaps it was a yearning for even more pleasure than he was already getting from it. Another form of greed, maybe. And so it was that, as ever, pleasure produced pain. A simpler level of appreciation might have stopped with the pleasure, but you are what you are. And Michael was the sort of person to chew on anything which moved him.

He had no inkling of the passage of time as Allen played through the set of nine pieces. His mind drifted, occasionally being brought back into focus as the music demanded. Tim really had a wonderful touch, he thought.

Allen finished and sat in silence for a while. Michael made no effort to announce his presence. Had Allen looked about him, he would have seen him, but he didn't. After a while, he returned to the shelves, returning, after some riffling, with sheets for Schubert's Moments Musicaux. Michael's emotional response to these was, by contrast, more a feeling of peace, of bathing in light. They were very familiar pieces, of course, but that was no criticism; probably the reverse. Allen's even playing over some of the extended runs had lost none of its old dexterity, at least to Michael's ears.

In his youth, Michael had wished and wished to be able to play the piano. He no longer pined to play the instrument. He knew, inside his head, that he *could* play it. He knew every note of those pieces and was playing them to perfection inside his skull. Escapism takes many forms.

As Allen reached the end of one piece and was about to begin the next, he looked up from the music and saw Michael for the first time.

'Please don't stop, Allen,' Michael called out. 'I'm having a bath over here!'

Tim knew what he meant, and with barely a break, continued his concert. All in all, he had played for nearly an hour and a half before he finally stopped and carefully replaced the music on the shelves behind him.

'This is a lovely instrument, Michael,' he said.

'And you do it justice, my friend,' Michael replied, walking up to him and taking his hand. 'It is *so* good to hear you play again. Maybe you would be willing to give a small concert for our guests in the next day or so?'

'I don't think I'm good enough for that,' Allen replied, ever modest.

'I'm sure you are, Allen. We really would be honoured if you would do it. Anyway, let me know what you think. I won't push. Let's go and have a wee drink now.'

Allen announced at dinner the following day that he would give a short concert in the music room in two days' time. Michael smiled and Rachael gave him a hug. Though cool outside, the forecast was for a sunny day, and Michael suggested that Allen and he might go for a walk around the village.

'We can check on progress with *The Pot*,' he suggested as they set out.

When Allen asked what he meant, Michael explained all about the fire, about Ken and Jill and about Nigel Plater.

'My goodness, you have been having a time!' Allen exclaimed.

'Oh, that's not the half of it, Allen. We very nearly lost the hall and, indeed, the whole of *The Hut*.'

Michael then began to tell his friend about the great trial of the year. Allen was aghast.

'But Geoffrey was your friend – your best man!' he exclaimed.

Michael slowly launched into the personal side of their trial. He broke off and directly asked Allen a question he had often wanted to raise with him but had never found the right moment.

'Tim, I hope you don't mind my asking you this question. I have often wondered about it but have always found it difficult to ask.' He paused. 'You have not risen very high in your church. I know you to be a very intelligent man. I *know* it. Your degree was very good, and there aren't too many people in the church with qualifications as good as yours. So why haven't you gone further? I do hope you're not offended by my asking.'

'Not at all, Michael, although it's not a subject I would discuss with many people. Firstly, I must correct one thing you just said. There are quite a few well-qualified people in the church. Well-qualified academically, I mean. Outsiders often imagine that churchmen only know about religion *per se*, but that is most certainly not the case. Backgrounds like mine – in philosophy – are, by no means, rare. Moreover, there are plenty of priests with doctorates as well. My fair bachelor's degree only gets me so far. Then, as you know full well, I'm a rather shy person – always have been. I'm not a fighter. I'll fight myself to work harder, do better, understand more. But I won't fight others. Maybe it's a form of cowardice. Maybe I'm frightened of losing. On the other hand, Michael, between you and me now, I do know my worth. I know my stuff. I also know that I know it better than many of my fellows. I have watched them overtake me over the years and, yes! I do resent it. Not so much that they have done better than me, but that they don't deserve to. That might sound like no more than simple envy. But I do know what I'm talking about. I have seen so many people go very high in the church on nothing more than their desire to rise and their belief that they should. I *know* that they have not deserved their rise.' Allen sighed before continuing. 'This is an old story, Michael. As old as the hills. "The meek shall inherit the earth." Eventually, maybe; but not, I fear, in this life.' He paused for a moment, before continuing. 'I can say this to you, Michael, and it is a great relief to find someone I *can* say it to, because of our long friendship. I know that you believe me, by which I mean that you accept my judgement, when I give you my self-assessment. You will also believe me when I tell you that, from time to time, it hurts like hell. And yet, after all this, I still cling to the belief that truth will out; that somehow doing the job well will yield justice. God knows why I still believe that. Literally God, for *I* have no idea. Intellectually, I know it's rubbish. The greedy, the incompetent, the lazy and the untalented inherit the earth. I'm sorry, Michael. I haven't talked like this to anyone before. That's the trouble for anyone in my position. If you complain, you sound like a whinger; jealous, small, a failure.'

Michael put his hand on Allen's back. 'I'm so sorry, my friend,' was all he could find to say, and added, 'but those who know you non-professionally, that is to say, without an axe to grind, all admire your quality – and qualities. Your honesty, the clarity of your thought, your kindness, your musical abilities. That is a formidable list, Tim. Many would kill for half of what you've got; for what you are.'

Tim turned to his friend, smiled a watery smile and clasped his arm gently but said no more, until he remembered that this line of questioning had come up while Michael was explaining about Geoffrey's actions.

'You were telling me about Geoffrey,' he reminded Michael.

'Oh, yes. You will understand me completely, I'm sure, when I tell you that I felt utterly betrayed by Geoffrey's decision to sell *The Hut*. I dare say that many businessmen would have agreed with Geoffrey's decision, for it was, by far, financially the least costly option open to him. But the way I see it is that Geoffrey made a big mistake in his business, borne of over-ambition – maybe even greed – and that he was about to throw me to the wolves rather than take the hit he richly deserved. It was a moral question, really. However, throughout all this, and particularly after I was rescued by some absolutely wonderful friends, I haven't been able quite to throw the thought that I live in a cocoon. That I am so privileged. Over-privileged. Why should I feel aggrieved when something I never really earned was to be taken from me? I really have no right to feel that way. Apart from anything else, even if *The Hut* had come to an end, I'd still be a millionaire many times over. How can any fair-minded person complain about that? Anyway, I have been in a deep place for many months, although Rachael has been doing her very best to extract me from my own self-pity. Actually, she has been succeeding, Tim. I wanted you to come here, frankly, to listen to my ravings and maybe to complete the job which Rachael began.'

They walked along in silence for a while. Their contemplations were interrupted as they came to the site of activities at *The Pot*.

'My goodness!' Allen said. 'It really did burn down!'

'I'll show you the plans when we get back home,' Michael replied. 'But look! They have actually finished strengthening the foundations and begun on the ground storey. That's wonderful! I must tell Rachael.'

After peeking through the safety wire surrounding the site for a while, they continued on their way in the direction of the wharf.

Allen returned to their earlier conversation. 'A good friend of mine – dead now – once reminded me of a fundamental truth in human affairs. "Life is not fair," he insisted, "and you can waste far too much energy wishing that it were." As time has gone by, Michael, I have thought more and more about those words. He was right, of course. It is often hard to swallow. Obviously so, if you're on the sticky end. But you must, if you want to keep your sanity. And you become stronger for it in the end. I am not an unhappy man, Michael. I might well have been if I had been promoted years ago. Who knows? But, apart from a dull regret, which only really surfaces when the subject is brought up... or is caused to come up, maybe,'

'I'm sorry, Allen. I didn't want to cause you pain,' Michael interrupted.

'That's all right. It does me no harm to throw up these thoughts occasionally. Usually, it's just me who has to listen to them – to myself. You asked, so I'm afraid it's your turn to be engulfed! Anyway, the point, Michael, is that feelings like yours and mine can be felt by anyone. Rich or poor. Deserving or not. Life is not fair. Instead, you must – *you absolutely must* – look for positives. I know mine. Indeed, you very perceptively listed them a few minutes ago. Are you as perceptive when it comes to your own qualities? You were born with the proverbial silver spoon in your mouth. Hardly your fault. As you have told me on many occasions, you met and supped with some incredibly interesting people – friends of your parents – during your formative years. Many a child would envy that experience. Sadly, many over-privileged youths have wasted the advantage. You did not, Michael. Death duties, which I know you agree were a proper thing for society to bring in and, in due course, to expand, meant that the lifestyle of your forebears could not be continued. At least, in the old way. You found a new way. But only by working at it. I know *The Hut* has a formal manager to organise the place in detail, but *The Hut* is *you*. The prices you charge – obviously, have to charge – put the place out of the reach of most people. Only the very rich – or those with some organisation behind them – can afford to come, except that you have so organised everything that you filter out, in effect, over-rich louts. Many of the world's great hotels would envy that filter, I'm sure. Even after that, many of your guests would not bother to come to *The Hut* if you were not around. They come to see *you*, Michael. Rachael too, but primarily you. You don't need to be at that wonderful dinner table in person every evening – a good job, too, or you'd never get a break – but often enough to provide the atmosphere that is intrinsic to *The Hut*. You know, it's not a hotel that you have built, not an escape or a secret club – although it's all of those things – it's a paradigm.'

Allen abruptly interrupted himself as a new thought occurred to him. 'Michael, you mentioned a little while back that your financial bacon was saved by some dear friends. I hope you don't mind my asking, but tell me about them.'

Michael was only too happy to explain and did so at length as they leaned over the rail in front of the wharf, where they had now reached, watching somebody fiddling about in their narrowboat.

'I wonder if you understand exactly why those friends helped you? I don't know them, of course, but their motivation shines clear to me. The American, Noah, had some family connection, or connection with your family's past, you say. On the face of it, that could be reason enough, but people don't risk that sort of money merely for historical sentiment. I can understand the Indian guy more easily, as he wanted to create a similar setup to *The Hut*, back home. Although, once again, he could have done that without buying shares in your enterprise. As for your ennobled friend: surely, there you have someone who really understands what it is to "come from nothing", or something close to that. He wouldn't normally be expected to risk a penny merely for sentimental reasons. No, Michael, it's clear to me that these wonderful people have placed a bet on you personally. I understand that their financial risk is not as high as it might seem initially, for they could sell their stakes and escape, but nevertheless, they have locked up funds which they might make better financial use of otherwise. It is obvious to me. They have bought into Michael Montayne. Not simply because they like you, for I'm sure they do, but because they have faith in you and admire you. You do not deserve their faith just by standing there. You have earned it. I understand this problem of yours inside out, my friend. You have been focussing on those parts of your personality and achievements which *you* see as being below par. Your friends simply don't notice those. They see the good, the worthy, the really meaningful in you. And that's enough for them. And for me.' Allen put his hand on Michael's shoulder and concluded, 'That's enough, my friend. Let's go back and smile for Rachael.'

The following evening saw Allen perform wonderfully for *The Hut*'s guests just as he had performed wonders for Rachael with her husband.

By the time that Tim Allen had to leave them, Michael's demeanour had very obviously changed for the better. Rachael breathed her profound gratitude into Allen's ear as he climbed into his car.

'Come and see us again soon, you miracle worker!' she whispered.

36

Halfway through November, and *The Hut* was gearing up for Christmas. It was time to put up a tree. In the past, the tree had been placed in the entrance hall, but this year they decided that it should occupy one end of the dining hall. At the other, a roaring fire would warm everyone from this date until the gods favoured them with some less inclement weather. Rachael was supervising the tree decoration, surely a universally adored pastime. Some of the decorations were very old, having been used each and every year for the past hundred years or more. A few had been lost, damaged or even smashed to smithereens, but most had survived to be carefully rewrapped in soft tissue until needed the following year. Electric lights had replaced candles years ago, of course.

Michael had been declared "cured" by Rachael, and happiness reigned. It had been the case on many, though not all, occasions that *The Hut* had remained open to visitors over the Christmas and New Year period. This year, they agreed that they would close down their operation for two weeks as from Friday, the twentieth of December. It's always good to make firm decisions in life.

Not five minutes had passed after being so decisive when Rachael's phone beeped. An SMS from Isobel said that they were in the area and asked if she and Harvey might pop over for a cup of tea that afternoon. Rachael told Michael and immediately sent a reply.

'They'll be here around two o'clock,' she told her husband who was about to go out for his morning constitutional.

Isobel and Harvey arrived on the dot in the Porsche and were about to make their entry through the vegetable garden. As it happened, that's exactly where Michael and Rachael were at that moment. The men shook hands, and the ladies kissed cheeks. The Montayne's dog looked on in amusement. It was immediately apparent that something was afoot, as Michael recalled later, for both of their guests seemed to be a mite tongue-tied as they wobbled through trivial remarks about the weather and the time of year. Michael led the way into the private quarters and gestured to his guests that they might care to sit down. Harvey sat quite upright with an air of forced relaxation. Isobel, who was wearing a beautifully fitted skirt on this occasion (Michael had observed that she frequently wore trousers of one kind or another), smoothed her skirt with the flats of both her hands. Rachael saw it immediately.

'Are you…?' she began.

'Yes!' replied Isobel. 'You are the very first to know,' and she flashed the diamond on the third finger of her left hand.

Then Michael saw it and smiled broadly at them. 'Oh! Congratulations! I am so very pleased for you both.'

'And about time, too, if you ask me,' Rachael said, as she rose to take Isobel in her arms for a hug.

Michael took Harvey's hand again and began to shake it like some sort of Union flag. 'I seem to remember your uncle and Hillary suggesting that this might happen. Mind you, that was a long time ago,' Michael said.

'Yes, we caught on to their matchmaking at the time, but they were – how can I put it? Previous,' Harvey grinned.

'Look, I hope it's not too early, but how about some bubbles?' Michael suggested.

Rachael nodded and it was done.

As they were all taking their first sips, Isobel began to talk. It quickly became apparent that this was the nub of their visit.

'I guess you don't usually do this at *The Hut*, but we were wondering whether we could hire the dining room here – and your staff, obviously – for our wedding breakfast. We are planning to get married in a few weeks, with just Hillary and Gerald as our witnesses, after which – by which I mean a week later – we hope, we could hold our bunfight here. As a lunch, that is, so that it wouldn't mean interfering with a *Hut* dinner. Except for the extra work. We know it's a lot to ask and, of course, we're happy to pay whatever you ask.'

'We'd be delighted,' Michael replied, without hesitation. 'Just two things, though. Do you have a date in mind, and how many people would there be altogether?'

Isobel came back: 'We plan on forty people all up. That includes us, Hillary and Gerald, you and Rachael and, therefore, thirty-four others. If we remember correctly, that is the maximum your table can hold. As for date, we were thinking of the Saturday just before Christmas day. Is all this too much to ask?'

'Not at all,' Michael replied. 'As it happens, five minutes before you sent your SMS this morning, Rachael and I had just decided to shut up shop for two weeks over Christmas. There will be no *Hut* guests to displace, and we can fit your lunch in on the day after they all leave. Nothing could be simpler.'

'And your lunch will be our wedding gift!' Rachael broke in.

'Absolutely,' Michael agreed.

'But you already shouted us a holiday here a couple of months ago!' Harvey protested.

'That was for the other thing. There's no connection,' Michael replied.

'No further argument!' Rachael insisted. 'Have you decided what food you would like? Why don't we pop down to the chef's office – that's Griff, by the way – when you've finished your drinks?'

A good hour was spent down there. Rachael and Michael left them to it all, content in the knowledge that Griff would do them proud on the day.

*

Isobel and Harvey did the deed one week exactly before the proposed lunch. Hillary and Geoffrey looked on like proud parents. From time to time, they looked at each other as if to say, "Well, we did it! A little nudge here, a little nudge there!" At least that was how their mincing ways seemed to Harvey and Isobel, who had no intention of disabusing them of their conceit.

It was a simple civil ceremony in a small town, not too far from Tomberwater, as it happened, although there was no significance in that – just the four of them plus the celebrant. It was how Isobel and Harvey wanted it. Afterwards, they walked down to a first-rate hotel nearby for champagne, champagne and more champagne. In due course, the four friends staggered into the dining room for a small but delicious lunch. By prior arrangement, all four of them stayed there for the night. In two rooms.

Of course, before the wedding ceremony itself, Isobel and Harvey had spent several hours making up their guest list for lunch at *The Hut* on the twenty-first. Amongst others, they each included their dearest friends from university days. Honey Blacket, for example, was a dab hand at illustrating various pamphlets and articles written for the university magazine. Since then, she had made a fine career for herself in the field of illustrations for both serious and frivolous publications. Isobel didn't know her husband at all well but thought he might be fun. On Harvey's side, Peter Forren, who had inevitably suffered from his surname as a youth and even as a young man and had read a general arts degree – Harvey couldn't remember exactly what – went into the commercial world and was now something pretty senior within a major food retailer in Britain. Harvey always associated Peter, however, with his hobby of chipping away at stone and things as a sculptor. As far as Harvey knew, he hadn't sold anything he had carved or moulded – which was a pity, for he was quite able – but had maintained his interest throughout the years. Peter had given Harvey a sizeable head made from ironstone which he kept outside amongst various plants on his balcony garden. Both Harvey and Isobel chose a precious handful of old friends such as these and established that they would be available on the day. They also agreed on another, rather special, guest known to them both, as well as to Michael and, indirectly, to Rachael. He accepted their invitation and hoped to find a partner to accompany him. So far as the lovebirds were concerned, everything was fixed up.

Meanwhile, Rachael and Michael had been getting the hall and gardens into the Christmas spirit. The tree in the dining hall had been erected and decorated ages ago, of course, as had the traditional mistletoe in unexpected places. Presents were being wrapped, ready to put around the tree. There were things to do outside, as well. They planned to have only a modest show of fairy lights immediately outside the front and rear doors, resisting the temptation to put them around the windows of the lounge bar which overlooked the Grand Avenue. They had something else in mind for that, something which Gordon had been working on for a few weeks.

*

And so, the great day came round and wonder of wonders, they were blessed with a pleasant, dry day. It was rather cold outside, of course, but if you must get spliced at Christmas, what can you expect? Isobel and Harvey greeted each guest as they arrived. Gordon and Barry attended to parking arrangements, although a number of guests had made arrangements either to come in bunches or to make use of various taxi services, while Rachael and Michael kept out of the way, quietly making sure that everything was as it should be and reserving their input, essentially, for the lunch itself. Guests were shown into the lounge bar where their whistles were wetted with a sensible quantity of good champagne. Those with a penchant for cocktails were charmingly told to behave themselves on this most special occasion. It wasn't long before the general hubbub of conversation reached quite powerful proportions. Isobel and Harvey had chosen their guests well.

The time came and the butler announced lunch. Isobel and her husband led the way through into the dining hall. It had, of course, been left pretty much in the style of the founder, Philippe Montaigne, even after the extensive makeover when *The Hut* was established. But that makeover, and the care lavished on the hall ever since, had established a remarkable atmosphere in the place. The roaring fire at one end and the great Christmas tree at the other, only served to make this a very special place. Harvey and Isobel were almost as proud of it as Rachael and Michael. Place cards had been distributed with great care and consideration around the great table, and it took a little time for people to find their seats. There was some hesitancy about whether to sit down or not until Michael waved everyone to take their place. Neither he nor Rachael had seen the guest list in advance, still less the distribution of the guest. Seated opposite them was a Chinese-looking gentleman, dressed impeccably and obviously in very expensive taste.

He leaned forward and offered his hand. 'Jim Chen,' he said.

Michael's mouth hung open for just a fraction of a second. He had never actually met the saviour of *The Hut* before, the man who had bought his shares in *Marchant Enterprises*. He gripped Chen's hand firmly as he welcomed him to their home.

'It is a great pleasure to meet you and to have the opportunity to thank you in person,' he said, and went on to introduce Rachael.

Jim Chen was charm itself. In a perfect English accent, which one could take anywhere, he, in turn, introduced his companion.

'This is a long-time friend of mine, a very dear friend, I might say, Mariana Pérez.'

Mariana was quite stunning. Obviously in late middle age, as was her companion, she had all the magic of authority and, Michael wondered, maybe of nobility.

Sitting to Michael's right were Hillary and Gerald, who neither he nor Rachael had seen since their stay at *The Hut* well over a year before. They were in fine form and obviously a little giggly. Michael wondered if they had indulged in too much champagne already. Surely not, at this early stage in the proceedings!

Isobel had insisted upon a light lunch. She had had to work quite hard to calm Griff's enthusiasm for his task, but then, Isobel could eat grits for breakfast.

Lunch began with a simple plate of figs and Parma ham. Isobel had been worried about being able to source figs at that time of year, but Griff assured her that it was summer somewhere in the world. The sommelier had suggested a fruity *Sancerre* to accompany the dish. The menu had a short phrase written alongside each course, obviously of humorous significance to the married couple. Associated with the first course was the phrase, *Every fruit has its secret*. No explanations were given for these phrases, but it didn't take too long before one of the guests announced that the line was to be found in D.H. Lawrence's poem, *Figs*. Plenty of time was allowed between courses, partly because everyone wanted to get to know their neighbours, but mainly, in all probability, because wedding breakfasts are like that. There was such an atmosphere of gaiety around the table. Rachael, for one, was so happy on behalf of the happy couple.

The main course offered a small package of lamb, cut from the loin, with asparagus, all wrapped in filo pastry, the whole accompanied by a selection of just perfectly cooked vegetables from the garden and from distant parts, as well. A *St. Emelion, Grand Cru* had been selected for this course. The text this time was a bible reference, *Isaiah 53 v 7*. Guests were catching on to these titbits more quickly now.

'I know!' someone called out. 'It's to do with "Lambs going to the slaughter."'

Someone giggled; many approved.

'Ah! But which is the lamb?' another called.

Yet another called out, 'You mean who!'

Plenty of time was allowed for the main course but eventually the table was cleared, and it was time for the third course. The associated text on this occasion was *Have it and eat it*. It was labelled *The Cake*.

'Neither Isobel nor Harvey like cake,' Rachael said quietly to Michael. 'I wonder why they chose this?'

The butler himself wheeled in a small, square table upon which was a four-tier cake, each tier smaller than the one beneath and each placed directly upon its predecessor rather than on pillars. On close inspection, every tier was coloured into four sections: white, yellow, puce, pale green. The butler spoke to Harvey, and both he and his bride of one week previous got up and went to the cake. They were presented with a large knife and asked to cut the cake together. It was all very traditional, and everybody applauded merrily. Thereafter, it was left to the waiters, as usual, to cut the whole of the cake into slices. Someone said something about leaving that till later when they would post off pieces to everyone.

The waiters began to attend to the guests. Only then was it apparent that the cake was made of ice creams: vanilla, orange, raspberry, pistachio, and so on. That was not going into the postal system. Guests were offered their choice of flavour. By great good fortune, everyone got a piece of his or her choice.

'Ah!' Rachael continued. 'How clever!'

Guests were then asked by the butler to vacate their seats while the staff cleared up and got ready for dessert, and Harvey suggested that, on taking their seats once more, guests should change places in any manner they chose.

'Just for the fun of it,' he suggested.

The table had been re-laid with plates of *petit pause*, the menu offering Petit Paws. The biscuits had been made in the shapes of cats' paws. The accompanying text was *Masters of depravity*.

'Oh! That's from Eliot's *Cats*,' someone called out almost at once.

'But why?' another asked.

'Because of Isobel's great love of cats, of course,' Hillary replied. All solved.

The table was also adorned with cheese plates and fruits. Each place setting had been provided with four glasses and, at several points on the table, were placed bottles in foursomes: An excellent dry claret, a *Chateau Fombrauge*; a Barsac in the form of a *Chateau Coutet*; an excellent port, *Quinta de Noval 1970*, and Scottish malt in the form of a Dalwhinnie. By the time everyone was seated, the waiters appeared for the last time, serving coffee.

'This should satisfy everyone, I would have thought,' Michael mumbled to Rachael. 'They had selected some rather inferior wines for dessert, but I found out and put a stop to that.'

After some moments, Harvey rose to speak. 'I am well aware that it is unconventional in the extreme for me to take the lead here, but it's our celebration and we'll do it our way! I would like to begin by pointing out to those who don't already know that Izzy and I were married exactly one week ago. If you don't believe me, I have a piece of paper – somewhere – to prove it. Well, let it be known… they said it would never last, but look at us! Hillary, who is Izzy's cousin, and Gerald, who is my uncle, were our witnesses last week. And they both got exceedingly drunk, I might add.'

'Hoffnung in Oxford!' someone called out.

'Quite right, David. Well done!' Harvey replied.

'We were not the only ones who were a mite squiffy,' Gerald interjected.

Harvey attempted to continue his speech. He managed to say how much he loved Isobel and how immensely grateful they both were to Rachael and Michael for the splendid lunch and for so many years of wonderful friendship. He began to say a little about each guest around the table but quickly became confused – though there were those who thought it was all a clever act – and surrendered the floor. After some minutes, Gerald rose to say his piece. It was not quite as everyone expected.

'First,' he said, 'I would like to confirm that Harvey and Isobel *were* married last week, and that Hillary and I do remember that bit very clearly. Several years ago, I introduced Harvey to *The Hut*, this most remarkable institution, let me say, and we met Hillary and Isobel on that occasion. Some might say that it was no coincidence. I couldn't possibly comment. It is, however, quite true that Hillary and I connived to bring these two young sparks together. They took a long time to ignite, I must say, but they got there in the end. However, while Hillary and I were playing cupid on Harvey and Isobel, Harvey and Isobel were playing cupid on Hillary and me. We did pick up the signals early on, even if the perpetrators didn't realise that we had. I must add that the youngsters took their time, more time than did we. I must further add that the youngsters are very unobservant.' Gerald turned to Hillary and said, 'Show them, darling.'

Hillary stretched forth her left hand, fiddled with her third finger and showed the group assembled a beautiful engagement ring – a twin diamond affair – inside a simple gold band. Rachael whooped with joy.

Gerald continued. 'We have been married for nearly three months!' he said. 'We wanted a quiet thing, which is why only now is the time of our announcing it, but I emphasise the unobservant nature of today's happy couple by pointing out that Hillary was wearing that jewellery when we were performing our duty as witnesses to their crime!'

Someone called out from the gathering, 'Happy, happy, you two, you four, all round.'

There followed a buzz of conversation. Isobel and Harvey rushed to hug Gerald and Hillary, and Rachael and Michael rose and went to hug all four of them.

'So I was right, last year…' Isobel said to Hillary.

'Of course you were!' Hillary replied, laughing.

The afternoon continued in much informality until Jim Chen rose, glass in hand. 'I hope,' he said, 'I may be permitted to toast the happy couple – sorry; couples – once more. I would also like to couple that toast with one to Rachael and Michael Montayne who created this place – or maybe I should say this thing – you all call *The Hut*. I had heard much about it even before Isobel came to me…' Michael looked surprised and Jim read his expression immediately, continuing, 'I keep my ears to the ground and my eyes open at all times. That's a difficult physical feat at times, believe me. Anyway, I already knew of *The Hut*'s existence, but today I have learned why it is great. So, if the happy couples don't mind, I raise my glass to Michael and Rachael, good friends of both couples.'

There was a general round of applause and silent raisings of glasses by Isobel, Hillary, Gerald and Harvey.

In due course, the party broke up as people wanted to stretch their legs and, frankly, go for a pee.

'Please go to the lounge bar, for there is to be more entertainment,' Michael called out.

Isobel looked sharply at him, with her head on one side, questioning.

'Patience!' Michael laughed.

*

Shortly after everyone was gathered in the lounge, chatting happily, there came a tremendous bang from just outside the windows on the right-hand side, followed by loud cry of alarm from someone outside. At the same time, the lights in the room were extinguished. An astonished silence reigned for a moment. It was dark outside by now, being well past half past five on that December afternoon.

'Oh no! Not an electric fault,' someone cried out.

The bar itself was still illuminated, so it was presumably on a separate circuit.

Then another loud bang, this time on the left, followed by several more at greater distances from the building, and there were sizzling noises and sparks coming from the places where the bangs had occurred. There were more gasps from outside the room to the right side of the building which, since now there was deathly quiet inside the lounge, were clearly heard by the wedding guests inside.

Peter looked out to the right. 'There's a large crowd of people outside,' he said. 'Maybe a hundred or more!'

The words were hardly out of his mouth when a line of bright-green – a rich emerald-green, it was – floodlights were switched on, illuminating the Grand Avenue outside, all the way to the T-junction at the far end. It was an astonishingly beautiful sight and brought forth a gasp of admiration from both wedding guests and those outside. There were no more loud bangs – presumably from thunder-flashes, someone suggested – but there came, at first soft, and then louder strains of Christmas carols from invisible sources all around the hall, and particularly from near the old oak tree on the left of the great lawn outside.

And then it began, gently at first but with a gradual increase in intensity and spread. Fireworks lit on cue. Close up were the family favourites: Catherine wheels on sticks placed around the great lawn; Roman candles spewing stars and flames from locations artfully chosen in the lawn and on both sides of the near end of the main drive; ground spinners, fountains and smoke bombs. A firecracker was tossed near the crowd of people outside, who were clearly visible now, being well-lit by all the fireworks around. There was a small area of panic there as onlookers backed away. Another firecracker was set off nearer the lounge windows, startling the guests inside. Attention then shifted back to the oak tree, but this time to streaming fountains of white and yellow from high in its bare branches. They burned out at almost the same time, and there came silence. Some people outside began clapping their hands.

'Who are those people?' one of the wedding guests asked.

Michael replied, 'They are people from the village. Everyone was sent an invitation to share the display with us. I hope they are well wrapped up in the cold!'

Suddenly came what can only be described as a shower of bangs from somewhere near the Grand Avenue. Being quite far away, they weren't frightening; rather they were signals, as if drawing the spectators' attention to that place. They were followed by more bangs, these from above, from noisy rockets wheezing through the sky above the trees. And then came more rockets, but these gave forth wonderful colours, cloudbursts and offspring, all forming a wall of ever-changing colour to proclaim Christmas for the more- and less-privileged onlookers alike.

Soon it was apparent that the display was about to end. The music faded as did the noises of rockets. A moment of silence came over the watchers. And then an enormous bang came from a place near the bird with two heads. Synchronised with the bang, a searchlight picked out a poster attached to that bird, the poster showing the faces of Isobel and Harvey, surrounded by stars. There began a loud fanfare from someone standing to the side of the poster. It was Barry with his trumpet. His fanfare came to an end and the crowd, outside and in, applauded loudly. He waited until they stopped before raising his instrument once more. He then played the fanfare all over again but, as he began, the poster changed – there was some mechanism which caused it to switch over – and now it showed the faces of Hillary and Gerald within a garland of stars. The wedding guests applauded wildly. When Barry finished playing and walked over to the villagers, the lights in the lounge were switched back on. The show was over.

Conversation inside began to buzz once more, the bar began serving drinks, and happy clinks became the norm once more.

Gerald and Hillary were gathered with Harvey, Isobel, Michael and Rachael. Gerald was looking puzzled.

'Michael, how on earth did you fix up that second poster so quickly?' he asked.

'Yes,' Hillary added. 'You can't have had more than half an hour – maybe three quarters – to do that.'

'Ah well,' Harvey answered for Michael. 'You oldies think you know everything. Did you really think that Isobel and I hadn't spotted Hillary turning her rings round on her finger at our wedding last week?'

Gerald looked at Michael, disbelief still in his face. The creator of *The Hut* shrugged his shoulders, smiled a little, but said nothing before excusing himself for a few minutes.

Michael went out of the lounge and into the main hall where he put on a warm coat before going outside to greet the crowd of villagers. There, he joined in serving hot punch to everyone, adults and children alike. He probably spoke to everyone out there before waving as he turned back to the warmth of the hall.

THE END

www.ingramcontent.com/pod-product-compliance
Lightning Source LLC
Chambersburg PA
CBHW060649190726
48289CB00002B/336